ACCLAIM FOR
THOSE WHO WALK IN DARKNESS

D0667851

What
Fire
Cannot
Burn

Also by John Ridley

Those Who Walk in Darkness

What
Fire
Cannot
Burn

JOHN RIDLEY

WARNER BOOKS

NEW YORK   BOSTON

Cover design by Don Puckey
Cover illustration by Herman Estevez

Warner Books

Time Warner Book Group
1271 Avenue of the Americas
New York, NY 10020
Visit our Web site at www.twbookmark.com

Printed in the United States of America

First Paperback Printing: January 2006

10 9 8 7 6 5 4 3 2 1

For
Jason

I'm alive for a reason.

I don't mean that with the cheap, feel-good populist existentialism daytime TV talk show hosts love to hand out: You're alive because even though you eat too much fast food and can't point to your own state capital on a map, we're all really unique and individual and specia-blah, blah, blah. I mean: in the world we live, with what I do, there's a reason I've remained among the living. A reason I've survived.

Actually, a couple of reasons depending on what kind of survival you're talking about.

Regarding my physical endurance, science is my guardian angel. Science by way of an O'Dwyer VLe. An all-electronic handgun that can fire a four-shot burst in just 1/500 of a second. Ordnance that is designed, specifically, to deal with the problem.

Funny. Kinda. It's that easy to turn the struggle for persistence into catchphrases. "The problem." "After San Francisco." "Freak hunting."

Too bad it's not as easy to solve the problem as it is to label it.

Nothing's ever easy.

Not in this world.

This world is hard, it's bleak, it's unsure, it is filled with risk. It's fat with weak sisters who look for obvious morals, comfortable politics, and clutch themselves hoping that hope alone will deliver them soft resolutions to hard situations.

Sorry.

And the world's got people like me. People who do, rather than subsist because of the deeds of others.

And people who do what I do; we're good as dead.

Accepting that, accepting my mortality: It's the other reason I survive.

Venice, California.

Venice, California, was beachfront land bought up by Abott Kinney and Francis Ryan at the end of the 1800s.

Venice, California, was an oceanfront attraction the two men built acre by acre, canal by canal, that matrixed the vistas of Rome with an American boardwalk.

Venice, California, was, long time ago, a tourist attraction. A place to ride amusement rides on a pier, go to an aquarium.

Then the pier burned down. Then oil got discovered percolating under the ground. Then the city of LA did a land grab, snatched Venice for its own just like LA did with everything it wanted. Water from up north. The movie business from out East. Venice was like that. Worth stealing. A sweet piece of real estate.

Things change.

Turned out there wasn't all that much oil in Venice, California.

So the city of LA lost interest in Venice, California, let her fall just about to pieces same as an ex-mistress tossed aside 'cause it'd grown tiresome. And when it didn't fall apart completely on its own, the city tore down more than five hundred historic buildings.

Five hundred.

LA didn't care.

Progress doesn't own any sympathy. Why should the city?

Venice, California, became kind of a shithole for bangers and dealers. Wannabes when they gave up and quit wanting to be anything but what they were which wasn't much. It was a haven for illegals coming up from Mexico who couldn't get to anywhere better than Venice, California.

But, real slow, Venice turned itself around. Some.

Just because it was cheap didn't mean decent people couldn't end up there. Decent people need affordable housing as much as bangers. More than bangers. Bangers aren't usually long-term customers.

With reasonable renting rates, a laconic beach vibe, into Venice flooded artists both visual and unique as well as crappy.

And Venice gladly took in the oddball, mainstream hating *artistes* because like a lonely boy who was otherwise without affection, Venice was really happy for anybody who came to be with her.

Venice, California, was like that; mostly about the little guy or the bohemian, the actor or the failed male beefcake who ends up pumping iron down at the beach, spending his considerable free time getting bigger for bigger's sake. Venice said to them: Forget about Brentwood or West Hollywood or Sherman Oaks or any of the parts of the city where people aspire to reside. Come here, live here. We'll take you as you are. Happy that you came, we will offer you little stress.

Things change.

Mostly, what changes, property values go up.

At some point the little guy, the little guy in Venice—the artist and the bohemian—has gotta get with the fact he's sitting on prime, oceanfront real estate. The little guy's gotta get with the program. The program: get outta the way.

The program: That's when the developers move in. The malls and complexes go up. The little guy is invited to move to Van Nuys or East LA or anywhere that wasn't *here* where we've gotta put up a mini-mall with a sixteen-screen movie multiplex.

Most, most little guys—small boutique shop owners, mom-and-pop businesspeople—they took the hint, sold out, went their way.

No fighting things.

Progress's got no sympathy.

But in Venice, California, against the odds, there was still the occasional coffee shop that wasn't a Starbucks, the bookstore that wasn't a B&N or a subsidiary thereof. Every now and then there was someplace other than a Gap, Inc., LLC, trying to make a stand, trying to offer people some other kind of joint where they could buy retail. And there was even a bank on the corner of Rose and Main that wasn't part of some massive, interstate fiduciary corporation. The tellers worked through lunch and the loan officers—David and Carol and Rick—looked at more than your TRW before deciding if you were an acceptable risk. ATM fees were under two bucks. Diane Woodward had been doing her banking there since her divorce—she'd left her stay-at-home-dad husband for a partner at her firm—had forced her to make some new financial arrangements. Regularly,

Mike Anderson strollered over with his two-and-a-half-year-old daughter before stopping by the newsstand to pick up a copy of *Chocolate Beauties*. And there was old Mr. Roth, the sweet, septuagenarian widower whom life never seemed to get the best of though life never shared with him the best of anything. The bank was, in a city of far too many millions of people, where you could go for a minute, do your business, get a smile in return that wasn't based on the size of your deposit. Wasn't charged against your account.

It was also the kind of place, like a lot of banks in Los Angeles, where a couple of guys—White. Gaunt. Sweaty with nerves, sweaty on the tail end of a hard meth jag that was crashing—walked in, stood for a second, stood for a second as their waning high gave them fake courage, then yanked nine-mils from beneath their jackets.

The usual bank robbery confluence of events followed.

Sweaty Guys: "Get down! Everybody get the fuck on the floor!"

Nobody moved.

"Get the fuck on the fucking floor now!"

No movement. Minds were processing what was happening—men, men with guns. Crazy-looking men waving their gafs around—while bodies waited for further instructions.

Except for the security guard. The security guard knew what was going on. The security guard was also getting paid minimum. The security guard went down like the class whore on prom night, hugged the floor. He never even bothered going for the gun he hadn't used in the year and a half since he'd capped his two-week private security training course.

"Get fucking down!"

Shots fired in the air.

Screaming. Crying. The mental/physical debate was over. People, finally, got down.

Time wasted. Time wasted by the Sweaty Guys getting the shouldabeen relatively manageable situation managed.

Old days, you couldn't take that kind of time to get a job handled. Old days, too much time wasted, all of a sudden you'd have the Adjudicator punching his way into the bank through a wall. The Sweaty Guys' guns? Useless. Bullets were like spitballs to the Adjudicator's kind. Then the Adjudicator would've been all over your sweaty ass.

That was the difference between then and now. *Now* there was time to scream at people just trying to do their banking to get the F down. Fire off a few shots if they didn't get the F down.

These days, when all you had to worry about were outgunned LAPD cops, seemed like there was all the time in the world for bad things to happen.

Unless you're jagged on crank. You're hopped on tina. Then time's got a way of being trippy, unnervy. No matter how fast things happen, they don't happen fast enough.

For Mike Anderson, with his baby in the stroller, it took a swipe of a pistol to the head to hurry up his downward progress. Wasn't really much of a blow. Mike Anderson more or less went with the swing, went to the ground on his own and covered his daughter knowing, beneath his body, she'd be safe.

David, Carol, Rick: still screaming, but learning well from the pistol-whipping demonstration the rewards of noncooperation. They pressed themselves on the tile behind and below their desks. Would have pressed them-

selves through the floor if they could have. The tellers
went down behind the counter.

In the whole of the bank only three were standing. The
Sweaty Guys. Mr. Roth.

Mr. Roth was old, didn't move so quick. Mr. Roth's
eyes were probably bad and his hearing most likely shot.
There was a real chance Mr. Roth didn't know, didn't
really understand, what was happening. For him it
must've been like trying to figure out what's going on
when you're watching the world from under five feet of
Jell-O. The "fucks" screamed, the pistol whips given: It
was all lost on him.

"Wha . . . what's—"

"Get down!"

"I, I don't—"

"Get the fuck down!"

It could be read in the Sweaty Guys' dilated eyes. Loss
of control was on the horizon.

Mike Henderson saw it.

From where he was on the floor Mike Henderson, sensing the badness to come, had a variation on a single
thought: I gotta do something. No matter his daughter was
there, no matter doing *something* wasn't . . . wasn't right,
wasn't safe, he could real easy see the sum of the equation
before him: Old man doesn't move fast enough, jagged
thugs don't react rationally. Bullets fly. Old guy dies.

"Get down on the fuck—"

"I don't . . . I can't—"

From the rest in the bank a modified Greek chorus
chanting in frightened wails: "Please, Mr. Roth! Get
down, Mr. Roth!"

One of the Sweaty Guys worked the slide on his gun.

Should've done that before he hit the bank. Anyway, a round was chambered. He was, finally, ready for business.

"Goddamn it, fucker! Get the fuck—"

Consequences didn't matter.

It was coming to that.

Consequences didn't matter for Mike Henderson. A life mattered. Not his own. Mike Henderson had to—

"Told you to get the fuck down!"

A gun yelled twice. Deafeningly loud in the tight space.

The screams, the screams from David and Carol and Rick, from Diane and especially from the security guard, spiked and died. The bank was filled with a bed of sobbing.

All looked.

Even Mr. Roth, still standing, looked and saw the two sizable holes in his chest.

A couple more screams from someone at the sight, the sight of Mr. Roth with those holes.

The two guys, the Sweaty Guys, they weren't high anymore. Not so much so. Shooting someone can do that to you. Sober you up. Shooting someone in California where they execute people for such things will slap the fuzziness straight out of you.

Mr. Roth looked up, looked from his wounds to the formerly Sweaty Guys.

And then the wounds in Mr. Roth's chest, which were not wounds, but truly holes—tunnels opened to allow the passing of a couple of slugs—self-sealed.

And then Mr. Roth gave a smile. A smile that stretched, stretched itself across his face. The corners of his lips seeming to . . . not seeming to. They did. The corners of his lips touched the base of his ears. Teeth filled his mouth, swelled to fill his mouth. Twisted. They went jagged. Looked more like ivory claws then dentition.

For a second Mr. Roth's smile . . . it quivered. It quivered. For a second it was like Mr. Roth's smile couldn't contain its glee, its perverted anticipation.

And then Mr. Roth's smile, his jaw, had at the two used-to-be/now-again Sweaty Guys who'd tried to rob a bank and had only gotten as far as shooting at a seemingly old man. Mr. Roth's smile bit at them, tore at them, ripped, ripped and ripped them. Did not slow for the shrieking, the screaming, the spraying blood and flying flesh. And meat.

And Mr. Roth's smile accomplished all this mayhem while Mr. Roth's body remained a good thirty feet clear of the slaughter.

Somewhere along the way darkness got a bad rap, got itself associated with fear and malevolence. Bad things only happen in the dark.

Perception, not truth.

The dark was safe and warm. People calmed and closed their eyes and slept in the dark. The dark was as solacing as a womb. It was coming out of darkness into the light of the day when you could see just how fucked-up the world was.

The APC doors opened. Harsh white sunlight hacked its way into the vehicle's bay.

Soledad held up a hand against it, against the light. But there was little blocking of the sun to be done.

Every time.

Every time she spilled out of an APC on a call Soledad felt like she was dropping out of a Huey into a hot LZ deep in Charlie territory or exiting a Bradley for some foot patrol in Fallujah, dodging random IEDs.

It was an assumptive feeling. She'd never done either of those: urban pacification or hit an LZ. Hadn't even been in the military.

But Soledad was pretty sure the feeling of dread, of imminent unavoidable death that came with taking either of those locales was the same as rolling out of her APC. The same, 'cept for the fact that across the street, in Soledad's war zone, was a Quiznos where she'd once had an exceptionally adequate lunch. On the far corner was a computer store where she'd had her PowerBook worked on three times because the first two times the twenty-something the joint passed off as a tech expert had not one idea in hell what he was doing. In Soledad's war the battleground was *here*. Not a desert city, not a rice paddy halfway around the world. Here; her city. And the enemy didn't wear a uniform or in any particular way identify itself as a combatant or insurgent. The enemy looked like Soledad, or the kid working at the copy shop, or the mother of two out running with her jogging stroller.

The enemy looked normal.

The enemy, however normal-looking, was anything but.

LAPD squads surrounded the bank at Main and Rose. Uniformed cops used the squads for cover. A growing crowd across the street from the police action stood out in the open. Overhead news birds from Channels 4, 7 and 9. Circling low. Making communications difficult. Ensuring the viewing public would get "live team coverage" if anybody got killed.

The shit was, most definitely, about to get rolling.

The uniformed Officer in Charge waved Soledad over. Her element was right on her heels. Her element, Pacific MTac, she'd inherited in a command shuffle when its most recent sergeant was KIAed. It'd only been his third call on point. Third time's the charm.

Pacific MTac: Eddi Aoki and Jim Whitaker on HKs. Jesus Alcala, a probee, working a Benelli. Alcala was a baby MTac, but he'd proven himself on four previous calls. Without fear, with smarts and deadly aim on the Benelli. All that and the fact Manhattan Beach had one less freak walking around courtesy of a one-ounce slug was proof enough of Alcala's skills.

Eddi was a known quantity. Her, Soledad; they'd survived going head-to-head—no pun—with a telepath. Eddi'd come back from a nearly shattered knee to get a slot on an element. She was a cop Soledad had no problem giving her back to.

Whitaker.

Whitaker had been transferred off Central MTac just prior to Central MTac being shredded by that telepath. Previously a little mousy, a little nervous, in the eight months since his almost near-death experience, Whitaker had gone at the job with a vengeance and without hesitation. BAMF twice in that amount of time. Knowing that you dodged a bullet by avoiding a telepath is a life-changing experience. Especially when it's just luck that kept you from standing in the spot where others died.

Soledad landed at the OIC, squatted, asked:

"What's the deal?"

"Two-eleven in progress. Turns out one of the civvies in the bank is a freak. Tore the shit out of the perps."

"Got an ID on the freak?"

"Won't do you much good. It's a shape-shifter."

Eddi, a noise of disgust, then: "Fucking shape-shifters."

Alcala: "One freak better than another?"

"Some are worse than the rest."

"Mouths shut, ears open." Soledad was all business.

The business at hand: getting intel, staying alive. To the OIC: "What do you know?"

"The guy's name was Sidney Roth. Ran him with DMV. Age listed was sixty-eight, widower. No priors. Was a quiet guy."

"The bad ones usually are. It's inside?"

The OIC gave Soledad a nod to the affirmative. "The civvies are accounted for. Perps are dead. Black-and-whites responding to the silent alarm had the perimeter locked down before anyone got out."

"Description of the freak."

"Told you, it's a—"

"Just give me height and weight."

"Five-eleven, around one-seventy. That's from the civilians." The OIC's meaning: Civvies don't generally make for great witnesses. "So it could go a little either way."

Across the street: Commotion. Loud voices.

Uniformed cops, on edge, overanxious, turned, took aim with their sidearms. Would've sent bullets into the lookie-lous if they'd had just a touch more jitter to them.

The lookie-lous: Their ranks had swelled by a handful of protesters. Voices raised, placards waving. Homemade signs. The sum total of their message: Fuck the Police. Let Freaks Be.

Alcala, re: the protesters: "You believe that shit? We're manning the line, and they're acting like we're the damn problem?"

"Forget 'em." Soledad was plain with her order.

Whitaker was snide with his suggestion: "How about we take a couple of them along, see if they're still freak lovers when some mutie's trying to rip their—"

"How about we concentrate on the job?" Soledad didn't have the time, didn't have the patience for her element venting. "It's the Westside. What do you expect but the liberals are going to turn out? Lucky Susan Sarandon's not here."

"I like Susan Sarandon."

Soledad looked to Eddi.

Eddi's smirk: Yeah. Really.

Still, Soledad was pretty sure Eddi was just messing with her. Much as Soledad respected the girl, there was no getting on with Eddi.

To the OIC: "Got a floor plan?"

"Bank manager drew one up." Flipping open his duty log, showing a poor sketch to Soledad: "Not much to it. About twenty-five hundred square feet total. Desk, chairs on the north side just past the door. Tellers' windows, manager's office back here . . ."

"Vault open?"

"Vault was open."

Soledad, facetious with herself: That'd be fun. Trying to corner a freak that could shift its shape just about any way it pleased within the restricted confines of the vault. It'd be like taking a swan dive into a steel coffin. She hoped, Soledad hoped it wouldn't come to that. She hoped they could nail the thing in the relative open. About all she didn't hope for was that the freak was already gone.

Other cops, the uniformed cops who'd be staying on the outside hidden behind their cruisers, guns pointed at the bank; probably they were hoping the thing had split. Hoping that they could make it through the day without having to deal with a mutie. But that's why they were, would never be anything but beat cops. Uniforms. Good men all. But when it came time to really step up they'd rather step behind their cars. By the time Soledad, her element . . . by the time any cop goes MTac they'd long since given up wishful notions of avoidance and turned their fancy to the hope that one day freaks would be relegated to a portion of a museum right next to *T. rex* and they as MTacs would get the chance to play a significant part in the extinction event.

From her belt Soledad slipped a yellow-marked bullet clip. Slid it into the back of her modified O'Dwyer. Her gun. *The* gun. The OIC watched her actions with the same mythic reverence for Prometheus grabbing fire.

Soledad to her element: "Listen up!" Her voice punched straight from the gut. The tone: This is it. The meaning: Pay attention and live. Maybe. "The space is tight. Be aware, and don't get yourself between the target and a gun. We go two-by. I'll give the Civil, but this one's already got a body count. You got the shot, take the shot."

No inducement for questions. Far as Soledad cared, at this stage of things there had better not be any.

One thing more: "The safe word is 'cardigan.' Got it? Cardigan."

The safe word was the first word that popped into Soledad's head. The randomness didn't diminish its importance. Not when the freak you were going after could real easy mimic, among other things, an MTac; reshape itself as the cop who was supposed to have your back. It was good to have a way, a word, to separate the real from the imposter.

This call: cardigan.

Soledad called for a mike check, heard her element count off in her earpiece.

Then they were moving, moving for the bank. As always, this situation, this call, different than the last call. Different freak with different abilities. And even freaks with similar abilities came wrapped in different psyches. Like snowflakes, no two alike. Like real deadly snowflakes. But every call, in some ways, was the same. MTacs vs. some kind of *thing*. The MTacs with their guns, the thing with heat vision. The MTacs with one-ounce slugs, the thing bulletproof. Four MTacs, the thing stronger than a hundred men.

The MTacs. A thing that could, with as little as a thought, steal their lives.

And for any MTac, no matter how many calls they'd been on, how many freaks they'd previously chalked . . . no matter how many times they're BAMF. Every now and again a little self-prepping is required.

Soledad, to herself, but loud in her head: I'm not dying today.

The sound track, the sound that came with action for the MTacs creeping into the bank, was the sound of each other's breath—short, sharp—coming through their earpieces.

The sight: Chairs overturned. Deposit slips spilled on the cream tile floor along with phones, brochures to inform customers in four-color gloss about direct deposit and certificates of deposit and free checking that actually hit you harder with jacked-up service fees.

Some cash.

Some cash just lying among bloody, shredded bodies. Body *parts*. What was left of the two sweaty guys.

The place was empty of people.

Probably, it still held a freak.

So now it was about looking. Looking for movement where there shouldn't be any. A sign of life where there should only be inanimation. The freak could've melded with the wall. Easy. Obvious. How about that shitty hotel-quality painting hung on one side of the space? Could a shape-shifter duplicate something that bad?

The spray of deposit slips on the floor?

Clever.

One of the dead sweaty guys: Was that really a freak in hiding?

Very clever.

A kiosk? A chair? The ashtray stand . . . ?

This; *this* is why, like Eddi'd said, shape-shifters were worse than other freaks. They're tricky. They play dirty.

Yeah but so could Soledad.

Soledad, to her element: "I'm giving the Civil."

Soledad yelled into the bank: "This is the police. You are in violation of an Executive Order from the president of the United States. You are ordered to surrender yourself immediately or face potentially lethal force!" The Civil—short for "Civil Rights"—was the freak version of getting Mirandized; a little speech mandated by the Supreme Court after a constitutional challenge of police powers by the ACLU for a metanormal rights group. "Freak fuckers" to the majority of Americans. The 5–4 decision required cops to recite the Civil when executing a warrant on anyone with "unique, metanormal and/or supernormal abilities not found among the common populace of the human race." The freak fuckers had complained that the cops weren't giving freaks a fair shot at surrendering. They'd complained that the cops with their guns that fired nothing more than bullets weren't giving freaks—flamethrowing, self-electrifying, supersizing freaks—an opportunity to give themselves up. So now Soledad had to scream the incredibly, legalistically stupid phrase "or face potentially lethal force" at the top of her lungs, doing the double duty of both embarrassing herself and warning the freaks: "Here we come!"

From outside the bank, from across the street, Soledad could hear the group of freak fuckers chanting for freak rights.

In the bank nothing. Relative quiet. Just the breathing of the cops in each other's earpiece.

Most times, with ornery freaks and muties, the lead officer delivering the Civil didn't get past "This is the po—" before fire or frozen air or animated metal came rushing for them, rushing to kill them.

Fine with most MTacs. They didn't care about freaks' so-called rights. They only wanted something to shoot at.

Alcala, checking the space: "Oughta just blow all this joint up."

No one responded to the statement.

"Oughta just—"

Soledad: "Heard you."

"Blow it up. Freak's in here, freak's dead."

"Good plan," Eddi miked back. "Every time somebody reports a freak, call in an air strike. Nuke the block."

"Just saying—"

"Not getting jitters, are you?"

She wasn't looking, but Soledad would take the bet

Eddi was wearing that grin of hers. "Aoki, Alcala, shut up."

Whitaker kept out of things, kept quiet. Kept his eyes on the space all around. Not scared. Not even anxious, having settled in his head that today, probably, was the day he was going to die. If not this call, then the next. Or the next. Sooner or later he was going down. Wasn't fatalism. It was, to Whitaker, being realistic. In anticipation of the moment itself, the prayer repeated in his head: Jesus, all I want before I go, let me chalk one more stinking freak.

Soledad's voice in all their earpieces: "Moving forward."

She crab-walked for the center of the space. Out into the open. Trying to use cover was without point. Cover could be the freak. Get too close to the kiosk, it could reach out and choke you. The garbage can could jump up and real quick beat you to death.

Whitaker kept near to Soledad. Aoki, Alcala covered. All of them, guns ready, fingers brushing triggers. The four black eyes of their weapons sweeping the space, looking without compassion. Looking for something to kill.

The doors of the bank were closed. If the AC was on, Soledad couldn't feel it. The air was full with the stink of the dead Sweaty Guys already going stale. To wrap things quickly would be a pleasure to the senses.

Soledad: "Rising up."

The element held their ground, did a slow sweep with their weapons. Black eyes searching . . .

Soledad stood from her crouch, had a look around. Nothing.

Not *nothing*. *Too many* things. Too many ordinary-seeming accessories of life that could be a homicidal, blood-crazy shape-shifter.

To her element: "C'mon up."

Aoki, Alcala and Whitaker stood.

Fingers brushing triggers, black eyes searching . . .

Soledad, inching forward, inching . . .

Something wasn't right. Something had to *not* be right. That something would be the freak: A section of wall misaligned. A chair where one shouldn't be.

Something had to *not* be . . .

Inching forward, inching . . .

Black eyes . . .

Sweat on her forehead, dripping across her brow. Why the hell would somebody shut down the AC?

The floor got tacky. Sweaty Guy blood under foot.

Something had to . . .

"Eddi . . ."

"Yeah, Soledad?"

"Tell me what you know about shape-shifters." Soledad didn't need a primer on transmogrifying freaks. What she needed: a voice in her head to help her focus, to walk her through facts, hip her to what she wasn't seeing.

"They have an evolved genetic ability to dissimulate. Every aspect of them malleable. They're able to alter shape, size . . ."

The carpet? The mutual fund display? Something . . .

"Not mass. Mass has to be maintained."

The loan area behind Eddi. The desks? The chairs?

"Altering mass would require a discharge of energy. Basically, the thing would explode."

The desk? The chairs?

Four desks. Three chairs.

There were three loan officers.

It wasn't right.

"Eddi."

"Yeah?"

"Move!"

She did. With speed, Eddi dropped low, twisted clear from Soledad's line of fire.

Soledad gave one tug to her O'Dwyer's trigger. Four slugs. All dead on target. All ripping, shrieking for the desk without a chair.

The desk moved. Its middle section dropped, torqued, pulled itself from the bullets' path.

And the party got started.

Alcala went to work with the Benelli, a hell's roar ahead of each one-ounce slug auto fired. Devastating most times. This time . . . The freak sucked itself in, stretched itself out. Took the form of something like a serpent. The slugs missed their intended target. One hit another desk, turned it into a vapor of wood chips, pulped paper. Another punched a fist-sized defect into a wall.

The freak, still shape of a serpent, sprouted tendrils. Lashed one for Soledad. She took it square to the face. Felt, tasted blood in her mouth from teeth driven through the flesh of her cheek.

Soledad went backward, went down, kept up the grip on her gun.

I'm not dying today.

Springing up, looking, assessing . . .

The situation: The freak had another tendril noosed around Alcala's neck, had his feet off the ground. His face already going from red to blue.

Eddi's HK went hot, but she maintained control. Fired in bursts. Regulated her ammo. In a gunfight with a freak what you did not want, you did not want to have to take a time-out to reload. Staying alive was hard enough. Running out of bullets? That kind of miscalculation got you killed.

The freak snapped its tendril, the one gripping Alcala. Alcala took air. Sailed for Eddi. Eddi had enough quick to her to hold her fire, keep from putting slugs in Alcala. Not enough quick to keep from taking Alcala full to her chest. One hundred ninety-six pounds of man. Fifteen miles an hour. Felt like catching a Hyundai.

Eddi's chestplate kept her ribs from busting. Eddi's chestplate shattered Alcala's wrist on impact. Both their weapons were lost as their bodies played a limp game of twister across the floor.

Soledad up, moving. Moving for the action. Two jerks on her trigger. Eight of her special slugs added to Whitaker's rhythmic bursts. A spray of blood signaled a hit on the freak. Whitaker's rounds, not Soledad's. Soledad's, and the thing would be down.

The thing.

The thing contracted, expanded. Went from looking like, from *being* a serpent, to . . . Scales into fur. Tendrils into claws.

Serpent into tiger.

A white tiger.

Soledad, to herself: Jesus H. Christ. It's a goddamn freak show.

And the tiger leaped, leaped for Whitaker. Whitaker fired, nicked the freak as it reached the apex of its arc.

Then it was on him.

Then it was tearing at his throat.

Sick joke.

Then Whitaker was screaming. Trying to. What he was doing, really, as he was failing, was gurgling. Blood was free-flowing. What wasn't pooling in his throat was just spraying. Whitaker kept up the fight, swung at the thing. Bare-handed, tried to beat it back. Whitaker was fighting for his life.

Whitaker was losing.

Eddi was sailing.

Like a Hollywood, A-list action chick, Eddi was sailing for the mutie. One hand out and groping at it, the other hand clutching her knife. *The* knife. The one her late father, a casualty of May Day, had legacied to her.

In all of MTac a single, nonreg weapon got the same dispensation and respect as Soledad's O'Dwyer. At the moment, Eddi was driving the weapon hilt-deep into a freak.

And blood fountained, turned the fur of the white tiger pinkish red.

And the freak went crazy with itself. It bucked. It kicked. It juked. It threw Eddi, finally, clear.

And good, Soledad thought. Good for that. Eddi was out of the line of fire. It was just her and the freak.

Soledad squeezed her trigger.

The O'Dwyer let slip its bullets. The bullets, four, nearly in unison found their way into the freak. Lethal on their own, Soledad's bullets carried a little something more. Hollowed, each with a flywheel. Air ramjetted against the wheel, which drove a microturbine that self-generated an electrical charge. Eleven hundred feet per second, the flywheel making 850 revs per one hundred feet. It made for a hell of a charge. On impact with the freak's body, inside the freak's body, the charge discharged. The freak got 675,000 kV of fresh-brewed juice. Per slug. That kind of electricity does a horrid thing to a malleable mass.

The freak snapped, contorted grotesquely against itself, voltage punching at it, ripping at it from the inside out. Its struggle made it seem as though, against its own will, it was trying to move in three or four or five directions at once. Limbs—ones that were properly formed and others, little mutated things that sprang from the tiger-form wherever they pleased—both reached for help and curled in pain. The whole of it twitched spastically and gave the impression of one of Satan's brood that, hellish as it was, fought the twin mortal afflictions of Parkinson's and epilepsy. From a tiger, from the nightmare tiger it'd become, the thing took on the form of a dog. A partial dog, partial humanoid. Then it, the humanoid portion of the thing, kind of started looking like John Madden if John Madden were melting. If his face were on the side of his head, if his mouth were pried open but incapable of delivering the scream it attempted to yelp.

Then it was a deformed John Madden with what looked like a goat making an escape from his thigh.

Jerking. Twitching. Slowing.

Then it was just a freak on the floor bleeding out.

Whitaker was bleeding out.

Aoki was curled, clutching herself.

Alcala was sitting, his right hand folded back in an incorrect manner.

Into her mic, Soledad: "Pacific to Metro! Eleven

ninety-nine; officers down! We need EMS at this location forthwith!"

And then she was over to Whitaker, putting pressure to his neck, lips to his ears. Talking to him but not telling him false promises—it's going to be all right. Don't worry, boy, you're gonna pull through. What Soledad was doing, Soledad was handing out orders.

"Hang on, Whitaker. You hear me? I do not lose operators! You hang the fuck on!"

And in herself she heard herself say, no longer as a command but as a sigh of relief: I will not die today.

And outside the bank, across the street, as the door opened, as EMS, as uniformed cops spilled in and got a look at the torn-up MTacs, Soledad heard voices chant: "Metanormals are people too!"

If the general public wanted to have a scare, they'd consider what happens immediately following a rough or south MTac call. A rough call is when one or more operators end up in serious condition. A call gone south's when one or more end up terminal.

Most MTac calls were rough calls.

And when a call goes south, when operators land on a bus to the closest ER, the nearest morgue, for a minute until a replacement MTac (or MTacs) can be slotted into an element—whether elements are shuffled or a cop is added to G Platoon, the LAPD unit that covers Metanormal tactical responses—the city, the people of the city are just that much more vulnerable. If freaks, if muties were a little more on the ball, if they really wanted to stir up some trouble, they could come at the MTacs in waves. We could take on a couple of them at once. I know we could. A few of them. Maybe. But sooner or later . . . There are about forty suspected muties in LA County. That's the best guess from DMI, the Division of Metanormal Intelligence, the spooks who keep a surreptitious eye on freaks.

Forty of them.

If the freaks really wanted to have at it, how long would it take for them to wear us down, wipe us out? My fear . . . well, honest, I've got a lot of them. But one that's becoming vivid to me is the one where I come off a call, I'm in a hospital healing up, or there tending to an operator who's gotten it bad, when we get a general alert: A flamethrower in Tarzana. A terraformer ripping up Carson. A UCM is flattening Century City. And when that happens, when that call comes in, I'll know, we'll know: It's not a coincidence of incident. It's the opening salvo. It's the beginning of the end. The race war we've been waiting for.

And when that happens . . .

When that happens . . .

I'll load up my gun.

I'll go to work.

Have to.

I'm alive for a reason.

Santa Monica–UCLA Medical Center.

Soledad's mouth had been stitched. Alcala's wrist was getting set. Eddi'd been bruised up, but that was it. No broken bones, cracked ribs. She was good. Soledad would've been clear of the hospital, clear of Santa Monica—its own city, a liberal city that brushed up against LA; that they had a different take on the "metanormal problem" was obvious from the cold looks Hypocritically oathed doctors openly sent her—except for Whitaker.

Whitaker was in very rough shape. Mauled about the neck. Massive blood loss. A stroke while under the knife. It was a mild one, but there's never, Soledad imagined, any good thing about having a stroke.

Best to be hoped for, out of surgery, Whitaker would get listed as critical. From there, the slow crawl from critical to serious was going to take a while. If it happened at all. And from there . . .

Eddi and Soledad sat in a waiting area just off emergency surgery flipping mental coins. The opposite sides: Whitaker was gonna make it/Whitaker was gonna expire.

And even if things landed right, even if he did live, what kind of living would he really have to look forward to? Months of physical therapy to get his jaw and facial muscles working enough to chew Jell-O. Vicious scars a reminder of the incident every time he so much as looked in a mirror to shave.

And mentally?

Forget about going through a near-death experience. *Just* a near-death experience. What Whitaker might . . . what he will, Soledad modified herself, what he *will* survive was something that would walk with him beyond a couple of sleepless nights and a handful of sessions with a PTSD counselor.

Jesus.

Soledad thought as she did after every call that went south: All this to take out one of them.

Just one.

Jesus.

She let her head fall back, rest against the wall behind her.

All this for one of them. How many were in the SoCal area? How many were there really? Those forty: a guesstimate from DMI. There could be, could be twice that. Three times . . .

Jesus H. . . .

"It's been good."

Soledad lolled her head on the wall, looked to Eddi.

Eddi, one more time: "It's been good operating with you again."

"Got a guy down, he's probably not going to be getting up soon if at all. It's been real good."

"If you hadn't been the senior lead, things could've

been worse. And more than that, I just mean, you know, personally. Personally, it's been good having you—"

Jumping in, cutting Eddi off: "If the brass got off its asses and approved the O'Dwyer departmentwide . . . Wait four more months just to evaluate my field test? That's a bunch of—"

"You're a piece of work, you know that?" Eddi smiled, but the laugh she gave was unkind. "All I'm trying to do, I'm trying to give you a compliment. I'm not trying to make a moment out of things. You don't want a moment, you want to avoid anything that comes close to you and me having a conversation? Cool. Fuck you." And she was very serious about that. "Now we don't have to have a moment."

The wall across from the pair got a steady look, got Eddi's full stare.

The wall was blank. Cinderblock jazzed up on a budget by a dull shade of green.

But Eddi gave it all her attention.

Soledad kept up a stare at Eddi . . .

Kept it up . . .

She rubbed her tongue over the stitches inside her mouth. Brittle. Prickly. Their alien nature begging to be scrutinized. Rejecting touch with a very standard form of pain, common to a hurt she'd had at one point or another in her arm, her chest, her back just below her scapula. Very, very common to her throat. The scars she wore there the first of so many forget-me-nots freaks would leave with her. This one, the mouth wound, it'd be what? A week or more of careful masticating before it healed? Even at that she'd probably end up biting the swollen meat a couple of times. At least that. Keep it from healing right. One of the hazards of a rough call. A minor one. The polar opposite of, say, being dead.

Being Whitaker.

Soledad to Eddi: "Let me see your shoulder."

"Fuck that."

"You've got a foul mouth, young lady."

"Fuck—"

"Want me to make it an order?"

"You're gonna order me to show you my shoulder?" Eddi gave a "yeah, right" smirk and bob of the head.

Soledad was without humor. "You want a write-up for insubordination, I will write you up."

"Like that's going to—"

"It'd sit you down for a while. And I know, for you, missing out on so much as one watch, one call, would tick you off royally."

Eddi's look shifted from the wall, the dull green wall, to Soledad. The two of them got into a quiet knife fight with their eyes.

They would've grappled forever.

Except Eddi, eventually, not quite backing down, but chewing her lips same as if she were grinding bits of lead—the job done with both grit and disgust—zipped down the front of her Nomex jumpsuit, started to reveal her right shoulder.

"The other one," Soledad instructed.

Oh, the disdain Eddi seeped. The petulant callousness of a young girl being called to task by her mom. Still, she shifted her suit, revealed the opposite shoulder. Flesh. Just flesh. No tattoo.

Eddi: "Okay?"

"Yeah. Okay."

"Got over it a long time ago." Eddi adjusted her suit, zipped, went back to looking at the wall with all the unwavering discipline of a Shaolin monk.

Soledad stared at it with her.

There was the occasional page for a doctor, a specialist. Hushed voices refracted by the acoustics of the space carried down the corridor. Mostly, there was quiet.

But elsewhere . . .

Elsewhere there were babies being born, spleens being removed. An organ or two being transplanted. Maybe. Being Santa Monica, there were mostly breasts being implanted, lipo being suctioned, tummies getting tucked. Probably at least one somebody dying.

But it all went on in a respectful quiet. Good news, bad news. Life. Death. Here it was held in the same clinical, objective manner. Perhaps we can save you, perhaps we cannot. Here is your child, but she needs a new liver.

Soledad struggled with: "I'm . . . It's good we got to work together again. You've become a solid operator, and I'm, I'm . . . that your first call got to be under my watch . . ."

And the difficulty Soledad had in communicating that little actually gave Eddi humor. It brought 'round that smirk of hers, that smart-assed variety of grin usually owned by frat boys playing pranks and kept women playing men. And Eddi when things tumbled her way. Very often things tumbled Eddi's way.

With as much shit-giving pleasure as anyone who's survived a fellow cop, *another* fellow cop getting maimed by a freak: "Damn, Soledad. Don't kill yourself."

He used to crack wise. Was always quick with a comeback. His word was the last word. His talent, his fetish was the ability to add with rapidity the final line to a conversation. If need be, or if he just had the desire, with an unblunted mocking of the person to whom he was speaking. Call it snaps, call it the dozens. Call it a sense of humor sharp as a brand-new knife. He could've been a put-down artist. He could've. In younger days.

Younger in spirit, not age.

Vin didn't crack wise much anymore. When he used his barbs, his jests were focused mostly inward. Self-deprecating. Sometimes self-destroying. What wit he had was leaden. His humor, his high humor, was ripped away along with his ego, his cockiness and his right leg by an animated engine block brought to life by a telekinetic freak.

Months.

After the incident—really, it was an ordeal—months followed of lying in the hospital recovering. Getting well enough physically, mentally, to just get out of bed.

Going half a day without pain was a miracle.

Going to the bathroom in something besides a bedpan became a minor victory.

Then there was the physical therapy. The physical therapist with his two good legs and easy platitudes who didn't have one idea in hell what it was like—how much it hurt—learning to stand. Learning to walk with crutches. Learning to walk with a fake leg and a cane. Learning to walk with *just* a fake leg.

Not so hard, the *just* walking.

It was walking without the gimp, the gimp that advertised to the world there was something wrong with him. Something different about him. Vin could do without the stares, without the pity. Pity from others. For himself, for himself he had plenty of pity. And his melancholy made him jaded. Stole his humor. Made him quiet.

Soledad didn't mind. She . . . liked? Preferred the Vin Vin was becoming, having been a perpetual target of the cocky Vin. The macho Vin. This Vin—unobtrusive and removed—suited her nature; isolated and detached.

It was New Leg Day. That's what Vin called it in a rare display of levity. Heavy as the levity was. It was the day he was set to get his permanent replacement leg. His phrase. Again, humor. Squarely jested from the thirteenth step of the gallows.

Soledad came around for the celebration. That made it a party of two.

Vin's permanent replacement leg was an Otto Bock Health Care C-Leg® with its patented microprocessor-controlled knee-shin system featuring onboard sensor technology, which reads the individual's every move by measuring forces at the ankle and angle of the knee fifty times a second. The C-Leg's microprocessor then uses this information to guide the knee's hydraulic stance resistance as well as swing phase to ensure that the user's gait is as natural and efficient as possible. The efficiency of the C-Leg's swing-phase dynamics—all this Soledad got from the Otto Bock Web site—even at varying walking speeds and uneven terrain, provides a more secure, natural and efficient gait. Using unique algorithms developed from studying how thousands of people walk, combined with input from multiple built-in sensors, the microprocessor determines the phase of gait. Then automatic adjustments are made to the knee's function to provide stability. The result is increased stability, ease of swing and greater efficiency with every step! The exclamation Otto Bock's own. There's even a knee-disarticulation version available.

Nifty. Really. To Soledad, having majored in emerging technology, it was all really nifty.

The days of prosthetics merely mimicking human ability were fading. Getting fucked-up and coming back at or below your birth abilities was yesterday's news. Science had found a way to improve on the Lord's work. The leg the Otto Bock was replacing had been a millimeter longer than Vin's remaining leg. The Otto Bock was the exact length of Vin's real leg. Science didn't make mistakes. Take that, God.

Vin jogged around his apartment a couple of times, displayed his leg for Soledad.

That ended his New Leg Day celebration.

After that, as was common, as was comfortable for Soledad and Vin, they sat together saying nothing. Physically close, they maintained distance. Incredible how much they dug that about each other: the ability to be in each other's sphere without taking up space.

After a while more, Soledad downloaded Vin on the previous day's call. The freak in the bank.

Never mind her facial bruises, Vin hadn't trespassed Soledad's privacy. Had asked no questions. He'd waited until she was ready to tell her tale.

And she told it.

She told Vin about leading the element against a thing that could alter its shape at will. She played back details of the freak getting taken down, finally, by a combo of Soledad's high-tech piece and Eddi's old-fashioned sharpened metal. It was a story that would've been—just a couple decades prior—fantastic. Before the likes of Nightshift and the Headman and the Miko.

Nubian Princess.

Much as Soledad despised all of *them* with their stupid names and ridiculous costumes, the thought of the Nubian Princess sometimes still gave her a thrill-chill.

Vin took it, the details of the call, as a matter of course, showing an emotional spike only when Soledad detailed the metanormal rights protesters.

"They've got an opinion . . ." Tight little shakes of Vin's head. "I don't care how stupid it is, okay, they've got their opinion. But . . ." Vin reduced his thoughts to a phrase: "Freak fuckers." Added: "Israel Fernandez; glad he died."

"Oh, no. Didn't die. The black copters from the special ops assassinated him." Sarcasm buttered with bitterness. "He probably killed himself just so we'd get the blame."

Then, talking about Eddi, Vin said: "She's good. She's a good operator."

Soledad said yeah to that, complimented Vin for having seen Eddi's abilities early on.

Vin was the one who wanted Eddi to join his and

Soledad's element as a probee to keep her hot head from getting taken off by a freak.

Ironic.

Vin thought it was ironic: He'd brought Eddi onto the element to help watch over her. Eddi ended up walking away from their bad, bad call relatively unhurt. And he had . . .

Vin looked to his bionics.

He thought of his days on MTac. Two-legged days. Days without painkillers.

Days that were only months ago.

Like she was dialed into his thoughts, Soledad: "What are you going to do?"

"Order a pizza. Watch *The Simpsons*."

"With yourself: What are you going to do? It's been eight months."

"Thanks. 'Cause a lot of times it's hard for me to keep track of how long it's been since I had my leg—"

"You're off rehab. You've got your new leg. So what are you going to do?"

"The only thing I've ever been is a cop, and that's done with."

"You could work Admin. You could work DMI."

"I was just thinking how much I want to hang around a bunch of other busted MTacs talking about how good things useta be when we had all our limbs instead of just a couple of them."

"So instead you're going to sit here, get fat off pizza and watch TV. If you were any more pathetic, you'd be a cliché."

Vin said nothing. Vin, fractured Vin, let Soledad have the last word.

And then, again, there was quiet between them.

And sometime after that Soledad said: "I was scared yesterday."

"Going against a homicidal shape-shifter, how are you not going to be scared? All the macho bullshit aside, I never knew an operator who didn't get tight on a call. You're crazy if you don't. You can plan on getting killed otherwise."

"I'm not talking that kind of scared. Scared that makes you sharp. I was scared to death. Vin, I was scared to where I *felt* Death. I felt it right there with me, crawling all over me same as a million ugly maggots."

"And you were wrong about it. Wrong about it for you, for the element." Thinking of Whitaker, thinking of him still lying up in a hospital between the here and the hereafter: "Maybe you were." Vin worked himself to where he was as sincere as he could be. Open as he knew how to be. "If you really felt Death, if that's what you really felt, fear, there's no shame in stepping aside. Bo was as tough an operator as there was. When it was time for him to get out of the bag and behind a desk . . ." Recalling a moment he and Soledad'd shared; their senior lead, Bo, telling them he was quitting MTac: "Nobody's done it with more whatever. Dignity."

Bo was still around MTac. Around in a big way. He was 10-David. Unit commander. He was the guy in charge of day-to-day operations. That meant a lot of pencil pushing. Politicking. A lot of filling out requisitions and forms. Begging one way or another for the couple of extra bucks in the budget that meant the difference between good equipment and the best equipment for G Platoon. And difference between good equipment and

the best equipment? Sometimes the difference was living
and dying. Soledad wasn't sure how other operators felt
about Bo's choices. But how she felt, how she felt when
she saw him knee-deep in paperwork: She felt he was
lucky. Not just lucky to be alive. Lucky to have the
smarts to know when to get out off the streets.

Maybe not just lucky. Bo, different from most MTacs,
had a wife. Kids. Probably, Soledad conjectured, having
something to live for keeps you from doing shit that'll get
ya killed.

Probably.

She didn't know. Not for sure.

From Soledad, a tick of her head, dismissing all that.
Getting back to what was what: "The way I felt wasn't
just about the call. I felt . . . it was like an O'Hara novel.
I felt like things were inevitable."

"Well, you're pressing thirty. Thirty, and you're not
married. Yeah, you're thinking about dying."

And Soledad laughed. A little. And this was why, despite their distant natures, she chose to spend time with
Vin. Vin knew her. Could slice the bullshit. Could move
her. Could touch her from feet away. Always could.

She wanted to kiss him.

Just a peck.

Maybe a little more.

Wouldn't let herself. And she wouldn't tell Vin that
when she thought of death, she thought of him. Thought
of losing him or being lost to him. Whichever. Thing was,
Vin gave Soledad something to live for. And the thing
about that . . .

"You think too much, Soledad." No idea what was
going on in Soledad's head, but Vin was precise with his

insight. "You think, then you let your thinking get to you. Yeah, you're gonna die someday. Somehow. You stay on MTac, it's gonna involve a mutie. But you're getting a cloud over you . . . what's got you feeling like that?

Like *that*.

What had Soledad feeling like *that:* Last time Soledad felt like she had something to life for, someone to live for, turned out to be a freak.

Hell if that was going to happen again, freak or normal human. Hell if it would.

Love = weakness all around.

Well, this was stupid.

Well, Eddi thought, this was just about insane.

She'd made it this far and she couldn't . . .

She'd made it this far, *this far* being from her duplex where she'd showered and primped and gussied up. Dressed in some hip couture that lacked the right amount of fabric in all the right places. She'd gotten in her ride, rode to Sunset in WeHo, overpaid for parking that wasn't all that close to where she wanted to be. Walked. Actually walked in the city of Los Angeles. And was standing across the street from what, according to her Googling, was real much "the joint."

The ridiculous part: She'd been cooling across the street from "the joint" going on four minutes. Four. Long. Minutes.

Couldn't make herself cross the street, go in.

It'll probably be too loud. She's not gonna know anybody. They probably aren't spinning the kind of music she's into.

Probably. Probably to all that.

But she had to get cleaned up, go out, spend dough to stand on a street corner to debate the act of going out in the first place?

Ridiculous.

And what really blew: This was supposed to be a . . . an "I made it through another call alive" celebration. Little more than eight months on MTac. She'd seen a grip of operators wounded, killed on the job. She'd almost done as much to one of her own on her first call. Somehow she'd survived.

Luck. Skill. Whichever. She figured she owed herself a little something for making it another day.

But standing outside a club alone? Ridiculous.

Eddi had actually thought about calling Soledad. Inviting her along. How weak would that've been? First off, Soledad was probably out doing whatever Soledad does when she's on her downtime. Dating a bunch of guys or kickboxing or bullfighting. God knows a woman like Soledad; her social calender was phat. God knows. Eddi didn't. Much as Eddi . . . appreciated Soledad, Eddi didn't know all that much about Soledad.

What she did know: Oh, the laughs she'd get from Soledad for asking Soledad to hang out.

So she went solo. And there she was . . . stupid.

Eddi made the cross. Overpaid, again. This time for cover. Entered the club.

Mostly, Eddi wasn't a drinker. Her parents weren't drinkers. At least in the time she had parents, she never much saw her father taking a drink outside of special occasions. Eddi grew up thinking that was the only time you were supposed to have a drink: marking an event that was memorable. In the time she was fatherless Eddi's mother drank. A little. Also to mark an occasion. An anniversary, a birthday, Christmas. Maybe not mark it. Dull the pain of it. So for Eddi, here was a moment to combine both habits of her parents. She drained some of her apple martini, which she knew wasn't strictly a martini but dug its candy goodness. She took in a little more, celebrated inside herself. Here's to eight months, six calls, two kills and no one to—

What was she gonna say? No one to share it with? She was in a club sick with people, the male percentage more than eager to share something with her. But she'd been sitting around, thinking about her past, her parents, what constitutes a proper martini. Eddi hadn't even been savvy to the three guys who were giving her the eye. One guy was clearly older than her but not old. Looked like he had means but didn't flaunt it. The other guy was gorgeous, and that was gorgeous measured against the average man in a city where the average man in a club at night made or hoped to make his living acting, modeling or otherwise engaged in a profession where a superior collection of features was an absolute requirement. The third guy didn't come off as being moneyed, was not nearly as gorgeous as the gorgeous guy, but was cute in the way he nervously, shyly stole glances at Eddi. He was a little country. In a good way.

In the way . . .

Yar was country.

Yar got killed courtesy of a piece of animated metal freak-jabbed through his chest.

Eddie finished her drink.

Marked the occasion.

Dulled the pain.

Went home.

People think about it. Average people. Real people. Normal people. They think about, surely every now and again, what it'd be like to be super. Average, real, normal people—as much as they hate superpeople, hate them for what they did to San Francisco, hate them for all the average, real and normal people who were killed when a couple of warring superhumans turned half the city to slag—they still think: What would it be like to have abilities beyond imagination?

After San Francisco—as people refer to the history of man since the tragedy—the response to the thought, at least openly, was disgust and revulsion and strong statements of contempt. Why would I want to be like *them*? Who the hell would want to be like *them*?

But the false plating on the statements was fairly obvious. Like racists who spent their time at the beach working their tans. Normal people couldn't help but think what it'd be like to be a god.

The real, true answer to the thought depended on who was doing the pondering. The real, true answer was sometimes banal: If I could make myself invisible, I could hide out in the women's locker at 24 Hour Fitness and ogle all the naked chicks I wanted!

The real, true response was sometimes, probably, noble: If I had superpowers, I could've kept that little girl from being hit by the truck, saved the space shuttle crew, put an end to the war in . . .

But those are the thoughts of normal humans. People who have to shield their eyes from the sun as they look skyward from the bottom of an unclimbable mountain.

Truth is, reality is, looking down from the mountain, the view's not all that better.

Yeah, you can turn yourself into a human torch, but when you do, you ignite, incinerate, everything within a ten-foot radius.

Superstrength is real nice. Except you have to work, actually concentrate on opening a door without ripping it from its hinges. Picking up an egg is an Olympic event. Your fear, your sweaty nightmare: someone saying, "Here, you want to hold the baby?"

If you're invulnerable—bones like titanium, skin like steel—sure, you could walk from a plane crash scratchless.

Physically.

But an invulnerable's still got pain receptors. It could survive a plane crash, but it would *feel* the associated trauma. The impact, the metal of the fuselage slamming into, twisting against its body. The shock of the explosion, the burn of the resulting fireball.

What would it feel? A shitload of pain.

For an invulnerable, at some point, a sustained influx of pain could overwhelm it, fry its CNS. Do to it what the physical force of getting plowed by a bus or hit by lightning couldn't. Kill it.

Anson Hall was feeling a lot of hurt.

Anson had jumped from an eight-story building, had been slammed against a brick wall, had a motorcycle thrown at him . . . And the running. All the running hurt like hell. His lungs burned from overuse, lactic acid nuked his legs. Brimstone in the body. Hurting like hell wasn't just an expression. Fact was, no matter he could take a hit from a semitruck, what Anson could not do was run any more.

Yet he kept on.

Adrenaline.

Adrenaline propelled Anson forward. Adrenaline brewed by panic.

Anson could die.

That he could die: It was a concept that hadn't so much as entered Anson's mind in the twenty-seven years since, when he was thirteen, a couple of rottweilers mauled him. Tried to. Ended up shattering their canines without so much as breaking his flesh. The thought of dying had no traction with Anson since Anson realized he was . . . different.

Special, his parents told him. They told him he was special. Then they told him to never say anything to anyone about being special because even in the Age of Heroes regular people had fear of superpeople. Special people. People who were different.

Then San Francisco.

Then "after San Francisco."

Then everyone who was special . . . different . . . just kept their mouths shut. Heads down. Acted normal.

Anson knew the score, played the game. But Anson also knew what he was and death wasn't a consideration for him. Never before.

Now death was a demon on Anson's back, chasing him down. The demon drove him on.

Run.

Run to where?

Didn't matter.

Just away. Run away from it. *It.*

Except *It* kept pursuing, and *It* could not be lost. *It* had followed Anson when Anson tried to lose *It* in that apartment complex, then jumped from the building to the street, crashed through the boarded window of an abandoned self-storage. *It* had been the one to hurl the motorcycle at Anson, pick Anson off the ground by his throat and slam him—repeatedly—into a brick wall.

Anson had broken away, run away, as he'd been running for the last eighteen minutes. Since *It*—middle of the night, at a lonely stoplight as Anson's car stalled—had run up on Anson, ripped the door from the frame and Anson from his seat. Introduced Anson to the asphalt of Chavez Avenue.

In Los Angeles, a city that traffics in random violence, this thing—*It*—had come specifically for Anson.

And *It* brought pain.

Fingers which crackled with electricity, electric fire which could not be detered by indestructible skin and bones. Forget the drop from the building, the thrown motorcycle and wall. Brought pain? *It* was pain.

So keep running.

Keep running.

Keep . . .

To where?

Anson had run, had been chased into East LA. Was like getting chased into Beirut. Abandoned cars, houses

shrouded behind metal bars and locked doors and
chained gates. Citizens living as inmates. Scared into
submission, driven to seclusion by bangers and crackheads and LAPD Rampart cops who were most times little better than bangers and crackheads. Sometimes they
were the same thing.

Farewell, age of heroes.

Who was going to help? Who among the timid, the
thuggish, the strung out would help Anson?

None of them.

Keep running.

Keep . . .

Climb!

Up, over a chain-link fence and then . . .

Keep running.

Never mind the hurt, the burn. Keep running.

Jesus.

Diane.

He thought of, Anson thought of . . .

Jesus.

Light.

Anson saw the light. Too late. Anson turned, but the
light was on him. The light and the wail of an air horn.
They were from the Gold Line, the light rail that cut from
Pasadena to Downtown. Anson was standing dead in its
path.

The train's horn shrieked.

That was what, a warning? Useless. The train was
rolling too fast to stop. Anson was too tired to move. Too
beat to care.

This was going to hurt.

And then came the impact: the grille, the steel of the

engine slamming into Anson, picking Anson up and launching Anson's body.

And then there was a moment, the pain so intense it didn't exist. It was off the agony scale. Anson's mind could not quantify it. The sensation did not register. Not immediately. Later Anson's head would find a way to process the hit, and the hit would hurt.

Later.

Now . . .

There was a moment when Anson was sailing in the air.

Sailing.

Flying.

And in the moment Anson thought, he thought: If there was a superhuman ability to possess, this, the ability to traverse without effort and with dispatch from one point to another, was the one to own. Anson thought: If he could truly fly on his own and unaided by a speeding train, he would not be *here*. He would be passing easily to Diane. He would go to her and take her in his arms, and together they'd sail away . . . God, Styx. When was the last time he'd . . . They'd sail to somewhere that people who were different and those who loved them weren't hated and hunted like rabid dogs. Wherever that mythical land was.

And then Anson's brain finished its processing. His receptors kicked in and he hurt like the devil. But even the devil didn't know hurt as detailed as when Anson took to the ground landing at sixty-plus mph. Skipping a couple of times, skipping along, whipping and twisting along. Clothes shorn on coarse earth. The repeated, repeated, repeated slap of flesh on road until there was a sound. The sound of an animal begging to be put down.

A few seconds or so. A few seconds. Then Anson realized the sound was his own putrid screaming. One more lesson in a night of learning. Being invulnerable ain't shit against hurting.

What Anson didn't hear was the sound of the train braking. It kept hard-rolling, the engineer not wanting to have to go through due process and the form filing for hitting whatever it was he'd hit. If he kept on for Union Station, pretended like nothing had happened, well . . . maybe he'd just hit a bum. That was the same as nothing happening.

LA. Even through the hurt of getting hit, Anson thought: Goddamn LA.

And Anson struggled up to his feet. Gingerly. Then he reminded himself, had to actually remind himself he was indestructible. He was not hurt. Not truly hurt. No need to be ginger. It was time, again, to run.

Run to . . .

Where would he run that *It* hadn't already demonstrated *It* would follow?

Run to the police? If they saved Anson from *It,* who'd save Anson from the police?

Home?

Diane? Run to her? Bring *It* to her?

No.

Run to where?

Tungsten. Anson thought of Tungsten. Anson used to want to be Tungsten, same as just about every metanormal—before San Francisco—dreamed of taking their gift and being something more than normal. Doing something beyond regular. Acting like a hero.

Tungsten had been KIA by King of Pain. King of Pain

had previously, in one of those used-to-be-common battles between the supergood and the superevil, put the otherwise indestructible Tungsten in a coma for five months.

Didn't matter.

To Tungsten it didn't matter. When it came time to square off with King of Pain again, he stood his ground. Knowing King of Pain had the ability to take his life, Tungsten didn't run.

Heroes don't run.

No more running.

No equivocation in what Anson told himself, ordered himself to do: no more running. No matter the outcome might be same as with Tungsten, Anson would stand. Anson would fight *It*.

I will be, Anson said in his head, something more than human.

A trick of the moonlight. Clouds cleared the sky. Up the street darkness seemed to part.

Coincidental. *It* was coming.

I feel no pain, Anson told himself. I cannot die. I am more than human.

The caller ID on her integrated cordless phone/digital answering machine that had every advanced feature except the one that allowed Soledad to walk more than five feet from the base unit while talking on the phone said it was Soledad's parents calling.

She didn't pick up. Wasn't Sunday. Wasn't the day Soledad had designated in her mind and by habit as being the day to talk with her folks. Sit on the phone while they talked at her.

She let the phone ring itself out, was through the door by the time the answering machine picked up and her mom started asking of Soledad's empty joint: "Are you there? Sweetie, it's Mom. Are you home?"

Melrose to Robertson. Down to Third, over into BH. That was the route Soledad was going to run. A five-mile loop. Same one, with slight variation, she ran the four days out of seven she did road work. Not too many places in LA offered decent scenery and a fair lack of traffic. The city was built for driving. Health nuts be damned. Soledad had found a course, and she stuck to it. Some Hybrid on her iPod to speed the miles along. The sun was, as always, up there. The heat from the endless pavement, the smog; they'd mix for a physically taxing workout.

A good workout.

Some sweat and ache to wear away that nagging, fucking . . . Death. Death was nagging Soledad. Shouldn't be. She'd gotten over, *thought* she'd gotten over, Death a long time ago. The day of San Francisco: Soledad, her family, were supposed to be in the city when a battle between the superhero Pharos and the supervillain Bludlust turned half the town and most of its citizens to slag and ash. But Soledad, her family, weren't there. They are alive. Alive, Soledad figured, on borrowed time. So what was Death . . .

Left on Robertson . . .

When Soledad was already dead? Should already be dead? That kind of thinking had kept company with Soledad, given comfort to Soledad as she jobbed her way through the LAPD academy, worked a beat, SPU and MTac without so much as getting sweaty palms.

Not once.

Until . . .

Right on Third.

And a thought came to Soledad, came like a frank observation that, being objective, was separate from her own thinking.

The thought: Know what you're scared of?

What?

You've been hanging around Vin. You're attracted to Vin. But you're scared you don't really care for Vin.

Endorphins pumping in Soledad. Runner's high coming on.

A high coming on.

Stupid, Soledad told herself. Losing herself in natural bliss, she told herself the thought was stupid. Why would it matter if she—

You don't care for Vin. Used to hate Vin. So you're scared Vin's just a bounce-back thing. You're scared 'cause if he is, then who you really love, who you're *still* in love with, what's really giving you unease—

No! It wasn't qualms or questions or misgivings on the ways of her heart. It was Death. Soledad felt Death creeping close and, yeah, it scared her because she didn't . . . she wasn't afraid of losing her life. She didn't want to lose the life she could have with Vin. *Vin.* Vin she loved, she told herself. And told herself. She could deal with Death and falling for a guy she used to hate. What she couldn't deal with—

A horn.

Soledad looked as she ran out onto Ivy. Looked too late. As she saw the massive front end of the Ford Expedition bearing on her, she thought: I hate SUVs.

There was laughter all around.

Rare thing. Odd thing.

Laughter from Eddi and Alcala. And from Soledad. Soledad laughing out loud, continuously. That was the bit that was rare and odd, and made more so by the fact that there were three MTacs cracking up and they were doing it in a hospital. Mostly, MTacs in hospitals meant cooling for some specialist to arrive from an ER, blood-covered, telling the rest—or the remainder—of an element, eyes lowered and with a mournful shake of the head, "Nothing we could do." Mostly, MTacs in hospitals meant waiting for spouses or family or lovers or life partners to come around, get the official word, then break down in sobs while the rest—the remainder—of an element wondered how long it'd be before their spouse or family, lover or life partner would be heaped on a dirty tile floor sobbing for them.

Mostly, that's the way it was with MTacs in hospitals.

But right then?

Eddi, Alcala and Soledad right then couldn't bust up enough. The situation was funny in a relieved kind of way. Everybody was relieved Soledad was still alive. Her left leg, specifically her knee, was fucked-up to a monumental degree by the hit it took from the Expedition. Beyond that, some scrapes and bruises she collected skimming over the asphalt on Ivy, the situation was funny. To a degree. After squaring off against flamethrowers, shape-shifters, even a telepath, Soledad had almost gotten taken out by a representative hunk of one of the worst automotive trends ever to get spat out of Detroit.

To the MTacs, it was hi-F'n-larious.

"Jesus, Soledad." Alcala joking. "Making all of us look damn near pathetic. An MTac getting put down by a station wagon."

"Wasn't a station wagon. You know it wasn't a—"

"Actually heard a traffic cop making cracks about MTacs. A traffic cop, Soledad."

"Hey, I had the right-of-way."

Eddi: "Yeah, you always have the right-of-way."

"I'm serious. Had the right-of-way, and this ass . . ."

"Shoulda hit him with one of your bullets."

"Guy barely brakes. Hate stupid SUV-driving sons of—"

"I've got an SUV," Eddi said, wearing that slick smile of hers.

"Figures. And he was on the phone too."

"You shoulda hit him with one of your bullets." Alcala saying it again. "What do you got for asses on cell phones driving their—"

"Lead. Nothing special. Just lead."

"Getting slow, Soledad." Eddi flicked through some food on a tray next to Soledad's bed with her index finger. Nothing worth trying. "You twenty-nine now? Might be time for your gold watch."

"Hell with that. I was making a move."

"Moving from human to hood ornament."

"Like to see you get out of the way of a speeding truck, *kid*."

"That's the thing: Us *kids* wouldn't let ourselves get boxed in first off."

Eddi and Alcala laughed, dapped.

What the hell, Soledad thought, was Alcala laughing at? She was older than him, but he was junior rank to her.

She was going to say something about that, but Vin walked in the room. Walked pretty decent for a guy with one real leg. That Otto Bock worked good. Vin walked in carrying some flowers.

Things quieted some, the laughing fell off.

Vin asked what was funny, what was the joking he heard before coming into the room.

Eddi and Alcala mumbled about busting Soledad's chops.

Then there was quiet. The uncomfortable kind.

Vin asked Alcala and Eddi how things were.

They said things were good.

The quad talked on about sports; what the hell was going on with the Lakers. The weather, the other night's episode of some sitcom.

Some more quiet.

Eddi announced she had some things to do. Alcala, too, said he had some things that needed taking care of. Both said their good-byes to Soledad, Vin.

"Good seeing you again, Vin."

"Take 'er easy, Vin."

Then it was just Vin and Soledad.

Soledad gave Vin an update on her knee. Torn liga-
ments. There'd be further surgery. There'd be physical
therapy, a limp that would, hopefully, diminish over time.
Time when Soledad couldn't work MTac. No matter how
she'd gotten busted, she was a busted cop. Being busted
was to be automatically inactive. Yeah, there was other
cop work she could do: file files, write up reports. Any
temp could do that. Doing *that,* the Admin work of law
enforcement, was not being a cop. And the feeling that
came with doing *that*—no matter she'd previously tried
to convince Vin otherwise—was one of supreme uselessness. A car with no tires. A fork with no teeth. A
Hollywood actress over the age of forty. It was a feeling
as discomforting as any Soledad knew. Her job was her
life, her purpose. It was her obligation. So no job . . .

No life?

No purpose?

And then Soledad got honest. "Scared me, Vin. Scared
the hell out of me."

"Screwed up your knee some."

"Thought I was going to die."

"If a freak can't kill you . . ." Vin maintained a stare at
the room door.

"That's what scared me. I've gotten it in my head I'd
go out in a general alert, gun in each hand taking on a
rush of muties. Put down as many of them as I can before
I go."

"John Wayne."

"Angela Bassett. But then you see mortality rushing at
you in the grille of a Ford . . . what the fuck, Vin? I was
going to die, and I was going to die for nothing. From

after birth to a stain on the asphalt, and what did I amount to in the between time?"

Still looking at the door: "This an ego thing? You figure your obit wasn't going to run enough column inches?"

"It could fill the paper, but right then I wondered, what would it amount to? That's what I was thinking: I was going to die without ever amounting to anything."

"Your gun, the telepath you took out . . ."

"I shot its wife."

"Another freak."

"I shot its wife. If I hadn't, would Yar still be alive? Would you still have your leg?"

"Wife or no, you want to talk about what the telepath would've done if you hadn't stopped it? Think about that."

"What I'm thinking, I'm starting to think . . . it's a war that breeds war."

"Jesus, Soledad—"

"It's the kind of shit that never stops. So my gun, how many of them I take out . . . doesn't matter. They'll keep coming at us, we'll keep going at them. So what I do, what we do, what does it amount to? Might as well pack the fighting up, move it to the Middle East."

"You almost got killed. I get that. But you don't—"

"It's not a near-death experience. It's more like a—" It was more like what? "More like a near-useless death experience. I'm just feeling a little useless right now."

"Tell me about it, Soledad. Tell me all about it and act like it's new to me." Through Soledad's self-assessment, her talk of her feelings and concerns, Vin maintained his stare at the room door.

When Soledad finished her venting, Vin said at the door: "I'm a bad memory to them."

Soledad knew who and what Vin was talking about. Alcala, Eddi. Their distance, their coolness when talking with Vin. From the second he stepped in the room the shift in their mood was obvious. Soledad'd hoped Vin would take it in stride. He didn't. This was not good for her. Bad enough she had her own concerns. Now she'd have to put some emotional work into dealing with Vin's as well.

Soledad said: "You're not a bad memory. Alcala wasn't even on the element when we went at the telepath. You're not a bad memory for him."

"Then I'm a poster child for what happens when things go south. Couldn't even look at me. Barely could. Eddi could barely look at me, and Alcala—"

"That's their own guilt; that it was you, not them. They're staring at you, they're staring at mortality. They look at you, and they've got to deal with their own shit, so they—"

"They were laughing with you. They can laugh with you, but with me . . ." Vin realized he was still holding the flowers he'd brought Soledad. He formally presented them to her.

"They're pretty. Thanks."

"Got them downstairs. Was on my way up, figured I shouldn't come empty-handed."

"Or you spent all day picking out ones you thought I'd love," she coached. "You don't have to be honest. Sometimes it's okay to lie a little." Soledad, touched, genuinely: "Thank you."

Again, Vin looked to the door. "How's Eddi?"

"Good."

"She good or just getting by?"

"She's good."

"I worry about her. She likes to talk tough, but she's more girl than man."

"I'm telling you she's good."

"She had a thing for Yar, you know. Watching him get killed like that—"

"You want to make her?"

"Do I what?"

Soledad was kidding on the square. A little jealous, never mind her jokes. "I can slip her a note, see if she's got a date for prom."

"Or you could talk to her, make sure she's good like you think. She worships you."

"She doesn't worship me." Adjusting herself, Soledad tried to turn down the volume on the throb in her leg. Meds had kept it subordinate for a while. Soledad had quit those. Wasn't some hard-ass ploy. Opposite of that. The painkillers were gooooood. Made Soledad feel as sweeeeeet as she had since . . . in years. She could see how people got hooked on the stuff. She could see herself getting hooked on the stuff.

So she quit 'em.

Soledad, finishing the thought: "She doesn't worship me. Not anymore, if she ever did."

"She get a tattoo?"

"No."

"You sure?"

"Checked."

"Checked everywhere?"

Soledad stared at Vin.

Vin: "She's not dumb. She knows you hate hero worship. She's not going to get a tattoo on her shoulder."

Soledad, still back at the head of Vin's statement: "Check everywhere like where?"

"Her ass, maybe. Maybe . . . you know how some girls like to get one right near the crotch."

Slow roasting. Soledad did some slow roasting. "No. I don't know. Why don't you hip me to how some girls like to get one near their—"

"Soledad—"

"Okay, just so we're clear on things: You really want to bang her?"

"Do you talk like a guy because you think guys think it's sexy, or—"

"Yes, and do you—"

"I think Eddi's a very attractive person."

Soledad opened her mouth to spew fire.

"But I think she's nothing compared to you."

No fire. No fury. Not a word. She didn't say a thing. Soledad's mouth maintained its slightly open position.

"So what are you going to do with yourself?" Vin asked. "I know you taking downtime isn't going to happen."

"I don't know." Soledad was talking to the wall opposite Vin. Forgetting for a second that her black skin didn't blush, humility made Soledad look away from him. "Was thinking of seeing if I could get assigned to DMI. Next best thing to being an active MTac, right?"

Vin shrugged.

"Figure it'll be good too, you know; doing intel. Find out what they know about freaks, how they track them, how many there really are out there. Now's the chance."

"Why don't you get assigned to HIT? You can keep your research going there."

"HIT is bullshit." Looking back to Vin, blush turned to heat. "Bunch of geeks who couldn't get jobs at Metalstorm or DARPA, sitting around with their bullshit theoretical science. 'Gee, maybe if we perfect a particle beam or a rail gun, we can take out muties.' Meanwhile, I'm in my garage making shit that works. Just because my knee's messed up doesn't mean I'm gonna go waste my time."

"But that's just your first reaction. It's not like you put a lot of thought into it."

Referring to Vin's causticity: "So what's the deal? Takes me getting just about run over to get you back to your old self?"

Rubbing at where his prosthetic and stump met: "The days of being my old self are good and gone."

And whatever trace Soledad had seen of the used-to-be Vin, cocky Vin, get-that-last-word-in Vin evaporated. Returned in brief, gone quick. By Soledad, bitterly missed.

She said to Vin: "You could come over with me. Real easy, you could get detailed to DMI."

"To do what?"

"To work intel. To get intelligence on freaks."

"Yeah, but for me; why?"

"Because you should be doing something. Because it's been eight months, and you should be—"

"You want to get married?"

Soledad managed: ". . . Married . . . ?"

"Do you want to marry me?"

In this second go-round, Soledad couldn't even muddle

out the one-word response she'd given the first time Vin asked.

"You don't want to marry me. You don't want to . . . You talk about what'd help me heal—"

"It's not that I don't want to . . ." No conviction there. Soledad quit talking, didn't even try working past what Vin knew, what she knew was the truth.

"If you're not going to marry me, and believe me, the question was more for shock value than meant as invitation, but if you're not going to really be part of my life, then don't try to orient my life."

Soledad wanted to say something counter to that, but short of "Yeah, I'll marry you," what counter was there?

Vin told Soledad he'd be back later to see her. He'd be back to quietly kill time with her as she'd done with him when the situation was exactly flipped. Exactly, except Vin's leg'd been chewed off, not busted by an SUV.

A kiss to Soledad's forehead. A squeeze of her hand.

The sounds of the hospital bled in through the open door, then died off as Vin left the room.

Figuring there couldn't possibly be anything on TV worth watching, Soledad passed time looking at the flowers Vin had bought downstairs, brought upstairs.

Her thought: Painkillers'd be real good right now.

What's the difference, the joke goes, between an MTac cop and a DMI cop?

You can see how fucked-up the DMI cop is.

That's the kind of interdepartmental ribbing that beat cops, SPU and SWAT cops think's funny.

It's not funny.

But like most jokes that trade on stereotypes, it's true. Kinda.

We're fucked-up, MTac cops; inside we are. Any MTac who's honest would tell you that.

Normal people—in the physical sense—who want to earn their pay busting superpeople . . .

You can say to yourself: Somebody's got to do it. Somebody's got to protect all of us from all of them. Yeah. You can say that. But most people, most cops included, would respond: Somebody, but not me.

There's something in us, people like me, that makes us respond: Okay, I'll do it. There's something in us that is, honestly, off. Not quite right. For some it's too much macho in their DNA. For some it's fatalism. Me, I feel guilty for my survival, and that guilt's informed or misinformed every other thing in my life. The choices I make. The ones that I do not.

Vin, for example. Why can't I just tell Vin I like him? Why can't I accept that I like him? When he asked me to marry him, why couldn't I just say . . .

Because I feel guilty. Because I won't let myself be happy. Because I can't commit.

For starters.

Yeah. MTac cops: fucked-up on the inside.

On the flip side . . .

DMI cops, cops who work the Division of Metanormal Investigations, you can see how they're fucked up. Mostly, they're ex–MTac cops who'd survived going up against a mutie, but just barely. Routinely, DMI cops had burned flesh, scarred flesh, were absent limbs or eyes or extremities. They limped. Sometimes they wheeled themselves. But they wanted to stay in the game. Fight the fight to the bitter, bitter end.

There was no way they could work an element, serve a warrant on a freak. But they could work with the brain boys who kept tabs on the freak community, gathered information to use against the freaks: identify freaks who thought they were passing; living as normal when there was nothing normal about them. Track the comings and goings of such freaks. Who they socialized with. What their abilities were. Most important: What were their weaknesses?

It's a hard little game trying to figure which muties to leave be, keep under active surveillance in hopes they'll lead you to something good — good being a boss mutie — and which muties are too dangerous to let walk around like they were free, white and twenty-one. The wrong pick, bad information getting passed up the line concerning which freaks were at worst a nuisance and which were a clear and present danger . . . that could be somebody's life.

Not a mistake that happened often.

Most of the men and women in DMI were there because of somebody else's bad intel or incorrect choice. Being a victim of stupidity makes you want to keep anybody else from suffering through the same.

DMI didn't suffer stupidity. They didn't tolerate slacking. They were arrogant about their work. They were more important—more self-important based on who was doing the talking—than MTacs. All MTacs did was shoot. DMI gave the MTacs an edge when it came time to pull their triggers.

Whatever.

You could go back and forth forever over who's the spearhead of the fight against muties. All I know, I'm not ready to give the fight up.

For a while, at least, I'll be working DMI.

Utilitarian, but as a style choice rather than a necessity of budget. Soledad hit the DMI headquarters in West LA and was, in return, hit with a mix of awe and resentment.

The awe: This is Soledad O'Roark. This is Bullet; the girl with *the* gun who'd been an operator on an element that'd taken out a telepath. Taken it out, mostly thanks to *the* gun. Hers. The one she'd made. She'd been BAMF a record number of occasions in a record short span of time. This was one of the best cops ever to wear a shield.

The resentment: Who's this girl, this slummer come 'round because her leg's bad—temporarily bad—and who'll go away soon as it's good again? Who's this MTac grunt who thinks she's got the smarts, the skills to work DMI?

Some of the resentment wasn't so territorial. Some of it was just garden-variety bigotry. A woman cop? A black woman?

The mix of awe and resentment fluctuated from person to person. And while Soledad could do without the awe,

she was surprised, from even those who admired her, to a
person they all carried some resentment toward her.

"Don't worry about it." Abernathy passed a hand in
the air, shooed away Soledad's concerns. Abernathy—
his first name, rarely used in-house, was Benjamin—
was, or would be for the time being, Soledad's CO. Her
lieutenant, her "lieu." He was physically, Soledad thought,
an unremarkable man. That wasn't a slight. There was
just nothing about the guy—his size, the cut of his hair,
the way his features were arranged on his face; nothing
biological or self-generated—that would make you give
him, if you passed him on the street, a second thought.
Except, except if you heard his voice. His voice was opposite his slight stature. It was deep and rich and boom-
ing. The voice of a beefy soul brother, not a negligible
white guy. Should be singing some R&B. Should've, at
least, been doing voice-overs for movie trailers.

"It's not personal," Abernathy said regarding Soledad
and the cold shoulder she'd been getting hit with tag
team–style from the minute she set foot in DMIville.
Abernathy said: "Can't take it personal. DMI cops, their
life is about being suspicious."

Soledad: "Even when there's nothing to be suspicious
about?"

A shrug. "You spend your days doing surveillance on
the corner pharmacist or a soccer mom who's actually a
freak that can take out a city block without producing a
sweat, suspicion's a hard habit to shake."

"I can deal with a little negativity. Compared to actually having to be the one to take down that pharmacist or
soccer mom, it's nothing." Soledad wasn't so much

displaying machismo as she was giving support to the whole of G Platoon.

Abernathy said: "There are bad habits all around. MTacs included. Again, nothing personal."

Cold. Distant. Unable, unwilling to allow people into their lives because their lives were, generally, short-lived. MTacs had bad habits to spare.

"I don't," Soledad said, "take it personally. Mostly." And mostly, Soledad didn't. She didn't take personally the ice, the propriety glances. Except for the cops that hit her with their straight-up old-school bigotry. Soledad personally wanted to kick that bunch in the teeth. Otherwise, long time ago, Soledad'd decided she wasn't in the give-a-fuck business.

Abernathy: "Would you mind?"

Just that said. Soledad knew what Abernathy was talking about. She pulled her O'Dwyer, removed the clip from the back. No need to eject a shell from the chamber. Didn't have a chamber. Handed it butt-first to Abernathy.

He looked the piece over, asked a couple of questions about it, and Soledad went into what'd become a standard speech on her sidearm. How Metalstorm had agreed to let her modify it, how the governor had okayed her field-testing it. Soledad skipped over the history of the field test: the disciplinary action against her and the trumped-up IA investigation that'd preceded it, her almost getting hung out to dry for getting a cop killed—a cop she admired, respected. A cop whose death she had nothing to do with, whose passing had changed her life. Whose tattoo, an exact duplicate of, Soledad wore on her left shoulder. Five simple words: WE DON'T NEED ANOTHER HERO.

All of that Soledad gave the go by to. She didn't need to bring it up. Abernathy knew about it. At least knew a version of it. There wasn't a cop on the force who hadn't heard the rumors filtered through the blue wall that's supposed to shield fellow cops from acrimony from the outside. Truth: All it does is make a cell where accused cops can get gang-raped from the inside by intimation and allegation.

So let others speculate and wonder. All that mattered, same as her encounters with a fire freak and a speed freak and any of the other freaks she'd gone against, Soledad'd survived that departmental attempt on her life as well.

Abernathy handed back the gun.

"I don't believe you'll be needing that much here."

"Never know."

Nodding to her assertion: "No, you don't. But the use of deadly force is the last thing events should come to. Here we watch, we wait, we note. We fight with our heads, not our fists. The grunt mentality stays with MTac." Abernathy wasn't accusatory. He was even. And that voice of his, he sounded like he was reading copy for a public service announcement.

"Don't have a grunt mentality," Soledad said. "With MTac or otherwise."

"That business with IA—"

"Was never carried through. An OIS that was investigated as required."

He was probing. Soledad knew Abernathy was testing her same as any lieu would an operator being rotated in who had a . . . a *situation* in their package. They'd want to know, not so much the details of the event, but could

the cop coming off the situation handle himself? Herself.
Or are they burned and bitter, full up with anger they're
just waiting to spew at a moment that's inappropriate?
Inappropriate, in a cop's world, is a moment that gets
someone killed.

"I guess the concern is," Abernathy said, "you have a
history of independent action."

"Independent thought and independent action are two
different things." Soledad was composed, quite controlled.
Soledad said: "I've been point on any number of MTac
elements, and on all of them my record speaks for itself.
I know how to work as part of a team. But I also believe
in thinking beyond the box. That's got its own rewards,
and it's got its own risks. But when it comes down to us
versus the muties . . . yeah, you play things smart, but
it's no good for cops to go at things overly cautious.
That's just as dangerous as being a hothead."

"If you do say so yourself."

"I do. But would you want a cop jobbing for you
who's not willing to take a stand?"

Nothing from Abernathy.

A moment more.

Abernathy said: "I don't mean disrespect when I talk
about the grunt mentality. It's not an attempt to put down
G Platoon. It's just, I don't know, call it departmental
hubris. We all work together, yes. Nice, as company lines
go. But as far as DMI is concerned, it's just a line. Three-
quarters of the operators here are here because the grunt
way of thinking got them shattered. Now they're ready to
use their heads.

"This is not G Platoon. This is not MTac. I have no

doubt once your leg heals you have no intention of continuing on with DMI."

No protest from Soledad.

"But you are here now. If you want to be effective here, now, then forget about G Platoon. They're not your family. We're your family. It's this family that has your back."

No flinching around with her gaze. Soledad gave Abernathy a stare hung on a taut tether eye-to-eye. "While I'm here, I'm here, sir. But I'm always going to be MTac."

What Soledad got for her forthrightness was sat down at a desk in an office empty of light that was natural and colors that weren't primary. What she got was a hard drive full of e-files that had to be cross-referenced with paper files that were prime for an incinerator. Most of the files were left over from surveillances that were shut down, a warrant having been served on a suspect. The suspect, the freak, probably dead by way of an MTac element. Occasionally, a freak was brought in alive and ended up housed at the SPA. The euphemistic way of saying they were incarcerated at the California state Special Protective Area located in the heart of the Mojave.

But freaks going to the SPA was very occasional. Mostly, when it came time for freaks to get arrested, freaks didn't do things the easy way.

The files, the cross-referencing, it was busywork.

For all the talk of brainwork, of how special DMI was, how DMI was the secret weapon in the war on freaks,

Soledad had been handed paper to shuffle. Duty buggery. Glorified secretarial fare, and that shit was what Soledad hated more than any single thing. Worse than being useless, it was the imitation of usefulness. For most cops their living nightmare was to get caught gun empty in the middle of a firefight. For Soledad . . .

So what was this? Was this a test too? Was this Abernathy having a look-see at how much banality Soledad could take? A gauge of how committed she was, despite her assertion of always being an MTac, to the job at hand?

That was a good thought to Soledad: that she was getting fucked with. That she was worth fucking with. That she rated some kind of initiation made Soledad feel special. Unique. Not, at least, like a cop too thick to be trusted with brainwork.

Soledad looked up from her papers. Outside the door was a guy she guessed to be in his early forties. Sandy-blond hair. Hazel eyes. One hand. He had one hand. His left. A prosthetic hook was the terminal device on the right. He was in the corridor lined up in the doorway staring at Soledad.

Soledad said: "Yeah?" And she said it to mean: Yeah, what do you want? Yeah, what do you need? Yeah, there's a black woman on leave from MTac working in your joint. What about it?

The guy's stare didn't beg any of that, but whenever presented with the air of confrontation, Soledad usually took things to the extreme.

The guy walked on, no words for Soledad.

Should've, Soledad thought, should've put in for HIT. Too late now. Not because she couldn't still get the transfer. Ego wouldn't let her leave. Leave and have others think she'd been chased off by the stares, the cold shoulders. The busywork DMI passed off as intellectual endeavors.

Soledad had the tenacity to survive all that was presented to her.

Soledad put all of her formidable tenacity into finishing her e-files.

The message on Soledad's integrated cordless phone/ digital answering machine was from Soledad's mom. Same hi-how-are-you-just-checking-in message Soledad had been getting, had been dodging, for six weeks. A month and a half. Little more than that. Soledad didn't feel like, could not take, talking with her parents. Loved her parents, her parents were great. Just couldn't handle at the moment the stress of their regard. The near-daily worry they heaped on her about her life, her work . . . Soledad could very much do without a repeat of five years previous when she'd been clipped by a car while out running. Her mom on the first flight out from Milwaukee, around all day every day for eight days solid to help Soledad recuperate when there was little or no recuperating to be done.

Her own fault.

Soledad knew the current state or her relationship with her parents—strained, distant, vague—was her doing. And it was as obvious as it was natural that the more Soledad pushed her parents off, the more clingy they became.

They clung to their daughter.

They held on tight to the little girl who inexplicably cried every time someone sang Happy Birthday and defiantly painted all her white Barbies black, shaved the heads of all her black Barbies 'cause "they look more kick-ass that way." Too young to even have a word like "kick-ass" in her lexicon. Soledad's parents hugged in absentia the young woman who—when others her age worshipped pop stars and teen heartthrobs—was in awe of the Nubian Princess, the greatest of the superpeople. Her opinion. And Soledad's parents quietly, daily, prayed for Soledad, the woman who shut down on the first day of May years prior when half the city of San Francisco and her citizens were removed from the planet along with Soledad's faith.

They loved her, Soledad's parents were there for her, and all Soledad had to do was reach out to them. Offer herself up as the daughter her parents wanted her to be.

Easy.

Sure.

If you could resurrect a city, 600,000-plus people. If you could basically hop in a machine that bent time and could carry you back to a moment before the demigods who should have guided aspirations instead sparked fears, then maybe Soledad could trade her solitude for effusiveness.

Wasn't gonna happen.

So, for another week, Soledad would put the dodge on her folks. Give them a callback when she was pretty sure they wouldn't be home.

From her integrated cordless phone/digital answering machine Soledad erased the message from her mother.

Couldn't see it.

Think about it.

You hold a magnifying glass over an ant on a hot day, you can't see the sharpened sunlight that fries it.

So . . .

If a person has the ungodly—extra-godly—ability to refract the light collected by their retinas into focused shafts of intense heat, you cannot see the hot death coming at you.

You can in movies.

In movies, people with heat vision are always lighting up the area around them with their death-beam eyes.

But that's movies.

Movie audiences have to have their fleshy minds entertained for them. The excitement's got to be obvious.

In real life, feeling your flesh start to heat up when a fire-eyes freak looks your way: That's all the excitement you need.

But you always got extra excitement thrown in gratis.

In a parking garage in the Bridge, in the middle of a firefight with a fire-eyes, Eddi and her element got melting glass and warping metal and bursting tires and instant heat damage to everything that was in the general direction of where the fire-eyes looked.

Good thing: In a parking garage, there was ample steel for the element to put between itself and the fire-eyes' killer stare.

"Where is the lamb for the burnt offering?" the freak screamed.

Bad thing: All that cover made it hard for the element to get off a clean shot. They swapped fire for fire, but they couldn't drop the thing.

"Reload," came the call from Tipden.

A hail of .45 Colt auto covering fire was Eddi's response. It was her present for being upped to the element's point in Soledad's absence. The most ferocious handgun in existence. One of 'em. Didn't hardly feel enough in Eddi's hand. And to think her max dream had been to thread every freak she crossed with her pop's knife. That she'd managed sharp-force trauma on any freak ever . . . Luck? A miracle? Stupidity.

Glass melting.

Metal renting.

Tires popping.

She wasn't going bitch, but Eddi couldn't put enough cover between herself and this freak.

"His word is in my heart like a fire, a fire shut up in my bones. I am weary of holding it in; indeed," the freak yelled, "I cannot."

"Reload," Eddi yelled.

Tipden and Allen picked up their rate of fire. Eddi crouched, popped the Colt's clip. Fed it another. She missed hefting an HK.

She sure as shit missed Soledad's O'Dwyer.

And she was up. She was firing. Three guns against a fire-eyes. Odds weren't hardly good. Three against one, and the MTacs were getting pushed back.

"He makes winds his messengers, flames of fire his servants!"

That was . . . Even as she jerked her the Colt's trigger, signaled Tipden and Allen to drop back, Eddi was working to remember. Sundays. Church with her mother, her father. "Winds his messengers." "Flames of fire his servants." Psalms.

And if Eddi could dial her rage, up it went. She wasn't the most Christian person. Not even close. Never much cared for church on Sundays. But her parents, her father, tried to put some God in her. Freak's acting like God had taken her dad.

And now this one was spouting the Word?

Unacceptable.

But just about unstoppable.

Eddi could feel the heat of the thing pressing closer. Cutting closer.

"Reload!" she yelled.

The freak just kept spouting pseudo-Bible. No reloading for him. No ammo out. No stovepiping, stoppages, jamming.

Just heat billowing. Steel bending. An Escalade sagged, bowed down before it.

The freak: "After me will come one who is more powerful than I, whose sandals I am not fit to carry."

Bad call. Eddi was starting to think she'd planned wrong.

"He will baptize you with the Holy Spirit . . ."

Planning wrong was gonna get her killed. Not so bad. She could take it. What made her feel like shit: Tipden and Allen were gonna get dead too. She saw the concrete of a vertical support char. She saw Allen make a move as hot light punched its way through the side of a German car.

How, Eddi wondered, would Soledad have played it?

"And he will baptize you with fire! Revelation is coming! The truth will—"

The standing theory with freaks, the one few normals were ever hoping was proved otherwise, was that the vast majority of muties only owned one significant fetish. They had one superpower. And it would be a very bad day for the normal human race when freaks started developing a second ability.

For a split second the fire-eyes looked like it had suddenly acquired the ability to rent open its chest and spit its innards outward. Would've been a useless superpower had it been a superpower. In fact it was a one-ounce slug fired from Alcala's Benelli punching its way through the freak's front carrying a good-sized mass of the freak's back and spine and lungs and whatever else it could grab up before heading out its chest.

And then it was like the freak was rushing to scoop up what it'd ejected from itself. Making a quick move to avoid a spill like some guy who'd accidentally dumped his martini at a cocktail party. Really, he was just falling over. Crashing into the garage floor. Splashing into a puddle of his own insides.

The fire in his eyes was out.

The freak was dead.

And then there was this moment, this blessed moment

that occurs only rarely and only when a call goes good. When the freak gets dropped, there isn't an operator down and what's left of the element's screaming into a radio for a bus. After the guns quit talking in their particular vernacular there is just quiet. Calm, halcyon quiet that is a harsh counterpoint to the raging hell that existed in the same space an instant earlier.

It made Eddi think or realize that it was just that much or just that little between chaos and calm. An instant.

And then the quiet was gone.

Tipden was calling in an all-clear to Command.

Alcala, easing for the freak—the Benelli giving the body a stare-down—called for Eddi: "Dropped it."

". . . Yeah . . ." Eddi's racing heart and spinning mind were a couple of gears that wouldn't sync.

"Dropped it, Eddi." Breathing hard. Words pitched between excitement and fear. Alcala sounded like a bull rider who'd just made his seven seconds. "Didn't even see me coming."

"Took your damn time."

"Only had one shot, wanted to make it count."

"Good call," Allen to Eddi. "Letting Alcala circle around like that."

Eddi to herself: It wasn't a good call. It was a gamble that turned out good. Most points would never hold a gun back against a freak. But she figured if three could keep it distracted, one could get the drop.

"Hell of a good one," Allen said, "for first time on point."

Alcala added: "Bullet wouldn't've called it any better."

She could see it. Beyond the dry prose of the perfunctory reporting in the *Daily News,* in the theater of her mind Soledad could see Eddi leading Pacific MTac—the element Eddi'd been elevated to point of upon Soledad's leg getting jacked—against a freak that could generate and discharge heat from its eyes. And they had taken it out sans casualty to the operators on the element, according to the *Daily News.* Usually, the *News,* the *Times,* local TV, didn't much bother reporting the details of warrants served on freaks, since warrants being served on freaks, no matter some flew and others spat fire, had grown over the years to be reasonably commonplace. Like gang shootings. Like politicians and their whores. Like Hollywood leading men getting outed. In this day and age what else was new?

What was new: a twenty-two-year-old cop, female on top of that, taking out a freak that could shoot heat beams with not much more than a knife.

That knife. That knife of Eddi's . . .

There was absolutely nothing in the article about the MTacs' procedure, about how they took out the freak. It was in her head Soledad saw Eddi putting it down, solo, with her blade. And Soledad could hear, again in her head, she could hear Eddi chiding: How about that, Soledad? Chalked a freak and didn't even need your fancy little gun.

That knife of hers . . .

Undoubtedly, it'd been multiple clips emptied by all of the element into the freak that'd dropped it. But Soledad, her feelings of uselessness that had festered in her leg and were now infecting her imagination, couldn't help but score the victory to that knife.

And Soledad'd been worried about Eddi worshipping her? Why should Eddi? Probably, Eddi made a better MTac than Soledad.

What was that Soledad was feeling now? Obsolescence doing an insect's crawl on her flesh?

Eyes.

It was eyes rolling over her, sensed so strongly they came to her as an actual feeling.

Beyond the doorway, in the corridor, the one-handed, one-hooked cop—that particular cop with one hand, one hook—was standing where he had a couple of weeks or so prior. Staring as he'd done previously.

And, same as before, Soledad: "Yeah?"

"O'Roark, right?"

"Yeah."

"People talk about you."

Soledad gave a shrug indicating how much—how little—she cared about other people's talk.

"People are saying—"

"Whatever." Soledad had no interest in the conversation and aborted it before it was fully formed.

The one-handed, -hooked cop kept up his stare, kept it going. And Soledad returned one. She maintained her intensity, not mocking him or imitating the guy. She was actively staring him down.

Then the cop came into Soledad's space. "Tucker Raddatz." He held out his left hand, offering an awkward shake.

Soledad joined his left hand with her right hand, didn't bother with her name. Obviously, it was known to him.

Raddatz said: "Welcome to DMI."

Where a thank-you would've been fine Soledad said, too honest for her own good: "You've got to come around, stare at me twice, two weeks apart, just to offer a hello?"

"Wanted to be sure."

"Of?"

"That you'd still be working here in two weeks' time."

Another shrug from Soledad. "Here's where I want to be."

"Which is why you waited until you got your knee messed up before making the move from G Platoon to DMI. A temp transfer at that."

"If I'd known the cops here liked to stand outside office doors like peeping pervs, I would have been here years ago."

Not so much as a smile from Raddatz. "Some gave a lot to be here." Signifying. He was obviously talking about his lost hand. Maybe some other wounds unseen. Those of other DMI cops. "Hard to take the sort-of-injured coming around for a temporary visit."

"I don't know if I'm supposed to feel a certain way because you're disabled."

"I'm not disabled. One hand, and I can still do more than—"

"I don't know how I'm supposed to feel that you're a gimp; if I'm supposed to feel guilty, or sympathetic, or what. Mostly, I don't feel anything. Not for you guys. You got the way you are because you were messing with freaks. Mess with freaks, sooner or later you get messed up. So I don't feel anything because, same as the rest of us, you knew the risk and you took it. And I don't feel anything because, well, how would you take the sympathy of a stranger anyway? Not well at all."

"How would you know?"

"Because I wouldn't take it well. I wouldn't want it."

Their mutual stare remained in a locked loop. Stayed that way.

Raddatz said: "Want to get coffee?"

Soledad said: "Sure."

Soledad felt better about Raddatz after he'd directed her to a Norms. Norms were diners. Old-school. Trapped in a Googie era. Value-priced. Highlights of the menu: a patty melt and a fajita salad and a California Reuben sandwich and a chicken-fried steak that Soledad had never had—she had never had anything of the kind anywhere—but promised herself to try before her death. She didn't care about seeing the Eiffel Tower. She didn't care about going skydiving one time before she bit it. She just wanted to try the chicken-fried steak. Only, not today.

Norms's coffee, porcelain-cup-served, varied only by the cream and sugar the drinker dumped in it.

Raddatz, deftly, used a combo of hand and hook to rip open his sugar, his little packets of cream. How many years of practice did it take to get good at mixing coffee like a two-handed person?

Soledad had tea. Regular Lipton. Lot of milk. Lot of sugar.

Panama had nothing.

Raddatz had brought a tagalong with them. Another cop. Chuck Panama. About Raddatz's age. Not a bad-looking guy. Only, he knew he wasn't a bad-looking guy and it had probably gotten him a lot of play in his younger days. So now he slung around his "ain't I fine" attitude same as some high-trading currency that ought to automatically buy him something.

Bought him nothing from Soledad except instant contempt.

And he was nondisfigured. He had no visible defect. No limp. No scars that could be seen. For a DMI cop that was remarkable to the point of being unique. Soledad's neck alone owned a souvenir—a palm-shaped scar of burned flesh—of her very first call. Panama's flawlessness was a curiosity to Soledad.

For a minute the three talked, mostly Raddatz and Soledad doing the talking. Panama seemed slightly above engagement. The talk was about nothing. The way smog was making a comeback in the city, the way the Clippers weren't and probably never would. They spent time on insignificance, but their talk wasn't about the conversation. Their talk, seeing who stood their ground, who held their convictions over matters of little consequence, served the function of a couple of sparring partners going around and around the squared circle waiting for the

other to demonstrate if things were going to be gentle or
if there was some pugilism to be done. In the process
Raddatz gave a little primer on himself. Married, a couple of kids. Boys. Was with West LA MTac four years
ago. Twenty-first call, eighth on point—and he remembered the exact number it was—a freak got the best of
them. Got three of the operators, got his hand.

Three cops dead, one gimped.

And here was the kicker. As the cops were fighting for
their lives—more rightly, as they were losing their lives
in a slaughter—one of the cops squeezed off a round that
went stray and did a through-and-through to some guy a
coupla blocks away. The guy died.

The *LA Times* ran an op-ed piece. Heavy-handed.
Anticop. Anti-MTac. MTacs were offing innocent people
in their cross fire. Israel Fernandez led a protest rally. Not
even a hundred people showed up. But that was a start.

Three cops dead. And the *Times,* the liberals were saying the cops were out of control?

Raddatz did his hand/hook thing, put cream and sugar
in some fresh coffee.

He took a sip, took in some of the brew. He let out
nothing but bitterness.

Raddatz said: "That damn Fernandez."

Panama nodded to that.

Soledad got where that came from. Here Raddatz was
with one hand, and other people with two good ones
wanted to wrap them around the freaks and give them a
big, sloppy, "oh, you poor victims" hug. And of them, of
that bunch of freak fuckers, the worst had been "Damn
Fernandez," Raddatz said again.

Soledad said something to the effect that it had been

how many . . . how few, really. How few years since San Francisco? Already people were starting to forget.

"That's the thing," Raddatz said. "You try to make people remember, they say you're wallowing in tragedy. You do nothing, they just let it slip out of their minds."

"Month after May Day, everybody's like: Yeah, we want the Feds to do something; yeah, we want DNA testing." By the string, Soledad bobbed her tea bag in an empty cup. Something for her hand to do. "A couple of years go by, people were already bitching the Executive Order's not constitutional. DNA testing's an invasion of privacy."

"How about we just let freaks back into the country? All of you in Europe, c'mon home." Raddatz's sarcasm was high. "How about we give them their spandex back? Let them fly around, get in fights . . . start knocking over buildings again. Shit, if we're just going to act like San Francisco never happened . . ."

Panama gave a laugh.

She knew he was just going off, agreed with Raddatz's core philosophy, but still Soledad shook her head to all that. "They think that way, the bleeding hearts; they just want to roll back the clock in their heads to the day before yesterday ended." Soledad got the psychology of the liberal fringe. At least, she was able to articulate the thought process she ascribed to them. "They want to believe, they want to make themselves believe . . . some of them, maybe they actually think they're doing right. But I think most of them just want to make themselves believe San Francisco could never happen again."

"How the hell could they—"

"They just want to feel safe. Ignorance and bliss, right?"

Panama: "Bullshit."

"Yeah, it's bullshit. Absolutely it is. So people like us, not only do we never forget what happened, we've got the added chore of having to remember *for* the bleeding hearts."

"That why you went MTac?"

"There another reason to try and arrest things that can make you burst into flames with a look in your direction?"

"Some operators are just action junkies." Panama was accusatory in tone. Slightly, but just enough. "They get off thinking they're BAMF."

"And those operators mostly never get past SWAT." Soledad was adamant about the point, having worked with enough jarheads, youth wasted on PlayStation and thinking cop work was nothing but a video game, to last a lifetime. A lifetime that was likely to get fractionalized when the jarhead found out too late that when you're going after a freak you don't get do-overs. "They can play badass all day, all night. Doesn't make them anything of the kind. Every other cop job, the odds are you're going to live, retire, get fat off your pension. MTac, every day you survive you've beat the odds. You know that. And you know, a job where being dead is the norm, you've got to be down for the cause."

"You'd stay with it, then; stay with MTac?"

Panama was probing. Soledad didn't care for it.

To Panama: "You ever work MTac?"

Panama nodded.

"So what's your story? You don't look like you ever got it bad from a freak."

"Maybe I'm too good for that."

"If you were so good, you'd still be MTac, so maybe you suck and got bounced to DMI."

"Lift your shirt," Raddatz said. "Show her your torso."

"The girl's eating."

"I stopped being a girl when I started kicking little boys like you in the teeth."

"She's not eating."

"I don't mean right this second she is," Panama said. "But she might want to eat again someday. Why spoil her appetite for life?"

"First call I went on an operator got a hole hand-burned in her chest by a fire freak. So unless you've got something else to show me . . ."

Panama lifted his shirt. What he showed Soledad was some whole, other, hideous thing. It was . . .

Just . . . some other, hideous thing.

Soledad had to make herself, make herself stare at the damage just so not to come off like a bitch.

Panama lowered his shirt.

"Would you give your back," Raddatz rejoined the conversation, "to an MTac who wasn't in things for the long haul?"

Shirt down, and Soledad was still staring at Panama's torso. Soledad shifted her look to Raddatz. "No."

"So you can see why we're curious."

"We?" The word stuck out to Soledad. So did the fact that, with Raddatz, it probably wasn't a casual slip of the tongue. He was tossing bait. She wanted to know: "When did I become a departmental concern?"

Pulling a laminated menu from a holder at the edge of the table: "You hungry, O'Roark? Can't ever go wrong with a five-dollar steak."

"I'm good."

"Think about things."

"And you're not talking about the steak."

A bit of a smile from Raddatz. He wasn't laughing, but he appreciated her, appreciated Soledad. Soledad had that effect on people. Usually, right before they tried to terminate her in some fashion, they gave her their regard. "I'm talking about what you're going to do with yourself. Think about that."

He put down the menu. With one hand—and for him there was no other way—Raddatz pulled his wallet, picked out some money, tossed it on the table.

At some point early on, almost all kids have a moment where they want to grow up to be policemen. They want to be honorable. They want to aid the community, and in return be looked on with gratitude for serving the public good. Then kids *actually* grow up, wise up, go for jobs that pay six figures. At least that. And where you don't have to dodge bullets in the process.

Most kids do that.

Not all.

Not Tom Hayes. At a young age Tom got caught in the wanna-be-a-cop frame of mind. Or rut, however you want to look at it. Got in it. Never got out. He'd been indoctrinated by the ads. Not just the slickly produced, near-Hollywood-quality ads the Los Angeles Police Department ran every recruiting season. He got caught up in the actual Hollywood-quality ads. Every movie, every TV show that portrayed the LAPD as the toughest roughneck shield-wearing MFs on the planet, drawing their guns weekly, wrapping up every crime, no matter how major, in some length of time between forty-four minutes and two hours.

Creative license, sure. But it had to be, Tom figured, an approximation of real life. And for Tom, for having grown up in a trailer park in Palmdale, a cop's pay was the icing that shined like all the gold in Fort Knox laid out end-to-end in the noon sun.

So Tom took the entrance exam, aced it, went to the academy, became a cop.

Then the boredom set in. Even in LA, even in a city of eight-plus million, there was mostly not a lot for a cop to do. Not a lot that was exciting. You could make traffic stops for minor infractions day-night-day. You could settle disputes between/among bums, alkys and vagrants of every known race, creed, color, ethnic and religious background and sexual orientation until you felt like you were working security at a skid row UN meeting. Occasionally, you could get into a beef with some scofflaw punks of the rich, white variety whose snobbery begged for reduction from the polished, forged aluminum of a Monadnock baton. And very, very rarely there'd be some actual trouble—the real-world version of movie/TV show trouble—that maybe just might require the removal of your gun from its holster. The chances of pulling the trigger? What were the chances of getting elected pope?

And even if trouble ever happened that it was so severe it necessitated the pulling of your piece, even in LA that was a once-, maybe twice-in-a-career kind of thing.

If you were a beat cop.

In LA real trouble got dealt with by SPU or SWAT.

Real, real trouble, and MTac got the call.

Everything else, every mundane thing was for cops like Tom Hayes.

Could've been worse.

Tom could've been a cop years back in the Age of Heroes.

Age of heroes used to be capitalized. Not anymore.

Back then, in the age, there was next to nothing for a cop to do. Drug dealers, gangbangers, carjackers got dealt with by the likes of Nightshift, Street Justice, Urban Legend. Guys—and women—with just enough super-normal abilities to be able to kick the ever-lovin' shit out of your typical punk-with-gun.

Bigger trouble—punks with automatic weapons, terrorists with bombs, superevildoers with particle weapons—got handled by the likes of Élan, GammaMan, Nubian Princess.

Cops worked crowd control, directed traffic around the inevitable damage done when supertypes mixed it up.

Then San Francisco. May Day. Then the age of heroes got written in lowercase. Then beat cops like Tom Hayes got elevated from doing absolutely nothing to doing barely anything.

So when Officer Hayes got the call from dispatch to "see the man" down at the LA River, it gave him no spike. Another bumfight. A couple of white kids, rolling on E, in need of an attitude adjustment.

When he got to the river—a river by name, in actuality a concrete ditch used as an aqueduct to flow the water the city stole from the northern part of the state—and talked to "the man" who'd put in a call to the Hollywood station re: a body he'd found, Officer Hayes didn't make much of it. Bodies, like abandoned cars, got found constantly.

But if he'd had so much as a sliver of an idea that, staring at the body, he was witness to a portion of a play that featured God and man, Officer Hayes would've made more of the moment. Probably, he would have bent over and puked in the face of it. More intrigue than his internal organs could handle.

But he was aware of nothing but a dead body.

He waited for a hearse from LACFSC to come and take it away.

Then Officer Tom Hayes went and got himself some lunch, writing up a moving violation along the way.

There was one message on Soledad's integrated cordless phone/digital answering machine. Her mother, Soledad figured. About the only other person who called at home—besides telemarketers who had no regard for the Do Not Call Registry—was Vin, and Vin hardly ever called Soledad.

Soledad played the message.

The voice she heard had all the distinctiveness of a Swedish automobile. So free of spirit and character it could not be recognized. So bland she had to listen—Soledad actually had to work at hearing—to absorb what the speaker was saying, the voice not self-compelling. Couldn't manage it the first pass. Halfway through, Soledad started the message over. A request for a private meeting, a sit-down to talk about . . . What was to be discussed was vague, as ill defined as the voice that spoke. At the end of the message: "Oh, yes. I'm sorry. I should have said: This is Tashjian calling."

Soledad had once been nearly dead and buried. Metaphor, of course. Actually, considering her job, not "of course." But in terms of living a life that made her feel alive, the business with IA had just about killed her. Could have landed her in jail too. And the guy who dug her grave—dug it deep, dug it well and was ready to toss the first shovelful of dirt on her not-even-cold body—was Tashjian.

Sapless, swashy, milk-and-water. Tashjian. His voice on her answering machine was reminder to Soledad of what little there was of distinction to the guy. Except for being quite the creep. And being undeniable. He was a fellow who got his way, got what he pleased.

What he wanted was to have a talk with Soledad. And never mind their history—or because of their history, because she ended up free and clear of him—Soledad was glad to take the meeting. To look the bogeyman dead in the eyes.

"I'm not scared of you."

Soledad, Tashjian, were at Pan-Pacific Park, strolling around under the LA sun that was—thanks to a population that refused to stabilize let alone diminish—again losing the fight against the smog that only a few years prior it had begun to get a handle on.

Tashjian responding to Soledad: "I would doubt there's very much you are afraid of. Certainly not me."

"You better believe I'm not."

"And I do."

"You tried to take me out. Didn't work. If you think I'm going to run and hide when you come knocking—"

"You have no fear of me. I take you at your word. But the more you talk . . . exactly who are you trying to convince, Officer O'Roark?"

At that point, to say nothing more was equal admission Tashjian was right. To let his comment go was backing down, and backing down never felt correct to Soledad. As middle ground: "Just so you understand where I'm coming from. It's not so much that I'm interested in what you've got to say as I am in letting you know I've got no problem with you saying it to my face."

"Understood."

It was odd being out of doors with Tashjian. He was, seemed as though he were, a creature of the shadows. More comfortable in dark than light where his designs could be more easily seen and therefore exposed. A requirement of prestidigitation is that actions be masked. Sleight of hand was Tashjian's expertise. The conceptual dark of others' ignorance was his stage. But here Tashjian was strolling around, walking in the sun just the same as anyone. No longer an object of apprehension, just more of what he really was. Incredibly normal. Maybe daylight changed Soledad's perception. Maybe it was the change of circumstances; the crushing stone of disciplinary action no longer hanging by a threadbare twine over Soledad's head. Either way, Tashjian didn't seem quite the creep.

"At any rate," he said, "my ultimate objective wasn't to remove you from the department."

"You put a gold medal effort into things for a guy who wasn't trying."

"I told you at the time, I might have been there to help you. You didn't believe me. My intention, my intention was not to bring a good cop to false justice for no reason. It was about getting to the truth. That's what detectives do, be they Homicide, Robbery or Internal Affairs."

"I don't have a problem with you getting to the truth. What I've got a problem with is that I told you the truth and you wouldn't take it."

"What kind of detective would I be if I accepted things at face value? It's in the looking you learn to appreciate what you see." As if to demonstrate, Tashjian took a glance around the park. A little spot of green and trees lined by the low-rise apartments, the orthodox business of the Fairfax District.

Tashjian said: "It's in these moments, the casual ones, that I see the reason we do what we do."

"We? You worked MTac?"

"No. I haven't. I was speaking of police work in general. *This*"—an arm arched before him—"is why we do what we do."

Soledad looked around, looked at what Tashjian was seeing. A bum, his whole world packed in the Sav-On shopping cart he pushed around the city. A couple of Asian guys, palish skin, shirts off, potbellies revealed, lying out sunbathing. Two softball-playing, Harleyriding, phys-ed–teaching dykes fornicating without care for, concern of, anyone who might be watching.

A cross section of the carnival Los Angeles. Small but representative.

In response to what she saw, to what Tashjian had said: "This? It's a freak show."

A tic of Tashjian's head. "You and I both know what a freak show is: things disguised as normal but far from. Things that fly, things that change shape or size. Things that can execute feats which you and I could perform only in our minds and with our best imagining.

"So the oddity around us now, within the city, these very people in the park: They are not so odd, Officer O'Roark. They exist, they are human. They perform simple acts of living. They search for love, companionship and meaning in life beyond the cycle of eat, work, sleep. It is these acts that make them human, that drives humanity. And though, per individual, we may not understand or wholly agree with the desires of others, the obligation that you and I and those who are like-minded have undertaken is to ensure normal people have the opportunity to fulfill their legal desires. Our obligation is not just, not merely to protect normal people but also to secure the acts of living to which they are guaranteed. Without that sense of guarantee, would we as people continue as a race or succumb to an emotional extinction? It is hope that gives us a future. So, in aggregate, our job is not to enforce the law. It is nothing less spectacular than to protect the future of humanity. We provide no other service except to ensure a certain peace of mind; that to the best of our abilities we will prevent acts of living from being interrupted. If they are threatened, we will protect. If the life itself is lost, then we will pursue the guilty.

For this social compact to work, you, I, people like us, must follow the letter of the law regardless of our feelings, our personal prejudices or favors. It is the law, as written and interpreted without bias, that must be our guide. Those you may have quarrel with out of uniform, you will offer your protection to under the color of authority.

"If this critical aspect breaks down, I believe—and I say this believing the statement is free of hyperbole—we will find ourselves on a path to anarchy. Worse. To our own destruction.

"We are on such a path, Officer O'Roark. I believe we are. But there is still an opportunity to correct ourselves. So I come to you to ask for your help."

There was nothing but confusion and questions for Soledad. "Help you how? With what? What . . . what anarchy?"

"You know, of course, of Israel Fernandez."

Soledad's nod "yes" became a head shake of disgust. A quiet editorial of what she thought of the man.

"His is a death which remains in question," Tashjian said.

"For the freak fuckers. If that's the anarchy you're talking about, as far as I care—"

"You don't. You don't care. For you, yes, that's the natural reaction. But the anarchy I'm talking about is more than *a* death, or the conspiracy theories that surround it. There have been, over the past fifteen months, several deaths involving people associated with the metanormal community. Some were certainly more questionable than Israel Fernandez's. Some, five of them quite frankly, were murder."

"They were sleeping with the enemy." Not knowing

the specifics, not caring for them, Soledad was unmoved, analytical. "Somebody wanted to, wanted to set them straight and went overboard. That's for R/HD. It's not my concern."

Then Tashjian added to the equation: "The five I believe were murdered were metanormals."

And that gave Soledad pause.

"What are you considering?" Tashjian asked. "How people with extraordinary abilities could be killed by anything short of an MTac assault? Or are you pondering the fact that most metanormals now live incognito and in fear of the law, police. If Fernandez was in fact murdered, he was an obvious and easy target. But how did the killer know his metanormal victims were in fact metanormals? The logical conclusion, the unpleasant one: The murders were carried out by those already collecting intelligence on metanormals. Those with an understanding of their weaknesses and how to exploit them, and with a severe desire to destroy them."

"Like a cop."

Tashjian nodded. Added: "Such as an officer within DMI."

"Does it . . . somebody's doing our job for us—"

"It is not 'our job,' Officer O'Roark. Executioners under the guise of the law is what the liberal media, the bleeding hearts wish us to be. But we aren't. If there was a . . . There is a child killer living down the block. You know this, you have evidence. You wait for him at night. And when he emerges from his house, as he passes, you press a gun to the base of his skull, and you—"

"That's not what I'd—"

"For the price of a bullet you save society the cost of

a trial, the family the incalculable agony of reliving a nightmare."

Soledad said nothing. Tashjian'd made his point.

"As rational," Tashjian said, "as it might seem, there is no rationale for vigilantism. Merely empty justifications. There is also no account in murdering metanormals or their supporters. Their supporters have a right to free speech, and metanormals have the right to due process, the opportunity to turn themselves in, receive reparations. They are incarcerated in the Special Protection Area, yes. At times deported. But they are not executed. They only face harm when they attempt to do harm, or when their identities are disclosed, a warrant is issued and they refuse to surrender peaceably.

"How many MTacs would still be alive, do you imagine, if they were allowed to fire first instead of waiting to be threatened or until they had delivered so-called Civils to a suspect?"

Rhetorical question. But Soledad gave a quiet accounting of dozens and dozens. And how many times had Soledad wanted to shoot first and not even bother handing a freak the opportunity to surrender? But she had not. Never once. Despite her feelings, that wasn't the way things were done. At least, it wasn't how *she* did things.

The case Tashjian was building was, as to be expected, undeniable.

What Soledad wanted to know: "So freaks, freak fuckers are being killed. Let the cops deal with it. Why do you and me have to take a walk in the park?"

"The murders themselves, quiet, spread out over time among a relatively disenfranchised community, have gotten little attention from the department. At least as of yet.

But what's nearly certain, sooner or later some intrepid individual at the *Times* or Channel 4 will piece things together: Metanormals and their supporters are being targeted, being killed by police officers. We are, Soledad, in a very precarious position. Less than a decade and a half since San Francisco, and people—"

"People forget," Soledad finished the thought.

"Worse than that. They have forgiven and are on the verge of shifting blame. The protectors become persecutors: We're too harsh on metanormals. We're too inconvenient in the public's lives. I've heard the word 'gestapo' used with the LAPD, with MTac programs. Hyperbole, but after a time extremism begins to stick. So metanormals, metanormal rights activists being targeted, murdered . . . which side, do you suppose, will gain advantage from this situation? Who will gain sympathy?"

"I get that. What I don't get: Why me? IA's got a department full of people."

"And you've been at DMI how long now? Already you've seen it's more like a fiefdom than a division. They don't even sit in Parker Center. To try and investigate by ordinary means is pointless. To try to infiltrate one of my officers would be useless. Everyone at DMI would see a plant coming as easily as if they were supervisioned muties. You're in a good position, inside DMI by circumstances beyond suspicion, and your credentials are beyond question. You've distinguished yourself in duty, and that you've been investigated by my department—"

"Tormented."

"Is well known. By rights you should hate Internal Affairs. Why would you ever work with us? You are perfect for what the situation demands."

"Like I was a born rat."

"We can play a game of semantics all day and all night. If you fear being a rat, don't think of yourself as one. Don't disregard the opportunity to exonerate innocent officers."

"And I could tell them that? After this is done, how do you think they'd take it that I spied on them?"

Tashjian made a show of looking confused. His version of sarcasm. "Why would you tell them?" he asked. "They have absolutely no need to know."

"I'm talking about—"

"Honesty. Fidelity. And I appreciate that. What I'm talking about, simply, is maintaining the structure of society as we know it for the foreseeable future. If the door of change opens slightly, it might as well be kicked down. I think so. You are needed to keep the door shut."

More than eight months since IA had gone after her. The bad taste Tashjian, the department, left with her was still strong in Soledad's mouth. "Won't do it. I'm not going to sell out other cops."

"If they're murderers, if they are killing people—"

"Freaks aren't people. They don't have rights."

"Neither do dogs, but you can't shoot one in the street. The transgression is the same. So is the threat to you and me and everything that we believe in."

"That's kinda much, don't you think?"

"Maybe. But is that the chance you want to take? Hate me, O'Roark. From where you stand, I deserve your hatred. But don't hate me so much you would condemn us all to returning to a time when freaks ruled and humans clung to relevancy. Understand, that is where we are now: a point of advancement or reversion.

"I don't know what destiny has assigned us. Whether it's to change the course of history as we know it, or just bust a few dirty cops. Honestly, even thinking like that . . . well, I stand on very ordinary legs. What I do know, for whatever reason, whatever the outcome, we have been delivered to this moment to do something or to do nothing. My question to you, Officer O'Roark: Which will it be?"

It started as a John Doe. A body, no ID, clothes partially burned away, found at the bottom of the LA River. Not that the LA River was particularly deep. More like the LA stream. The stiff was stiff, probably dead forty-eight hours by the rigor, the lividity, but lack of decomposition. A bum, probably. Dead from too much booze, too little shelter. The body got transported to the LA County Forensic Science Center. Fancy name for city morgue. Given the same deference as the inanimate slab which it had ended up, the body would get processed, paperworked, stored, then prepped for an eventual dump in a potter's field.

Routine.

In LA, in a city that manufactured 158.9 bodies a day, this John Doe was just more of the same.

Would've been.

Except for the mandatory autopsy that the assistant medical examiner finally got around to performing six days after the body arrived. Except that when the AME put a scalpel to the John Doe to open his flesh, the flesh would not open. Not with the scalpel. Not with a bone cutter. Not with a hacksaw. Not with a Black & Decker power drill the AME pulled out of the trunk of his Dodge Stratus.

Who the John Doe was, was still unknown. *What* he was, was becoming real clear. What he was, was a freak. An invulnerable. Dead, probably, a lot longer than forty-eight hours prior to its discovery. Impossible to know. A hundred years from now his body might, slightly, begin to decay. Somewhat. Nobody knew for sure. As there had only been a very few exanimate invulnerables as case studies, the rate of their decomposition was still being surveyed.

So who the freak was, how long it had been dead were questions. But neither was *the* question. *The* question, the one that got the examiners at LACFSC nervous as they called DMI, reported what they had: What is it that killed an invulnerable freak?

He's a freak."

Soledad and Donatell stood just inside the doorway of the house. Nice house. Really nice. Palos Verdes nice. Big. Ocean view. The house was nice to the point the guy who owned the house probably referred to his "inside the doorway" as a foyer or anteroom or something else classy-sounding.

The guy who owned it: Fong. An Asian guy with an English accent. Either born in Hong Kong or educated at Oxford. However it was, the end result, he'd ended up in the south bay area of LA with enough dough to live well. Real well. The only stress in Fong's life, apparently, was his neighbor.

"He's a freak," Fong said again.

Soledad and Donatell gave very little outward reaction. Donatell—Mike Donatell—might've reacted the hell out things. His face, hard to tell. Donatell, when he was MTac, had ended up on a bad call against a fire freak. Donatell had been severely burned. Donatell's skull looked like it had molten flesh poured over it. Ears and nose made out of melted, discolored wax. He was a sight. Not a pleasant one.

Donatell: "When you say he's a freak . . ."

"When I say he is a freak, I mean that he is a freak. I'm not sure what else there is to say."

"What kind of a freak?"

Hesitation from Fong.

"What are his abilities?"

"Well, they are subtle. But they involve his vision. I believe he has, has the ability to see through solid objects."

"X-ray vision," Soledad prompted.

"I believe. And he is superstrong."

"Thing is, freaks only have one metanormal ability. So which is it?"

Hesitation from Fong.

Soledad, again: "Which is it?" Soledad had been "graciously invited" along on the interview by Donatell. Strictly, she wasn't sure she should be asking questions. But, response by response, she was getting a sense of things. Her sense, her time was being wasted.

"X-ray vision. I believe."

"And you know this because . . . ?"

"Because I've seen him use it."

"You've seen him use X-ray vision? How were you able to see someone use X-ray vision?"

"Why would I lie? What reason do I have to lie about that . . . that freak being a freak?"

"Did I say you were lying?"

"Mr. Fong," Donatell stepping back into things, "before we deal with the situation, we need to be absolutely sure of what we're dealing with."

"And I have told you." Fong did not, could not look at Donatell. Donatell's aspect too severe to handle.

"Yes, you have." Donatell's mouth was nearly fused shut. His words were permanently slurred, and every sentence uttered ended with a slurping sound. Donatell sucking in air and sucking back saliva. A couple of scenes from *The Elephant Man* jumped into Soledad's head. "But we have to be sure of what we're dealing with. Every detail has to be considered. Can you give us a description of the individual?"

"He's Mexican."

And Soledad got it. No matter the guy was doing well enough to afford a place in Palos Verdes—which meant he was doing better than ninety-five percent of the working stiffs in America—Fong figured his property value was going to take a hit having a Mexican living next door. So what do you do? You call him a freak, call DMI, have them send him off to a new place to live. Like the SPA.

Standing right where she was, Soledad settled back within herself. Let Donatell do the work, conduct the interview. She was done with getting her time wasted.

The queer thing about it all, one guy was accusing another of having the ability to see through solid objects. Soledad thought he was lying, but in the world she lived in he didn't sound insane.

The waiter took the order of the Chicken Saag, the Lamb Tikka Masala. Onion Kulcha. The waiter, taking the order, stared at Donatell. Barely looked away enough to write on the pad he carried. He stared at Donatell like he was clocking one of those *Night of the Living Dead* zombies trying to figure what was the best way to kill the beast. And on top of all that the waiter was obvious with the speed he took down the order, got away from the table as if he had to rush off to puke. Donatell didn't seem put out. Then again, as before, it was hard to tell what was going on behind that permanent mask Donatell wore.

Soledad, eating some katchumber: "What do we do?"

"About the call? Write it up, turn it in. Surveil the guy."

"Even though the complainant was lying?"

"You know he was lying?"

Soledad gave a laugh. "C'mon."

Donatell, again: "Do you know he was lying?"

"Back in the day the complaint would've been: He's a dealer. A banger. Whatever. Whatever to try to get the cops to do some redlining on the city's dime."

"Do you—"

"I know it's a waste of time when DMI ought to be looking for real freaks."

"Good of you to educate me," big slurp, "on how DMI works."

No matter the damage, the scarring, the flesh around Donatell's lips retained his right and real pigmentation. Darker than his burned skin. He was sort of a reverse minstrel. So badly burned. A few more seconds, a few more, Soledad wondered, and would he have been killed rather than left to live as he is? Does he ever, she wondered, look in the mirror and wish the couple of seconds had broiled him into oblivion?

"Do they bother you?" Soledad asked. "Ones like the waiter. The ones who just stare."

"Two kinds of people. The ones who stare, the ones who don't. The people who stare . . . hell, I would stare at me. The ones who won't look are the ones I hate. How are they not going to look? I know how my shit is. But they won't even acknowledge me, like, like if they don't look, I don't exist and who the hell am I screwing up their beautiful world with my hideousness? Anyway, you get over it. I scare kids and I can't get laid by anyone but whores I've got to overpay. You learn to deal."

He sucked in some katchumber.

"I used to be," Soledad said, "the same way with my neck. Self-conscious like that."

Donatell laughed, blew slightly masticated food out of his mouth. "That's like a hangnail, O'Roark. That little bit of scarring you've got's like a hangnail."

"Yeah, well, I used to be beautiful. For all I know, what you've got's an improvement."

A little light in Donatell's eyes. If he preferred those who stare over those who don't, he really dug those who could give a good ribbing no different than if all he'd gotten was a bad trim at Supercuts.

Getting back to what's what: "Maybe it's bullshit, O'Roark, but we still do things by the book because that's how the book says to do them. I know you've got issues with that."

"Issues with . . . ?"

"You don't always do things how they're supposed to be done."

"You know that?"

"I know the talk."

"And I care for talk the way you care for the people who won't even stare."

"You gotta understand," taking up a napkin, whipping drool from his chin, "things are different at DMI. Yeah, I know you've heard the talk; cops here think they're superspies. Most of that, most of that is self-arad . . ."

"Self-aggrandizing."

"I was never good with big words. Shouldn't even try. We're busted cops and we want to feel good about ourselves. I was MTac. Most of us were. But I'm just talking from my POV for a sec. When I was MTac, I saw things different. Mostly, I saw how the book was written by guys who were safe behind a desk telling us how to take out the freak of the week. You get bad advice a couple of times and you—"

The waiter brought the food. Set it down. Asked if the pair needed anything. When he got their no-thank-yous, the waiter left the table. All of that, his eyes never left Donatell.

Donatell, going on: "Things go bad for you a couple of times, sure, you do what you've got to do to keep you, keep your element alive."

Probing: "Not here. You don't use any independent thought?"

Donatell didn't say anything to that.

So Soledad let it lie. Had some saag.

Donatell ate too. It was not the most attractive thing in the world.

After a minute, taking a break: "I think if we go off the page, *if* we do . . . different from just doing something on our own, it's more about leadership here," Donatell said.

Soledad kept chewing, gave a quizzical look.

"Not like going head-to-head with a mutie, collecting intel is straightforward. Pretty much it is. But once you've got the intel, what do you do with it?"

"Merits a warrant, you get a warrant. Give it to MTac."

Donatell went back to eating.

Soledad was struck by his lack of affirmation. Being roundabout: "When you talk about leadership . . ."

"I'm talking about Raddatz. He's got respect coming to him."

"Other cops don't?"

"There're some of us who respect him a lot more . . . *even* more, I should say. Even more than others. The reason you did things your own way back on MTac—and I'm not telling you, I'm saying ask yourself: Was it because you couldn't trust your leadership? If you had real reason not to, if you just felt like you couldn't, it was the leadership you couldn't follow. Not when it got down to it. But Raddatz . . ."

"Him you can follow. No trust issues?"

"You're lucky enough to work with him close, you see why."

"How many work closely," a little something on that word, "with him?"

"Me, Tony Shen."

Soledad gave a shake of her head. Shen she didn't yet know.

"You'd remember him if you met him."

"How's that?"

"He makes me look good. Chuck Panama."

"Him I know."

"You're curious to him, to Raddatz."

"And is that how I ended up taking a call with you? Are you giving me a field audition?"

"You've got nothing to audition for. How you handle yourself only matters if you're going to be DMI. You really going to be DMI, O'Roark?"

Donatell cast a line, waited for an answer.

Soledad ate.

When it was real clear to him he wasn't going to get a response, Donatell joined her in getting back to eating.

Throughout lunch Donatell sounded like a suction filter on a pool. Bugged the hell out of Soledad.

There was one new message on Soledad's integrated cordless phone/digital answering machine. From her mother. The message had barely started playing and already Soledad was reaching to erase it, thinking of what would be a good time to return the call. "Good" meaning a time when most likely her parents wouldn't be home.

Her hand stopped, hung in the air, held up there by her mother's message.

Soledad's mother wasn't calling from Milwaukee, wasn't in Milwaukee. Soledad's mom was calling from the Radisson Hotel at LAX. Soledad's mom was in the city.

Sunset Plaza was a strip of boutique shops and al fresco eateries that lined the north and south sides of Sunset Boulevard in West Hollywood. Very LA. Very LA in the way folks outside LA think when they think LA: Beautiful people. Expensive cars parked along the curb. Really old guys with their hot young girlfriends who clearly weren't hanging out with their men because they actually had a thing for guys thrice their age. Minimum of thrice. Lot of flamers. The occasional actor who could still do box-office. All very ostentatious. High-end. And it was all just pretentious enough to give the tourists something to talk about when they went back home to talk about "those people" out West. All in all, Sunset Plaza was about as decent a place Soledad could think to take her mom for lunch. It was also, Soledad hoped, filled with enough "look at that over there" value to intrude on her and her mother's conversation. The crappily little conversation Soledad knew she'd be able to muster.

Things would start badly, Soledad figured, when her mother saw her on crutches. Bring on the worry. Then the "Why are you doing this, why don't you get a regular job" talk would start free-flowing. After Soledad macheted through that tangle of nonsense, things would really get going southward with all the questions her mom would send at her fusillade-style about the love life Soledad didn't have, the friends she didn't own. Question after prying question about bullshit, bullshit, bullshit . . .

Driving up La Cienega for Sunset Plaza. Soledad gripping the wheel of her car. Choking it.

God, how she hated this—

Tenser, tenser with each block traveled.

—having a sit-down with family. Having to open up and share because somebody wanted access to her life even though that somebody had given birth to her. Not that Soledad wasn't . . . appreciative; was that an expressive enough word? Not that Soledad wasn't appreciative of that. Her existence. Thank you very much, Mom, now here's a card for Mother's Day and a bunch of flowers. But why did coming from her mom's gene pool entitle her mother to more than Soledad wanted to give?

Jesus . . .

Her mother had to come to LA, had to come unannounced? Soledad said to herself—and it was hyperbole, sure, but there was a kernel of truth to her emotion— she'd rather go at the worst of the freaks—a telepath— than have lunch solo with her mother.

Sunset Plaza.

Soledad parked in the lot looking south over the city. Clear day. Warm weather. Decent view. LA wasn't all bad.

Soledad limped up the hill from the lot to Sunset, crutched it over to Le Petite. Her mother, Virginia—

Gin—already there. Looking good. Soledad thought her mother always looked good. Wasn't just a daughter's assessment. Gin was handsome the way Maya Angelou was handsome. The way, the way early pre-glam-makeover Oprah was handsome. Strong black women whose greatest strength was primarily their intelligence.

The future as Soledad had predicted did not materialize. Her mother greeted her warmly. Said how good it was to see Soledad, made a comment on the quality of the day. She did point out an actor sitting three tables over who'd had a hit TV show six years prior and hadn't much worked since outside of commercials for some kind of snack chip that wasn't made out of potatoes.

Gin said nothing about Soledad's crutches other than to ask: "Hurt yourself?"

"Twisted it running," Soledad lied. What she figured to be the first of many she'd be spinning over lunch as she prepped herself for the continuing cover-up of her leg injury.

But Gin had nothing more to ask concerning her daughter's leg, was more inquisitive with the waiter regarding the specials.

Soledad absentmindedly ordered the Santa Fe salad. She'd had it once years ago. It was decent. She figured it couldn't've changed all that much, and if it had, probably not for the worse.

A thank-you to both ladies from the waiter. He went to place their order.

No assessment as point of entry into a wider conversation about Soledad's love life from Gin to Soledad re: the waiter's looks and what Soledad thought of them. If Soledad found him attractive. If she'd consider dating him. If she wouldn't, was it because she was already seeing someone?

Unusual. Highly unusual, the lack of question asking.

In the time between the food order was placed and its arrival, Gin took charge of the conversation, apologized for coming to the city without forewarning but it just seemed the two of them kept . . . missing each other.

Signifying. Saying without saying she was on to Soledad's long-running scam.

But Gin abandoned her grievances there. Barely started, she let them go no further. All that came from her were pleasantries. About her flight, about the city. To her daughter, and about life in general.

Lilac.

She thought she smelled it when she sat down. Now Soledad was sure. There was lilac in the air.

Soledad didn't know of any growing on Sunset. The smell had to be drifting down from up the Hollywood Hills. Near the intersection of Sunset and Holloway—six blocks away—in a car that was made in Korea a cover version of a song by Fleetwood Mac played on the radio. Somewhere on the Blvd. a woman cried, but they were tears of joy. For a brief moment a near portion of the entire world was received with exceptional clarity by Soledad.

It wasn't right. The situation was incorrect. A background as a cop wasn't needed for Soledad to know her mother suddenly showing up in LA by herself was messed up. As her mother talked, Soledad half listened, half tried to figure the most natural, the least abrasive way to ask what she needed to know. Except if Soledad was ever nonabrasive, she'd long ago forgotten how to be. Probably about the same time she'd forgotten how to be patient.

So Soledad blurted: "What are you doing here?"

"I came to see you," Gin said.

That didn't come right away. There was a pause ahead of it. Brief, but it was there. The hesitation her mother had taken, the thought she'd put into a simple answer: Gin was lying.

Having spoken enough of them, Soledad knew a lie when she heard one.

"For no reason? You just get on a plane, fly a couple thousand miles—"

"To see you, talk with you. Not over the phone and not in, in vagaries."

"You and Dad splitting up?"

A laugh from Gin. A bitter one.

"If you are, you can, I guess, stay with me if you want."

"I never should have let you be an only child. You needed more family than your father and I could give you."

Soledad didn't know what to say to that, didn't know where it came from.

The waiter stopped by with the Santa Fe salad, the sea bass Gin had ordered, asked the ladies if they needed anything further.

A couple of curt noes.

Soledad fumbled with her silverware. Gin cut her food with a knife, forked a piece and ate. Ate another bite. Then she set the fork at the edge of her plate.

She said: "I have cancer. Ovarian cancer."

The handle of the knife she held, dull as it was, hurt

Soledad with the force which her fingers gripped it.
Drove it into her palm. Her throat went dry. And her eyes
as well. Someone else hearing that, hearing their mother
was potentially terminal, most likely their eyes would go
slick. Soledad's did the opposite.

Her voice, Soledad's voice was steady. "You should be
in the hospital."

"I will be. I'm scheduled to go in Monday."

"You're going to wait until—"

"I wanted to see you. I wanted to tell you."

Soledad started to say: You could have called.

Except . . .

Her mother *had* called. She'd called and called, and
Soledad had ducked and dodged.

Soledad felt a slow and steady drip of guilt water-
torturing her. She knew she'd feel it for years.

Fucking cancer.

Gin: "I came to tell you . . . well, I came to say how
much I loved you. How proud I was of you . . ."

Was.

Was?

"This is . . . you're, you're sick, and you come all the
way out to tell me—"

". . . but it sounded so odd, vapid to tell someone you
loved them. Under the circumstances." Gin had to fight
with that word some. Circumstances. "When you say it
like you're making a final declaration. If they don't know
it; if the person you're saying that to doesn't already
know that you . . . and it sounded, and it sounded cliché.
I'm dying, and therefore I have to . . . well, probably I'm
dying, so I have to tell you that I . . . but I wanted to tell
you."

"Stop it!" Soledad barked loud enough people four tables over looked in her direction. The has-been actor among them. "Stop talking in the past tense. It's like talking to a ghost."

Amazing even to herself; her mother had cancer, the bet was it was killing her, she'd picked flying to LA over going in for immediate surgery or treatment or whatever science was up to that was—in terms of fighting cancer—little better than a good leeching, and the only emotion Soledad could show was anger.

Unbelievable.

The waiter returned, asked the two ladies if everything was to their liking.

Soledad's head shook.

The waiter thought one of the meals was lacking and started to go into a WeHo hissy fit.

Gin set the guy right, sent him off. She ate. She put an effort into eating, going to the trouble not hardly out of hunger as much as to give Soledad a minute to collect herself. Food was poor distraction. Gin didn't have an appetite, hadn't since her doctor had sat her down, looked her in the eye and told her with all the compassion of a guy who's told a hundred patients some HMOified version of the same spiel: You've got an illness which could very much end things for you, and it's pretty much beyond us.

Gin pushed her plate away. She looked to her daughter. "What I want to say, I wanted to say face-to-face. I'm going to be selfish, Soledad. I don't want you coming home."

"What?"

"I don't want you dealing with my sickness." In that

sentence Gin put the emphasis on "my." "I don't want you watching me waste away."

"You're not going to die."

"You talk as if it were a matter of choice. If I choose to live, I will. That's hardly the way things are."

Except, in Soledad's world it was. In Soledad's world she had to believe it was.

Soledad: "Please quit the bullshit acceptance of the—"

"It's not . . . bull." Knocking on Death's door, Gin wouldn't sully herself with foul language. "I'm fifty-eight years old. My time is coming. Today. Tomorrow. It is. I can cry, or I can . . . I can get what I'm able to out of the time I have left. If that means taking a few days, flying to see my daughter . . . My fear, Soledad, my living fear was that something would happen to you while I was still alive. I didn't want that. I didn't want that as badly as possible. There is something so horribly out of sync about a parent burying their child. And I take comfort in knowing the manner I will end. It won't be by a bullet from a, a thug or some such. Or getting run down by some drunk. This way when it happens it will be just like, like slipping under water."

Soledad was realizing there was so much more to her mother than she knew. Was it some kind of law of nature you had to be close to losing something to appreciate it?

"How's Dad taking it?"

"Well. He's well in my presence. I think he cries alone, wishes that he could do something. I haven't . . . There are some things you avoid talking about, but I know it must be horrible for him. When you marry, you take a vow to love, to protect. Then there comes a time when the vow is useless."

"It's not useless. He still loves you."

Gin appreciated her daughter's insistence. But she was in a place of frankness. "Not useless, then. Hollow. How much does it hurt to love someone, to say you'll always protect them . . . I know he'd give his life for me. But he can't. He can't, and that's a hurt beyond imagination. I've felt it about you. There have been so many times where I've felt—"

"Do people know? Have you told people?"

"No." A slight smile. Even at this juncture Soledad steamrolled her mother, kept the personal conversation from becoming too intimate. "I told . . . do you remember Mrs. Schoendorf? Her daughter was in your class."

Soledad remembered the girl, her mother. She indicated so to Gin.

"Right after," Gin continued, "I got out of the doctor's office, in a store I ran into her. Don't even know why I'd gone shopping except so that I could pretend everything was normal. Pretend the doctor *hadn't* told me what he told me. So there I was. Mrs. Schoendorf, she was talking, going on about . . . whatever. About nothing, really. I don't know. Maybe it was important. Maybe it was the most important thing in the world to her. But once you know you have, you have this thing, you have this thing that's actively trying to end your life inside you . . . once you know your self is trying to kill you, that's the only thing that's important. And I said that to her. I said: 'I can't talk now, I have cancer.'"

". . . How did she, what did she—"

"Well, I think I shocked her. I did. I know I did. You say something like that . . . but not so badly that . . . I saw her again. A day later. She shunned me. She actually shunned me."

"What do you mean?"

"She . . ." As if it were a cat lying on the table, as if it could feel and respond to her movements, Gin's hand, the tips of her fingers, moved up and down over the fork that rested near her discarded plate. "I don't know how else to describe what she did. She did not wish to encounter me, and did everything she could to keep from doing so. Because I was sick. Just because I was sick, she treated me like I was some kind of—"

"I want to come home. I want to go home with you." Soledad was forceful with that. Put the same energy into her words she would if she were kicking in a door, executing a warrant.

Her mother, not as forceful, was equally indisputable. "No."

"This isn't . . . we're not taking a vote."

"Soledad, I love you. There it is. The cliché I didn't want to . . . I love you, you're all the daughter I could have ever wanted."

A lie. It hurt Soledad that at such a moment her mother was so mindful of her feelings she felt compelled to engage in emotional subterfuge. That Soledad, despite, in spite of her faults—her baggage that she portered poorly. The distance at which she kept people—could be as a daughter anything close to all Gin could have hoped for was beyond Soledad's comprehension. Both her self-perception and her perception of her mother were that badly adjusted. When she looked in the mirror, all Soledad saw was a cop who did work. That she was a cop who was honest and true and selfless was as lost on her as it was precious to Gin.

And that it was lost on Soledad made her all the more

beloved to her mother. Tears free-flowing from her. The cloth napkin not nearly enough to contain them. Giving effort to rejoin her own thoughts: "But since the day you left home you've been your own woman. I haven't agreed, I haven't even liked every choice you've made. But I've let you live your life the way you wanted to." She was pointed with that. "All I'm asking, if I'm done, let me end my life the way I see fit."

Soledad tried to think of a time—after Reese had a pit burned in her chest by that fire freak. After the tag team of a metal morpher and a telepath had cut through half her element. Even when a weather manipulator, for a minute, looked unstoppable to the point Soledad thought for sure she was staring death in the eye—she did not want to face a day of work.

Couldn't come up with one.

Her work gave her purpose. Even being benched from MTac, maybe especially *because* she was benched, her work gave Soledad a sense of purpose.

She wouldn't, could not consider *not* working, even though the stats said her work would eventually catch up to her. Kill her.

There were, yeah, times alone when Soledad found herself with the shakes. The night after going against that telepath she'd gone home and vomited. Spilled from her gut contents she didn't even know it had. That reaction was human. It was a reminder she hadn't actually "seen it all." Like Vin had said: the kind of nerves that keep you on your toes.

What Soledad was feeling now . . . competing needs: the need to come up with a reason to pry loose her grip on her Prelude's steering wheel, get out of the car, cross the parking lot and go into the DMI offices. Into work.

Vs.

Come up with an excuse not to do all that. Flip the ignition. Go home.

Her mother's dying of cancer. A reason. No excuse needed.

But telling people, telling Abernathy about her mother meant opening a door a little. Letting people view a sliver of herself.

Wasn't going to happen.

So there had to be something else; another reason to go in or drive off. Stay or leave. Do work or—

Metal tapped the glass right next to Soledad's head. Unexpected, but it didn't startle her. Not that she was startleproof. She was in another space where sound took its time traversing, and when it had, it was garbled among thirty-three other sensations coming to her on a lag. Even turning her head was a process where thought and action were filtered by delay.

At the window of her car: Raddatz rapping his wedding band against the glass. He said something. Through the door it was just a fog of wordless sounds.

Soledad dropped the window.

"You good, O'Roark?"

"Yes," she said. Quick, but without conviction.

"Sitting in your car alone? You sure you're good?"

Soledad's eyes drifted over Raddatz. Over his body. She wondered: What did he look like naked? What kind of damage did his clothes hide? Massive scars? Burns?

Twisted flesh that would never be a well-tailored suit again? She wondered: Was it better to have your wounds on display—a missing arm, a leg gone—was it better to look damaged than to walk around normal on the outside only to, end of the day, have to strip down to the truth of yourself?

"O'Roark . . ." Raddatz tossed out her name trying to catch her focus.

"I'm not okay," Soledad said.

Raddatz squatted, came down to Soledad's level. "Got issues you want to talk about?"

Soledad took what seemed the appropriate amount of time she figured it should take to work through the pre-articulation of a difficult thought.

She said: "Talked to my physical therapist this morning. My knee's only going to get so much better."

"How much?"

"Not enough to go back to MTac."

"What are you going to do with yourself?"

"That's what I'm sitting here thinking about."

"What would you like to do with yourself?"

"I guess . . . what I've been doing with myself for the last month. Working DMI."

Coming up off his haunches: "Make it sound like we're a consolation prize, and not much of one."

She wasn't an expert on such things, but common sense told Soledad the best deceptions are the ones that aren't deceptions. The best deceptions are truths that hide lies.

"If you're asking me, yeah, it is a consolation prize." Soledad modified herself none. Didn't plane any edges. As such she sounded as though she spoke with honesty.

"But a prize is a prize. And a job where I can still help do something about muties is a whole hell of a lot better than working security at the Beverly Center. I'm still in the fight. If this is the way it's got to be, I'm good with that."

She put up the window on Raddatz. She went back to sitting alone. She was pretty sure the lie about her knee would stick. And just that quick she was working for Tashjian. That quick she had purpose again.

The thing is, the thing is how right she was."

"Mothers have a way of being annoyingly correct."

Soledad was with Vin. In his place. Lying on his couch. Staring at his ceiling.

Vin was across the room, in a chair. Same chair he'd been sitting . . . planted. As much time as he spent there, "planted" was the better, was the more accurate word. Same chair he'd been planted in last time Soledad'd been over. If Vin hadn't opened the door for her, Soledad would've figured Vin and the chair were never apart.

"And the way she said it." Soledad giving color to the context of her conversation with her mother. " 'I don't want you to come home.' So to-the-point. So . . . harsh."

"The apple doesn't fall far from the—"

"Don't give me that shit."

Vin kind of mumbled something. Back when he had two legs, when he had two legs he didn't mumble. His comments, always sharp, were never gagged by self-pity.

And then he kind of eked out: "She wanted to make it stick."

"She could have just—"

"Just what? If somebody told you to breathe, you'd suffocate yourself just to be your own man." Force to the thought, but not much to his tone. "She doesn't want you to watch her die."

"Don't say that!"

"That she's going to die or that she doesn't want you around?"

"Any of it. Take your pick."

Vin's head dropped back, sort of lolled around. "I didn't. Didn't say it. She, she did." That last bit was slurred slightly as it gimped its way off Vin's tongue. Something besides pity was washing out his words.

Soledad looked to Vin. He was slumped some in the chair. Was as if, even sitting, he needed all of the furniture to keep him propped up. A little sweat was on his brow, collecting on his upper lip. It was there never mind the AC being on.

Vin, like he was waking up from a snooze, realized he'd caught Soledad's eye. "So . . . so what are you going to do?"

"Stay on the job. Stay here. Mom made it real clear what she wants."

"Do you care? If someone told you to, to breathe—"

"You said that. You said that, Vin. You said it already." Soledad drifted where she lay. She drifted to the day prior, to her lunch with her mother. Before, like a little girl who'd messed her best dress, Soledad feared having to explain her damaged leg to her mom. But at lunch . . . "She didn't even ask about my leg. Barely she did."

"She's got cancer."

"Cancer'll kill you. It doesn't stop you from being a

mother. Nothing does. She knew I didn't want to talk
about my leg; she knew the boundaries I'd set."

"So she knew."

"All this time I'd been pushing her away. Didn't have
to. She knew to keep some distance. But I kept pushing
when I should've been—"

"Soledad, you've got a unique ability to make everything about you."

Vin's words didn't set Soledad right. Just made her
more morose. "The death I was feeling . . . thought it was
mine. It was hers."

Vin: "How is your leg?"

"Good. Recovering good. Moving to a cane in a couple of weeks. I could put in for active duty." And on the
subject of limbs: "Where's your leg?"

Vin flipped a finger, indicated across the room.
Through a doorway Soledad could see the prosthetic
lying, surreal, on the floor. Some kind of exhibit on loan
from MOCA.

She said: "Doesn't do much good parked there."

"Doesn't do much good at all unless I've got somewhere to go. I'm not going anywhere."

"If you had it on, maybe you would."

"And one day I'm going to put your little theory to a
test."

That was that. So Soledad moved the conversation on
by returning to the central subject. "I couldn't even cry. I
sat there feeling like I should. Feeling *it,* knowing *it.* Was
like I went through a checklist—heartache, guilt, denial—but I couldn't finish the emotion."

"You're shut down. That's what we . . ." Vin was
mealymouthed with that, feebled the word "we" as if

ashamed at the attempt to equate himself with working cops. Doing an edit: "That's the way you get through things."

"This isn't cop shit. I've been shut down since May Day. Since San Francisco I've been about taking a stand against the freaks to the exclusion of every other thing around me. It's like I was so set on dying I took out a scorched-earth policy on the rest of my life."

Pathos with such pretty words.

Putting spin on it, Vin: "And good for it. Well, not good, but . . . good came, came out of it." He stumbled a little. "If you hadn't taken out that telepath—"

"Some other cop would have."

"Without that gun you put together? Doubt it. And even if . . . we only lost Yarborough. How many cops would've been lost if things were different?"

Despite what Vin was putting out, Soledad's lament stayed constant. "My own mother . . . Tell you something: You're looking at the end of things, you realize you weren't even decent with your own mother . . . Sometimes, Vin, sometimes I feel like—"

"Don't get sentimental. You'll regret it tomorrow."

"Sometimes, sometimes I feel like I'm fighting for normal humans and I traded my humanity in the deal."

"And you talk about me going soft. Act like you don't know what love is just 'cause some guy broke your heart."

It was as if, what it was like was Soledad had been gored from gut to chest. Some guy. Ian. He was unaware, but Vin wasn't just talking. For Soledad, he was séancing demons. And the twist in her Soledad felt . . . it wasn't that she had her heart broken. What was hurting her was the *how* of her heartbreak. It's one thing to fall in love and have love not work out. It's a very, very different thing to fall in love, have the love force you to question yourself to the core, only to find out who you love is the thing you hate most.

Soledad had fallen in love—she'd use the word in the quiet inside her, but she'd never speak it, regarding Ian, aloud—she'd fallen in love with a freak.

"How'd you know?" Soledad asked regarding Vin's knowledge of Ian.

"You make a big deal about a guy for months, then all of a sudden you don't so much as speak his name. Not since I got out of the hospital. Maybe you're being sensitive to me, knowing how I feel about you. But the next time you're sensitive to how I feel'll be the first time."

"Fuck you." Playful with that. Relieved, really. Vin didn't know the specifics of Ian, was just tossing out suppositions on some vagaries of Soledad's heart. Coming back at Vin, deflecting things from herself: "You want to be a detective, put your leg on and get back on the force."

Just a little smirk from Vin that said he didn't want to play anymore. From the way his shoulders slouched, his body hunched, he didn't want to do much else than sit where he was for another hour. A couple hours. Seven years. It was all the same for Vin.

But it was okay Vin didn't want to play. Soledad was ready to get serious about things as well.

She said: "Were you for real about what you asked before?"

"What I . . ."

"Do I want to get married? Do I want to marry you?"

"Yeah," Vin said.

"Okay," Soledad said.

My motivations are screwed.

I know that.

I don't know if I came out of the box screwed up, or if I got that way after San Francisco when getting sick kept me from taking a trip to the city. Kept me alive when 600,000 other people got killed.

That's a shitload o' guilt to be carting around.

So I quit living for me and started living for the give-back. Paying off a debt I didn't really owe to people I'd never met. And from day one, if that wasn't wrong, I knew what I was doing at least wasn't quite right.

Thing is, knowing you've got a dysfunction and doing something about your dysfunctionality sound the same, but are nothing alike. Maybe with years of therapy and religion, tons of medication you can break patterns.

I didn't go in for any of that.

So the pattern repeated.

With MTac.

With the tattoo I wore for Reese.

And now, again, with Vin.

I didn't love him. I liked him, cared about him. The

little bit I understood of love, I know I didn't feel that way for Vin.

What I felt . . .

Pathos.

I felt it for this cop, used to be so strong, who'd let himself devolve to the point of being a gimp. Not just physically. There were all kinds of people, fewer body parts than Vin, who amounted to so much more.

That sounds harsh, but sometimes the truth hits like Ali.

What was damaged on him, it was his spirit that was handicapped. The most obvious indicator was he'd casually, quietly become a lush, thinking his slowed movements and slurred speech went unnoticed. Same with the perpetual glisten of sweat that he now wore. Or worse, he knew the signs were obvious and didn't care.

I think, really, Vin's romantic about the idea of being cliché: the busted cop who melts to an alky.

Not romantic. Just pathetic.

I couldn't let Vin be pathetic.

No matter saving Vin is an unactionable task. Like the costumed freaks from years prior who I've come to hate so well, I felt I had to—had to—try some difficult heroics. So I tested Vin. Took his offer of marriage. Any other man, receiving a belated yes to a proposal right after talking about a woman's former love would say two things to her. The second is "you," the first, "fuck." Any man wouldn't let himself, so obviously, be relegated to sloppy seconds.

Any real man.

Any self-respecting man.

Any man who hadn't let himself devolve into a one-legged drunk.

But Vin, Vin had said okay. Vin passed the test. Or flunked it. Vin needed saving. So here's Soledad the anti-hero to the rescue.

God, do I need more religion.

Or medication.

Soledad was crutching through DMI, crutching to her office. Raddatz was on his way somewhere else.

Their paths crossing, Raddatz stopped. Said to Soledad: "Got anything pressing?"

"No."

Raddatz said: "Want to head over to LACFSC?"

"Sure."

Humanity is self-modifying. It adjusts to constants of its environment.

Death.

See a dead body once, be shocked. Revulsed.

See another body, a few more. You might be revulsed, but shock's no longer part of the deal.

A few more bodies, revulsion is a quaint notion that's remembered, if at all, with effort.

See a dozen bodies or more, no matter they've been shot, no matter they've been burned, regardless of the decay or level of stink, the viewing sensation is nothing more spectacular than seeing a late-model Ford creeping along in the slow lane on the 405.

But even the jaded could be, if not astounded, affected. There are, after all, a lot of ways to die. But Soledad didn't know, wasn't sure until she hit the Los Angeles County Coroner's Office at the Forensic Science Center, that there was any way to kill an invulnerable metanormal.

Michael Han, the county ME, found it all fascinating as hell. Fascinating enough he didn't pawn the inquest off on some junior on his staff.

Raddatz . . . ? Hard for Soledad to tell how he took things. Maybe he was shocked into submission by the confirmation of an invulnerable's mortality. Maybe he didn't care just as long as the freak was dead. But if there was a spike in him emotionally one way or the other, it was indistinct beyond normal curiosity. By choice or by accident he was tough to read as a player at the big table at the World Series of Poker.

Raddatz asked: "How did it happen; an invulnerable dead?"

"Dead by a means other than natural causes." Han tossed out the obvious.

Hard to say if an aptitude for working with the corpses was a product of nature or nurture. The Hans could've been a case study. Michael's father, Chise, had jobbed in the Coroner's Office. As an assistant ME, but never as *the* coroner. That left a way for the son to surpass the father. Assuming being better at dealing with the dead than your old man was an aspiration. For the Hans, for a generation of Hans, apparently, yeah, it was.

"Other than natural causes," Raddatz acknowledged.

"If you were," Han continued, "to consider which superability would be the most desirable, I think many would say invulnerability. Skin that's impregnable. Bones that are little different from titanium."

Han gave an odd gaze to the thing on the examining table below him. It was the longing look of reverence. Han was all about death. With the John Doe, he'd almost met something that could kick Death's ass.

Almost.

Han, continuing: "It's about as close to immortality as can be achieved. You would never need fear a traffic accident, a plane crash, let alone slipping on a patch of ice. Only age. Only God's work itself. And even that may not come on a schedule normal humans are accustomed to."

"And this one, it didn't die of natural causes?" Soledad was circling the examining table, giving herself a guided tour of the freak, the examining light overhead raining down a harsh luminescence. There's your God light: the light people who've had near-death experiences claim they've floated toward. The light of the guy who looks at your body with a cold disinterest before he cuts it open 'cause that's what his paycheck tells him to do.

A shake of the head from Han. "Not that we can determine, Miss O'Roark."

Soledad stopped, looked up. Looked to Han. Miss O'Roark. Not Officer O'Roark. Not operator. Not Bullet. Miss O'Roark. When was the last time she'd heard that? Long enough ago that hearing it now sounded pleasant.

"What about poison?" Raddatz asked. "Poison'd take it out, yeah?"

Han answered: "We were able to empty the contents of its stomach, run a tox screening. It came back negative."

"Suicide?" Soledad asked.

"A possibility." Han leaned back against a wall. He looked up, looked at the ceiling as if he were giving the question a little thought. "If anyone would know how to kill such a thing, it would be . . . it would be the thing itself. But that adds why to the question how."

Raddatz: "You're a freak, you've got no prospects, the law says you're not human. You end things."

Soledad: "We should be so lucky the muties start taking themselves out." Soledad added harshness to a sentiment she already held, put the edge there for Raddatz to see how he'd take it.

Nothing. No effect she could read on him.

On the freak, on its side, on its bare flesh: defects. Soledad saw them as she circumvented the body. Little . . . little divots. Four on one side.

Soledad: "What are these?"

Han stepped around, took a look at what Soledad was talking about. "Actually, I was hoping you might know."

"How am I going to know what you don't?"

"If it was any other metanormal, I wouldn't expect you to. But as you can imagine, not a great many invulnerables make their way to my part of the world. And not too many officers have had as much experience with metanormals as you have."

Soledad gave a careful look to the defects. She said to Raddatz, guessing: "Scar tissue?"

Raddatz shrugged.

Soledad split her focus between the freak and Raddatz. Here they were checking out a dead invulnerable, and all Raddatz could do was shrug? Was he one of those cops who said little but took in all they saw? Was he a cop that had prior knowledge of what he was looking at and was therefore bored by questions he knew the answers to?

"It's a possibility. The meta gene," Han said, "becomes active in most metanormals around puberty. He might have been injured as a child."

Soledad asked: "Has the body been cleaned?"

"Before the autopsy. Before," Han corrected, "the attempted autopsy."

"Where the scar tissue is, was there any flaking?"

Han picked up a notepad, flipped through it. "Yes."

"A lot, a little?"

"Minimal amount."

"But there was, there was flaking there?"

Han said to Soledad: "Yes."

"Dead flesh," Soledad said. She said: "This wasn't an old wound."

"That just," Raddatz said, "narrows it down to a million other things it could be."

Soledad stepped up, put her hand to the invulnerable. No matter that it was dead, except that it was cold, it was human to the touch. Not hard. Not alien. Nothing exceptional other than the marks on the body. Marks like . . . they were like . . . Soledad's fingers slipped neatly into them.

It had started to rain. Just a little. Anywhere else, any other city, a little rain would be an annoyance. Slightly bothersome. In LA anything more than a misting is a plague from God. A disaster of the highest proportions. The motorists of the city, suspect of skill on good days, were utterly deficient in the short-term-memory department. Between the annual sprinkles that came around in January and February, then took the rest of the year off, LA drivers had a habit of forgetting real quick that water is wet and wet pavement is slick. So idiots would take the Laurel Canyon speedway—a twisty road that ran over "the hill"—at the limit plus fifteen. Same as they did on hot dry days. Launch their vehicles over the center line or into one of the houses that bordered the road. Occasionally, they took flight over a guardrail and down the Santa Monica Mountains where they sometimes went days, months . . . wasn't weird for a launched vehicle to go well more than a year without getting spotted in the thick growth despite an organized search by the LAPD.

And Soledad was fine with that. Other than innocents potentially getting hurt, the people who ended up in a porch or over an embankment were the same ilk who, millennia ago, would've been stuck in the tar pits watching the rest of humanity pass them by.

Instead, here, now, Soledad and Raddatz were stuck in traffic courtesy of a Neanderthal with a CA driver's lic.

"So what do we do?" Soledad asked.

"Sit here like everybody else. What do you want me to do, hit the lights and siren?"

Soledad wasn't sure if Raddatz didn't catch her meaning or was giving her shit. Either way, her true question wasn't answered.

"What do we do about the John Doe? What's the procedure with DMI?"

"Write up his particulars, log it. Try to track his family, any other freaks he had contact with—"

"But the John Doe; what do we do about him?"

"We keep surveillance on living freaks. We don't deal with dead ones."

"And when they die of questionable causes?"

"Don't think anybody said it was questionable."

"Nobody said anything, because nobody knows what happened. You can't give an answer, to me that counts as questionable."

The radio was playing. Old-school rock and roll. Raddatz reached over. Lowered it. "From your dealing with things one time that's your professional opinion?"

"Yeah, 'cause I've never done cop work before. Never even went to the academy."

"What you do—"

"Got a gun and badge high-bidding on eBay. The rest was a free ticket."

"What you do, what you *did,* I've done it. I've worked

both sides, O'Roark. MTac and DMI. So don't think you know more than me, know better than me. You don't. Doesn't matter how much legend you built in G Platoon. This isn't G Platoon. This is a whole other thing."

And Soledad let that sit for a while, not caring one bit for being talked to—talked down to—like *that*. And if they were in G Platoon, if they were on an MTac element . . .

But they weren't.

They were stuck in a pool car going nowhere.

So Soledad could, should, just let things go . . .

Instead: "Why am I here?"

"You busted your knee, you put in for the hours."

"Are you obtuse, or do you just want to see what it takes to—"

Raddatz made an awkward cross-body reach for the radio, reached to turn it up.

Before he finished the motion, Soledad had slapped the radio completely dead.

"Because if you're trying to set me off," she said. Soft and low. The quiet adding its own emphasis, "you're doing it. Why am I here? Why are you bringing me along for the ride?"

"Testing the waters. You say you're done with MTac."

"The doctors say I'm done with MTac."

"However it is, it's a new beginning. So now it's a matter of are you up for this, or are you just doing things to do things?"

Raddatz and Soledad rolled up on the accident that was slowing a good portion of LA to a crawl. Squad cars. Flares. A BMW welded by its own fire to a tree.

The sight, the smell of the burn. Sense memory came on hard to Soledad.

She said: "Here's the thing: I've been tested every way you can think of. I've passed all of them, so throwing me any more of them is a waste of time. Mine and yours. I'm gonna be here. If I'm part of your cadre or not—"

"I don't have a—"

"If I'm a pariah, I don't give a fuck. Honest; you, all of you and your supercreep attitudes get on my nerves. I'm keeping freaks in check however I've got to do things."

"That's a good speech, Soledad."

"Christ . . ."

"Is it done? Is that it?"

"Yeah, that's it."

"Procedure; that's what you were talking about, right?"

Soledad and Raddatz slid past the accident. Traffic picked up. Most of the drivers went right back to speeding.

"Here's procedure," Raddatz said. "ID the John Doe. Run his prints, try to match him up to a missing person report, take things from there."

"'K." A fraction of a word that stood for: whatever.

Raddatz turned up the radio. Flooded the car with old-school rock.

Soledad moved up—or down, depending on how you looked at things—from crutches to a cane. Cheapest thing she could find at a medical supply store. An old-man cane. Wasn't very cool. As unaffected as she liked to think she was, she still figured if she was going to have a cane, maybe she oughta get a cool one. For a hot second Soledad thought about getting one of those canes that have a sword hidden in them. But then she thought she might end up using it. Worrisome. Not that she'd some-how get in a situation that was cane-sword necessary. That didn't worry her. What was worrisome: She'd use the sword and people would start comparing her to Eddi and her knife. She could live without the comparison. She could live real well without that. She got the old-man cane.

No getting past the feeling of clandestineness. The hour was odd, the location obscure. One-forty in the morning, a bar in Hollywood. Not a glam bar. A small joint off Ivar where drinking was done by a select few night, morning and high noon. Drunks who couldn't remember their names, let alone unfamiliar faces. Perfect for clandestineness. The meeting Soledad was having with Tashjian was on the extreme DL. IA cops were not cops that cops wanted other cops to peep them talking with even if all they were rapping about was the price of tea in China.

Soledad didn't like playing in the shadows. Up until recently her cop life had been about being in the open, being direct. A show of force. That—coming on strong about things—was as much of a weapon for MTacs as their HKs and Benellis and Soledad's own home-brewed piece. Working DMI was all about rooting around, rooting around. Being a mole for IA on top of that was . . .

It was what?

If DMI was about kicking over stones, was IA the slug under the rock?

Only days Soledad had been perpetrating a lie. Already she was sick of it.

"It does take getting used to," Tashjian counseled.

"I'm not going to be doing this long enough to get used to it."

"My hope was, in time, you would at least see the value in what you're doing."

"I see the value, but to me it's like seeing value at Kmart. Taking advantage and taking pride are two different things."

"I miss that, O'Roark." Tashjian tipped his glass to her. "I miss that sense of humor of yours. So slight as to be unique."

Whatever Tashjian was drinking—a mixed, lime-greenish thing—it was the girliest drink Soledad'd ever seen. A queer alky mick going dry on St. Paddy's Day wouldn't touch the stuff.

Yet . . .

The drink fairly glowed, was nearly hypnotic. Hard drinkers—and the few flies in the bar at that hour were nothing but—stared at Tashjian each time he raised his glass. Watched him as he lowered it. Licked their lips in sympathetic pleasure. Whatever Tashjian was drinking, before the night was done, everybody in the joint would most likely have one.

"I mean"—Tashjian returned the glass to the bar—"I'm assuming you're joking. I can't imagine you having something against value-priced shopping."

"We're talking about the job." Soledad kept on point. Soledad didn't want to string things along, spend one more minute where she was and doing what she was doing any more than necessary.

"We're talking about the job," Tashjian echoed. "Tell me about the job."

"You heard about the invulnerable John Doe?"

"Very slightly. I know the ME has the body, but DMI is in control of the situation."

"It's being . . . I guess it's being investigated. I'm not sure how the hell things work at DMI. Anyway, I'm on it."

"How did you manage that?"

"A senior lead was going to check out the body, I got an invite."

"And it went all right?"

"All right how? All I did was look at a body."

Tashjian stroked the condensation on his glass. "This senior lead; he trusts you?"

"He doesn't like me. My experience, someone doesn't like me, they're taking me at face value."

"I'm glad for that. Don't agree, though. I don't take you at face value, and I like you quite a bit."

"Don't get ideas. I'm engaged."

"I have none. But I'm flattered you think enough of me you have to put me off."

"I'm not . . . I don't have to put you off. I'm just telling you."

"And all the protest you're putting into the telling: Is that for me or for you?"

Fucking with her. Tashjian was fucking with her. Some guys golfed. Some built ships in a bottle. Tashjian's hobby, Soledad was pretty sure, was fucking with her.

"Can we talk about the freak?"

Tashjian nodded. "Has anything come to light?"

"I've been out one time on this, and I was lucky for that much."

"Do you have a sense of the circumstances? Was it murder?"

"It's inconclusive. No poison, at least as far as the ME can tell. But how else you'd kill an invulnerable freak I don't know."

For a minute Soledad and Tashjian said nothing.

The sound track playing in the bar was ESPN from a TV. Ice kicking around in glasses. Hacking coughs.

Soledad didn't like being there, in the bar. She wasn't a drinker. Drinking reminded her of Vin. And that didn't feel real right; that she didn't want to be reminded of her instant fiancé.

"Tashjian, how long you been with the PD?"

"Thirteen years."

Something funny about that to Soledad. Figures. Tashjian's been around thirteen lucky years. "Seen a lot in thirteen years?"

"My share."

"But not a dead invulnerable."

"Can't say that I have."

"So if you did, if you did see one, it'd get your attention."

"And, finally, your point?"

"Seeing a dead invulnerable didn't much get Raddatz's attention."

"Raddatz? Tucker Raddatz is the senior lead you're working with?" Tashjian's thumbnail scratched at his chin: acknowledgment of the curiousness.

"Something I should know about him?" Soledad asked.

"Very distinguished officer. A short but memorable stint with MTac. Memorable mostly because he was the

sole survivor of a warrant served on . . . what's the collo-
quialism for metanormals with accelerated production of
adrenaline?"

"Berserkers."

"Tore through the rest of his element as though they
were rice paper. He was lucky to get away with just losing a hand. I think that's all he's lost."

"I can think of one other thing: any and all regard for
freaks whatsoever."

"Is there something hinky to you?"

"I'm not a detective." Soledad, no permission asked,
reached over, took Tashjian's glass, took a drink. Girliest
thing she'd ever had. And it was good. "But I'm not sure
I blame somebody who's been torn up by a freak for having absolutely nothing but hatred for them."

"Careful with your sympathies."

"I know what's at stake. I'll do the job."

"You misunderstand me. Whoever is responsible for
the killings feels personally threatened by metanormals
and is acting upon his or her feelings. And if they have no
fear of freaks, do you think they would be afraid to deal
with you? For your own sake, I would be gentle with this
Raddatz."

The threat of things getting physical. The threat of
violence and possible death that would have to be met in
kind. Suddenly, Soledad was starting to like her new job.

Might as well have been talking with God. Maybe not God. How about the Holy Ghost? If nothing else, Officer Tom Hayes felt like he was talking with that one model on the cover of all those fitness magazines he was desperate to meet. Not that he felt sexual toward Soledad. But in a cop's life that was less than he'd dreamed of, sitting across from one of the most talked-about operators on the LAPD was a dream come true.

He wanted to ask Soledad about some of her exploits. Not fan boy–style. He honestly wanted a firsthand breakdown of truth from fiction. He wanted, he wanted to get her take on the job, on being MTac. He wanted very badly to know—her opinion—the best way to work up to G Platoon. Tom Hayes had a thousand questions for Soledad.

Sitting with him in the coffee room at Hollenbeck station, Soledad had only questions about the John Doe Officer Hayes had found.

The first had been: How'd you find him?

"Didn't really. Some kids had gone down in the river, were doing some boarding on the concrete. Saw the body, made the call."

"Your report said his clothes were burned away."

"Yes, ma'am. Looked like it."

"But not his flesh. Wasn't that weird to you?"

Officer Hayes flipped his hands up but wasn't flippant. He tried to be respectful with the gesture. Added a look that said: "Didn't think about it." He would have said as much himself but was afraid Soledad'd pick up the crack in his voice. He was nervous. Soledad was the kind of cop who could, down the road, have sway over his getting into G Platoon. And the way she was asking questions: How come he didn't do this, didn't do that . . . He shouldn't be nervous, Hayes told himself. Maybe he should have been more observant, but wasn't like he'd fucked up. Right? He hadn't. Had he?

Hayes said: "He looked like a vag to me. He looked like he had on, you know, bumwear. Half the time stuff that's burned or torn is the best they've got. I thought he died of exposure or drink. He was stiff as hell. Thought it was rigor at the time."

Soledad felt stares. She'd always been sensitive to other people's eyes. The locked looks she was getting now didn't, they didn't feel like the ones she was usually most attuned to. The "it's a black woman!?" ogles she got when she had the audacity to stick herself right where somebody thought a black woman didn't belong. Still, she felt eyes rolling over her. Probably 'cause in the open and out of uniform she was having a chat with a uniformed cop. Some of the cops staring maybe thought Soledad was just a friend. A chick friend who'd come around for some palaver with Hayes which he'd get some good-natured shit about later. But some probably considered Soledad was official in some sense. Admin or IA.

That made every other cop in the joint instantly, reflex-ively reassess their relationship with the blue who was having a sit-down.

Hayes didn't hardly seem to care. To Soledad he came off a little nervous, but other than that, his head was level all around. Soledad figured if he ever had his shot, he'd make a good MTac. A real solid one. His odds of surviving serving a warrant on a freak were probably 60/40 in favor. Better than the 70/30 most MTacs rated.

"Anything," Soledad asked, "at the scene that'd make you think it was foul play?"

"Nothing. But LA River, if there was anything, it might have gotten washed away. I imagine DMI gave a look once they found out it was a mutie."

"They didn't find anything."

"What about at one of the other incident sites?"

Soledad looked right at Hayes. She didn't answer the question. The question didn't make sense.

She asked: "What incident sites?"

"One of the other . . . well, you know, where he was hit by the train. It was in my report. You read it, right?"

Soledad went back to just giving a stare to Hayes. The question didn't make . . .

"Just walk me through everything," she said. "Take me through it."

Officer Hayes didn't bother with any orientating. Soledad had questions, he gave her what he knew to be fact. "Got the call on the John Doe. Went over, spotted the body, called it in. Right?"

Right, meaning: We on the same page so far?

"Right."

"Previous to that, the station had taken a report from

the MTA. Something got struck on the Gold Line. Engineer thought maybe he'd hit somebody, but couldn't find a vic. No blood or flesh on the car. Way the train was tore up, engineer thought some joker might've put a store mannequin on the track or something. It's LA. Wouldn't be the craziest thing somebody ever did. I found out later the John Doe was a mutie. Did the math. The mutie must've been the one that got clipped by the train. I know DMI handles investigating freaks. But it's my beat. I know the neighborhood. Thought it couldn't hurt to do some talking to people, see if anybody saw anything, heard anything. If they did, maybe they were more likely to talk to a cop they knew than one they didn't."

And it was a good way for a beat cop to score some points too, Soledad thought. And she thought: Hayes was all about the ambition. Forget MTac. He was going to be brass.

Prompting him to go on: "So you talked around, talked to some people."

"One witness said he saw someone running through the area on foot. Another guy thought he saw someone fall off a building. Fall or jump. Thought he did, but the guy got up and ran off."

"Our John Doe."

Hayes nodded. "Way I see it, our freak was going crazy. Tearing up buildings, walls . . . looks like he slagged part of a mailbox on one street. I don't know. He was drunk, I guess. Maybe high. Lucky the only thing that happened was he ended up dead. Anyway, that was all in the report I gave to DMI. Should have been."

Yeah, Soledad thought. Should have been. But not a word of it was.

Jealousy. That was the thought for Soledad's drive home. Jealousy was the logical reason she'd come up with for Hayes's report getting redacted. DMI officers were resentful that a beat cop'd done a better job investigating things than they had. So left out what he'd said—removed what he'd written—from their report.

But the jealousy theory required some serious denial. There wasn't a cop in the PD who wasn't territorial about his or her department. But you'd have to believe that DMI cops—grown men—would get bitch jealous of a flatfoot doing some flatfooting in the first place. And say they were, whatever, jealous or resentful of the work Hayes'd done. No reason they couldn't just stick his work in their report, claim it as their own, and that would be that about that.

Irrelevance. That was another possibility. What Hayes had come up with, those additional incident sites didn't merit inclusion. But to not at least reference them was sloppy police work. In her short time at DMI sloppy wasn't something she found the cops there to be.

Reality: What Officer Hayes had offered up had been purged from the DMI report.

Why?

Did Soledad have to ask herself why?

Yeah.

Because she didn't care for the obvious answer. The freak had died a questionable death. Probably, it was murder. So the obvious, the unsettling answer to the question why was that the people who purged the report were conspirators after the fact. Or worse. They're the killers.

East LA was a fairly shitty place. Drugs free-flowed up and down the streets. A bromide against the better life that wasn't so much better for the people who'd risked everything—everything being their wives, their lives, their well-being—to get to America so they could clean toilets or clean pools, stroller around rich people's babies or hang out on street corners hoping some shifty contractor would roll by offering work at cut-rate pay before the INS came around offering an all-expense-paid trip back to their country of origin. A few weeks, a few months, a few years of that and, yeah, you'd be a hophead too. So, in East LA, there were drugs. There was everything that came with drugs: guns and gangs and stealing to get drug money and whoring to get drug money and the shooting of people because they got in the way of drug money being exchanged. It was shit cops should've handled. But in East LA the cops worked out of Rampart. Comparing the two, Rampart cops made East LA gangs look like castrati.

Soledad was a cop. But no matter her badge and gun, or maybe because they were of principal significance, her current proximity to East LA—looking at it on a map in her office—was as close as she cared to get to that part of town. But in her head, at least, she had to get close to it. She had some concepts to calculate.

Soledad was a cop, but she wasn't a detective. She didn't have years of know-how when it came to asking questions. She had instinct. She had a nurtured ability to look at things a couple of times in a couple of different ways asking each go-round: What's wrong with this deal? Under the circumstances that'd have to pass for being a detective.

Soledad backtracked the final hours and last minutes of the mutie John Doe. His place of dying, or at least where the body was found, got an X on Soledad's map. The action made physical her thoughts, gave her focus. Made it feel like she was doing something besides waiting for answers to come.

The Gold Line.

JD got clipped by a train crossing the track. Maybe that was enough to put down an invulnerable. Maybe this freak, maybe JD was only *kind of* invulnerable. Titanium skin wrapped around garden-variety innards. Gets hit by the train. Internal damage. Dies.

The Gold Line got highlighted.

But Officer Hayes had said a witness saw him drop from a window. Jump from a window? If that didn't kill him, would a train?

And what was JD doing on the tracks? This guy wasn't a bum scrounging for food, looking for shelter. So what was he doing on the tracks?

He was crossing the tracks.

To?

"To the river" wasn't answer enough. To the river for what? Crossing the track to the LA River. Why go to the river?

Why go from point to point to point?

Along the way something happens. He ends up slamming into a wall. Soledad had dug up a photo of the wall. Cement. Graffiti-tagged. Now with a body-sized divot where the Doe's invulnerable self took out a chunk of it.

And the mailbox Officer Hayes'd told her about. She had a photo of that too. The mailbox used to be a big blue stump same as you'd find on the corner of any street in Anytown, USA. It used to be a symbol of a citizen's right to communicate in the slowest way known to man that didn't directly involve animals. The unit was wrecked, bent, misshapen.

So . . . what? The Doe goes nuts, has an emotional meltdown, slams a wall, wrecks a mailbox, takes a run across the tracks . . .

Maybe he wasn't just going nuts. Maybe he was scoring. *In need* of a score bad.

Sounds very dull for an event involving a freak.

But the first freak Soledad ever took a warrant call on was a flamethrower jacked up on crack. Maybe they were the next step in evolution, but a percentage of them, no different from a percentage of normal people—be they lowlifes living in the hardest urban centers, be they lofty talk radio hosts—just wanted to get high.

The burned clothes?

Maybe if the freak was freebasing, he lit himself up. But Officer Hayes didn't report any paraphernalia around the body, and Officer Hayes had proven himself to be ass-kissing thorough. And who the hell freebases anymore?

Jumping from a window, running the streets, crossing the tracks, running . . . He was running.

Why do people run? 'Cause they're getting chased.

The Doe was getting chased.

Somebody wants to kill a freak, so they give it a gas bath, flick a match at it.

Reasonable if it was some don't-know-any-better hate group. But if it was murder, if it was the cadre, if they had targeted the Doe, wouldn't they know he was invulnerable? Wouldn't they know gas and fire wouldn't do much more than scrub him clean?

With her pen Soledad drew circles on the map. Circles overlapping circles. Lines of confusion. There were bits of nonlogic, but that the JD was targeted was clear. A police report had been sanitized. The only people in position to do both were cops from DMI.

The really ugly part of all that: If it was true, Tashjian had been right.

Tucker Raddatz had a decent life. He had a decent little place in Studio City. Nice lawn. Some trees. A pool. Little but decent. He had a very decent wife: Helena. She was from Spain. Born there. Grew up in America. She was pretty. Or rather, decent-looking. Two kids, boys, seven and five. They weren't at the age yet where everything their father did embarrassed them. They actually liked being around their dad, and on the surface, at least, didn't seem to be moving toward a time when they wouldn't. There was none of the gloom around the edges of Raddatz's homelife that he seemed to slog with him in his cop life, in the life Soledad was familiar with. A palpable lack of affliction was the first thing Soledad noticed when she rolled up to Raddatz's house. She noticed that, and she noticed Raddatz didn't come off as being real happy to see her.

Helena didn't pick up on the agitation. Or if she did pick up on it, could act the hell out of seeming to welcome the unwelcomed to her home. She greeted Soledad, walked Soledad out to the pool to wait while her husband finished up whatever Soledad'd interrupted with her arrival. Helena brought out some lemonade. Homemade and fresh. Offered it to cool Soledad's wait.

And Soledad sat, sat some . . .

She'd left her sunglasses in the car. Mistake. The sunlight kicking off the water of the pool was nearly painful.

The patio door opened. Raddatz's kids. Not him.

They jumped in the pool, the younger boy wearing orange floaties. Splashed wildly. So much happiness. So much, despite the fact they would never know a world in which a full and whole city of San Francisco existed. What was such joy, unfiltered and undamaged? The bliss of ignorance? The resurrection of hope? Kids who just didn't know better than to be happy, splash and play? That was the thing, wasn't it: that life was malleable, able to conform itself around its circumstances? Simply: No matter how fucked-up shit was, people thrived. In example was modern history, as within modern history is when man's come the closest to—remained within reach of—making himself extinct. But even when Europe was mustard-gassing itself into oblivion, when Hitler was Final Solutioning everybody in sight, when it was about the Greater Southeast Asia Coprosperity Sphere, when it was all about the cold war or ethnic cleansing or the war on terror, up to the war between normals and metanormals you could still pick up the paper and read about how the local team had blown a ten-point lead and gotten eliminated from the play-offs. You could still turn on the eleven o'clock news and catch a piece about the dog or flower or auto show coming to town. There was a girl somewhere with her girlfriends all giddy with themselves as she tried on wedding dresses. There was a guy at a newsstand, eager, because the latest *FHM* had just rolled off the presses with a neatly airbrushed ass shot of that month's It Girl. Even at the edge of forever there were attempts at normalcy. Forays into happiness. The human spirit conforming to chaos.

What had Tashjian called them? Acts of life.

Acts of the human spirit. *Human* spirit. Not the metahuman spirit. Human spirit survived. Humanity survived.

It would if Soledad had anything to say about it.

The patio door again. Raddatz. Hook off, stump showing. He crossed right to Soledad, sat next to Soledad on an adjoining lounge.

No preamble: "What?"

For a second Soledad thought about cracking wise on Raddatz not even giving her a hello. But she didn't feel like jokes, and jokes weren't about to buy her anything.

So getting right to it: "Know a beat cop named Hayes?"

"No."

Lie. Didn't even think about it. An absolute assertion needs consideration. A lie you know is untrue. What's there to think about?

Soledad: "He's working out of the Hollenbeck station. Same area the John Doe was found. Know him now?"

"What's the problem, O'Roark?"

He'd gone from lying to evading.

"Here's what I need: I need people to be straight with me. I show up at DMI, nobody wants to touch me. Then you give me the hand. You and your cadre. I know about them; the guys you keep tight. You take me out to look at a dead freak, only that's all you do. You don't let me in on any investigation, if there is one. Then I find out a cop's report has been purged. Why?"

Raddatz looked off somewhere. Nowhere in particular. Just not at Soledad.

Soledad didn't care for that. "When I said be straight with me, I meant now, not when you felt like it."

"Or . . . ?"

"Do not fuck with me."

The sound of the words shrieked against the air. *Chop. Chop. Chop.* A swinging blade that metronomed in a manner not to be ignored.

Raddatz: "I feel like, why do I feel like this is a setup?"

"You think this is more than me just asking for answers, then send me walking. Whatever the reason: I don't fit in, I'm a pain in the ass, I've got no skills for this, I'm a crazy black chick . . . whatever. Don't admit to anything, don't say anything. But give me a way out before I get buried with the rest of you. I've been down IA road. Didn't care for it. All I'm looking for is a little self-preservation."

Raddatz looked away from whatever it was he wasn't really looking at. Not back to Soledad, but to his two boys going nuts in the pool.

"What do you want, Soledad?" Only time she could recall Raddatz using her first name. "I don't mean why are you here right this minute. What's your big objective? Why'd you go MTac?"

"Could ask you the same—"

"But that wouldn't get us any closer to anything, so I'm asking you. Why?"

"To . . ." How to say it? How to put into words what

she felt, but so rarely articulated? "Save lives. To save *life*. Human life."

"And that's what's most important, right? That the . . . the, I don't know. The cloud of death that's been hanging over us since San Francisco, since before that, that it gets blown away."

Soledad looked to where Raddatz was looking, to his boys.

She said: "Yeah."

"And would you try to carry out that objective without holding back?"

"If I could keep freaks from taking any more lives? I'd go after that any way I had to." The statement only at its outer edges was any kind of cover for Soledad's current career as a provocateur for IA.

"Then what we're working toward is the same thing."

"You and me?"

"You, me. Others who are like-minded. How are you on trust?"

"I suck at it."

For the first time since he'd sat down next to her, maybe since they'd first crossed paths, Raddatz showed anything like lightness. With a smile: "You and me both," he said. "But I've got to ask you for some. You have a problem with allocating a little trust, well, then here's the out you were looking for."

And for a sec Soledad considered things. Considered how many lies she was living. The cop lies. The personal-life lies. If she had any honesty left in her, anything similar to trust, if she felt it, would she know it?

"What," she asked Raddatz, "are your boys' names?"

"John. Jason. John's the older one."

"You like being a father?"

"Love it."

"Like being married?"

"I love my wife."

"Not what I asked. Like being married?"

That question didn't get answered so quick.

When it did: "You get married, it's like taking a picture. It's two people at one point in time, and same as a picture nothing's supposed to change. Maybe that was all right when somebody invented marriage ten thousand years ago, or whatever. Ten thousand years ago people lived until they were fifteen. Nineteen. You get married, it's not good . . . fuck it, you're dead in a couple of years anyway.

"People don't typically die anymore at fifteen or nineteen, O'Roark." Back to using her surname. "People go till they're eighty, ninety years old. I don't care how much you love somebody, you try going fifty or more years of navigating being who you are and who your partner's looking to make you into."

"Your wife, what did she want you to be?"

"A guy who cared more about living than changing the world."

Soledad, bringing things back around to the issue at hand: "And if I can show a little, show some trust?"

"You get to witness something amazing."

"Something . . . ?"

Raddatz, looking right to Soledad: "You get to witness the end of fear."

There's no cure for cancer. All the docs can do is sledgehammer it into submission. Remission. But even when it's gone, it's not really gone. It's always there. A sleeper agent waiting to be activated same as an embedded terror cell. And that's the thing: It's waiting. It's patient. Cancer is death. A form of it. Death in all its forms is hard to beat. Ultimately impossible to beat. Life is finite. Death's got all the time in the universe.

Taking that into consideration, Gin's surgery, her early phases of recovery looked good. The docs thought they'd gotten all the malignant cells out. All that science. Best they could say was they *thought* they'd gotten them all out. Anyway, they were happy with the probability.

Gin'd always prided herself on looking as healthy as she was for her age. Not looking young for her age. Looking young was an illusion. She was healthy and she liked looking healthy. Fit and relatively trim. So along comes the chemo. There goes her hair. And how chemo makes most patients lose weight, it worked opposite for Gin. Gin ballooned. The thing that kept her alive distorted her nearly beyond recognition.

The ironies of life.

Soledad got all that from e-mails her mother sent. E-mails. Very complete, and completely removed from any kind of emotion.

E-mails.

And Soledad used to think a once-a-week phone call was cold.

Your husband disappears. You go to the cops, file a missing person report. Unpleasant. Unsettling. But that's what you do. It's what you do if you ever want to see your man again. You do that. And you pray.

For Diane Hall, filling out that report must've been the hardest thing in the world. She did the job with two competing hopes: that her husband would be found, but not found out.

The finding took a while. At least, it took a while for all the paperwork to line up, for the people who track bodies and names and fingerprints and dental records to realize that a John Doe cooling at LACFSC was Anson Hall, reported missing six days prior by his wife. They finally had a name to go with the body and the one other known fact regarding it. The John Doe was a freak.

Normally, a missing person comes up dead, a loved one can expect as sympathetic a dial-up as you're likely to get from cops who make bereavement calls three or five times a week. Maybe, if things are slow, someone on the city payroll might actually swing out to the survivor's place and deliver the news in person. As death goes, things are rarely slow in LA.

What Diane Hall got, Diane Hall got an MTac unit rolling on her house backed by a full complement of uniformed cops. A police bird overhead. Diane got ordered from her house hands up. Diane almost got shredded because she came out of her house clutching her six-year-old son rather than, as cops had ordered, with hands skyward. MTacs moved in, Diane got shoved to the ground, the muzzle of an HK pressed—jammed—against the side of her head. She and her boy got cuffed. The six-year-old got cuffed. Put into separate APCs and whisked to a secure lockup in East LA. The only part of town that allowed for a temporary holding facility of metanormals. Not coincidentally, East LA had the highest population of illegal immigrants who were just trying to get by in life, but couldn't much complain about superpeople getting incarcerated in their backyards because if they did they were likely to get a little incarceration thrown their way prior to being shipped off to whatever country they'd border-hopped from.

DNA tests got done on Diane and on her son. Both came back negative. Diane was transferred to the county lockup. Her son got sent to Children's Services.

A cop came by at some point and informed Diane of all the laws she had broken that revolved around harboring a person she had known to have metanormal abilities. She'd pretty much broken all those laws twelve years prior when, in a chapel in Vegas, she said before immediate family and God "I do."

The knowledge itself, the *knowledge* she was cohabiting with a metanormal, was illegal. But a senator from

Texas was sponsoring an amendment to the Constitution banning the whole concept of such unions. Turned out to be more trouble than it was worth. The only thing the citizenry disliked more than freaks was the Constitution getting fucked with.

A public defender came by at some point and informed Diane her best bet was to cop a plea, cooperate with investigators and inform on any other metanormals she was aware of.

Diane asked the lawyer when she was going to be able to see her son again.

The lawyer didn't know when. Or if.

Diane spent the following just-shy-of-a-day crying, and did a real poor job of trying to kill herself by swallowing a spoon that came with her next meal.

The spoon got removed.

Diane got removed to a hospital ward, strapped down and put on meds.

Her mind floated. Vegas. I do. Happiest day of her life. C-sections hurt like hell. Do it again. She'd do it all again. Even the spoon down the throat.

Raddatz and Panama and Soledad came by at some point and informed Diane they were from DMI and they had questions for her. They had questions and she, for her sake, better hope they liked her answers.

And in the private visitation room in the county jail Diane said to the three cops:

"I think we were . . . it must have been about two years we were dating. Even though that was back in the Age of Heroes I think he, I think Anson was scared. I think he thought I wouldn't . . ."

In the room were a table and four chairs. Raddatz and

Diane were the only ones who sat. Diane looked too empty of strength to do anything but sit. Raddatz had been through enough interrogations to know they could go for hours. Might as well take a load off early.

Soledad was on her feet. Sitting made her feel relaxed. She'd gotten hip even in the most innocuous of situations—especially in the situations that seemed to hold the least amount of peril—being chill could get you killed.

Panama was on his feet because it allowed him to slink around the room, edge the perp up by his ever-shifting presence. Tough-Guy Cop one-oh-one. And pointless. Diane, looking like she'd been poured into her chair, had all the edges worn from her. To Soledad, Panama going to one wall of the room then crossing to lean on another came off like a monkey making its way around a cage.

Diane, finishing her thought: "It was so silly the way I found out. Saturday on an afternoon. He was making lunch, cutting meat. The knife slipped, ran across his fingers. I gave out this yelp, but when I went to Anson . . . the blade of the knife was bent. Not a scratch on his hand. I remember holding his hand. I remember, no matter what I had seen, his flesh felt normal to me. I knew regardless what he was, to me he was, all he was, was *just* a man. Just a man I loved."

From his spot behind Diane, Panama: "I think you misunderstood the question. We didn't ask about your love life. We asked if you knew what happened to your husband."

"He's dead." She was flat with that. Beyond acceptance. It didn't matter. Nothing did. The fact that her husband wasn't around to share her life made life not matter.

Without him, without their son, she didn't have a life. They were all, in a way, dead together.

To herself Diane wondered if she could get another spoon. Diane wondered if she could get another spoon or a sharpened comb or maybe she should just take her bedding and . . . then they really could be dead together.

But that, that was the thing. They weren't really dead together. Their son was alive. Somewhere. He was being processed by some municipal agency. He was at some location being given all the perfunctory love and attention a minor could get from a civil servant who was just trying to rack enough hours to make retirement worthwhile.

Diane was going to leave him to that? She was going to leave their son to the city? The moralists and the demagogues could label her an unfit parent. They could assail her for breaking the law. The law. Yeah, she broke it. She broke it in favor of a promise made before God. But only a truly unfit parent would abandon their child to a system that did not recognize love. That legislated, that institutionalized bigotry. A system that gave birth to, and moved to the sway of, the euphemized organisms of hatred. The White Citizens Council. The Moral Majority. People for the Ethical Treatment of Animals. Focus on the Family.

So in the room, sitting in the chair, wearing her county lockup jumper of bright, bright orange, Diane gave herself strength with a thought, with a mission: Keep it together. For *our* son, keep it together. And get him back.

"Do you have any idea how?" Raddatz asked.

"What?" Diane had lost track of the questioning.

Raddatz reminded himself the flightiness of interviewees is the reason he'd taken a seat. This shit could go on for hours. "How your husband died; do you know how?"

"You told me. The police did. The other ones. They told me he was dead, and that's all. How would I know anything more?"

"You're good at keeping secrets." Panama, from a corner of the room different than the one he'd most recently occupied. "You kept it secret your husband was a freak."

A scoffing sound from Diane. A pitying sound.

"Kept that a secret, maybe you're keeping other secrets."

"Why did you file a missing person report." Soledad. "You knew if he was found, your husband could be exposed. You could be."

"I was worried about him."

Panama: "Guy's bulletproof, and you're worried about him?"

Soledad, to Panama as he wandered: "Only four corners in the room. How about you pick one?"

The look from Raddatz to Soledad: Be cool.

Panama kept on. "Something must've given you concern."

Diane asked: "You're not married, are you?"

Soledad laughed.

"He's, he was my husband. I don't need any other reason to be concerned about him."

"You'd have reason to be concerned if he was involved in—"

"Where is our son?"

"Don't worry abou—"

Raddatz cut off Panama with: "Your son is in protective custody."

"Being taken from his mother, he's protected how?"

"You go for a ride in the car, you don't put your kid in a child seat"—Panama kept up a stroll as he talked, did the walking just to be contrary to Soledad—"you get pulled over, the state can take your kid 'cause you kind of suck as a parent."

"I am not a bad—"

"You leave a kid around a freak—"

"Stop calling him a—"

"You leave a kid around a goddamn freak, what do you—"

Diane was crying.

Soledad's cane was covered with blood, as was one wall of the room. Panama's head was literally split open. Really, really, it was more cracked open, or crushed but in a way that left a separation in his skull. Soledad was ready to run a marathon. Compete an entire triathlon. She had that much energy. That much power. Killing Panama had been that invigorating. As much violence as she had delivered in a limited lifetime, this violence was positively delicious.

In her head it was.

In the room where she and Raddatz were, where Diane was crying and Panama was leaning against yet another wall, all the more violence Soledad would allow herself was to say:

"She's a mother. Leave her alone."

"I don't care if she's—"

The sound of her flesh twisting up around the cane in her grip, her own blood ripping through her veins. Soledad was going hypersensitive again. Death was coming.

"Take a walk." Raddatz giving orders to Panama.

Even from Raddatz, Panama didn't take orders well. "What do I need to—"

"Chuck, go get some air."

The sound of Diane sobbing.

Panama stood around. His way of showing he didn't let himself get pushed around. The more he stood, the more ball-less he looked.

That became obvious to him. Eventually. The flat of his hand slapped the room's steel door. A CO opened it. Panama went his way muttering slurs.

Diane cried on.

Soledad had said, talking about—defending—Diane: She's a mother. The emotional connection to a mother, as Soledad was in the process of maybe/maybe not losing hers, is where the compassion for, the defense of Diane came from, Soledad told herself. The woman had knowingly maintained a long-term relationship with a freak. Put how many lives at risk just to satisfy her own base emotions? There wasn't any other compassion to be had for her. How could anybody ever love a . . .

So what Soledad was about to do wasn't about compassion, she told and told and told herself in the span of a couple of seconds. It was about, it was just a bone being tossed.

What Soledad tossed: "Mrs. Hall, if you cooperate with us, we can make your cooperation known to the right people."

Soledad got eyebrow from Raddatz.

Diane asked: "The right people? What does, what does that—"

"People with authority. People who could get you back with your son."

"O'Roark."

"I can't make guarantees. But if you help us, I will talk to somebody. Just so you know, my word carries weight."

Raddatz's hand worked his jaw, rubbed all around it, wiped down his mouth. Maybe he was suppressing a scream. Maybe he was trying to keep from saying anything because Soledad seemed to be on to something.

"Help you how?" Diane's voice was no longer flat. It was raised just slightly by hope.

"We've got reason to think your husband was murdered."

Raddatz stepped back in, took over again before Soledad could hand out any more freebies.

Soledad was wordless. That Raddatz was openly backing a murder theory was news to her. For the minute she was just listening.

"It'd take a hell of a lot to kill a man like your husband. We need to try and find out exactly what."

"I don't know what I can tell you."

"You can tell us the names of the other freaks he hung around with." Raddatz was direct with that, sure in tone. For him there wasn't any doubt Anson consorted with others of his own kind, no matter Diane said otherwise.

"He didn't—"

"You want to see your kid again or not?"

Like a knife to Soledad's gut. That Raddatz had taken the hand she'd extended Diane and was using it to slap her . . .

"He didn't talk with other metanormals. He wouldn't take a chance like that."

"Like *that*?"

"A chance letting anybody know he was different.

Even others like him. When you people arrest them, when you torture them—"

"We don't torture—" Soledad started to say.

Regardless of the bridge of fidelity Soledad was trying to build, Diane didn't care about Soledad's POV of the world. "When you do whatever you do. When you do to them what you're doing to me now, he didn't want to take the chance his name would ever be given, or that he would name names. Mostly, he didn't want to take the chance you people would take Danny from us."

"Danny," Soledad said. "Your son?" she asked.

Diane said: "Do you know what . . ." She had to take a couple of seconds, get herself back together. "Anson used to wear bandages. Every three or four months or so he'd put a little bandage on the back of his hand or a finger or one on his neck. Never made a big deal out of it. But he wanted people . . . he wanted it in their minds they'd seen him cut, hurt. He never wanted people to suspect he *couldn't* be hurt. He was that careful. I know there are other metanormals in the city. Everybody knows it. If Anson ever talked with them, that I don't know about."

If Diane was a liar, she was a helluva one. But knowing you could close the separation from your child with a lie well told could give any mother a tongue of gold.

"All I can tell you," Diane continued, "I think he knew."

"Knew?" Soledad asked.

"That he'd been found out. Or . . . or something bad was going to happen."

"Why? Why do you say that?"

"Maybe I'm just using hindsight. But Anson had been

carrying . . . concern. For weeks it seemed. It seems. And more than what I'd come to accept as normal."

"What," Raddatz asked, "were his normal concerns?"

"That he'd be exposed, hunted down by the police. You see on TV every other month, somewhere someone is being exposed as a metanormal, assaulted by police—"

"They can turn themselves in." Maybe she had some compassion, but for Soledad it stopped short of allowing for police-bashing. "How many years after San Francisco, they can still do what's right. If they don't . . ."

Yeah. If they don't. Diane nodded. Didn't rejoin the argument. She wasn't going to win hearts and minds in an interrogation room. Why bother trying?

Diane went on with: "All those were his usual concerns. He had his brighter days. Always he was bright with Danny. But mostly, he lived in fear. But these last few weeks, month . . . he was quiet, distant. But I guess I'd say serene also. Like he'd accepted . . . whatever. Whatever there was for him to accept."

Acceptance.

Soledad thought: the last stage of death. Anson knew there was a chance he was going to die. Was he aware of the other murders? Does that kind of chatter bleed through the underground freak community? Had he seen Death in his mind? In his heart? Had he seen Death watching him, following him? To a freak, to an unkillable freak, how does Death appear?

Soledad looked to Raddatz.

"He tried to hide it from me," Diane said. "But in the quiet moments, in the moments he thought I wasn't watching him . . . you know the regard of someone you care for. You know when it's wrong."

Raddatz came forward in his chair, leaned on the table. "Do you remember how long he'd been feeling that way?"

"I think, really, since Israel Fernandez was assassinated."

"He died in a car accident," Soledad pointed out.

She didn't laugh, but Diane had a sick humor to her. "Sure. One of those accidents where a man loses control of his car on a dry road in good weather and crashes into a tree."

Raddatz: "Happens all the time."

Diane agreed. "It does happen all the time. It happens to political leaders, people who want change. An accident. A lone gunman. A high-tech lynching because the people who don't—"

Raddatz was up out of the chair moving for the door.

"The people who don't want change make accidents—"

"Guard!"

"They make them happen!"

For a minute Raddatz's hand slamming on the metal door, Diane's voice nail-on-chalkboard screeching in the air, fought each other to a draw.

A CO opened the door.

Raddatz bulled his way out of the room. Soledad merely followed.

Diane, alone, wanted to cry. Was too spent for tears. She just sat. Until a CO took her back to her cell.

*   *   *

Soledad and Raddatz made their way through the lockup, through sliding steel doors and partitions and past guards and surveillance cameras . . . All that to keep normal people incarcerated.

She'd never been to the SPA.

She'd bagged a lot of freaks, but Soledad was thinking right then she'd never been to the spot in the desert with the sweet-sounding acronym that housed freaks brought in off the streets. How you keep them from getting back on the streets . . . it must boggle the mind. Soledad figured at some point she ought to take the trip. Her mind could stand to get blown every now and then. Or at least reassured.

Panama wasn't around. Soledad and Raddatz would run into him sooner or later. The later, for Soledad, the better.

As they walked, to Raddatz: "Who would he have called attention to?"

"What's that?"

"If Hall wasn't consorting with other freaks, if this guy felt like he was in for some trouble, the trouble didn't come from nowhere. He must have at least felt like he'd caught somebody's eye. Whose?"

"People who want freaks dead."

Feeling Raddatz out: "A hate group?"

"Enough of them around."

"My experience is they're full of talk. They march, they burn their symbols, but what yokels in White Trashville don't do is go after vics that might actually fight back."

" 'Yokels in White Trashville.' But you're not biased."

"I'm not PC with shitheads, and shitheads don't have what it takes to bag a freak."

"Yeah? What's your theory, O'Roark?"

With her nonresponse Soledad made it plain she didn't have one. Not one she'd articulate.

"Then forget about leading," Raddatz told her. "Learn to follow."

Up at a CO's check-in Panama was talking with a couple of corrections officers. From the body language he was being confidential. Soledad approaching. The COs looked up, gave a look: Shh, shh. Here she comes.

Part of Soledad wanted to give a grin to their frat-boy antics. Part of Soledad wanted to walk up, coldcock one as a roundabout way of wiping the shine off all their smirking ivory faces. Even the one Latino CD was right then ivory to her.

Raddatz collected Panama. The trio started heading out. Before they cleared the joint Raddatz pulled off. Said he had to pee. Soledad thought more likely he wanted to give her time with Panama. Let things get hashed now so they wouldn't have to be dealt with on the drive back.

A couple of seconds of standing around before Panama looked like he was working his way, working his way toward clocking Soledad.

And right when he was at the very least going to smack her with every hard word he could think of, Soledad cut him with: "Good play in there; you taking it rough, me looking soft. Scared of you, Panama. She was scared to hell of you. Soon as you left she opened up like a wet paper sack. Don't ever think I've seen a cop play things so smooth. You know what you're doing. I don't have to tell you that, but you know what you're doing."

Panama stood where he was. Flesh pink. Rage useless. No way to get satisfaction. A eunuch watching a porn flick. So he huffed and puffed at Soledad. Balled a hand into a fist.

Soledad took a stick of gum out of her pocket and unwrapped it and started to give it a chew. Then, finally, she gave Panama some attention. Both eyes straight to the face. Her forbearance mocking his fury.

By the front of the building, back from his faux piss, Raddatz called to Panama, to Soledad.

Panama, Soledad; they wouldn't take their eyes off of each other. It's like they were worried in a moment's flinch the other would reach for their gun.

Soledad said: "Go. You don't get to walk behind me."

"You're a fucking cunt."

"Respect it. It's where you came from. Go."

Panama went, went right past Raddatz, out for their car.

As Soledad arrived to him, Raddatz asked: "You two done?"

"Done. Unless we're just getting started."

I live for simplicity. MTac afforded me a very simple lifestyle.

Find a freak.

Kill a freak.

Unless it kills you first.

Simple.

Your life's not cluttered with a lot of friends because civvies don't understand you and coworkers tend to die off with regularity.

Simple.

You shut down, you close up, you isolate. By yourself in your apartment, on the Santa Monica promenade high noon on a Saturday. Either, or. You're alone.

That makes your life all about you.

That makes life simple.

So all this complexity is driving me crazy. Sensing death, knowing it's coming for me, only to find out it's hitting my mother instead. Working undercover against guys who might be doing a more proactive version of what I believe in.

Dealing with a woman separated from her kid. That hurts. I know. My mother had separated herself from me.

And, oh yeah, I'm getting married.

I would say it's looking like a Vegas wedding, but I think it'll take more than a couple of quick "I do's" at the Little White Chapel to cover the sham of things.

But making my situation with Vin legal's the least complex part of my life. I don't really love him, I'm just going to marry him. So really, I'm just like a thousand other chicks who've quit love and are only looking to graduate to a state of blind permeance in their lives.

What's complex:

A cop whose head I wanted to beat with my cane, a freak sympathizer I actually feel sympathy for. Violence and death unseen but all around. It's all that which I can't figure.

I don't care for my inability to navigate my own life.

As I approach thirty, I don't need for my life to require an ever-increasing amount of attention.

But then, as I approach thirty, I realize I never thought I'd live this long.

A shower. Hot water. Some kind of a soak. She had, Soledad had a tangible urge to physically do something about the dirty way she felt.

Felt.

Felt, just from the "you so smart, Joe"-ing she'd done with Panama. The cowering, the virtual bootlicking to avoid conflict and maintain good graces had left in her mouth the taste of Panama's filth. On top of that the tack hadn't particularly worked.

Jesus.

This wasn't, she was sure, the way Tashjian operated. Tashjian, Soledad was damn sure, didn't lower himself for anybody for any reason.

But Tashjian came at people head-on.

Soledad was working a cerebral Delta Force, coming up out of the mud on someone's intellectual rear to . . .

To stab 'em in the back.

Right when Soledad was coming to grips with her choices, she had an annoying way of queering her own deal.

So, she proffered herself, here's the new bargain: do

your work, Soledad. Get to the real. If real was Raddatz and his cadre were on the bad end of things, well, then, take 'em out.

Then kick 'em.

What the hell? They're down, right? Might as well get a few shots in. To Panama for sure.

Panama was top of Soledad's list of people to which she'd hand out a few nasty blows.

But that was for later.

For now: the truth, and getting to it.

Officer O'Roark?"

"Yeah?"

"This is Officer Hayes. I was the one who found the freak," he said in case Soledad couldn't put name with face. Wasn't an issue. He'd very much been in her thoughts.

"What's doing, Officer?"

"I . . . I wanted to give you a call. Wasn't sure if, if this is strictly right."

Soledad gripped the phone. Her anxiety: A request for a date was coming.

"I wasn't sure, but there's some things going on I think you should know about."

The call wasn't about the two of them getting together. Some other kind of shit was imminent. Shouldn't be a surprise. Soledad couldn't recall, seemed like she couldn't remember the time the phone had ever rung with some good news.

She asked: "What's going on?"

"I'm not real sure, ma'am. That is, I know what's going on, but I don't know what it means. If it means anything."

"Just play things back for me."

"Is it safe to talk on the phone?"

Jesus Christ. Soledad hadn't even thought about that. And the fact that Hayes had . . .

Shit was most assuredly coming.

For any ears that might be listening, playing things off: "Course it is, Officer."

"Of course it is," Hayes parroted. "I only meant—"

"Just play things back."

"Had an investigator come around the other day, asked me if I had ever talked with you."

"An investigator?"

"DMI."

"What was his name?"

"It was Raddatz, ma'am."

Soledad held down her phone for a sec. She brushed the antenna over her teeth. Finished with that, with a mindless act that bought her space to think, putting the phone back to her ear:

". . . O'Roark? Officer O'Roa—"

"Yeah, I'm here. So Raddatz comes around, talks to you. Asks you what?"

"Asks me if you and I ever talked, and about what. I told him."

"You were straight with him?"

"Straight all the way. No reason I shouldn't have been."

"No. No reason."

"But I don't go in for the DMI types. I don't care for them. You're decent and all, Officer O'Roark."

"Thanks." Kiss ass, she thought.

"But the rest of them . . . So I figured I give you a heads-up because something about him stank."

"Yeah. Like Old Spice."

Soledad gave her thanks and good-byes. Started to. Hayes cut her off with a query as to whether or not Soledad liked to shoot pool.

Soledad said she did, but that her leg was still barely in fair shape. Now wasn't a real good time to go stand around shooting a few games. But, and this she stressed, she really appreciated Hayes having her back.

Hayes said he understood. Maybe another time.

Maybe. Soledad hung up her phone.

Raddatz coming around behind her, asking questions. No matter what she was putting out, Raddatz wasn't taking it at face value. Same as he'd said he was short on trust, she was going to have to be long on caution.

And right then among other stuff she was thinking, Soledad realized in her excuses to Hayes as to why she couldn't go out with him, the fact that she was getting married wasn't one of them.

The earth is a beautiful thing. Mother Earth, Gaia, depending on what kind of Old Age hippie, New Age guruism you believed in. However you called her, she's a real decent home. Not just the green and the blue and the white of the trees and the sky and the clouds. A modest girl, her true beauties are hidden.

The earth moves.

Around the sun, through the universe. The earth was in a constant state of adjustment. Of resonance. The seismic plates, the fissures, the volcanic rings. Moving. Shifting. For billions of years. Creating, as it created topography, a song of folklore that spoke, almost cried in longing for a time before man and machine and clear-cutting and chemical dumping and toxin pumping. And the song was beautiful.

If you could hear it.

People couldn't hear it.

Normal people couldn't hear it.

Metanormals couldn't hear it.

Except for metanormals with the ability to terraform. The ability to touch the resonance, affect the resonance.

Alter the land. Move rock and stone. Literally the ability to make a mountain out of a molehill. It was an art. Magic. Here's the trick: Terraformers didn't actually do anything. Like geologic Dr. Dolittles, they encouraged the earth to alter herself. There had been a few, a very few, heroes who terraformed—used their abilities to move earth to fight wrongs. But mostly, terraformers had been, were, pacifist. They felt, they *felt* the violence earth had known since her birth. The impact of massive meteors. The extinction of entire species. The attempted extermination of whole races. It was all in the song. If you heard the song, if you felt the song, you didn't much want to cause anyone, anything, the slightest tribulation.

But the thing about nonviolence: It's a good concept, but it doesn't much stand up to the need for self-preservation.

Tiesto Moore was just finding that out.

He found that out, really, about eight minutes prior when . . . when *It* came after him throwing off electricity, throwing bricks and metal and whatever *It* could get *Its* hands on and pick up and whip at speeds which turned the objects into deadly projectiles. Speeds that forced the projectiles through the earthen walls Tiesto yanked from the ground for his protection.

That was before he completely quit his pacifism.

That was before Tiesto started ripping rocks and then boulders from the earth. Moving them like buried marionettes. Making them rush for *It*. What else was there to call . . . *It*?

Maybe . . . Tiesto was getting delirious. He was starting to think maybe he ought just call it fear. Call it, maybe, Death.

Delirious. The running, the shifting of the earth he was doing. *Was* doing. Too tired now. Too tired to move earth anymore. Just run. Just stumble. Just keep ahead of *It*.

Just keep alive.

He'd miss the song. Tiesto thought about an empty eternity without the song. And the thought was pretty shitty. And *It* was rushing up somewhere behind him. *It* was coming to end things.

Really going to miss the song.

And Tiesto came stumbling around a corner.

And there it was waiting for him. Death. Four MTacs. Weapons ready. Fingers on triggers.

Eddi: "You are in violation of an Exe—"

Tiesto raised a hand for the MTacs. Maybe to attack. Maybe to defend himself. Maybe to use the flesh of his palm to shield himself, feebly, from the inevitable. In that sliver of a second his thoughts too capricious to discern.

The MTacs took it as an act of aggression.

The MTacs opened fire.

Tiesto was dead before he touched earth.

Raddatz did the talking. He was the one who asked the questions. He handled or at least took the lead of the debrief. Standard. It was Raddatz and Panama, Soledad third-wheeling it as they went through the call with Eddi Aoki. Her written report would follow. But it was SOP to have a face-to-face with the senior lead of an element soon as possible after a warrant was served. Originally, on-site debriefings'd been established to wring every piece of intel there was out of the responding officers while memories were fresh. Guns are good, but knowledge is power. And any piece of info could be the key piece when it came to going after a similar mutie on some future occasion.

But . . .

More and more the on-sites were done to get an official story out quick as possible to placate the freak fuckers and, worst case, contradict any altered version of the incident bleeding hearts might try to virus through the liberal media.

The call had been fairly standard as warrants go. Someone had 911'd about a freak. Pacific MTac rolled. A terraformer, but Pacific got the drop. Chalked the kill.

Soledad was humiliated.

Standing there, Raddatz and Panama doing the talking, Soledad felt unpurposed. Added to that they were talking with Eddi. It was Eddi being witness to Soledad's lack of purpose that elevated her disconcert to humiliation. Every second that passed sank her with shame.

About three-quarters of the way through the debriefing Raddatz got a call from back at DMI—Donatell was Soledad's best guess—and stepped off to talk. Panama, not looking to kill downtime with Soledad, took a minute to go do something. Go pretend he was doing something.

Soledad and Eddi.

Soledad offered: "Nice job on the freak."

"Wasn't much, but I'll take the easy ones."

It didn't overly show, but Soledad rated Eddi's modesty as false.

Eddi asked: "How's things with you?"

"Different. All different."

"Like it?"

"It'll take getting used to."

"Good thing is you won't have to." Eddi did some cheerleading. "Your leg gets good, you'll be right back where you belong."

"We'll see." Then, one more time: "We'll see."

"I was actually glad to see you today."

"*Actually?* You make it sound—"

"A little backhanded, yeah, but I mean it. Worst thing about serving a warrant is you've got to deal with the DMI creeps afterward."

"Worst thing besides getting killed, you mean."

A little bit of a smile from Eddi. "Maybe not even.

Swear, there're days I'd rather let a freak go than have to sit across from DMI."

Soledad shared the feeling. Maybe it was just departmental fidelity for G Platoon, but since making the transfer the feeling'd gotten stronger, not weaker. She was ready to agree with Eddi.

But Soledad had put work into looking loyal to the new boss no matter how sincere or fake they gauged that loyalty to be. There was no sense in queering things with loose lips, on having her true feelings come back to bite her in the ass.

She said: "They're not creeps."

"Yeah. They're normal guys who—"

"They're not creeps."

The smile slipping from Eddi's face: "Just joking around, Soledad."

"Except what we do," hitting the "we," making it very much come off as "not you," "isn't a joke."

"You get DMI branded on your ass too?"

"I've worked both sides. Maybe you ought to before you start making judgments."

From Eddi, a cold, cold look. Then a smile, but that, too, was frozen. And sharp.

"Know something, Soledad? One day you and me are going to talk. Maybe not long. Couple of minutes. But we're going to talk about something. And when we get done talking, we're going to realize we went that couple of minutes without just about getting into a fistfight. Then we'll go out and celebrate. Only, it won't be much of a celebration because, I'm guessing, before we get to the champagne you and me'll get into an ass-kicking contest."

"Other than I think champagne is for little girls, I'm looking forward to it."

"The lack of argument or the ass kicking?"

"Sweetie, we get into some ass kicking, you'll be too busy getting your ass kicked to argue."

And that turned Eddi's smile warm.

Raddatz came back around. Seeing that, Panama felt comfortable enough to quit faking like he was doing something else and reengage.

Raddatz asked of Eddi: "Anything else for us, Officer?"

A moment's thought. A shake of her head. "I was saying to Officer O'Roark this one was pretty average. We got it, and everybody gets to go home. They should all be this good."

"Write it up and get it in."

"By tomorrow."

Raddatz departed without salutation. Panama and Soledad followed.

"Soledad."

She turned back to Eddi.

Eddi didn't say anything else, made no move to close the distance between her and Soledad.

By her lack of action Soledad got that whatever else Eddi had to say wasn't for other ears. She made the cross back.

"This is going to sound a little weird. If it was some other DMI cree . . . If it was some other cops besides you, I wouldn't bother."

A little shrug, a little shake of the head from Soledad. She'd take it as it came.

"When we hit the terraformer, it looked scared." Eddi

stood close to Soledad, went quiet. For eyes that might be watching she tried to come off like she was being casual: a little leftover girl talk that had to get finished. "I don't mean the kind of scared four hot MTacs put into a mutie."

"Then scared how?"

"If I knew how, it wouldn't be weird to me."

"Why are you telling me this and not Raddatz?"

Rocking on her heels, Eddi faked like she was without concern. "I guess I've got ego the same as anybody. So making something out of nothing; I can do without DMI thinking I'm all hysterical. But I've looked in the whites of enough freaks to know this one was, was scared of something besides us. Maybe it means something. Maybe it doesn't. More than those guys, I trust you to come to which is which. Get healthy, Soledad." A flick of her hand as a wave good-bye. "However you feel about me, I feel better when you've got my back."

Watching Soledad limp away, Eddi got an ill feeling. Her insides real quick got morbid and unwell. Eddi'd never seen Soledad so busted up. Wasn't just that she was watching Soledad cane away with an odd rocking gait that was same as Vegas neon announcing Soledad was jacked. Wasn't just that Soledad'd been injured at all. Plenty of times Soledad had gotten the bad end of things. Less, maybe, than some MTacs, but enough so that the image wasn't alien to Eddi.

Soledad was busted in another way. She'd been always to Eddi a single-minded MTac out kicking ass. She was still emotionally myopic, was still putting her foot to tailbones. But she wasn't an MTac and didn't seem to be one in the most severe way possible. In a change-a-day world, Soledad had been a constant. The extreme variations between life and death Eddi was pretty sure she could handle. But in the day-to-day, aside from being extant or extinct, it was nice that some things always remained. Lucy was always going to screw things up, Ricky was always going to forgive her. Politicians were always going to set aside the public trust for cash or whores. Soledad was always going to be an MTac.

Or not.

And what really made Eddi's ill feeling putrid, it wasn't going a few rounds with a mutie that changed things. It was not looking both ways when Soledad ran across a street.

It was extreme chance. It was real bad luck. It was not much of anything that changed everything.

Eddi was ready for major life changes. Eddi'd been through the sudden loss that robs survivors of good-byes, makes closure a quaint notion. That kind of shit makes every other unchanging thing a minor miracle.

Soledad limping away was one less miracle in Eddi's life.

Thursday was off for Soledad. She got up late thanks to the little white pill she took to help induce the sleep that otherwise rarely came to her. She went swimming. Worked out her bum leg. Hurt like hell. But she wasn't about to let herself go to waste. Laundry. She gave thought to going to a movie but couldn't find one she figured she could sit through without later regretting the two hours of her life, the nine dollars of her hard-earned she'd tossed away. She gave thought to calling Vin. Couldn't particularly think of anything to say to him different or new or somehow meaningful that wasn't covered in their last pseudo-conversation three or four days prior. She did send off an elongated e-mail to her mother. Soledad had plenty to say to her mother. A dark part of Soledad wondered if her mother was even really sick, or had just tumbled onto a grotesque way to build a relationship with her daughter. Errands were run and Soledad ate and watched the news. She eked out a few more pages of the Mailer book she'd spent closing in on a year and half "reading." She fucked around on the Internet for a while.

Eight months after his seventy-third birthday a guy fell in love for the first time all over again. A mother was told her child would not live to see the morning. An NBA hoops star who hadn't started let alone finished college, but still managed to pull in more than twenty mill a year, was refusing to take no for an answer from some girl he'd known all of three and a third hours. A guy who'd never wanted kids was taking his sons to the amusement park for the third time this year thanking God for them every step of the way as, ironically, they were the only things that gave his life meaning.

All this was happening across town, somewhere across the country. Somewhere beyond Soledad. Physically beyond her. Emotionally. In her time and space it was the most ordinary of days that passed utterly without significance. The kind of day, in another forty-eight hours, there would be little of it she would be able to recall with distinction if at all. With absolutely nothing else to do, having wrung herself empty of every approximation of purpose, she lay in bed and let sleep come.

Sleep ignored the invitation.

Soledad debated taking a little white pill. Wasn't worried about getting hooked. She was worried only that when she ran out, more would be hard to come by as more required a prescription she didn't have. And taking the pills built up a resistance. As it was, beyond just the sleep they gave her, Soledad dug the knockout that came with the drugs. Made her think that death . . . yeah, it had to be respected, but there was no reason to fear it.

That quick, that easy, Soledad was thinking about death again.

Getting her mind off that, she settled on skipping the

pill. Better to go a few sleepless nights than have them lose their sweet, sweet effect.

Soledad lay in bed. Ignored the urge to check and check and recheck the clock. Over a few hours maybe she slept a little, but probably she didn't. The phone rang. It was late. Or really early. Either way Soledad knew she wasn't going to care for what was waiting on the other end of the line.

"It's Raddatz."

"Hey."

"What kind of shape are you in?"

"Tired. I can function if I have to."

"What I talked about before: the end of fear. Do you want to be part of that? Is that something you want to be part of?"

"Well, I don't know what it is. I can't say I want to be part of something when I don't know what it is."

"It's the right thing, Soledad." He was being oblique. "You've got to know, inside you, the truth is you want to do what's right."

She lay in the dark. Not a word. Not a sound. The day had come so close to being insignificant. Now it was on its way to being monumental. An invite from a rogue cop to be part of "what's right."

"Soledad . . . ?"

"It's a bullshit question. Yeah, I want to do what's right."

"I'm going to come around. Be ready. And, Soledad . . ."

"Yeah?"

"Have your piece ready too."

Not that Soledad had ever put much thought to such things, but in passing she never figured a clandestine meeting regarding murder—murders that had occurred, murders that might—would take place in a Jamba Juice.

That's where she was with Raddatz, with Panama, with Donatell, with Shen. All of them with their scars and missing digits. And Shen with his . . . his head. It was where a head goes on a regular body. Right up there on top of the neck. That's where its similarity to normality ended. Shen's was all stoved in on the sides. Pushed in at the front. Features violently asymmetrical. At some point something had crushed it severely. And all the king's horses and all the king's men . . . The kid clerking the counter unable to keep eye contact with Shen while he took Shen's order for a Mango-a-Go-Go. Donatell had been right about Shen. Shen did make him look good. Sitting around as they were, they looked like busted war vets come out to drink smoothies, reminisce and try and convince each other the sacrifice they'd made in some desert or jungle or European city thousands of miles away'd been worthwhile.

Except for Soledad. In the company she kept, the burns on her neck made Soledad look like a security guard who'd gotten scratched breaking up teens scuffling at the mall.

Somber. The group was somber as they took a minute to put down their blends of fruit and ice and nonfat yogurt, and it would have been hi-F'n-larious to Soledad— grown men, boozers all probably, drinking their girlie drinks—except their avoidance of liquor and caffeine signified they were keeping clean for work. And not a one of them was at the minute on the city's clock. The work that was coming was extracurricular.

A little bit of bullshit was slung back and forth. Home talk. Cursory personal matters. There was subtext to it. Reminders to all: There's something I've got to go home to; a family, a life. Somebody. Something. So when we hit it, I got your back. Make sure you got mine.

From an envelope Raddatz slipped a photo. Surveillance photo. Black-and-white and very, very grainy. Very snowy. The camera that took it was apparently shit. In relation to the doorway he was passing through, the subject was a man of average size, though his weight appeared above median compared to his height. Vague as that was, it was also as detailed a description to be gotten from viewing the photo. Wearing a sweat suit, a hoodie with the hood pulled up over his head, all the more to be said was that he (or she; it was impossible to be absolutely certain of the subject's gender) resembled those FBI sketches of the Unibomber, and those FBI sketches of the Unibomber never quite resembled anybody, which is why the FBI caught the Unibomber only after the Unibomber's brother ratted him out.

The photo got passed and passed and passed. Everybody took a look. Nobody said a thing.

Except Soledad.

Soledad said: "Who's this?"

"It's the guy," Raddatz answered, "we're looking for."

"Didn't know we were looking for a guy."

Shen hit the bottom of his cup, slurped up the last of his drink.

Soledad said again: "I didn't know we were—"

"He's a person of extreme interest."

"That says a whole lot. How do we find Mr. Interest? If this is all we've got to go on . . ." Soledad flicked the picture over the table back to Raddatz.

"Run a watch." Panama made it sound like Soledad's lack of savvy was tightening up the muscle around his neck and head, causing him pain.

"We're going to watch over the whole city? The five of us?"

Donatell: "We know where to look."

"How do we know where to look, 'cause I don't know shit except for what you're telling me."

"You gonna give her everything?" Shen asked of Raddatz.

Raddatz kept quiet.

"Good intel. That's what DMI's all about." Panama gave DMI one-oh-one. "You get good intel, you get your freak."

She wasn't trying to be contrary. For the sake of her true objective, Soledad was trying to front acceptance of the offered vagaries. She nodded a little. But the reality she wasn't buying what was being passed off didn't need articulation, was obvious beyond words.

"I think what we wanted was to give you a taste of how DMI works." Panama was coming across, was trying to come across soft. Not one time before had he been anything less than tough with Soledad. Every word he was saying now: bullshit. "This is just us processing a tip." He didn't trust her. He was trying to shove her off.

"Middle of the night in a smoothie store is where you all process your info." She made it all sound stupid, wanted Panama to know how stupid he sounded. "If I'm in or I'm out, that's up to you. But if I'm out, don't call me up and drag me around way after dark anymore."

As he got up from the table, Raddatz to Soledad: "You ride with me."

So here was Soledad in a car parked off a street in Westlake. Waiting. Watching, supposedly. But she knew she was on the hunt. No matter the convolutions Raddatz was taking her through, she knew that she and the cadre were on the edge of a badness. At the low end was acting without authority. The far end was targeting a metanormal for execution.

Simply, murder.

To Raddatz: "This guy we're watching, is he a freak or is he a freak fucker?"

Raddatz said nothing.

To Raddatz: "If this is a freak, if you're thinking about doing more than just watching him, we need to call in MTac."

Raddatz kept looking straight ahead. Right out the windshield. His gaze went down the block, over the horizon. It was that distant.

"If you've got solid intel, it needs to get passed to—"

"We're getting a little more."

"It takes the five of us to eyeball a freak? They only send four MTacs when it's time to take one out."

"I'm taking a chance bringing you along."

There were a lot of ways to take that. Best, Soledad thought, not to take it any one way in particular. No assumptions. Let Raddatz explain himself. Let him help her figure what to do.

"You're good-cop, Soledad. From what I know, as a cop, there's not one thing wrong with you. You remind me of me."

"You complimenting me or you?"

"If it's a compliment, it's backhanded. When I imply I was a good cop, I was the kind who didn't ask questions. I believe . . . I believed in the job—"

Believe. Believed. The tense shift stuck out to Soledad.

"I believed, and I followed orders. I didn't question things. I could be trusted to do right."

"That's what good cops do." Soledad slouched against her door. Kept up the outward appearance of being relaxed. She eased, very much eased, a hand for her piece. For whatever was coming she'd feel better gripping it.

Raddatz: "It's also what your average Nazi did: act without consideration. Just follow orders."

"That's not a backhanded compliment. That's backfisted."

"As much against me as you. But same as me, I think you can change."

"Change to what? The opposite of good cop is bad." Her fingers brushed the butt of the O'Dwyer.

"Being a better one."

"What's better than doing right?"

"Keeping from doing wrong."

"Jesus Christ, it's like talking to a fortune cookie."

"Leave your gun."

Soledad quietly gave props to Raddatz's good eyes. His hand was resting on the steering wheel. His hook was in his lap. Unless he started swinging it, he wasn't a threat.

Soledad, getting a strong grip on her O'Dwyer: "It's too late for that."

"Never too late." Raddatz, looking to Soledad: "You've got a reputation for being cold and hard. More so than most of the MTacs."

Soledad didn't take that badly. It was fact, one she'd gotten comfortable with a long time ago. She got a comfortable grip on her gun too. It was carrying her green-tipped load. Slugs gel-capped with contact poison. Soledad wondered, if she had to take the shot, would it put Raddatz down before he got off one in return? In close quarters what were the odds Soledad would get back-splashed by her own poison? Right then she kinda wished for a regular gun. Didn't have to be big. Just deadly in a conventional fashion. While she was thinking that, Soledad checked her back side. Made sure none of the cadre were creeping on her.

"But only once," Raddatz went on, "have I seen you quick to anger. When I threatened Hall's wife to keep her son from her."

Before she could even process the thought an answer fell out of her: "A kid needs his mother."

"So you see."

"See what? I throw somebody a break, you think I can't do what's—"

"You see the gray."

Soledad flicked her free hand like she was deflecting a useless thought.

She said: "The law, justice, doing the job; there's gray all over those. If this is supposed to be an academy primer, it's years too late."

"You believe in a better world? Hell, you know you do. You want a better world, it starts now. Tonight."

An invitation. An open invitation. With her hand on her gun, knowing she was ready to kill him anyway, Raddatz was still offering her to join the cadre.

If just in theory she took the offer, *if* she jettisoned her expressed obligation to Tashjian and threw her allegiance to the cadre, what she did this night wouldn't be her first kill. Not hardly. But it'd be her first without sanction. Without the letter of the law backing her. And that, that "little" thing—the law—made the difference. Maybe not ultimately a true moral difference. That's what cable TV shoutfests were for: pundits to go back and forth on right and wrong before the moderator got in the last word after the final commercial break. But the law gave Soledad and every other cop justification. And justification, under the circumstances, after San Francisco, allowed her to execute her obligation: protect normal humans.

It allowed her to protect normal humans and still sleep the sleep of the innocent. On the occasions she slept at all.

This night she couldn't let things go to murder and feel the same way. Clean.

Could she?

Unbelievable. The situation had advanced to the brink, and still Soledad was conflicted. She would have complicity, or she would be duplicitous. One or the other. And only just then could she even vaguely pick which.

"I don't believe in vigilantism." Fuck being a rat. She'd pick Tashjian's side, but she wasn't going to be surreptitious. "Being a better person means we're not like *them*. We follow the law. We don't make our own rules. We're not gods. We don't hand out life and death whenever we please."

"You're with us more than you know. I've got a high regard for life and death," Raddatz said. "The power to take it is awesome. The power to preserve it is humbling. And the ability to know which to apply scares the hell out of me. If I could explain this in a word . . . I need you here."

"That's a strong way to put things."

"I need your skills, but if you don't want to use them, I need to know where you are. I can't take a chance."

"Not when you're going to do some coloring outside the lines. How about we do this: How about we start up the car, head back to DMI?"

"I can't."

"I hate them as much as you, as much as a person can. But all this does—"

A laugh from Raddatz. Snide.

Soledad rode over it. "All this does is give the power back to the freaks."

"It's not about power, except the power to do what's right. And I honestly believe in the crucial moment you'll do what's right. I believe, I have to, you can't do otherwise. But I need your trust. I need—"

A little electronic chirp. It was muffled under the fabric of Soledad's coat, but she and Raddatz both heard it. It was audible confirmation from Soledad's gun the safety had been flicked off.

There was her trust.

She said: "I'm telling you one last time: Start the car and—"

Raddatz's radio came up weakly, barely able to read Shen's call.

". . . spotted . . . pretty sure . . ."

"Shen!" Raddatz did a one-handed fumble with the radio, adjusted dials, tried to squeeze life from it. The movements so quick Soledad nearly pulled out and took the shot. "Shen, you're coming in weak. Repeat."

Static. A little. Then not even that.

"Raddatz, it's Donatell, you read?"

Soledad: "Raddatz . . ."

Ignoring her: "Donatell."

"I read." Donatell's voice came strong, the radio signal clear. "You get that last from Shen?"

"Negative. It came garbled. Crawl up Union toward him." Raddatz lit the car's engine. "Keep your mike hot."

"Roger that."

"Raddatz, call it in."

Raddatz looked to Soledad. In the look he made himself naked emotionally. He cast off anger, any trace of a tough-guy stance. The irradiate musings that had dominated his tone. All that, all that was set aside. It was quite a trick, though it was not an illusion. It was replaced by a sincerity beyond honesty.

"Soledad," Raddatz said, "shoot me or get out." Wasn't an order. It was a request to do one or the other.

Soledad had to let him be. Or she had to let him die. If he could not complete his task, then—and this she got from his tone—all there really was, was for Raddatz to be dead.

Shoot or get out.

Soledad did neither.

Raddatz put the car in gear, drove. He took the street at a solid creep. Even at the hour there was activity. People coming and going from something that was open all night. A pharmacy. A club. A porn store.

Rounding a corner where Shen's car should be but wasn't: "Where is he?" A useless question, but it fell out of Raddatz's mouth just the same. "Shen?" No response to his call over the radio. "Shen, it's Raddatz, you read?"

Nothing.

To Panama: "Panama, anything?"

". . . on the . . . back around . . ."

More static than words.

Soledad's grip on her gun stayed constant, though the gun itself had moved from beneath her coat to a spot in the clear where it would be more ready for action.

"Eyes open" was Raddatz's order to Soledad. She didn't need to be directed. That things were hinky was obvious.

Raddatz kept up the creep of the car, kept it up, but even as it slow-rolled, it rolled with an urgency. Something was not right. Very close by, some things were ill. Heading for terminal.

Soledad spotted it. Parked on a cross street facing opposite of traffic. Shen's car.

"There!"

Raddatz was already angling for it. Both cops out of the car before it stopped rolling.

Raddatz drew out.

Two-handed grip. Gun forward, muzzle down. Soledad came around the car. The car in drive. Engine dead. Door open.

Raddatz did a quick assess: The target wasn't on the street or sidewalk.

An alley behind an apartment block. Raddatz took it, Soledad right behind.

Creep, creeping along. Cautious, but not too slow. Things were happening somewhere. Raddatz, Soledad had to get to them.

And mariachi music played from a radio and candlelight danced from a low window and a baby made its hunger or tiredness or displeasure known by its wailing.

The world was one sizable distraction.

Creep, creeping . . .

An odor. The odor was . . .

Puddled water. Shadows. A stray cat with a wound on its leg that was home to an extended family of maggots.

Shen.

Up ahead in the alley Shen sat on the ground. Legs splayed. Arms dangling at his sides. A gun spilled from his right hand. That odor: The air was sick with cordite. He'd gotten off a bunch of shots. No blood on the ground. If Shen had hit the target, the bullets didn't slow it any. The bullets didn't stop the target from getting close enough to Shen to punch a hole into his chest.

Into his chest.

Torn flesh and busted bone and flattened organs bent in on themselves like the heart of a black hole. That's what it was. The center of Shen was just a hole into which life had collapsed.

The expression on Shen's face, the one he wore when he exited existence: disbelief. He knew in his last half seconds he was going to die in a spectacularly horrid way. He wasn't ready.

Who is?

Soledad, voice above a whisper: "What is it?"

Raddatz didn't have an answer.

Unmistakable. The rapid, successive pops of nine-mil gunfire. The echo effect of the alley working against pinpointing the shots.

Raddatz, Soledad took their best guess. Ran.

On the street: screams and scurrying civvies.

Soledad, waving her badge at a tattooed cholo who was running like a *muchacha*.

"Esa manera! Esa manera!" And the cholo kept running.

The two cops went in the direction they were given, Soledad hobbling hard against her bad knee. Didn't have far to go before they saw what the running and screaming was about. Two people. One a corpse, one nearly.

Panama. Skull crushed. Dead. And Donatell'd be joining him shortly. A few wheezes—dying breaths—from his burned body. Freshly, very badly burned. Even for Soledad, rock-hard Soledad, what a horrible, horrible . . . to take on fire once, to live, just so fire can catch up to you, give you all its hurt again.

The wheezing quit.

Shen. Panama. Donatell.

Soledad to Raddatz: "You fucking ass!" Cadre or not, Raddatz had gotten them killed.

Raddatz took a step, a step for Soledad.

Soledad's hand rushed up, out—swinging from her shoulder. Her shoulder's where she felt the impact. Back of her fist, center of Raddatz's face. She felt the cut of his teeth through the flesh, the commingling of their blood.

He dropped, Raddatz dropped straight down popping up only some when Soledad's swinging foot caught his jaw.

Most of that was straight anger. Three cops dead. Part of the aggression was self-preservation. She'd rather pursue the freak solo than have to keep one eye on Raddatz.

Swapping the green clip for the orange. Semtex-tipped slugs. No fucking around. Soledad was going to blow the shit out of the freak.

To her left, civvies standing, gawking. Something had gone by them eastbound.

Back to running. Yelling as she ran: "Police! Get on a phone. Nine one one. Get an MTac to this location!"

LA. Maybe the good citizens would make the call. Maybe they wouldn't.

Bum leg be damned, Soledad tore north on Union. Rounded the corner onto Shatto.

Apartments. Apartments. Apartments. Boles to shovel humans. Built tight to each other. No space to run, to hide. Windows barred. Doors locked, gated.

Soledad's thought: This is what comes of being a rat, a mole—running in the dark in the Valley, three dead cops behind you. A freak in front of you. At your side a cop you can't trust and the only thing you can—your piece.

Apartments. Apartments . . .

. . . construction.

A new building going up. Multi-unit. Bordered by chain-link. Part of it torn away. Wasn't damage a human had done.

It was inside.

No hesitation. Soledad pursued. If inside was where it was, inside was where she'd kill it.

Inside:

No light except what the moon was giving off. The moon wasn't giving up much.

Her knee *was* stiff, *wasn't* throbbing. Should've hurt like hellfire. Soledad's adrenaline was high. Kept the pain low.

Oughta keep steady. Oughta wait for MTac. Soledad thought she ought to . . .

Oughta what?

Back down? Hold off? Let a freak run wild, kill some more people?

Nah. Her adrenaline was BAMF high. Too high for fear. Too high for reason. She started to creep.

Fuckin' Raddatz, Soledad thought. What in the hell had he stirred up?

She brushed something. Jumped back, turned. Didn't fire. Just a work light. Minor miracle. Groping for it, groping a wire, she flipped it on. A string of lights went hot. The visual improvement marginal. The space was strung with thick plastic sheets. Dustcovers. Dust shields. They muted the light. Perception got messed with. Everything opaque. Gave the space a fun-house quality. Minus the fun.

Inching along. Gun out.

Like being wrapped in a chrysalis. Like moving through a fog of substance. Like living in oblivion. The unreal. It was all unreal. Except for the three uniquely dead bodies. The thought of those made everything truly real again.

Things got realer.

Something moving through the plastic haze, moving for Soledad. Big and heavy, but it didn't lumber. Big and heavy, but it traveled with speed.

She turned, sidestepped. Twisted to take aim.

What Soledad felt: a punch by a hand so big it could drape her body in a single hurt. Make her twitch, lurch. Make her spasm. Make her see a serpent that ate and ate and ate its tail.

Wasn't a punch.

What it was:

What it was, was an electric charge popping—slamming—the air all around her.

Picked her up.

Threw her down.

Was only seconds that she jerked, flopped across the kind-of-finished floor. Only seconds that she could feel the tight of the muscles that clinched her jaws. Felt her eyes zipping around their sockets.

Only seconds that residual electricity flowed through her. Long enough the thing that was big and strong and fast should've been on her, finishing the job of trying to clean her clock.

Hearing coming back to her: the sounds of stumbling and grunting. The thing caught up in the sheeting.

Now. Shoot it. Kill it.

Shoot it, but she couldn't see.

Shoot it, but Soledad could barely command her movements.

The thing stumbling close, grabbing. The sound . . . the sound of a hiss. A whine. A hiss and a whine with its movement.

Soledad moved to shoot. The thing gave in return a blow. Physical this time. This time not electrical. The blow lifted Soledad, sent her slapping, slapping, slapping through the hanging plastic. Wrapped her up, but was no insulation from the splintering wood that waited to collect her. Puncture her. Or maybe it was just a busted rib ripping through her flesh. The agony of breathing was the same either way.

Slipping on the plastic, slipping on her own blood.

And then it was on Soledad, pulling Soledad close. Pulling her tight, tighter. A rush of air forced from her. Sounded like the collective wailing gasp of raving, exedout youths losing themselves in the first shared bliss of an oncoming tsunami of euphoria. With that: popping, snapping. More ribs busting. Arms pinned, Soledad couldn't get her piece up, couldn't get a shot. Too close anyway. The Semtex going off: Wouldn't it kill her?

Did it matter?

Kill the beast.

Both thoughts running in her head: Did it matter? Kill the beast.

If she had to go, she'd take it with her.

Get your arm up . . .

Squeezing tighter. Crushing her. Killing her.

Not going to die today. Get your arm up. Kill the beast.

Use your head, she self-counseled. Use your fucking head.

She used it. Soledad reared her head back, drove it forward. Drove it.

Cartilage snapped, blood sprayed her face. The beast wasn't so tough.

Its grip slipped. Soledad slid, tried to slide away.

The beast still had speed. It took her by the throat with a hand like steel. It got back to squeezing, added twisting to the action.

Soledad felt the bones of her neck collapsing.

But the beast had her arm's length away. She could take the shot. Probably she'd live.

Didn't matter.

Her arm came up.

Kill the beast.

There was a click. The gun did not fire.

There was a snap. Soledad's head being torqued until her spine broke. She heard that. Soledad survived just long enough, just the fraction of a moment of time that was required for her ears to fill with the sound of her own death.

Eddi thought about going to the gym. Thought about lifting. But the weather was decent. A good day for cardio, for some outdoor running. But Fred Segal was having a sale and better—in LA—to get there early than try to go late, have to fight the crowds, the traffic. No matter. Nine point eight million people in the city. If a fraction had the same thought, the store'd be sick with bodies. So skip shopping. Skip cardio too. It was going to be the gym, then on to IHOP for a little . . .

Then Eddi remembered. Soledad was dead.

Soledad was *dead*.

Soledad was . . .

Eddi could repeat it as much as she cared, as many ways as she could. Her brain wouldn't take to what it rationally knew.

Soledad *was* dead.

Whatever else in Eddi's world that would evolve, grow, differ from day to day, what would not change was the reality of Soledad. That was beyond alteration.

Just awake, Eddi hadn't gotten out of bed. The thought

of Soledad dead fresh again in her head, she couldn't exit the sheets.

She wanted to cry.

Wasn't going to happen.

Eddi had bartered off her emotions a long time prior. Tears for fearlessness. Softness for survival. The amputation of her frailties kept her, ironically, whole. Gave her the ability to act and react without the burden of emotion. Such a condition had kept Soledad alive too. For a while. For Soledad "a while" ended. Then what? Literally ashes to ashes. Soledad cremated. Tears Eddi couldn't cry. A feeling seeping through her that regular people call sorrow and that Eddi, hard-guy cops like Eddi, passed off as nothing more than an inner call for activity. Cops needed to be working, doing, enforcing. What she was feeling was just the malaise of passivity that all cops got when they had too much downtime, and not when they lost one of their own.

That feeling: How do you shake it?

Ten days since Soledad's death. Four since she'd been cremated. And every time Eddi did that count in her head— adding a couple of hours, adding a day to the bottom line—it still hit her like she was getting bitch-smacked with the news for the first time as it was hand-delivered from a drunken wife beater.

Soledad was dead.

How do you shake that ill feeling? Most times, most other cops she'd known and lost the feeling never even came. Death was sad, yeah, but it was part of the job. It was a done deal before you even put on a badge and blues, so why go crying little girl–style after the fact? You didn't. You didn't take on feelings, you didn't have to get rid of them.

And as much as she . . . not hated, Eddi didn't hate Soledad. As much difficulty as she'd had with the girl, as much friction, what Eddi felt now was like a shiv to the soul delivered with a quick, vicious, surreptitious jab. Unexpected, and unexpectedly painful.

How do you, how do you shake such an ill feeling?

There had to be something. Some way more than just the cop send-off Soledad'd gotten. The obit that'd run deep in the *LA Times*.

Nothing that Eddi could figure at the minute. At the minute she couldn't figure anything besides lying in bed a little bit longer. A little bit longer being, like, the rest of her day off. The month. The reminder of her life, which, considering Soledad was one of the heaviest hitters MTac ever birthed and she didn't make it past thirty years of age, seemed like it might not be too much longer.

But Eddi wasn't going to ditch the effort. She'd figure out something to do for Soledad.

She'd figure it out.

Later.

Eddi rolled over, tried to sleep off her malaise.

Eddi rested her hand on the door. It was slightly open. The door. Her hand too. Splayed over the wood. From beyond the door came sounds. Things scraping against cardboard. Objects being packed. A life being put away. No voices.

Her hand on the open door. It opened no wider.

Eddi had kicked in how many doors on the job? Solid wood, steel-lined. Rarely, though sometimes aided with a ram, had she ever had a problem knocking her way through any of them. This door, already partly open, she couldn't pass through. She knew what was on the other side. Soledad's mom and dad. The primary grievers. Eddi liked to think she was in, or at least she self-elevated herself to, the number three spot.

A distant third.

And she knew she really had no business being in breathing distance of numbers one and two.

But . . .

There was a but. Always is.

But Eddi had already called the O'Roarks, offered condolences. Had wanted to keep things brief but didn't know what to say and ended up saying way too much. Blathered on and on about what a good person Soledad was and what a good cop she was and how much Soledad would be missed and couldn't be replaced and would not be forgotten and shut up already, Eddi. But they, Soledad's mom at least, had been so gracious on the phone. Had said they would be in Los Angeles to collect the remains of their daughter. The consumed remains and the remains of her life. The clothes and the photos and the books and the this and the that. They—Soledad's mom said "they"—very much wanted to meet Eddi, put a face with the voice that spoke with such grace and regard for her daughter.

Grace?

So in that phone call Eddi had formed a loose bond with people she had only one connection to. They had among them Soledad's death. As much as she did not want to go into the condo, tenuous as it was, breaking the connection was beyond Eddi.

Hand on the door, she pushed it open.

Inside the condo: a man kneeling before some cardboard boxes; a woman standing taking knickknacks from a shelf. The woman was a little on the heavy side. Or, or the bloated side? Wore a scarf covering her head. The man, although of a height and girth that would be considered above that of an average man and though his health seemed well for a man of his age, his presence was weak and tired. As a life had been taken from him, liveliness had been drained from him.

From the man: "Yes?"

"I'm Eddi Aoki." Looking to the woman. "I think I spoke to you on the phone. I'm a friend of Soledad's."

"Soledad didn't have friends." A little mournful smile on the woman's lips. Gallows humor.

"Well, next best thing, then."

"Thank you for coming," Gin said.

"I wanted you to know your daughter will be missed. She was a good person, and she sacrificed herself for her convictions. Anybody would tell you Soledad was one of the best cops to ev—"

"I'm going to take this down to the car." Soledad's dad, Richard, hefted a box, brushed passed Eddi without a word, left the apartment.

A chill lingered.

In her mind Eddi damned her blather.

"My husband doesn't think Soledad died for her convictions. That she died for any good reason, really."

"I'm sorry. I didn't come here to upset anybody."

"The thing about losing someone, I'm learning," a little laugh, "is dealing with other people's sympathy. Everyone wants to tell me that things are all right or that Soledad's gone to a better place. Things are not all right. I've lost my child. She is not in a better place. She's dead. And all the well-wishes just remind you of what's gone."

Eddi didn't know what to say, didn't want to say she was sorry. Again. She did not want to be where she was. She was not touchy-feely. She wasn't a people person. It was as if she'd inserted herself into the heart of a painful situation for pain's sake, the hurt inflicted as a substitute for the ache she couldn't otherwise feel for herself. Trying to make peace with Soledad's mother for Soledad was a losing proposition.

"You come to give me your sympathies, and I reject

them. It's not very polite. I think my own guilt is working on me."

"Guilt?"

"I've been ill. I told my daughter . . . I told Soledad I'd
rather her not be around while I was recovering. But it
wasn't . . . I didn't know if I would recover. I didn't want
her to watch me die." Gin could read the look on Eddi's
face, answered the question there. "The surgery went
well. The doctors think I have a good chance of surviving."

"You wanted to save her some hurt. You shouldn't feel
guilty for that."

A shake of her head. "That's not why I feel guilty. If
I'd let her come home, let her be there for me—"

"She'd still be dead." That was harsh and sharp,
maybe more than Eddi had meant it to be. Definitely
more. If she'd thought about it, she would have planed
the edge off the statement. But maybe in her self-pity Gin
could use a reality slap. "Soledad was going to fight this
fight long as she could, and long as she could would be
right up to her end. I know that doesn't make losing her
any easier. I work the same job, and having a like mind
doesn't make . . . God, Soledad was a tough one . . ." One
tear from Eddi. Just one. But it was one that up till that
moment wouldn't come to her at all. "It doesn't make her
not being around any easier for me."

"A parent shouldn't outlive their child. It should not be
this way." The depth of the observation was matched by
a dispassionate delivery. The summary of a grad-level
thesis. A truth that could not be equivocated.

And the quiet returned.

Fat, uncomfortable quiet.

Gin asked: "Would you like something, something to remember her by?"

"I couldn't."

"I don't know how to do this." Just heavy with a certain "Jesus, end this" defeat. "I don't know how to close out a life. All of this," nodding to the boxes in various stages of being packed, "we'll just take all this home, put it in a room and never touch it again."

Eddi understood that.

"You were her . . . ," lightly, "friend. It would be a nice way to help keep her memory alive." Gin started for the door. "I'll give you some privacy. And thank you."

She left.

It was like, it was like being in a museum exhibit. A room set up to approximate the real world, but empty of actual life. And this, ladies and gentlemen, is where Officer O'Roark would have sat and watched television. Right here is where she is believed to have lain on the floor and read a book or a magazine. Over there, the supposed location she partook breakfast. And to our best estimation, this very location is where she developed her modified O'Dwyer VLe that was one of the most effective weapons in the fight against the hegemony of the muties. Right up until it misfired and cost Officer O'Roark her life. Soledad's ghost was all over the place. Warm and vibrant. Quite present. It felt to Eddi she could, with patience, wait out this dark, sick joke Soledad was playing—'cause that's all it was—and catch her sneaking from a hiding place in a closet into the kitchen for a sandwich.

Just a feeling.

Soledad was dead.

And how to keep her alive? What thing was there that would remind and inspire and comfort and not depress too severely? A photo? A book? Soledad's favorite book? How the hell was Eddi supposed to know what Soledad's favorite book was? Yeah, there were books around, but did Soledad particularly read any of them? Like Eddi, did she just buy books because it made her feel not so bad about wasting nights watching reality TV? Maybe something Soledad had made herself, some craft or something.

Weren't any around. Probably, Soledad wasn't a craftsperson. Except for her gun. With her gun she'd been real crafty.

On a table was a book, but not one that had been published. Eddi reached for it, opened it. Not a book. Soledad's journal. Eddi read for a few pages. Stopped. Held the book, clutched it. Clutched it tight in her hands, then to her breast.

This.

If Gin was gracious enough to share her daughter, this—Soledad in her own words—is what Eddi would take.

The end of fear.

Sounds good. That's the problem with catchphrases and manicured sound bites: They sound good, but they don't add up to anything. They sound good because they're honed and shined by politicians and zealots with badges, but with sophistry like that, all you end up with is shine.

I'm getting shined. Getting shined three-sixty.

Raddatz is perpetrating with his "end of fear." Don't know what or exactly how or why, but I can feel in my gut it's below the boards, not above. Problem is, that's the shine I came into things being told to expect.

The shine I can't divine: Tashjian. Maybe it's a false reading that I could, I should pass off to our history. My natural distrust and paranoia. But the feeeling I have is that there's no way Tashjian's being straight with me. Yeah, freaks are getting killed and somehow Raddatz, the cadre, they're part of it. But that I should so conveniently find myself in the middle of it, that so quick I was able to hook up with the guy Tashjian needed to put in his sights . . . there's something else, something more going

*on and I don't know how the hell I'm supposed to figure
what. And I'm thinking, maybe, maybe that's the point.
Why put an MTac cop and not an IA investigator into the
mix, and I'm not going for Tashjian's "they'd smell 'em
coming" line. Why is because the MTac cop can't—at
least she isn't supposed to—figure things. Or maybe it's
'cause she's got a way of being a lightning rod, and it's
time for lightning to strike.*

That's cute.

Lightning rod.

How about target? How about dupe?

*Whatever. People are trying to fuck with me, not the
first time I've been fucked with. I've been had at plenty by
freaks and normals the same. With freaks, I got technology for them. With normals, well, the rearview mirror of
my life is littered with people who made the mistake of
getting on my bad side.*

That was it. That was the last of Soledad O'Roark. Eddi read her journal again. Not, as with the first time, in a sitting. The second time there was a good deal more flinching involved. The second time Eddi had to read until she was full up with, with all she could take. Toss the journal aside. Then allow herself over a period of time to gravitate closer, closer to it, almost throwing off a front of indifference—I can handle this, I can handle it—before picking up the journal, reading to her level of tolerance and going through the process again. Reading to completion a second time.

And when she had, Eddi said: "Fuck."

Eddi wanted to meet outside somewhere. It'd been nice to walk on the beach, along the Santa Monica promenade. It just would've been nice—not nice, but more tolerable—to deal with bleakness under some daylight.

Vin wouldn't have it.

Yeah, he wanted to see Eddi. Would love to hang with her. But go out of doors? Han, he didn't much feel like going out.

Why don't you come on over? he invited. C'mon, we'll sit. We'll talk.

Eddi had come to know Vin liked to sit and talk. Sit and watch TV. Sit and veg, and especially to an increasing degree sit and booze. She'd got that reading Soledad's diary. Journal. No way Soledad would've ever called it a diary. Eddi'd gotten Soledad's take on Vin's descent and wanted to avoid the opportunity to support his further degeneration by being audience to the cheap theatrics of his one-man drunk show.

Wasn't gonna happen.

So Eddi came around to Vin's.

Vin hobbled from the door after opening it. One leg.

Too lazy, too drunk to put on his prosthetic. A technological wonder purchased through the generosity of others, and it did nothing more spectacular than prop itself against a wall.

A look around the apartment upon entering. You gotta, Eddi thought, be kidding. A scattering of newspapers that worked as something of a floor guard, as a layer of receptacle for whatever rubbish Vin seemed to feel had to be discarded right *there*. And Vin seemed to feel there *was* a lot of rubbish that needed to be discarded right *there*. Fast-food wrappers. A gang of empties. A bad stink was all around. All of that was noticed after Eddi got past, finally got past how bloated Vin had gotten. A repository of bad eats, fermented drink, with nothing like ambition to burn any of it off.

Once Eddi found a spot to settle, Vin got into some dry crying remembering Soledad: Can't believe she's gone. Iron woman. She was like some kind of . . . Christ, never thought she . . . I can't imagine life without . . .

And Eddi just sat where she was, sat and gave a couple of "C'mon, don't do that's." She was patient with Vin's drunken exudation of woe. Patience was a chore. At the core Eddi got his hurt, had once shared it, but she had already put it on display with Soledad's mother. Wasted it on Soledad's father. Eddi couldn't go back to that well a third time. Now her needs were more practical than cathartic. What she needed, she needed information. Vin probably had some, and she didn't feel like slogging along miles and miles of self-pity to get at it.

Swatting aside all of Vin's blubbering: "What was Soledad doing over at DMI?"

". . . Wha . . ."

"At DMI. You know what she was doing, what she was working on?"

Vin sat a moment. He was waiting for a translation. From English to . . . whatever it was he was capable of comprehending in his state.

"She was . . . it was DMI stuff. I guess it was. If she was at DMI, what else is she going to—"

"But what? What kind of an assignment? Did she talk to you about it at all?"

"No."

Brushing fingers across her lips, taking a minute to think. "What about . . . you ever hear her say anything about the end of fear?"

". . . I don't . . ."

"C'mon, Vin. A phrase like that? You'd remember if you heard it."

"I can't—"

"You're a cop. Think. Remember."

Mopping a hand over his sweaty face.

"Vin, remember!"

Nothing from Vin.

Eddi was up, moving around the room. Newspaper crunching under her feet. Riding wild frustration. Working at keeping from kicking down a wall.

Vin knew he was the eye of her ire. Like a kid that'd done wrong, he tried to explain away his delictum.

"It's a bad time for me," Vin said. "You come in here demanding shit. And I'm, I'm going through—"

"What are you going through that nobody else is except a dry-out?"

"I lost my wife." The words left a trail of saliva that flopped around on his lower lip, dripped to the floor.

"She wasn't your wife."

"She was gonna be!"

"You know why?" Moving right at Vin, rolling right up on him. "She felt sorry for you. She felt so fucking sorry for you and your one-legged booziness she would waste her freedom on marrying you. Not even marrying you—"

Vin tried to get up, move away. One leg. He wasn't going anywhere. Eddi, hot, grabbing him, throwing him back in the chair that was his domicile. No, he wasn't going anywhere at all.

"She wasn't marrying you, she was throwing you a lifeline. And what do you do with her memory? Nothing. Not a goddamn thing."

"Don't fucking say that!" Vin squirmed around in the cushions same as if he was trying to dodge Eddi's words. "She loved me. She did. I lost her, lost, lost my body," rubbing at his stump, "lost everything. You stand there, shit, you *stand,* and you tell me how I gotta feel? You don't know how much she meant to me. You didn't lose what *I* lost."

She moved. A step back. One more. Eddi slipped off her jacket. Without hesitation, preparation, pulled up her shirt. Reached behind and unhooked her bra.

Vin didn't look, couldn't look. Scared of Eddi, naked but standing unashamed.

She said: "Look at me."

Vin could not.

"Vin, look at me."

His head came up, a tangle of his hair was foreground in his vision. The wet in his eyes made Eddi look so slick she glistened. A warrior princess with a Hollywood shine.

Eddi cupped her hands over her nipples. Her left breast was pulled back slightly. Along the curve, tattooed in simple letters: WE DON'T NEED ANOTHER HERO.

From Reese to Soledad.

Soledad to Eddi.

"Told her she should've checked you more carefully," Vin said. "She would've hated that. She hated hero worship."

"I don't worship her."

"Just woke up one morning with that on your tit?"

Eddi slipped back on her bra. She put back on her shirt. "I know what you've lost, Vin. I've lost as much. But I'm not going to be careful with your hurt, hand you any soft, feel-good bullshit about her. I've read her dia . . . journal. Whatever. And the shit that's in there . . . Soledad was, she was empty. She was an empty human being. It's like emotion was beyond her. Only thing that filled her was guilt for being lucky enough to live when half of San Francisco died. Can you imagine that, Vin, hating yourself because you're not dead? And it was killing her. Guilt was killing her. Before that freak snapped her neck, guilt took her life way back."

A very lonely thought. Lovely in its pathos.

"I admire what she stood for. But don't tell me I worshipped *that*." Eddi asked again: "Tell me everything you can about Soledad and DMI."

"Soledad . . ." Vin pulled back his hair. Tangled. Dirty. Uncombed. It just flopped over his eyes again. "I don't know any more than you. They were doing surveillance on a freak. The cops got caught out. The freak killed three of them. And Soledad."

"You know a cop named Tashjian?"

Vin shook his head.

"He's IA."

There was a thick booze haze Vin's memory was nearly useless against. He hacked at it, hacked at it . . .

What came to him: "He was . . . he investigated her. It was before you were MTac."

"She was cleared. The investigation was over. Why was Tashjian back in her life?"

Vin didn't know.

"The end of fear: You never heard that?"

"You asked me already."

"I'm asking again. Did you ever hear that from her?"

"I don't . . ." Vin realized: "She didn't talk to me. Not really. She'd spend all day sitting around with me, but she never . . ." And he knew: "She didn't love me."

"No, she didn't." Moving straight on from that: "Soledad wasn't working DMI just to work DMI. She was there for a reason."

"Why would you, why would you say—"

"Because it's the truth." Eddi refused to care about Vin's feelings, only wanted to know: "What was the reason Soledad was working DMI?"

" 'Cause her leg . . . I was . . . her leg was messed up. That's why."

"Yeah, getting hit by the car was an accident. Her being at DMI; Tashjian was taking advantage of the situation. She didn't trust him."

"What, what situation?"

"If I knew, I wouldn't be here. Christ, dry up and help out."

"Help what? Help you be bitter?"

"I'm trying to find out what happened to Soledad."

"She died. She got herself killed!" Vin's delivery dived in and out of rage and extreme sorrow. "And you can't deal with that. You can't deal that your goddess was dark and cold and a brute. You can't handle she let a freak get the best of her. So you've gotta start dressing things up different than they are. Gotta, gotta get it in your head the same guys who took out the Kennedys and King got Soledad. Otherwise she was nothing but normal, and all the time you spent jerking to her was wasted." Vin was taking a spiral right for sloppy, starting to process the truth about Soledad: Her affection for him was just more of her own guilt. "Well, here's the deal, Eddi: Soledad was just like the rest of us, life-sized and not an inch bigger. She was a cold bitch and she fucked up and now she's dead. That's all there is."

Fighting Vin's belligerence with evidence: "It was in her journal."

" 'There's a big fat conspiracy going on, and I'm in the middle of it.' That what she wrote?"

"She wrote . . . she'd written—"

"I'll tell you . . ." Vin curled up in the chair, tired from the effort of dealing with Eddi. It was a reminder of all the effort that had gone into dealing with Soledad. "There is no way Soledad'd ever have anything to do with Tashjian."

"You barely remembered his name."

"I remember *her*. I'm sitting here crying over her. That's more than you're fucking doing."

Kinda lit or not, Eddi could've gone across the room, put a fist to Vin's head. Done it again. Then one more time.

Vin was oblivious to Eddi's passions. The only thing

tangible to him was the need to freshen his melancholy. "Let's remember her, Eddi. Sit down, have a drink. Let's recall the girl."

All folded up, Vin was a little mass in the chair. Wanting a drink, too messed up to be able to go get one.

Eddi would have none of it.

"She didn't love you, Vin, but she cared a hell of a lot about you. If you felt any of the same for her, you'd clean up."

Eddi took off.

Eventually, Vin got himself up, got himself that drink he was wanting.

Years working IA had inured Tashjian to a lot of things. Dirty cops. Dirty cops ratting out other dirty cops. Dirty cops ratting out clean cops 'cause they've got to give up a name, any name, to keep from doing hard time. Cops eating bullets as a substitute for doing any time at all. Never understood that. A cop's tough enough to kill himself, but not tough enough to do a stretch inside? Didn't seem equitable.

The dirty, the greedy, cops with holes they'd put in their own heads: Tashjian had gotten real used to all that. A sad comment on his life was that he was very unaccustomed to a woman calling his name.

"Hey, Tashjian."

He turned, looked behind him.

Heading in his direction from across the street as he made the walk to his house was an Asian woman. Though hardly tiny—for a female she was probably just above average in height—her presence far exceeded her stature. Her mien bulled toward Tashjian over the width of the street. Formidable at a distance. It was, to Tashjian's sensibilities, an attractive quality.

The woman asked: "Tashjian, yeah?"

As if he were required to, Tashjian gave the woman careful visual exam and then, sure of things: "I don't know you."

"Eddi Aoki. I'm an officer with MTac."

"I still don't know you."

"I'd like to talk."

"Is this official? If it's official, then it needs to go through the bureau."

"It's not official."

Tashjian's features seemed to be double-jointed in that he made an expression yet expressed nothing at the same time.

"It's not official," Eddi said again, "but if you've got a minute, I'd like to talk."

"And what would you like to talk about?"

"Soledad O'Roark."

Another look from Tashjian equivocal as the previous.

"You had a run-in with her, yeah?" Eddi tried to make herself as unguessable as Tashjian. Had to work at it.

"I had business with her once."

"Well . . ." A look up and down the street. A casual look, not to spy anything in particular. Physical action, no matter how slight, gave Eddi a moment to do some mental calculations. "This is just personal stuff, okay? She was a friend—"

"O'Roark didn't have friends."

"Been hearing that a lot. Anyway, I call her, I *called* her a friend. Just some blanks I want to fill in. Maybe you can do it."

Hesitation. He shouldn't bother with her. Tashjian should not bother with this woman. But how many times did he ever have a woman call his name? She had some questions, he'd give her what answers he could. That'd be the total of their interaction. Tashjian knew it would. But he liked the way his name sounded coming from her. It compelled against his better judgment.

"There's a diner up the block."

"Don't you live here?"

A smile from Tashjian. Suspicious, not salacious. "An unfamiliar woman alone in my house? I can see my name all over a harassment suit."

"All you IA guys have as little trust?"

"I'd say."

"I'm just here to talk. If you want me to sign an affidavit . . ."

Tashjian's smile remained constant. Remained constant. Then it changed. How, Eddi couldn't say. But it changed.

Tashjian went for his keys.

He said: "You'll have to forgive the place. I don't usually have company over."

Tashjian's house—decent-sized, decent-sized for LA, Mediterranean style—was, to Eddi, spotless. A place for everything, everything in its place. So either his comment to her re: its state had been a joke, or to him the place was a wreck, meaning his mind was obsessively-compulsively beyond anal.

Tashjian didn't offer Eddi a beverage, didn't offer her a seat. His unspoken way of making it quite clear he didn't expect her to be around long.

He asked, very much to the point: "What is it you want to know?"

"Most people," Eddi said, "they meet somebody who's just lost a friend, they offer condolences."

Tashjian said, again: "Officer O'Roark didn't have friends." And, again, very much to the point: "What is it you want to know?"

"You were handling Soledad. Why?"

No confirmation. No denial. Just: "It's time for you to leave."

From under her sweat top, from the holster on her hip, Eddi slipped out her off-duty piece. A Glock 17. A harder weapon than a whole gang of on-duty pieces some cops toted. If the sight of it had any sway on Tashjian, if it evoked unease or anxiety or any kind of concern, in line with every other emotion he seemed to own, it wasn't evident.

He said to Eddi with all the knowing condescension of an Ivy League professor to a first-year student: "That's not particularly smart."

The blow was hard enough to rattle a man of typical heartiness. The blow, Eddi's gun to Tashjian's jaw, was more than hard enough to stretch Tashjian out on the floor. To send his eyes rolling back in his head for a good fifteen seconds. Fifteen seconds when his senses took a little vacation. When they finally returned to him, auditory being the first to get back to work, they heard:

". . . how it starts. That's *just* how it starts. From here it gets worse."

"Made a . . . you made a . . . ." Talking with blood in his

mouth. Inhalation made him choke on his own fluids. Tashjian learned, quickly, he had to spit first, keep his mouth faced toward the floor, then try to talk. The day was filled with new experiences. "You have made a sizable mistake." Better. It'd be a while before he had the act down cold. His mouth bleeding as it was would offer him time to practice.

"Yeah, I was just thinking that while I was watching you flop all over the floor."

"I'm going to have you swimming in char-*aaaaaah! ahhhh! ahhhhhhh!*"

One hundred and twenty-eight pounds of Eddi. All of it converged on her knee. Her knee converged at the center of Tashjian's groin. Not for nothing was he screaming.

And screaming.

Loud, long and hideous.

But he was screaming in his house in Los Angeles, in West Hollywood. A lot of men go screaming in that part of town. With pain. With pleasure. Tashjian's screams went unnoticed.

When her knee got sore, Eddi got up from Tashjian, stood over him.

She said: "It's my day off. I've got nothing but time and desire. We can talk about you handling Soledad, or we can, well, not talk."

". . . lost your mind . . ."

"I lost my friend. And if I'd just lost her going against a freak . . . that's what happens. But this wasn't about some freak. It wasn't only about that. She was into something, and you put her there."

"I ca—I can't . . ."

"Yeah. You can. 'I put Soledad at DMI because . . .'"

The thing about pain—and Eddi was thinking from personal experience—quick, sharp pain you can deal with. It's already dissipating by the time your receptors even register its peak. A lower grade of hurt that's prolonged over time . . . that's when real agony begins.

She wanted to give Tashjian some agony.

What Eddi did was guttural. Straight National Geographic animal. But Eddi was in an animal state of mind. Instinct, base emotion, had more claim to her than higher thought. She'd come to talk, not torture. Talking, as little as she allowed for, was proving futile. So, yeah, she got animal.

She got on her knees.

She bit, and bit, and bit, and she bit at Tashjian's earlobe.

More screaming.

No lights. No sirens. No cops. Nobody cared.

In forty-eight minutes Eddi would look at herself in a mirror in the bathroom of her duplex, see blood on her sweatshirt, caked at the corner of her mouth. Her mouth? She would wonder what the hell she had done. What the hell had she let herself do, let herself . . . her mouth? And she enforced the law? She was given governance? She would look at herself and she would see that her professed obedience to order was a suit she labored herself into daily. Ill tailored and convenient, and the moment she didn't need it anymore . . .

Her fucking mouth?

In just short of an hour's time Eddi would consider all

that as she rinsed herself. The water in the basin tinged red.

Now . . .

She wiped the blood from her face with one hand, threatened toward Tashjian with her gun in the other. "I'll hurt you any way I . . . Tashjian. Tashjian!"

He held down his whimpers. Listened.

"Any way I have to, I will hurt you. You understand?"

A nod from him. Blood seeping from the hand that clutched his torn ear. A dam of digits useless against the tide. But it made Tashjian forget about the blood from his mouth.

"There . . . there are, there're . . ." A bad motor sputtering itself started. "There are cops in DMI, we believe they've, we believe they're a hit squad targeting muh-metanormals. The media, the liberals find out before we can clean it up it'd make us all look like killers, not cops."

"Why Soledad? She wasn't IA."

"That's the point!" Pain made Tashjian impatient. "They never would've seen her coming. Nuh-never should have."

"But they did?"

"You knew her, knew what she was like. I'll never believe suh-some freak got the best of her."

Like a riptide. Concepts coming so strong Eddi could hardly think against them. Had to force herself not to just accept them.

"What aren't you telling me?"

"That's all there is."

It was like her gun jumped out, jumped at Tashjian, at his head, and her hand just went along for the ride.

From Tashjian, a corresponding scream to the blow.

From Eddi: "What else?"

"There is nothing else! I sent her inside DMI, she didn't come back."

"What's 'the end of fear'?"

"The end of fear is when we get every freak there is off the streets of every city in America. Be they live, or buh- be they dead. That doesn't happen if the bleeding hearts . . . if they can turn things against us."

Heavy breathing. From Tashjian, yeah. But Eddi, chest working hard, was just then realizing how much labor was required to make even a weak man submit.

From where she stood, she said: "I know you think when I'm gone, a couple of hours from now, tomorrow at worst, you're going to crush me. You're going to get IA all over me, if you don't just go ahead and swear out a warrant. I know you're thinking that."

Heavy breathing from Tashjian. Just the breathing.

"Nothing's going to happen to me, okay? Nothing. Something happens to me, I don't get a chance to find out what happened to Soledad, I swear to Christ, swear on my father's grave . . . you hearing me, Tashjian? I swear I will put a bullet in you. I have to do five to fifteen for taking a piece of your ear, I might as well do twenty-five to life for killing you. Got that?"

Just the breathing from Tashjian.

Eddi holstered up. She made her way from the house, to the street, to her car.

Traffic was bad.

The nine miles to her place took thirty-four minutes to drive.

A little bit later Eddi was looking at herself in her

bathroom mirror, looking at the blood on her sweatshirt. Her mouth.

She took up a spot on the bathroom floor. Her head dropped between her legs.

It'd been forty-nine minutes since she'd taken a bite out of Tashjian.

The shower had been pointless. The kind of cleaning Eddi needed wasn't going to come from tap water. Standing on the balcony of her duplex, letting the sun and the air do work on her hair, the thing Eddi recalled most about the last few days—trying to give condolences to Soledad's parents, spending time with a boozed-up Vin, talking to Tashjian. Attacking Tashjian—the thing she recalled from all that was being told time and again by people connected as well as could be with Soledad was that Soledad didn't have any friends.

So why did Eddi care what happened to Soledad? Why travel the road that'd started with a pistol whipped against Tashjian's head and a hunk of meat pulled from his ear?

Because, she answered herself, someone somewhere ought to give a fuck about Soledad's passing same as when *her* time came—and Eddi knew sooner or later her time was going to come—she'd hope to God someone somewhere'd give a fuck about her.

But giving a fuck—

Blocks away, a siren. Moving in Eddi's direction. She

could tell by the pulse it was a cop's, not fire or EMS. The feeling teeming just under Eddi's flesh: It was coming for her. She swore at Tashjian for being ballsy enough to call her bluff, put the heat on her. Five to fifteen for losing herself, for losing control. Doing battery on a cop. The only thing—the siren seconds away—that was killing Eddi was that now probably she'd never know what really happened to . . .

The siren passed. Diminished. Faded.

The balcony railing. Eddi consciously loosened her grip that had tightened without her being aware.

So she had been thinking . . .

"Giving a fuck" about Soledad meant getting even closer to the whys of the situation. Getting closer to DMI.

And getting closer to DMI . . .

Getting inside DMI.

What Tashjian had said: They'd see an IA cop coming a mile away. They'd smell a rogue before he got planted. And, anyway, Eddi didn't have the authority, was never going to get the authority to do a job against DMI.

On her own, how was she going to get close? Get inside?

And then she had the answer, the answer being absolutely ridiculous. But the ridiculousness of it was immediately shoved aside by the very logic of the irrationality. No one would know. No one would suspect. No one could contest. No one could stop her. Except Tashjian. If he was going to, she'd be in cuffs already.

Then it was too late for debate. It was too late for trying to figure another, better way to do things. Eddi was already over the edge of her balcony and sailing for the ground a couple of stories below.

I've never done anything like this before. Actually, I'm doing a lot of stuff I've never done before. In particular I've never previously expressed myself to myself in writing. And I'm not doing this because Soledad did it. I'm only doing this because it seems like a good idea, a good way to keep track of things. Seemed like a good idea until I realized the first thing I had to document is that I'm losing my mind. To jump from the balcony of my place? For a while, in the hospital while I was getting X-rayed I tried to sell myself that by dumb luck I'd stumbled off the balcony right when I'd come up with the idea of taking a header. But the self-denials just made me think I was all the crazier. So just admit it. I'm losing my mind. At least, I've lost direction. Direction, previously, had been easy and obvious. Straight ahead. Don't think about anything else, don't look around for some other road to travel. Just keep straight on because dead ahead for me was MTac. Ahead for me was a chance to pay back the freak community for killing my dad on the first day of May all those years ago.

And for a long time, for me, there wasn't much

distraction. A couple of guys I'd call boyfriends. A couple
of days thinking about the beach or skiing or something
besides the knife my dad'd once given me that I swore,
improbably, I'd use to kill at least one mutie. Beyond
that . . . there wasn't a beyond that. Just school, the academy, whatever assignments I could pull that'd better position me for MTac.

And then I heard about Soledad.

It was like hearing about the heroes again. Only, she
was our hero, not some mutie.

Then I made MTac and I met Soledad. It was like meeting the queen bitch. She was cold and single-minded. She
was also genius enough to make her own modifications to
an O'Dwyer. She was unstoppable by any freak that'd
been stupid enough to show its face to her. And I thought,
damn. Really. That's what I thought: daaamn! That, and
how much I wanted to be like Bullet. Only, don't let her
hear you call her that. Don't let her know you respect,
admire . . . call it what it was. Don't let her know you
worship her and want to be a third of the cop she was so
you can be a thousand times the cop most others are.

And I knew she wasn't really cold as she played. I
knew, or at least I figured when I got to know her, I'd see
the soft to her. Hadn't she cut me major slack when I accidentally put a couple of slugs into Vin?

But I never got the chance to really know Soledad.
Don't know anyone could.

Then I read her journal. Should've taken something
else when her mother offered. Should've taken her favorite sweatshirt, a hat. Should've taken something that
wasn't page after page of bitterness and scorn and lone-
liness and guilt and a whole lot of self-hate.

That fucked me up. Not reading Soledad's true nature in her writing. What fucked me up, what I read, I could've been reading my own words. It was my life she was writing, lived at arm's length and by rote. I had to actually look in the mirror, had to stare at myself and tell me that I wasn't like her. Bristled when Vin insinuated I was. I was human and normal and functional. Then I reminded me I'd thrown myself off my own balcony trying to collect an injury. I'd lost my mind. I'd lost my direction. I had gone on an excavation looking for signs of life and found nothing but a warning from beyond the grave in the here and now.

Someday a freak could very well kill me. But it was my own life I was taking.

Page after page after page after page. I expected something more from Soledad. Something better. I expected, in her private moments . . . she didn't owe me anything, but I expected where I thought she was callow for callowness' sake toughness because tough is what an MTac, a black woman MTac in particular, needed to survive.

What I didn't expect . . .

Page after page after page after page of more of the Soledad I already knew. From the day she started keeping a journal it was filled with entries about her hate of the freaks, her disdain for freak lovers, her adherence to the law because the lack of law gave rise to the freaks in the first place.

I'd hoped maybe there'd be some levity, some light. Some life.

I wanted that from her.

I wanted it for *me.*

I wanted to know we could do what we do, but remain whole and human.

I wanted those things.

But I had bitten nearly clean off the ear of someone I wanted intel from.

To be like Soledad? I had evolved—devolved—way beyond that.

Soledad only carried the guilt of living through May Day. My loss was tangible. My wounds deeper. I didn't need to worship Soledad to have my rage. Reading her journal helped me to see all that I could do with it. Or all the rage could do to me.

It could help me become one of the best MTacs to ever job on the LAPD.

It could also turn me into a cop who dies wondering if there's anyone anywhere who gives a fuck about her.

Here we watch, we wait, we note. We fight with our heads, not our fists. The grunt mentality stays with MTac."

Couldn't be sure, but Eddi was willing to make book this was the same speech Soledad, same speech every ex-MTac got when they arrived for duty at DMI. Abernathy's perfunctory delivery like the corporate-approved greeting at a Holiday Inn or the requisite "bye-bye" as you disembark a major carrier's jetliner. It was made all the more passionless by Abernathy's movie-announcerish voice. It was like preparation for watching a once active career go stale.

Not stale. Doing intel on freaks was important work. To Eddi it just wasn't as significant as being an MTac. And Eddi would double down her bet that rather than smiling and nodding to the sentiment, when Soledad'd gotten "the speech," she'd opted to make her true feelings known to Abernathy.

Eddi said nothing.

Eddi threw off a serious, by-the-book, "I get your meaning" expression. Tightening of the eyes. Furrowing

of the brow. A hearty nod of her head. She exuded all in-
dicia she was DMI-ready. It was like doing theater. It was
like Eddi'd studied and studied a part, then walked out
onto a stage. Before a self-fractured wrist landed her
there, Eddi had never been to DMI HQ. Only knew a few
DMI cops in passing from the job. But she knew from her
journal these were the halls Soledad had limped along
with her bad leg. One of these offices had been used by
Soledad to push paper. Soledad'd worked very briefly
with Raddatz and a small group of cops. Those cops,
Soledad chief among them as far as Eddi cared, were
dead. Tucker Raddatz was alive. Raddatz was center of
Eddi's sights. From what she could take from Soledad's
journal he was most probably a thug. And he had almost
certainly killed Soledad. A freak had taken her life, but
Raddatz had maneuvered her into that situation. Eddi
wasn't buying it was just a surveillance gone south.
The stats were against it. The circumstances just too
convenient.

A DMI inquiry said otherwise. How F'n surprising
was that; cops clearing their own?

A court. A review board. The law. They weren't about
to come down on Raddatz. But if Eddi proved things to
her satisfaction . . . Used to be all she wanted was to
drive her daddy's knife into the heart of a freak. A
farewell to her father. Holding on to that pledge, Eddi'd
crawled from a life of devastation to a new normalcy. She
wasn't feeling normal anymore, was thinking taking her
knife to Raddatz would cure the feeling.

But as close as she was, close as Eddi was to the edge,
that's all she was. Close. She wasn't over all the way. She
wanted blood, but the want was a base desire. What she

needed, to confirm what she believed: Raddatz killed Soledad or got her killed or had her killed. Whatever variation was truth, the truth Eddi wanted to know. To know, she had to get next to the one person who'd walked from the incident. To get next to him, she had to fake like she was a good little DMI cop.

"I understand, sir." Keeping up the by-the-book, "I get your meaning" expression. Eddi said: "I know, at least I think I know what's going to be required for me to make the grade. I just hope I live up to it." Might as well have had her thumb on a page in a script.

"You have to be aware of the situation," Abernathy said. "Your post here is temporary. We get temporary posts. We get them constantly. But when the arriving officer only looks at their post as temporary, circumstances can become problematic. Do you understand?"

"I do, sir."

"I'm sure you must have felt distance coming from some of the other officers."

"A little."

"It's not personal," he said. Abernathy said: "Can't take it personally. DMI cops: Their life is about being suspicious."

"Appreciate that. I hope I get a chance to show while I'm at DMI, I am DMI." Looking Abernathy dead in the eye. Liars have shifty eyes. Liars look around a room when they're lying. Eddi was speaking from her heart. Or so she perpetrated. Eddi did not lose contact with Abernathy. Eddi would not be, wouldn't let herself be farmed out or shunted to one side. She needed to be in the heart of things. And compared to grinding a knee into a man's balls, amputating part of his body with her own teeth, what was a little rallying around the flag?

Slightly, Eddi smiled.

Eddi's welcome to DMI: paperwork. Sorting and filing, transferring from hard copy to digital file. What she got was a taste of the struggle against the freaks waged from the very bottom of the totem pole. The part that was stuck in the mud. And this is what Eddi got for being the "good" transfer, the obsequious MTac arriving to the brave new world. She could only imagine what Soledad, filterless Soledad, got handed. She couldn't imagine Soledad putting up with busywork. They were very crappy chores.

Also eye-opening. The numbers. The stats on the freak population. Eye-opening in the way your eyes spring wide in the bloody climax of a horror show. Eddi was giving consideration to the idea that Abernathy was at least partially correct in his assessment of MTacs: They were nothing but grunts. Eddi'd never really thought about how many freaks might be in Greater LA, how much they might be communicating with each other. What those communications could be. Like, some kind of call to arms. DMI thought about that kind of stuff. Ran through all manner of threat matrixes. Worst-case scenarios. Calculated for every sort of bloody encounter. All the thinking, the considering and predicting made Eddi long for MTac. Just point your gun, pull your trigger.

She felt comfortable in G Platoon. Eddi felt like she belonged. No matter that she was hiding her designs, her sense was to a person DMI had no trust of her.

And they shouldn't. They shouldn't trust her. But they didn't know they shouldn't. Or maybe they did. Maybe they were that good. They could suss the untrustworthy. Or maybe in their job it just paid to not trust strangers. Which was fine to a degree. Eddi was sure in time she could earn trust.

Despite lingering animosity, she'd earned Soledad's.

Just needed time.

But Eddi didn't have time. Really, she had time, but she didn't have patience. Didn't have the desire for her abhorrence to diminish. She had to get into Raddatz's sphere. But at the end of nineteen days of trying she'd gotten to file and sort. She'd gotten hit on by a double amputee. She gotten told "Don't worry about it" when she'd asked a couple of officers how exactly they postulated their threat assessments. She had not gotten anywhere close to knowing the truth about Raddatz. She had been unable to surreptitiously work her way close to him, and he certainly had not approached her. No reason. Unlike Soledad, Eddi brought no real celebrity with her.

Raddatz remained a distant, lonely cipher. A cop on the job going through recovery after the loss of fellow officers. The rest of DMI cut him a wide swath as he worked his way back to zero.

All the while Eddi was sure he wasn't going through shit. Was pretty sure he was only faking his remorse.

Unfortunately, pretty sure didn't cut it.

Waiting around wasn't working.

So forget subterfuge. Forget doing things on the sly. Navigate the situation, Eddi coached herself, like she'd handle a call. Straight ahead and in the open.

T|ell me about Soledad."

In his chair, in his office, Tucker Raddatz turned from the window he was staring out of, looked over his desk, across the room. Eddi was in the doorway.

"Tell me," she said again, "about Soledad O'Roark."

"You a friend of hers?"

"She didn't have friends. I operated with her on MTac."

"Then you know her good as me. Probably better."

"She had a way of—"

"You're Aoki, right? Just came on."

"Eddi Aoki."

"Tucker Raddatz. You were saying?"

"She had a way of pushing people off. A habit more than a trait."

What Eddi was noticing: Raddatz wasn't paying any more attention to her than to whatever he'd been looking at out his window. He was slow, unfocused. A guy permanently waking up.

Sure he was.

He was weighted down. He was slogging around the burden of murder.

Eddi asked: "What happened?"

Raddatz went back to looking out the window.

"You all were surveying a freak. Then what happened?"

"I've been through all that with a review panel."

"I wasn't on the panel."

"You've been on calls that've gone south."

"Yeah."

"You want to spend your time rehashing the bad ones?"

Truth was, Eddi didn't.

"You tell me about her," Raddatz said, redirecting. "Curious what kind of cop I lost."

I lost. Eddi considered that a queer way of putting things. Queer in the sense Raddatz sounded more like a man guilty of error rather than volition.

She said: "I told you, we weren't friends. Not in any real sense."

"Whatever you recall. Anything."

"I recall . . ." Eddi let herself into the office, took a seat. "I recall Soledad didn't want me on her element. She didn't . . . I gotta tell you, she didn't care for me."

"Didn't care for you how?"

"On the force, you're a woman, you're a minority, yeah it's hard, but you can stake your own territory. You work your way up to MTac, you can pretty much be a celebrity. I don't think she cared to share the spotlight."

"She didn't strike me that way; the kind that wanted attention."

"You're not a woman. Or a minority."

As if to say otherwise, Raddatz held up his missing hand.

"Yeah, well, around here that pretty much puts you in the majority. Look, I don't think Soledad wanted attention. I think deep down she wanted to make a point. The point gets muted when there's somebody like you doing the same thing."

Raddatz said: "What changed with you and Soledad?"

"What makes you think anything did?"

Raddatz's phone rang, rang, rang. It rang itself quiet.

Taking up the conversation where it'd been left, Raddatz: "I think, I *thought*. I thought she was the kind who could change. I hoped for it."

He was being cryptic. Eddi wondered if it was a dodge. Was he being veiled to get something out of her? Did he have something to say and wasn't sure in what way she would take it? "How did you hope she'd change?"

"She came with a mind-set. I hoped she'd see things another way."

"Yeah, but what way do you—"

"There is a line of thinking: In a republic only soldiers should have certain rights. Only people who've served their country should be allowed full and complete suffrage. It's, uh, extremist, you know. But I'd say I understand the philosophy. The philosophy being only those who've defended the republic can really appreciate the responsibilities that come with running it."

"If you want to enjoy freedom, you've got to pony up."

Sort of a nod, sort of a shrug from Raddatz.

"Sounds kind of Spartan."

"Look at our country. We're in a time of crisis. It's almost cliché to say we're in a state of war, but we are. It's a struggle for our survival. You know that. And yet, what are the concerns of the people, the citizens? Their concerns are whether or not they can get their meals supersized. How big of an SUV they can drive by themselves on their long commutes over smooth-paved roads to work and back. They forgo news for reality shows that are anything except real. They can't tell you the name of the vice president, but they can tell you to the person every character on their favorite sitcom. They are invested in the having, but couldn't care less about what it takes to earn what they have, protect what others have earned. They've never known sacrifice. Not self-sacrifice. So how could they ever really appreciate the sacrifice of others? They can't. Once you understand sacrifice, once you're willing to sacrifice, it changes your perspective. How many times have you been driving, you've been shopping in a mall and you find yourself angry at the sight of a regular American? The overweight-by-sloth, underinformed-by-choice American? I sound bitter, don't I? I am. I'm bitter that I've had to put good cops in the ground when indifferent people keep on being indifferent. But I'm also . . . I guess I'm defiant. We've earned the right to do as needed in the interest of all. We have to. Because even if we win this war, without change, what chance do we really have to survive?"

For all his rhetoric, Raddatz had been easy to follow. But at that moment he was drifting lanes. Eddi, trying to get perspective: "You don't think we have a chance against the freaks?"

"Do you know what it takes to survive?"

"What does it take?"

"Inspiration. The belief there's something better."

"How would you inspire?"

"I would take away the thing that people fear."

Eddi knew.

She sat in Raddatz's office nearly eight minutes more small-talking about DMI and what she would need to get acclimated. But as Raddatz finished his dissertation, his high-minded babble, she knew. His words were his manifesto. It was all like Tashjian had said. Raddatz was an elitist. An extremist. He thought he could kill freaks as he pleased. Was privileged to the right. Soledad, for all her faults, was the law. The law got in Raddatz's way.

Fine. Fuck the law.

Eddi knew.

Raddatz killed Soledad.

She was going to kill Raddatz.

It was the lack of internal debate that was most queer for her. That she had the capacity to take a life, Eddi had long since gotten over. Third week on the job. Still in uniform. Responding to a two-eleven at a convenience store on La Brea. Perp comes out, perp swings a gun in Eddi's direction. Perp took two in the chest, one in the throat, was dead less than thirty seconds after hitting the pavement. Not the day after, not in the years since, Eddi never once felt bad about the circumstances of the shooting. If a guy's got a gun, if the guy points the gun at you, you drop him. That's it. End of story. No issues. You make the choice to be a cop, you better already have made the choice to take a life.

And being MTac, that reality was merely magnified. Long before she hit G Platoon she'd heard all the rhetoric, all the back-and-forth about the EO, whether it was constitutional, unconstitutional . . . Always, when she even bothered to do an internal debate, Eddi came back to the same thing: She didn't know constitutionality. Was hazy on morality. But Eddi knew it was wrong for her father to have died because a couple of muties felt like getting into an ass-kicking contest in San Francisco.

So Eddi went MTac and never had guilt when she was standing over the writhing husk of an expiring freak.

With Raddatz she figured she might've had some questions for herself: Is this the thing to do? Is there any other way? She knew it wasn't lawful, but was it right?

She had no questions.

If it wasn't about reprisal for Soledad, and it very much was, then it was merely about stopping Raddatz before the left could hold him up as a poster child for their perceived gestapoism of a system broken. Tashjian couldn't touch Raddatz. Legal channels had been useless and probably would be for lack of hard evidence and fear of public opinion. The only thing that would really be effective was a bullet. Maybe two. However many it took to kill Raddatz.

She really had gone animal. The truth of that didn't matter to Eddi in the least. The consequences didn't matter.

If she went to prison for the crime, as she had said and meant to Tashjian when she'd . . . done what she'd done to him, that was all right. Acceptable, at least. She would have committed a crime. And little as she cared for Raddatz, she knew the law would feel different.

Eddi did have a problem with getting caught for killing a cop in a state where she'd be looking at taking a poison needle for the act. She didn't mind killing, she could handle prison, but the strength of Eddi's convictions stopped way short of giving up her life to square things for Soledad.

So Eddi planned.

A murder is predicated on three things: means, motive and opportunity.

Motive Eddi had.

Means. Her knife was off the list. There would be visceral pleasure in the act of putting steel to flesh and watching the results. There'd also be a lot of blood. And unless Eddi struck with speed and stealth there'd be a lot of screaming. Probably, she could complete the job without the screaming. But then where's the pleasure? What's the point?

She had to sit for a moment, let that thought pass. Going animal was okay. Going insane was unacceptable.

But Raddatz was taking her there. Taking her there with his talk of citizen soldiers and a higher objective and the end of fear. All he was saying: a police state. A final solution. All he was doing: taking what she believed in, believed was hard but necessary, making it into genocide.

So means. A gun. Not her own. She'd have to get another. South Central. East LA. Either was good for it. Gangs loaded up with rods they were looking to unload. Rods with history, stolen rods. But getting a piece down there also made it real easy to get caught up in some unpleasantness. To get caught between gangs or between gangs and cops. Eddi didn't need high drama. Just a gun.

She'd do it Beverly Hills–style instead. In BH there were all manner of rich kids—or at least kids who lived well under the wing of their parents—who needed some extra cash of their own to score OxyContin and were more than happy to lift one of their daddy's guns and put it up for sale. The BH police were weak. Eddi was less likely to run into an SPU running a sting there than in Compton. And rich white kids? To them all Asians looked alike. Even one identifiable by her busted wrist. If things really went south, the chances of one of them picking her out of a lineup were just about nil. So Eddi took a trip to BH. A CI Eddi was tight with told her just where to spike herself. She ended up copping a .38 off a teen girl. Her parents shelled out eighteen thousand a year for her private school, but her last John had shorted her and she needed some ready to pay off her pimp.

Wasn't Eddi's problem. Really, better—Eddi propagandized—she had gotten ahold of the piece and not some crackhead. What Eddi would do with the gun, it wasn't a crime. It was justice.

Means, motive . . .

Finding the opportune time to hit Raddatz—when no eyes were looking, a moment she could wrap an alibi around—wasn't going to be easy to come by. Would take charting. Watching. Watching Raddatz. Where he went and when he went there. That meant sitting on him, tailing him, timing him. That meant opening herself to getting spotted watching him. Not by Raddatz. Eddi was sure she could elude him. Pretty sure. But with eyes focused forward there's always the chance some neighbor, some merchant . . . somebody would notice that one particular car with that one particular driver with a bad wrist who seemed to be hanging around all the time. It was a chance, yeah, but murder . . . *the administration of justice* was a chancy thing to begin with. Still, the odds favored Eddi. The stats in LA said seventy percent of murders went unsolved. Seven zero percent, higher or lower by some margin depending on what part of town the killing took place. Still, better odds you couldn't get in Vegas.

So, chancy as it was, it was a chance Eddi was going to take.

She held her conviction. She held on to her new gun. She watched Raddatz. She clocked him on duty, his comings and goings. Clocked what time he hit DMI on watch and what time he left. When he was working a watch, he was punctual. Same time in. Same time out. Every time. Raddatz was almost military-like with his adherence. Good for her. When Eddi finally figured the right moment to do things, Raddatz would most likely keep his appointment in Samarra.

Occasionally, after work and before going home Raddatz would stop to take a drink alone at a sports bar in the Valley. An actual sports bar. Not a strip club sports bar. Eddi didn't go in. Besides not wanting to make herself obvious, she couldn't watch him in the act of consumption. She had no interest in taking a read on what kind of solitary drinker Raddatz was. If he needed a little something to help him unwind, or a boost to help him through what remained of the day. She didn't know if it was a happy drink or one laced with bitterness. If the booze in the glass was really just a reflecting pool—something for Raddatz to look down into and see what stared back.

Eddi watched Raddatz at home. What Eddi found out, what she figured but wasn't previously sure of: Raddatz had family. Wife and two boys.

The first time Eddi got any kind of conscience about what she was planning was when she learned that about Raddatz, learned he had family. Was she really going to make a woman a widow, take away some kids' dad? Probably, at some point on some call she'd already done

as much to the family of a freak. But under the circumstances she had the law backing her. She had the reasoning that the freak could've chosen to turn itself in, but did
things a different way. A family had ended up husband-
less, fatherless for the choice it'd made.

This time there was no law backing Eddi's play. Still,
what she was doing was purely predicated on Raddatz's
choices. He'd decided to set himself aside from the law.
Jeopardize the war against the freaks. He'd put himself in
this place.

That his family would suffer . . . well, would they?
Honest, Eddi thought, they'd be better off without him.

Yeah. Right. Like she was better off without her dad.

She was comparing Raddatz to her own father?

She wouldn't have that. Not even from her own conscience.

Conviction was good, conscience was unacceptable.

Sundays.

Sundays, early evenings—at least three of them
running—Raddatz took himself a walk to the newsstand
on Laurel Canyon blvd. It was a couple miles there and
back. A little exercise, a little air. The streets were mostly
quiet, mostly residential. But there was an alleyway, a
shortcut behind a block of shops. Two hundred yards.
Maybe. But back there, there were few eyes. Back there,
there was less light, more shadow and a better op for Eddi
to shoot a guy and escape conviction for it. Back there,
the alley behind the block of shops, was where justice
would get put into the back of Raddatz's head at 111 feet
per second.

The waiting. That was the part that cut. From the
Sunday she decided when and how to kill Raddatz to

the Sunday she would do it were seven days in which she would pull three watches with Raddatz. *With* him. Watch by watch she knew what he did not. That he was a dead man. Seeing him, seeing him go through the motions of living not knowing that the time and place of his death had been stamped . . . for Eddi it was like watching a documentary of a life famously lost. King or Lennon or pretty much all the Kennedys. You see some footage of them at some innocuous moment laughing or smiling. Living, with no idea there was a bullet milled and waiting for them in Dallas or Memphis or just outside the Dakota. It was like watching a slasher flick and wanting to scream at the screen, useless as it was. Even with Raddatz, even knowing why she was doing what she was doing, Eddi nearly wanted to tell the man to get out of the way of the badness coming.

She had to avoid him. Three watches out of seven days a guy she previously barely crossed paths with on the job Eddi had to work at avoiding for fear Raddatz'd be able to decipher the look in her eyes, gain warning from it. But she wouldn't let herself avoid him too much, paranoid he could read her evasion as well.

One watch down. Another watch down. The third watch down.

She kept way clear of him on that last watch. Totally. She felt like a bride giving distance to her groom. She felt like she was dodging some kind of ill karma. They'd meet up later. Sunday evening. Sunday evening they'd consummate things.

Friday night. Saturday. Saturday night. Eddi had no idea what navigating those hours would be like. Rough. Anxious. Full of impatience. Reality was, it wasn't any of that. Eddi was less, much less keyed than she thought she'd be.

She also drank more than she usually did. Easy to do as she mostly never drank. But she was home, alone. It gave her an activity.

She thought about calling Vin. If she was going to drink, you know, why drink solo? Why let some other guy be an alcoholic by himself? But weak boozer that she was, what she didn't need was to put down one too many, get weak with her mouth and start spewing her plans. Much as Vin loved Soledad, as much as he regarded the struggle against the freaks, Eddi didn't figure he'd get with the idea of killing Raddatz. He wouldn't rat her out, but what Eddi could live free of was hours and hours of Vin throwing liquored reasoning against her plans.

A waste.

She'd worked herself up. She was ready for the kill. There was no going any other way.

Sunday. It felt like Christmas was coming. Not a child's Christmas with the static electricity of excitement permeating every single element of life. It was an adult's Christmas. Everything seemed rushed, harried, and no matter all the preparations Eddi felt horribly unprepared. Incredibly, though she slept poorly, she woke up late and felt as if even with taking a life the only thing on her calendar, she was running behind all day.

Then the day was gone.

It was getting on evening.

Eddi got in her car and drove to the Valley and parked a short distance from the alley off Laurel.

Shoot him in the head, walk to the car, go.

That was the plan. What little there was. What little was needed.

Shoot him in the head. Walk to the car. Go.

More waiting. Close now. Eddi could feel, could *feel* the passing of each second. No need to look at her watch. The sweep of her internal second hand was a razor to flesh, hacking off the time. Literally keeping score. Raddatz would come. Just wait. Be patient. He'd come.

Shoot him in the head, walk to the car, go.

The scent of arriving moonlight. The sound of clouds in the air. The laugh of a child who wasn't even born yet. In her journal Soledad had written about her sense of death: an elevated level of perception that made the world hyperreal. As many calls as Eddi had been on, as many times as she'd walked with mortality—hers, other operators', freaks'—Soledad's words were, to Eddi, just inflated talk. Eddi'd never felt anything of the kind. But now things beyond the normal senses were coming real and real clearly to Eddi.

What she did not sense was Raddatz at the newsstand. Her essence spread across the city, Eddi hadn't seen him arriving. Didn't notice when he started thumbing a copy of *Road & Track*. She'd only caught him as he picked up a copy of *Evo*, flipped through it, put it aside knowing there was nothing in there for him.

He shared some friendly talk with another browser, got a copy of *In Style* magazine. It was probably for the wife, but that purchase alone of glamorized vogue-trash wrapped around the cult of celebrity was enough to remove any qualms Eddi had about what was to come.

Raddatz moved from the newsstand.

Eddi moved across the street.

Raddatz jammed the magazine under an arm.

Eddi put hand to pocket. She closed on Raddatz. Not too quickly. Casually. Steadily. Just a girl out for a stroll. Keep a little distance. Let him make the alley. Let him hit the center of it. Then give it to him.

Hand on the .38's grip.

Give it to him quick.

Her finger brushed the trigger. Feathered. Easy to pull one-handed.

Give it to him twice, to be sure of things, right in the . . .

He kept going. Raddatz didn't make the turn up the alley. He kept north on Laurel. Went west on Maxwellton where cars passed at a steady clip, where a couple of old women walked their dogs. Eddi watched Raddatz walk off, toss off a wave to some guy in-line skating. She stood there hand in pocket, hand gripping gun, watching a man who was supposed to be dead walking home.

She was . . . what was Eddi feeling? Disappointed. Queer as hell, but that's how she felt: spending so much time working up to something that didn't happen even if what didn't happen was . . . Pissed. She was pissed Raddatz took a walk, literally walked from justice.

Eddi sat in her apartment. Lay on the floor. Lights low. Assessing herself, her feelings.

Scared.

Eddi was real scared that Raddatz had switched up his routine, would never again head down that alley. Scared not that she wouldn't get to take another run at Raddatz. She'd make that opportunity. She was scared she'd have to take a run at him somewhere less clandestine. Somewhere she'd be more likely to get caught. And something she hadn't even considered: When she got caught, what was her story going to be? Not the truth. Taking things public defeated the purpose. Shit, she didn't want to rot in jail. The only thing she wanted less was to go out as a crazy cop who killed for no good reason. It came to Eddi maybe a hotshot was the better way to go. Twenty-five to life in a California prison? A ruined rep? Better she should ride out on a mix of state-approved, lethally applied meds.

Eddi felt tired, and that feeling was an emotional preview of the week to come. Another week of waiting. Another week of three watches she'd have to work around Raddatz. Another week of psyching up, of foreplaying toward the real deal. The thought, just the thought of it wore the shit out of her. But the juice to do the job was already building in her. It was seven days, at best, away and Eddi was already fidgety. Antsy.

She needed, this time she really needed a drink and did not need to drink by herself.

Eddi wound up at Vin's. She didn't bother calling first. No need. He'd be home. And he was. In the dark. In the same chair he'd been in that last time she'd come around. At least, he'd done a one-legged hobble over to the chair after letting Eddi into his joint. But Eddi figured he was just returning to his roost.

If he was surprised to see Eddi, Vin didn't show it. If he was surprised by her request for some liquor, it was covered by a casual "Help yourself." Mostly, Vin registered nothing greater than numbness.

So Eddi did as offered, helped herself to a selection from Vin's ample collection of drink. A hit of Stoli vanilla. Downed the flavored vodka. Poured another, taking just enough time to open a window. The recycled air was killing her.

She polished her second drink, then Eddi took up a seat in Vin's general vicinity.

Be cool. Eddi told herself to be cool. Drink what you like, what you need, but keep your mouth shut. Keep your designs to yourself. Vin served his purpose—a little human connection. A reminder of the whys of what she was planning: too many having given too much for the struggle to get fucked-up by a guy like Raddatz—just by being around. Beyond that, talk was not needed.

The two sat. The only thing going on between them the occasional clink of ice in a glass.

"This is how we used to be."

"What's that?" Eddi asked. In her head she'd been watching Raddatz walk up the street instead of down the alley.

"With Soledad. Hours like this. Sitting. Not saying a word."

"Hell of a thing you had going."

"Best kind of thing. Two people so tight they don't need words."

Eddi lay back on the floor, looked up at the bad Spackle job on the ceiling. "You're positively delusional."

"If you're going to take my booze, then fuel my lies. Soledad called it . . ."

"What?"

"Some Japanese thing. You don't know it?"

Eddi turned her head. Free juice or not, she shot Vin an "oh, fuck you" look for the assumption that because of her heritage she was supposed to be aware of all things Japanese. Vin missed the visual chastisement. He was slouched, face half buried in the fabric of the chair. The way he was, head up he still probably couldn't see ten feet in front of himself.

He said: "They've got this thing in Japan, people talk without talking."

"Talk without talking. That's not talking, then, is it?"

"Anyway, that's what she told me."

"Where'd she get that?"

"I think it was from her guy. She was seeing a guy before we started . . . started whatever. She was telling me about that Japanese thing, rambling about it. When she realized what she was saying, she got all quiet. Bitter. Bitter for her even. Just figure, you know, thinking about her guy set her off."

"His name was Ian."

Head coming up from the chair. "How do you know?"

"Her journal."

"What'd she say about him?"

"Not much. She wrote about him steady for a while how she felt about him. Then nothing. From one page to the next it was like he didn't exist anymore."

"He must've broke her bad."

"I guess."

"Did she . . ." Vin paused, didn't want to sound too jealous. But then, hell, he was a one-legged drunk. Who was he saving his pride for? "Did she love him? Not like she loved me, did she really—"

"Yeah."

They went back to two people quietly sharing space.

Eddi poured another drink. Drank it. Fixed another before going back to the floor.

"You look butch, Eddi."

"Excuse me?"

"Not dyke, butch. Tough. That cast—"

"Not a cast. It's a splint."

"Looks like a gauntlet. Looks tough. That leather?"

"Yeah. It's comfortable. And I figure if I'm going to be a victim, might as well be a fashion—"

"I think she cared about me some," Vin said.

"She did."

"I think she really did. Her eyes used to go green. She thought I wanted to have sex with you."

"Maybe she wasn't jealous of you. Maybe she was jealous of me."

And Vin melted some. "Jesus, Eddi. Let me have one fantasy."

"Was she right?"

"Right about—?"

"Do you want to have sex with me?"

A yes-or-no question. But Vin's answer was: "I think you've got nice tits. I was never a small-chest guy. I was always, I mean, guys are guys. They go for girls who've got it. But yours—"

"There a compliment in there somewhere?"

"Yours are beautiful."

"What about my stomach?"

"That's tight. Serious. That's, like, fitness-model good-looking."

"And my butt?" Eddi was definitely drunk. But she wanted to know. She wanted to feel wanted.

"Yours is . . . I don't think of women's asses sexually."

"C'mon."

"No, I mean, I look at them, but I was never . . . some guys are into them in a hard-core sexual sense."

"Some guys?"

"A lot of guys. Whatever. Not me. But yours . . . it makes me think about it."

"What's my cootchie make you think about?"

After about eighteen seconds of silence, after Eddi's brain was able to process that time had passed in silence, she looked to Vin. Vin was looking at her. Just looking at her.

Eddi: "What?"

"What are you doing?"

"Asking you what you think of me."

"Are you getting off? This a, this a tease or something?"

"When you talk about me, you sound alive. I like it when you sound alive. And . . . I like how I feel when a guy is talking about me. It makes me feel . . . I don't want to be Soledad. Having a guy like me, knowing I could like him back; it makes me feel *not* like Soledad. It makes me feel like I got some human in me, and I'm not . . . I don't know that I got much left."

"What's that mean?"

Like she feared, Eddi was on her way to saying too much. So she followed it up by saying nothing.

Vin, remembering: "*Haragei* it was called. In Japan when people talk without . . . whatever, without talking. *Haragei* is what it is."

Eddi stayed with Vin a little less than two hours more. They engaged in a little less than two of *haragei*.

Life in reprise. Waiting was the repetition, was the slow torture. One watch down. Another watch down. The third down.

No diminishing of desire. No cooling off. If anything, like a frat boy that'd been cock-blocked, frustration made Eddi hungrier for the act than previously.

Friday night. Saturday. Saturday night.

Eddi was back to drinking. Back to drinking alone.

Vin'd been a good booze buddy. But getting comfortable with him was not her desire. Vin's inclination was downward. Clearly, when this—"this" being murder—was over, Eddi was going to have issues to deal with. Getting caught up in Vin's wake wasn't going to help her deal.

She smiled. The first she could remember in a while. The first she could remember since . . . the phone call. The news. Soledad was dead.

Eddi smiled and realized it was thinking of Vin that'd brought it on. An alky with no desire to be anything other. But Eddi thought of Vin and she smiled.

Sunday.

Eddi sat on the floor of her joint, played some Chicane on her multitasking CD/DVD system. Watching the sun pass through the sky was all the more assignment she'd given herself.

The sun in the sky.

What was it she'd learned? Long time ago. High school was it? *Not even the sun . . .* How did it go? *Not even the sun will transgress his orbit but the Erinyes, the ministers of justice, overtake him.*

And she rubbed her left tit. Beneath the gray cotton of her undershirt, through her bra, Eddi could feel, could *feel* her tattoo. That hyper sense again. Death was coming.

In the nightstand was a photo book. In the photo book was a picture of her father. She kept it close. No matter tough little MTac she was, she didn't have the fortitude to display it, keep it in constant view. She could barely ever look at it. But it remained always near. Near enough that in the middle of the night she could reach out and take hold of it and clutch it to her chest and cry in secret. She'd done that. Done it plenty.

The sun made its way to the edge of the sky.

The ministers of justice, overtake him.

Day was gone.

It was getting on evening.

Eddi got in her car and drove to the Valley and parked a short distance from the alley near the newsstand.

Shoot him in the head. Walk to her car. Go. Same as the Sunday previous. Except she expected more substantial results.

Eddi was vigilant this Sunday, saw Raddatz heading up the block, hitting the newsstand. She had a fear that

the hitch this week would be Raddatz'd have his kids
with him. She wasn't about to do the job with his kids
close. That much, or that little—that sliver of morality—
humanity Eddi had left.

Raddatz was consistent.

He arrived on schedule. Without family. He flipped
through *Esquire*. Flipped through, again, *Road & Track*.
Same as with just about all newsstands the automobile
magazines were displayed next to the porn. One-stop
shopping for a demographic. Two Sundays in a row
Raddatz had looked at the car mags without so much as
considering the porn. That bumped her some. Maybe it
was stereotyping, but it seemed to Eddi a guy like
Raddatz should have more visible vices.

Raddatz stood, stood reading an article. It felt to Eddi,
timewise, he was reading *The Fountainhead* in a sitting.

He stood reading.

He stood reading.

Raddatz put back the magazine.

He chatted some with somebody.

He started off from the stand.

Eddi made the cross.

Raddatz stopped. Looked at another magazine. *The
Week*.

Eddi didn't want to double back on herself in the middle of Laurel Canyon, call attention to herself. She kept
up the cross, landed on the far north end of the newsstand. The porn mags Raddatz had skipped over. Eddi
gave them a perusing. That she was making herself seem
engaged in other women's bare bodies was lost on her.
Head down, face hidden, she let her senses travel, touch
and feel Raddatz as he read through the newsweekly,

took it to the cashier, paid, started his walk again. Giving him a bit of a lead, Eddi fell in behind him.

This Sunday Raddatz took the alley.

Shoot him in the head. Walk to her car. Go.

Eddi closed on him.

In her pocket, hand on the .38's grip.

Give it to him quick.

Her finger brushed the trigger.

Give it to him twice.

Eddi pulled out, picked up the pace. Kept her hand down, gun at her side, hidden. Hidden, but ready to do work.

Raddatz oblivious.

Shoot him in the head.

On him, nearly on top of him. Close enough she wouldn't miss. Close enough she couldn't help but kill.

A sound, behind her.

A witness?

Eddi turned.

A man. Wispy. Reedy. He barely registered, yet somehow reeked menace. Not a witness. Something bad.

Eddi brought her hand around, started to bring her gun up. The guy caught it, caught her wrist. Wispy. Reedy. But his grip was like getting caught up in steel rails. Couldn't move. Eddi could not even start to move her arm.

The wispy guy twisted her wrist. A machine going to work on her. The hurt the same as her limb getting torqued by mechanical rotors. Pain made her open her hand, her gun clanking to the ground. Her grunt drowning out the gun.

From behind her, from Raddatz: "No, no!"

Eddi's left hand came up, whipped out, caught the thin man hard in the head. Square in the face. Her fractured wrist fractured a little more. There was blood from the guy's nose, from his mouth. On impact his head hardly moved.

The thin man made a fist.

Sleepy time for Eddi.

Eddi was cognizant. She wasn't sure how long it took her to figure that out. A while.

She realized she was awake, that it was dark. The room she was in was a basement, a cellar. If it was day or night outside she didn't know. Couldn't tell. She'd taken a blow to the head. Beyond the accompanying hurt she didn't feel as though she'd been drugged or otherwise roughed up. Probably, she'd been loopy only a short time at most. Probably, it was still Sunday evening. Sunday night.

So she'd narrowed the time frame. Like that was some F'n victory.

The space was windowless. And it stank. The choking stink of rotting flesh. Vermin probably. Maybe, Eddi considered, human.

Eddi realized she was staring up close at the print of a magazine. She lifted her head. Tried to. Her head told her real loudly to lay it the hell back down. Eddi didn't argue. She asked her eyes if they wouldn't mind focusing and, eventually, they responded.

The magazine: *The Week*. It'd been shoved under her

face as a pillow. Or a drool cloth. Eddi had, she was coming to notice, done a lot of that while she'd been out.

She was coming to notice she was cuffed too. The steel of the restraints particularly painful to her already fractured wrist.

The cuffs, *The Week*. Eddi only had to do a short replay to catch herself up to things: Her trying to kill Raddatz. The thin man who threw a punch like he was throwing a small car.

She'd fucked up. Raddatz knew she was coming. Or just, rat that he was, had his back continually covered. However it was, Eddi had fucked up. And now there'd be some kind of very nasty retribution. If Raddatz was just going to turn her over for attempted murder, she'd be in custody already. That he had no problem killing she knew already. But she wasn't dead. To Eddi that meant her death was going to come at a particular time and very likely none too quickly.

So she was going to die for her actions. It'd always been a possibility, though she'd thought it'd come by way of the state, not at private hands. She was going to die. Okay. Not okay, but . . . more immediate, more important, in her passing was there anything she could do to trip Raddatz up? Get him caught? Anything, same as setting a delayed fuse, that would after she was gone do to Raddatz what he was going to do to her?

If there was—*if*—Eddi's head was in no shape to think on it. Anyway, that kind of logic was Movieville superspy thinking; the incredibly complex trap sprung from beyond the grave. Eddi was no superspy. At the moment she was little better than a screw-up cop.

A padlock popped. The rattle of a chain. Eddi couldn't

tell in which direction the door was. Her senses were not working in concert. She heard the door open. She heard it close. She heard it lock again. Footsteps. Couldn't see from where they traveled. A voice came from directly above her.

The voice, Raddatz: "I'm going to tell you something; something that happened a few years back. I'll tell it to you, then we can talk about the way things are."

As long as he'd lived in LA Raddatz couldn't remember spending any significant time on Rodeo Drive. Why should he? It was Beverly Hills. It was the priciest bunch of blocks in LA County. Sick with high-end boutiques. Not stores, not shops. Boutiques. Armani, Gucci, Christian Dior, Chanel, Ralph Lauren, Valentino, Cartier and Tiffany. The priciest store on the planet—according to its own press—was on Rodeo. Bijan. Don't show up without an appointment. Don't show up without expecting to pay a min of a hundred grand. A pair of socks starts at fifty bucks. The rich bought on Rodeo. Tourists threw away good money on Rodeo so they could say they bought where the rich buy. Angelenos, regular Angelenos, didn't go anywhere near the street. Unless they had to. Unless, for instance, they were MTac cops and somebody'd put in a call on a sighted freak.

Somebody'd put in a call.

Raddatz was leading his element south on Rodeo.

The call had come in as a two-forty, an assault. That part was sketchy. What wasn't: One of the combatants picked up the other one and threw him a couple hundred feet. The area of eventual impact being the side of a store.

A boutique.

Threw him hard. What was left of the vic was still splattered, some kind of sick art, over the brick facade. There were a couple of the BHPD cops on patrol. They drew out, opened fire. Boxed the freak, but then backed off. It was Beverly Hills. BH cops rousted the homeless, kept the blacks and Hispanics from wandering the flats. What they didn't do, they didn't handle freaks. For that they called the LAPD.

LAPD sent MTac.

The streets'd been cleared. The civvies had been evacuated. The area was a quarter mile in circumference of ghost town. Maybe the freak had slipped away in the initial confusion. Maybe it was holed up in a dark corner next to overstocked, overpriced goods. It was up to West LA MTac—Raddatz and Carmichael and McCrae and Tice—to figure out which.

That meant going slow south on the drive.

That meant going boutique to boutique.

That meant getting into tight little spaces where cover was minimal, and getting caught in another operator's fire was a genuine concern.

And behind any door, any counter, in any dressing room, could be a freak cooling. Waiting to do damage to the cop who was a little too slow with his trigger.

Haute urban warfare.

"Clear?" Raddatz called to his element.

Down the line, over throat mics: "Clear."

"Clear."

"Clear."

That was what, twelve boutiques down. Twenty-five to go? Plus a couple of restaurants. Just as cautiously as when they'd entered the joint, the element was as much so coming out. Had to be. Relax a split second, plane your own edge, that's when you were begging for trouble.

Gloved hand under his Fritz helmet, Tice whipped clear sweat that was spilling over his brow, filling his eyes.

Raddatz, calling his progress in: "West LA to Central."

"Go ahead, West."

"We're clear. Move D Platoon down another fifty."

"Copy that, West. D Platoon moving fifty yards."

D Platoon. Special Weapons and Tactics. They were good. Plenty of them had elevated to G Platoon. Problem was, the ones who hadn't, they were okay doing overkill on the disgruntled employee of the weak huddled up in some office building looking to hand out some payback for his pink slip. Those cops'd avoided going MTac for a reason. The reason was usually fear. So D Platoon— SWAT—being the only fail-safe against a freak that got past his element didn't help Raddatz feel any better about the situation. Just more pressure. Either they got the freak, or the freak was likely to not be gotten at all.

Next up: Harry Winston's.

The four MTacs went for it, eyes moving. Always moving, sweeping, looking . . .

Enhanced strength. That's what they were dealing with. The perp fused the vic with a wall from two hundred feet away. That takes some kind of muscle. With freaks, what you were going up against was never certain. But, yeah, probably it was a freak with enhanced strength. That meant not *just* looking for somebody. That meant keeping an eye out for a truck or a generator or a main-frame computer . . . whatever the thing might feel like picking up same as a kid's toy and tossing your way. That possibility was obvious. But the thing could just as easily flick a paper clip at you with enough force, even with a vest, it'd tear through the Kevlar and hit like a Teflon bullet. And should you be lucky or unlucky enough to dodge what it was thrown, get close to it, if it got you in its paws, it could crush you. Rip clean your limbs. Snap you in two. Dealer's choice. The freak being the dealer.

Sirens. Getting closer.

Raddatz: "West LA. We've got sirens?"

In his earpiece, the OIC: "Car fire on Wilshire. Fire responding. Unrelated."

Raddatz let a breath slip from his mouth.

Keep on your toes, keep your eyes rolling. Raddatz whispered as much over his throat mike to the rest of the element as they slipped into Harry Winston's.

The House of Winston.

The King of Diamonds.

Jeweler to the Stars.

There was, there had to be, fifty mill in rocks in the place easy. Necklaces, rings, earrings, pendants, gold settings, white gold, platinum . . . The actual market value of the gems was maybe half that fifty mill. The cheapest . . . the *least expensive* piece went in the neighborhood of forty grand. But if you bought at Harry's, you were paying for the name, the legend, the zip code. If you were a tourist, you paid. If you were a Hollywood wife, a kept girl, your sugar daddy paid for you. On that business model Harry's had been in operation a lot of years.

Raddatz's element paid zero mind to the bling. Getting

caught up in it could get 'em killed. At any price was there a rock in the joint worth losing your life over?

A lot of glass. Display cases filled the center of the boutique, ringed the edge. Should've been an easy look-see, but the sunlight pouring in refracting off the glass and the diamonds did tricks with the eyes. Dazzled. Was like doing recon in a kaleidoscope.

Raddatz: "Tice, hold back. Cover us from the door."

Tice was schlepping the Benelli.

Raddatz put Carmichael and McCrae on the edges of the boutique. The pair toted HKs. Sexy in black.

Out front was Raddatz carrying just his Colt .45. *Just* the .45. A precision kill weapon that hit harder than a Glock. For most cops in most situations it'd be more gun than they needed. Against a freak, at best it was adequate.

Raddatz inched his way forward, every step feeling same as bait on a hook. If the thing was present, he was making himself available for it. Hope was he'd get it first. If not, the hope was one of the other operators could put it down.

On the walls: shimmers of light like sunshine kicked back from a pool. Constant movement. An optical distraction. In all his years Raddatz had never squeezed off a jumpy round by mistake. Today might be the day.

Forward, peeking, peeking around a display case. Nothing. Jewels, riches. No freak. Forward. Forward some more. Eyes fluttering from dripping sweat. The heavy breathing of three other MTacs in his ear.

He should clear his sweat. Raddatz thought he should. Light on the walls.

Thought he should. Probably not a good move.

His choices had come down to that: Take his hand off

his gun to clear his vision. Have his vision cut by the sweat, but keep up a solid two-handed grip.

Breathing in his ear.

He hated self-debating; what to do or not. Just do it or forget it.

The light, the light dancing.

A door up ahead. A storage room? Back office?

Raddatz, into his throat mike: "Going for the door."

Behind him the sound of shifting bodies. Red dots slipped over the wall. Guns taking up new aim points.

And the sound of breathing.

Left hand out, reaching for the door. For the knob. Raddatz took hold. Tested it. Unlocked. He opened it slightly. Opened it . . .

There was a single scream split in two, both parts heard simultaneously. The vocalized one behind Raddatz. The transmitted one in his ear and stabbing into his heart.

Raddatz whipped around.

Tice was off the ground. Elevated inches above it by the thing. The freak. Elevated inches off the ground by the freak's hand jammed wrist-deep into Tice's chest.

Tice: squirming, screaming. Blood gushing. Dying.

Raddatz didn't need to give the go. Carmichael, McCrae already doing work with the HKs. Thirteen rounds a second X 2. Flying hot. Scorching air with a *ffft, ffft, ffft* as the slugs sourced for the target. Missed the target. Both MTacs missed. The freak was already moving. The bullets it dodged rapid-punched walls. Little as they were, they dug out fist-sized divots. Bricks chipped. Powdered. Clouded the air.

All that was behind the freak.

The freak was leaping, hauling Tice—or Tice's

body—with it. The freak landed on a display case. Shattered glass sent gems flying, scattered sunlight through the diffused space.

Pretty.

Then the freak leaped again, leaped for McCrae. Moving too fast for Raddatz to keep a bead.

Then it was bloody hell.

Bare-handed, the freak tore, literally tore into McCrae. Fingers like hooks. Arms spinning like blades. Old-school Warner Bros. cartoon Tasmanian. Without the funny. Tore up McCrae, tore up what was left of Tice at the same time.

Fountains of crimson.

Chunks of meat.

Walls got painted.

Slaughterhouses were more genteel.

Screams coming, seeming to come from everywhere. Screams of death, of rage. Wails that begged God and woke the devil.

The freak was strong, was fast. Impossible. Freaks didn't own multiple abilities. One. All they had was one. If they had more than one . . . straight fear talking to Raddatz: If freaks had more than one ability, how was a cop supposed to have a chance in hell of going against it and living?

Carmichael held fire, didn't want to hit Tice or McCrae. Bad-cop fidelity. What was left of the cops was dead.

Raddatz jerked his trigger two, three times. The bullets took the target. Raddatz saw the hits, saw flesh rent, blood spurt.

To the freak three bullet wounds were nothing. Interfered with his continued violence none.

Carmichael got over his concerns, got to shooting. The low boom, the deep roar of his Benelli. Hell coming for the hellion. Came too slow. By the time his slugs got to the freak, the freak was gone. The slugs beat the shit out of a wall. The freak was taking air, arching for Carmichael. A *whoosh,* a streak as it slashed an arm forward. Then Carmichael's head, separated from his body, was shattering through a glass display case. Coming to rest among a collection of eighty-plus-carat diamond pendants. Carmichael's body did about five seconds of a headless-chicken dance. Dropped to the floor. Danced a little more. Purged some more blood from the top of its empty neck. Joined Tice and McCrae in being dead.

Strength, speed. Nearly invulnerable. Freaks didn't have multiple abilities, Raddatz told himself. How was a cop supposed to have a chance in hell of going against it and—

The thing put feet to a wall, sprang off. Arching again. Arching for Raddatz.

Raddatz's finger jerking the Colt's trigger. Three more bullets for the freak. Two more hits. Same as before. No difference. The freak was not stopped.

The freak landed. The freak was right in front of Raddatz. Looking human, but so far removed from humanity. Chest blowing, eyes burning, bleeding but not dying. Hell-born, but a thing hell wouldn't want.

And then it moved. Fast, like before. Violent. With its hands it grabbed. With its teeth it bit, cracked. Tore away the bones of Raddatz's wrist. A sucking, popping sound.

And a scream from Raddatz. He saw his own hand, gripping his gun, flipping through the air.

And the freak: blood flesh-spilled from its mouth that curved with a smile.

Raddatz stepped back. Thought he was. Thought he was stepping back. He was falling backward. Took the ground hard. Instinct—a cop's instinct, plain survival instinct—told him to get up, get back into things. If you're gonna die, die. But die fighting. Die taking the thing with you. So Raddatz tried to scramble off, push himself back up. He slipped on his own blood. His stump useless for helping out in the effort to stand. Good for nothing except causing him pain, bleeding massively.

No getting up. No getting back into the fight. The next couple of seconds held nothing but the remainder of his life. Just time enough to consider: eyes closed or open? Does he go out like a man, watch death coming? Does he shut his eyes and pick that one last image to ride to eternity with?

Eyes closed. He conjured his wife, his boys.

Please, God, let 'em know my last thought was of them.

He calmed none. Held his family tight in his mind. Took a quick hit of every emotion he'd ever felt.

Please, God.

Please . . .

Thunder is its own thing, he'd always thought. When Raddatz was a boy, when his father taught him, as good fathers do, to count the seconds between lightning and thunder to figure how far off a storm was, Raddatz just got it into his head thunder is different from lightning. And it is. But they're partners. It takes lightning to make thunder—the sound of a vacuum collapsing when air is riven by electricity. So when he felt it, when Raddatz felt the sharp bite of charged particles racing above him, he knew it was lightning when he heard the thunder. Heard the animal scream of the freak as it fried. Smelled flesh that was bone-roasted.

Then there was nothing but the sound of breathing.

His own. His own was all that remained.

His shaking, convulsing diminished. Volition returned. Raddatz used it to open his eyes. The world swam around him. A mile away, maybe just ten feet, was the freak. Burned, obviously. Skin charred where it wasn't just cooked away. Probably dead. It was motionless enough to be dead. There were bodies about, body parts about. Blood everywhere. All that remained of his former fellow cops. Raddatz's head moved in some direction. Actual geography was lost to him. Upside down to him was a woman. A female anyway. She was little older than a girl. A teen. She wore a shirt that both quoted some urbanism and showed midriff. Baggy pants that peekabooed the thong her parents must have hated her wearing. Such a normal girl. Other than the arc of electricity that crawled around her clenched fists. Three cops dead. Raddatz dying. The freak that had done all that stopped by a youth with tricky fingers.

Her mouth moved. She spoke to Raddatz, her voice lost to him. His senses failing him.

Fading. He was fading. Blood was flowing from him. Life was slipping from him.

As he traveled on, Raddatz caught up with the words of the girl as both her voice and his life headed for eternity.

The girl had said: "Don't be afraid."

There's something about dying, Eddi. There's something about it that—"

"That drives you insane?" Eddi talked through the pain in her head, the pain in her wrists; the cuffs biting into her flesh. "You didn't die."

Raddatz didn't take Eddi's acid as insult or sarcasm. He took it as point of fact.

"I died, Eddi. I did die. If not technically, then I had the NDE that changes you. How could I die and not get changed?"

"You're not changed. You're fucked-up!" Words delivered with a spray of the blood that filled her mouth.

"You've never been pushed to a state above and beyond every other thing you used to believe, Eddi?"

"Stop saying my name!"

"There's never been a time you've done things never mind the consequences, others might find . . ." From a picket: Eddi's .38. The gun that was meant to kill Raddatz.

"You deserve to die."

"I do." No argument from Raddatz. Just an expression of sadness. "But not how you think. I deserve to die because . . . They aren't freaks, Eddi. They *are* different than us. They're—"

"They're fucking mutants!"

"They're not afraid."

"They ought to be scared. Kill me, but that's not going to stop us from taking out every last—"

"They're not afraid as we know fear. That girl: If she'd been identified by the police, what would have happened to her? A warrant would have been issued. She would have been hunted. Maybe killed. Her family sent inside just for being her family, for never having turned her in to the cops. but she knew she had to try and stop the metanormal that was in the middle of killing me. That is, if it didn't kill her. If the police didn't kill her. There's a difference between us and them. Not in their abilities. Not in being genetically better. What sets the best of them apart from us, sets them to a degree above us, is so basic, but beyond you and me. Metanormals, the ones who believe in good aren't scared of doing what's right. Facing persecution, without regard to self, no matter the law, they're not afraid of serving a higher cause. Serving mankind. Isn't that what lifts our species above common animals; to do good without regard? And isn't that what holds our species back; the inability to give selflessly? And I know you're thinking: Cops; we do that. Give of ourselves. We put our lives on the line to fight them. But we fight from a place of fear. Stop them, or they'll destroy us. Stop them, or they take over. Stop *them*.

"They don't fight *from* fear. They fight *for* right. For all. They fight to end fear. That young girl, when she gave me life, she took my fear."

"You've got no fear. That makes you a, a traitor now? She saved your life, so you kill cops."

"They're using you, Eddi. Do you understand? They used Soledad, now they're using you."

Just the mention of her name. Soledad. Enough to slow Eddi down. No matter she'd been pummeled, no matter she was on the floor cuffed, for the first time since she'd gotten her sense back Eddi listened.

"What do we fear?" Raddatz asked. "What are we all scared of? A return to the days before San Francisco. The metanormals—the good, the bad—going at each other in the middle of Downtown LA, or New York, or Atlanta. We're scared of this 'cause we've been told to be scared."

"Because more than half a million people got killed on May Day."

"And do you think if Pharos hadn't gone after Bludlust, things would've turned out different, the city wouldn't have been torn in half? When that happened, we said to our leaders: Not again. Do what you have to, but never again. So there was the Executive Order, there were the MTacs and the deportations and the SPAs. The government could do what it wanted, when it wanted, in the name of security. I know, Eddi, I know what you're gonna say. It was, it *is,* a time of war. We need to protect ourselves and do so extraordinarily against an extraordinary enemy. But do you think the desire for power is limited to metanormals? Ordinary people want to be extraordinarily. What genetics hasn't given them, the law grants them. The Executive Order gave men power.

"But memories fade, Eddi. Every day the past slips farther and farther away. People don't remember May Day as much as they recall the sight of cops with HKs taking out metanormals in the middle of the street. You've seen it, the rise of what's called freak fuckers; the liberal fringe. How much longer before their voice takes hold, the Exceutive Order gets rescinded? Metanormals get rights again? There is that fear. It cuts deep among normal men who value their power. It's why someone like Soledad got persecuted for taking half a step outside the law."

"She got roasted because the brass was trying to cover up kickbacks."

"They tried to punish her to hide others' crimes. So you get it? People in power will do what they can to keep their power. Power never cedes except by force."

Eddi was getting the feeling she was going to be where she was for a while. She was losing the feeling in the arm she was lying on. She rolled, tried to find comfort. All she found was more hard floor. More hurt.

"I'll tell you honest, Eddi. I've used my position to advance my objectives. I won't participate in hunting metanormals anymore. Not ones who aren't a threat."

"They're all a threat."

"If they were, I wouldn't be standing here."

"And you decide that, you and your cadre? Which ones are trouble and which aren't."

"If we knew of a metanormal who committed a crime, was in the act of planning the commission of a crime, then we processed him. Got that intel to MTac. Otherwise, we lost a number of metanormals in mountains of paperwork."

"You're protecting them."

No denial. Not even a modifier. "Yeah. Myself, a few others I was able to persuade."

He was doing a lot of talking. Giving up a lot of information. Eddi knew things were heading in one of two directions. Raddatz was going to offer her some kind of a deal, or he was going to kill her. As she wasn't dead yet, as Raddatz was rapping like a Buddhist monk on E, Eddi held out hope.

Raddatz: "Careful as we were, we couldn't keep ourselves off the radar forever. People were getting suspicious."

"People?"

"The department. IA."

For Eddi IA equaled Tashjian. She was hurting again. This time in her gut.

"And then," Raddatz went on, "the killings started. Metanormals, sympathizers. Fernandez, maybe."

"That wasn't your people?"

"No."

"If you're going to tell me it was IA . . ."

"It's not them. This is . . . we are on the edge of a whole other destiny."

"Quit fucking around!" Hurt. Humiliated. Whatever was coming Eddi was ready to get to it. Enough with the setup. "What's the situation?"

"Someone's killing metanormals. Those I'd call innocent. Harmless. But as harmless as they might be, they're not defenseless. It's a single perp. As far as I believe, one-on-one, it takes a metanormal to kill a metanormal. But if this went public—"

"Freaks going to war again."

"The fear of another San Francisco. That'd be the end of the liberal voice and the push for the return of metanormal rights. It would give more power to the guys in power."

"You, your little cadre: You hid this info."

"And we tried to find the killer. But somewhere, someone started to see a pattern: intel they weren't getting, information that was being misdirected. They couldn't prove anything. They seemed to believe they couldn't put any of their people inside to watch us."

"But Soledad was at DMI."

Raddatz nodded. Up and down, but the motion was sideways to Eddi's skewed view of the world.

Raddatz said: "She got the charge to get evidence, to shut us down. Or, better, if things worked out that way, to stop us with force."

"To kill you."

Nothing from Raddatz this time.

From Eddi: "That's bullshit. That's the most fucked-up . . . I've had perps popped red-handed who could spin better lines."

For a minute, for nearly that, Raddatz stood. Just stood. He took Eddi's words, her crack about all he'd said being bullshit, about as well as a boxer—beaten, beat up, struggling through round fourteen of fifteen—would take a long-delayed but well-laid blow. He was done. He was through. A husk that'd just had a hole riven through it exposing it as the empty vessel that it is. Raddatz could not reach Eddi, and that finished him.

He put Eddi's gun down on the floor. "Do you remember"—Raddatz empty in spirit, empty in voice when he spoke—"how you felt the day after May Day? The hate I had is still so clear to me." With his hook Raddatz pushed Eddi's piece toward her. "When the girl saved my life, everything I used to believe was taken from me. But what I believed in was hate. My hate was replaced with the burden to . . . not to do what the law said was right, but to do what I knew was right. I fucked that up, and my fucking up cost people their lives. Now I'm alone in my efforts. Maybe I've got a chance to make things correct, but if it's a chance at all, it's a slim one. Before the guys in power can make a grab for more I have to buy the metanormals time."

"Time for what?"

"For the truth to come. For revelation to set them free. But now's the time to do something, or do nothing. To do right or just let evil play. What's it gonna be, Eddi?" With her gun still lying on the floor before her Raddatz stepped around behind Eddi. She felt him work her cuffs. She felt the metal give up its bite.

The gun right there. A trick. Had to be.

"What's it going to be, Eddi?"

"I pick up the gun, I try to shoot you, what: Your superfriend's going to crush my skull?"

Ra shook his head no.

The gun.

"Maybe all this is just to test me, to see if I'd flip over to the freaks' side."

"Or maybe all this is the truth. Maybe, crazy as it is, you and me ended up here for a reason. Even if the reason is just to kill me. And if that's the way things are," nodding for the gun, "pick it up, do your job. Tell your bosses you got a freak fucker. An insurgent. You've preserved the order of their world for them."

Eddi picked up the gun, couldn't feel it. Just the throb of blood pumping back into her hands. Pumping hard. Her heart was exhausting itself. She was swimming in gore. Eddi was, in her head, back in the alley on the edge of doing what she'd come to do. Make things right, yeah, but make things right for Soledad.

The blood in her hands felt like it was going to purge from her flesh. Bust right through it.

Raddatz stood where he was. Gave off nothing. If this was it, this was it. Whatever was coming he was ready to take.

Not a trick. He was okay to die.

Kill him. For Soledad, kill him.

Her head, hands ached. Fucking ached. Eddi felt her hurt so clear . . .

But she did not feel . . . she could not sense what was outside, what was a mile away. She couldn't smell the fragrance of a freshly perfumed girl sitting in her car on Beverly Boulevard, or hear the whisker-snap of a shaving guy in Torrance. All that was lost to her. She was just in a little dark room somewhere. She was not hyperaware of anything. She did not sense or feel death. For the minute there wouldn't be any killing.

"One more time, Raddatz. Tell me everything."

She sat looking down at the tabletop, staring at it. Through it. It was glass. So, really, it was the floor at which she was staring. The kitchen floor. A stain from some Chef Boyardee ravioli that one of the kids had spilled onto the tile and she'd managed to miss since . . . Raddatz's wife asked herself when was the last time the kids had eaten Chef Boyardee?

She was calming down. But still she asked: "Why?"

"Same as always. Nailing a perp is only half the job. It's the paperwork that—"

"Why now?"

There was some world-saving to be done. Double-dealing by the establishment had to be put down. But before all that, Raddatz had to do some damage control with the missus. He was only supposed to have walked a few blocks to grab some magazines. A couple hours had passed. A couple of hours Raddatz had spent doing a nasty dance with Eddi Aoki in the basement of a half-built/never-finished apartment building in Studio City. A cop's wife, her man all of a sudden does a fade, no matter how many years she's been living with possibilities, it's understandable if she goes a little nuts. So Raddatz had to tell a few lies about an incident that'd gone down in plain view. Lies about having to step in, assert himself as the law—as cops are never really off-duty—until some uniforms hit the scene.

Helena bought it. Through her love of her man, her fury at him for maybe having gotten himself hurt or worse, she bought the lie.

Raddatz did a quiet thanks to God. Helena being a cop's wife, he knew her intuition—or her enhanced suspicion from years of proximity to a DMI officer. There was a chance she wouldn't have gone for word one. Then would come questions and recriminations. Accusations. Was he off drinking, was it another woman . . . Raddatz really only had the time and temperament to douse a small fire, not to deal with a whole forest set ablaze.

So in a way it was a little ironic. She'd bought the big lie of her husband stepping in and helping out. What she couldn't get past: him telling her he had to go out and push paper. Right now.

"Somebody else can't do it?"

"I was a witness."

"So do it tomorrow."

"The time I sit here talking I could be done and back."

Head up, looking right at her husband: "You were dead."

"I don't . . ."

"I said to myself he's dead. Not *maybe,* but . . . I wanted to accept it. Be *done* accepting it. I wanted to be ready for it."

"Those days are over. I'm not MTac anymore."

"It doesn't matter. If you know the feeling once, you never—"

"I was gone a couple of hours."

"To me, Tucker, you were dead."

Just then he realized she was cupping his mangled wrist. Hook off. Raddatz was letting it breathe. His nerve endings were pretty much useless. The whole of it, the stump, the scars, the remnants of surgery—surgeries— was a hideous sight. Never, never once that Raddatz could remember had Helena ever recoiled from it or from its touch to her body. Never that he could recall did she hold back from making contact with it.

She was such a good woman. No pejorative there. No marginalization regarding her gender in relation to modern society. What was right and fine, what was the core of all vows that a man and woman take when joined before God and the law was what Helena owned and regularly put into practice.

Raddatz asked himself: Would she—if Helena knew the truth of things, if she knew that he was helping the kind who'd tried to turn her into a widow, had done as much as they could to turn the human race into a distant memory—would she finally recoil from him then? Would her anger still be a combination of love and rage, or just the rage?

Or maybe, know what might shove her away? The fact her husband didn't trust this "good woman," this woman of her vows . . . he didn't trust his partner, his wife, the heart of his life enough to be honest with her. That would most likely set her back same as a fist to the face.

"I'm telling you those days are done." Raddatz hoped he'd go to his grave not knowing what the revelation of the lie would do to his wife. He could endure, had endured a lot of pain and loss and suffering and come away from it a version of whole despite his scars. What he could not take, what would leave him a wreck: breaking Helena's heart. "I'm not that kind of cop anymore."

"So you get in the middle of, of—"

"A punk acting like a man. A kid running around high with a knife. His knife, my gun. You don't need two hands to win that fight." An attempt at humor. It got Raddatz nothing. "I sat on the kid for a minute until the—"

"It wasn't a minute."

"I had to wait for uniformed cops. I told you."

"Go two hours without hearing from me when I'm supposed to just be running an errand. How would you feel?"

"Jesus. By the time it was all done—"

"How would you feel?"

Like he'd been hacked open. Like his insides were being lifted from him for no greater purpose than being spilled onto a floor. Like he was dying, which he might as well be because he wouldn't want to go on living. And all that would pretty much be his initial reaction.

But Raddatz said, calmly, evenly, covering his true concern: "I'd be worried as hell. But my worry wouldn't let me keep you from doing what you had to do in life."

"Paperwork?"

Raddatz's exasperation was turning real. "I'm going to go to the station, I'm going to do some work, I'm going to come home. You need anything from Ralph's?" He was already moving for the garage.

Helena mumbled a no.

Raddatz gave the most casual good-bye he could. The kind a wife'd get from her husband cop off to do paper-work and a stop at the store on the way home. The kind he'd given her a thousand times previous. Now he couldn't even be sure he was faking it well.

Raddatz pulled out of the driveway, rounded a corner, stopped his car and picked up Eddi.

Re: the time it'd taken Raddatz to deal with his wife: "Home issues?"

"Cop's life, cop's wife. Always issues."

"Where are we going?"

"To Hayden's."

"Who's Hayden?"

Raddatz kept mum to that.

Eddi, again: "Who's Hayden?"

"You carry grudges well?"

"Why?"

"Hayden's the one who laid you out."

Eddi'd always wondered . . . not always. Not even sometimes. Occasionally, when she was taking the Sepulveda exit off the 405, the La Brea exit from the 10, almost any exit off the 101 between Chauenga and Sunset, Eddi wondered: the little apartments? Dirty, ratty apartments tucked close to the freeway that absorbed the continual roll of rubber on road, the noise pollution associated with it, the toxic fumes that came from it: Who lived in those? Who the hell would live in those?

The answer, obvious: anyone who couldn't live somewhere else, somewhere decent. The poor. The transient. The unbalanced. The undocumented.

And now Eddi knew to add to the list at least one superhuman who would otherwise, living normal, risk being exposed and hunted down. Killed.

Standing across from that superhuman, Hayden, standing in his shithole of an apartment, Eddi wasn't sure what she should be feeling. The hate she'd always felt for the kind that'd made her fatherless. Hate with some added resentment for this freak that put a single, unanswered punch on her that still left each pulse of her heart throbbing in her head. Some kind of awe that she was spitting close to a metanormal and they weren't actively trying to kill each other.

Or maybe she should be feeling pathos. Not so much for the freak, but for his wife and for his kid who was maybe three years old. Old enough he should be starting preschool. He should be outside playing, running, laughing. He was doing none of that. Probably never would. That kind of life was reserved for kids who didn't grow up hiding out in crappy apartments near off-ramps 'cause at least one of their parents was a freak.

Not a social worker, Eddi told herself. She wasn't there to hand out pity. Contrivances were in need of being conceived. Conceive them. Make things correct. Move on. Eddi told herself quite firmly: You are not part of this world.

"It's difficult sometimes." Hayden was doing the talking. "With my abilities, enhanced strength, it's difficult—"

"To know how hard is too hard to hit somebody?"

"I'm sorry."

Eddi recognized him. Beyond being the wispy, reedy guy who'd knocked her loopy, Eddi recognized him as the guy Raddatz had chatted with a couple of times at the newsstand. Chatted. Passed information with. Eddi should've been a little more observant.

Queer. Here was a guy, Hayden . . . trim and slight as he might have looked, here was a guy who could punch his way through a concrete slab same as regular people could poke a finger through tissue. Here was a guy that could've taken off Eddi's head using any two digits of one hand. And here was this guy apologizing to Eddi. Standing back away from her. Cowering slightly, unconsciously, now that she stood opposite him. This is how badly the MTacs had freaks scared. This was the legacy of Soledad, of Yar, of Bo, of Reese, of every MTac that'd ever chalked a freak in the name of the law.

Eddi, making sure everybody's on the same page: "So you got freaks getting killed. You wanted to know if freaks're going after each other, starting back with their old ways."

Raddatz nodded to the affirmative. "But we've got no motive for the attacks."

"One superhuman wants to kill another. How much more reason do you need?"

"On the job, how many times did you come on really random violence? Guy robs a liquor store, he wants money. Guy jacks a car because he wants wheels. A girl gets killed because she jilted her man. I don't care what kind of powers metanormals have, you've got to look at the crime same as any other. Besides . . ." Raddatz looked to Hayden. "If one of their own went off, they would know."

They would know. Raddatz was acknowledging what the establishment feared: Metanormals weren't just hidden among the normals. They had a network, an underground. As far as the establishment cared, that was one step removed from having a resistance. Forming an army.

And Raddatz was actually trusting Eddi with this information.

If he was trusting her. If he wasn't handing her misinformation. Disinformation. But, really, wasn't the trust Eddi's to use or discard? She could keep on with Raddatz, hear him out, back his play. Or she could keep a metaphorical hand on her gun ready for betrayal.

"Okay, so this isn't random . . ." What was the phrase Eddi was looking for? "Freak-on-freak crime."

"No," from Hayden. "Whoever it is, or they are, they've . . . they've made targets of us."

"The last guy to get killed, Anson Hall, he'd been stalked. We got out the word among the metas: Mind your back for anybody who's watching you, clocking you. That's how," Raddatz said, "we knew to stake the house where the last murder attempt was."

"Melinda thought—"

Eddi asked: "That was the intended vic?"

Hayden hesitated. He used her name in front of Eddi by accident. He'd just outed to an unknown quantity a fellow freak.

"It's all right." Raddatz vouched for Eddi. Went out further on the limb.

Hayden said: "Melinda Franklin. She has the ability to alter thermal degrees in a microclimate."

"A weather girl," Eddi slanged.

"She thought she was being watched. She got a message to some other metanormals, to me. I told Tucker."

Hayden was so insubstantial. He was in his mien, he was physically. Going from the gut, Eddi'd always figured a guy who was superstrong would have muscles the size of small bull calves. But if you could lift almost anything and everything that was set before you—from engine blocks to locomotives—how could you ever develop musculature? Couldn't. No more than pumping five-ounce weights would land Eddi on the cover of a fitness mag. Metagenetics had their own, odd rules. And admittedly, for Eddi, even in this short amount of time seeing them from the inside out held a certain fascination.

A semitrailer coming down the off-ramp took Eddi's attention. She looked to Hayden's wife. Hayden's wife had been watching Eddi stare at her husband. She didn't care for the way Eddi was staring, studying her man as if he were a control animal at a university lab. Hayden's wife made her feelings plain in expression alone.

Eddi to Raddatz: "Why are you involved? Besides your guilt or near-death experience or whatever. Freaks've got—"

"Do you like 'chink'?" That from Hayden's wife. "You call us freaks, do you like to be called a chink?"

"Chinks are from China." Eddi calm enough to be commenting on a recipe for soup. Directions to the mall. "My family tree goes back to Japan. So *they've* got all the power this side of God. Why don't they just take care of the problem themselves?"

"That's what the people up top want."

"They don't fight back they get killed. They fight back they get blamed for using their abilities and end up hunted." Eddi, flippant: "Kinda sucks to be a *meta-normal*."

Hayden, not sarcastic, serious: "Yeah. Kind of."

The boy, with his mother, just sat and listened. Grown people standing around talking about the thousandth variation on hunting season on the unique, and he just listened. The thing was, even if both his parents were metanormals, it wasn't a sure bet he'd have an active gene. Wouldn't know at the earliest until puberty. For most that's when the gene went active. And how would that be for this kid? Early teen years, getting zits and pubic hair and maybe the ability to rip sequoias from their roots or see through brick walls or have control over the metals of the earth. What do you do then? You try to live "normal," or do you take your abilities and pay back the normals for what they did to your kind? It occurred to Eddi that maybe this moment was merely a polite introduction to the boy. Their severe meeting was years and circumstance away. And what would the circumstance be? Violent, hopeful? Would it end in death or inspiration? Eddi was getting with the idea the future was beginning right then. And right then Eddi got, or was at least starting to feel, the weight of Raddatz's words: It is time to end fear.

Okay, so what did Eddi have? Eddi had nothing. Raddatz had little to give her beyond what was known. What was obvious. Freaks were being killed. Tashjian had given her that much coming in. All Raddatz had added was a long-winded assertion freaks were the vics in the situation. Backed it up with nothing more than the word of a freak itself. Eddi didn't take it. She didn't disbelieve Raddatz, but she wasn't going on trust anymore. She was also going to jettison the gut instinct that almost caused her to commit murder. She would start acting like a cop. A cop alone, for sure, but a cop.

And where'd that put her? Nowhere. The freaks were no help. No matter the underground they had going, they didn't know—at least the way Hayden told things—who might be responsible for the killings. And Raddatz really only knew—again, according to story—what the freaks were feeding him. Raddatz had been hiding intel, been chasing tips, but had been able to do little investigating. And what amounted to his investigating unit, the rest of the cadre, they were zero help where they were.

And yet, ironically, the only help Eddi had was

coming from beyond the grave. Soledad. Her journal.
Whether Tashjian was lying to her or not, using her or
not, she'd come into the situation to collect intel—go
back over Raddatz's work, be it honest or otherwise, vivi-
sect it and hand the pieces to another. Like with everything else in her life, Soledad'd come at the chore with
frigid dispassion. Sentimentality is fine when you're reflecting on things. But in Soledad's world attaining a
point of reflection would have been impossible being
sentimental. In the end, for Soledad, sentimentality
wasn't possible anyway.

So here was Eddi hoping what Soledad left behind
would give her the perspective Soledad never had.

Accurately, succinctly, on the pages of her journal
were summaries of Soledad's conversations with Anson's
wife, with Officer Hayes—a notation about him trying
to hit her up. There was her retracing of Anson's steps,
his running from his attacker. The burns to his clothes,
as well as the possibility the attacker had thrown Anson
into a wall, actually tried to beat him with a motorcycle.

That was troubling. A freak displaying multiple abilities. The thing that had taken out Raddatz's old element,
the berserker, had increased strength and speed, but it
was just the meta version of a druggie on PCP. A mutie
that had actual separate, distinct abilities . . . It signaled
the next step in evolution. It harbingered the end of normal humankind.

And wouldn't that be . . . ironic, poetic? As the freaks
were a threat to normals, the superfreaks were now ready
to wipe out the freaks.

But that was just theory. The very first one Eddi arrived at. Really, all that made it substantive was motive. It at least gave meaning to the murders.

Back in the day, in the age of heroes—Age of Heroes—those kinds of murders were easy to explain and so very public. One-Eyed Jack trying to prove he's a badass by taking out the Egyptian. Death Nell trying to pay back Red Dawn for what'd happened to the Burningman. Every endowed evildoer on the planet trying to assassinate Pharos in the belief that if he fell, the Age of Heroes would pancake with him.

In a way, in the wake of San Francisco, that seemed true.

Eddi was getting sentimental. Hadn't she warned herself against it? Jesus, she wished she were Soledad. Maybe the first time she'd ever admitted that. Even to herself. Conflicted, yeah, but Soledad was rarely confused. Never distracted. She had her burden, but she carried her burden. Incorporated it. Eddi for all her toughness didn't take loss well. After May Day her development arrested. She'd forever remain daddy's little girl. And after the loss of Soledad . . . She knew she'd always be trying to prove herself to a woman who couldn't care less what Eddi did or how she did it as long as the execution was fuckup-free.

Christ, Eddi muttered. This wasn't an investigation. This was an exorcism. It was evidence that ignorance was the most blissful thing this side a hit of ketamine.

This was not something Eddi could at the moment deal with.

What she could deal with, what she needed or at least felt as though she needed . . .

Wouldn't it be nice to waste some time with Vin?

The hell of it was, it was so comfortable down there. The shag of Vin's carpet was fairly thick and took Eddi's body well. The lack of conversation stressed her none. And the liquor . . . Eddi'd only had a little, but a little was all that was needed to make her numb. She almost could have envied Vin's existence. But this was a treat for Eddi. A life lived oblivion-style on a daily basis, that's not really living.

Then again . . .

If you're oblivious, how do you know?

The alcohol was slackening her brain, allowing for elevated thought. Eddi felt herself caught in an ever-expanding yet closed loop of logic.

Wasn't good. She needed to pull out of it.

"How do you go on like this, Vin?" Assign negativity to the whole scene. That should crush it.

"Sweet, huh?"

Was like Vin was reading her mind. Or just feeling her true emotion.

Eddi, deflecting: "Not really."

"Haven't moved in forty minutes."

"How would you know? You've been passed out."

"Yeah, right. I'm a little bit too much of a pro for that."

"I'm serious, Vin. How do you take this? It'd be different if you were—"

"If I were what? I were really messed up?"

"Yeah." Not backing down. If anything, sobering some. "A hundred years ago . . . I'll even give you thirty years ago, missing a leg meant something. What you've got lying around here somewhere is almost better than human, and you mope like you were paralyzed from the teeth down."

"I love it when people like you show up telling me about me."

"People who are trying to get you back on your . . ." Feet? She was drunk.

But Vin laughed at the near pun. Made the flesh of his face tight. And for a second, under the bit of flab, behind a growth of beard, Eddi could reconstruct Vin's good looks. Could see in her head again the senior officer who'd given her the nod for MTac. And the guy she'd accidentally shot in the chest.

"Sorry."

"It's just a turn of phrase."

"I mean for shooting you."

From his expression it seemed he actually had to recall the event. It was more that he was confused as to why Eddi would even bring it up.

"I know I probably blurted it a thousand times in the moment," Eddi said. "But I don't know if I ever really looked you in the eye and told you that."

"I'm pretty sure you did."

And then the two of them were quiet for a moment.

And then the two of them were quiet for too long.

"You want to ask me something," Vin said. Then prompted: "Ask." And when Eddi said nothing, he prompted again. "It's all right. Ask. Whatever it is, it can't be worse than that foot crack you were—"

"Do you like me?"

The feeling when Eddi's bullets hit him. The unexpected kick from a hundred mules. The rush of air from his lungs. Vin had that feeling again.

"Do I like you as a person? Do I—"

"You know what I mean."

"Do I . . ."

"Simple question."

"The hell it is."

"Simple answer, then. One word. Two choices. Yes or no."

"Let me ask you a question."

"This is going to go on forever, isn't it?"

"Just one question, then I'll answer yours."

"Remind me what my question was, because I don't even—"

"You're putting on a dodge, Eddi. You asked the question, are you afraid of the answer?"

It was weird to Eddi how perspicacious Vin could be. Always had been. But now that he was still, as in a variation of nearly motionless in life, he seemed even more astute. The one-legged man in the chair was really a sage on the mountain. Maybe he wasn't wasting himself. Maybe the disregard he displayed for every other aspect of his outward being allowed him to focus—and, yeah, this sounded a little ethereal to Eddi's own ears—on his inner self. Ot maybe drinking just took away whatever filter he had left.

It was really repugnant to Eddi that she found herself continually cruising by the conclusion that booze elevated rather than deflated.

"Ask your question," she said to Vin.

"If I said I liked you, would it make you feel good personally, or would it make you feel as though you'd outdone Soledad?"

Eddi's answer was quick and honest. "I don't know."

And Vin didn't need to rejoin the statement, as it was obvious Eddi knew the significance of her answer. He did, however, compliment her candor.

To which Eddi said: "Thank you."

"You're welcome. I like you," Vin said.

Eddi didn't know how to take that since, as Vin had pointed out, she didn't know what she wanted from his answer. She really wished she owned Odin's eye the way Vin seemed to. She didn't. Probably never would. Settled instead on having a drink. Another couple of drinks.

And it got late. Vin slid to sleep right where he sat. Eddi began to drift as well. As she departed, right before her she saw the answer to her original vexation. She'd said as much to Vin, who was beyond response.

Eddi knew what she was hunting.

Know what a No-Contact jacket is?"

Raddatz felt like it was a trick question. He was starting to learn that Eddi seemed tricky by nature. When they were done with "all this," she could do worse than stay with DMI.

"I don't know."

"It's a jacket, actually pretty stylish. Its major accessory is that it can surge an 80,000-kV pulse to anyone who tries to attack the wearer. The attacker gets fried, the person wearing doesn't feel a thing. Know what a Power-Assist suit is?"

"What you wear when your No-Contact jacket's at the cleaners?"

Not that the crack wasn't mildly amusing, but Eddi was on her way to something. "It's a digitally controlled exoskeleton that uses air pressure to enhance the wearer's strength by a factor of six. It's got a level detect to counterbalance the additi—"

"Where's this going?"

"The theory coming in was freaks were being targeted for murder from inside DMI. Made sense. DMI maintains surveillance on freaks, DMI would have the intel to take them out. Except the freaks seemed to have been killed by something with superhuman abilities. So your theory: A freak was going after other freaks. That it happens is a historical fact. But that left motive. That left your freak buddies not knowing what was going on. So, maybe, both theories are wrong. And both are kind of right."

Raddatz and Eddi were in a booth in Raddatz's sports bar. Good a place as any to do some talking away from any curious ears. Between sips of nothing stronger than coffee Raddatz was piecing together what Eddi was handing him. Trying to. Was too anxious to do the work himself. "Explain."

"Metas are like gods on earth. What do normal people do every day, except try to imitate God? Fly in a plane. Cure the common cold. Prenatal transplant surgery . . ."

"We're not after a metanormal? A normal's doing this?"

"A normal who's geared himself up to be more than normal."

"I never heard of this stuff before. Where the hell does a guy get hold of a no-touch—"

"No-Contact jacket. A Power-Assist—"

"Where does he get 'em?"

A cocktail waitress making her rounds. The drinks she was hauling looked reeeeeal tasty to Eddi.

Eddi said: "Might have gotten some prototypes, modified them. Probably, he just cooked up his own version of them."

"By himself, basement workshop, he comes up with stuff the rest of the world's never heard of."

"They've heard of it if they've crawled on the Internet. So, yeah, by himself, basement workshop or garage he does it up. Same as the guys who invented the airplane, the better home computer, the intermittent wiper . . . Same as Soledad did with her O'Dwyer. Look, Raddatz, you know how it works with HIT: Everything goes through committee, gets bid out, the development cost gets jacked up so everybody can get their kickbacks, long ass approval process . . . By the time anything gets done there are new administrators who don't want anything in development from the old regime. So cops like you and me get shoved out onto the street with hardly better than our bare hands. Meanwhile, Soledad's gun is up, running, and evening the score."

"If you're right—"

"I am. That surveillance picture you had of the perp. That sweat suit? Just enough to hide the Power Assist under it. Add some Kevlar to that . . . Think about how your cadre got it. Beaten, ripped apart, burned. Soledad's head snapped nearly clean off. Multiple abilities aren't a trademark of freaks. It's the work of man. I'm right."

Raddatz appreciated the confidence, didn't fight it. "How'd you come up with all this?"

I was getting drunk with the ex-lover of the dead woman I'm in postmortem conflict with when I had a boozy thought about the superhuman/man-made leg he has but won't use? Was easier for Eddi to say: "Just did."

"That doesn't give us who."

"It points us in the right direction. The killer's still got to know his vics. If he killed Fernandez, that was an obvious target. But how did he know about other freaks liv-

ing in hiding? Where would he get that kind of intel?
Who's got the hardest ax to grind, then swing at freaks?"

"Somebody who's DMI."

"Is," Eddi said. "Or was."

You wouldn't believe that someone who could reduce himself to the size of a microbe would be all that dangerous. Wagner didn't. Course, Wagner never thought anything was dangerous. He was such a roughneck. Was that way straight out of the academy. And let me tell you, when I was in the academy—"

"You were talking about—"

"One of those freaks with molecular-reduction abilities. Wouldn't think one of those was particularly dangerous. Wouldn't think that."

Eddi could hardly think at all anymore. More than an hour, almost an hour and a half of stories. Stories from Blake about Blake's days with MTac and Blake with his element going after this kind of freak and that kind of freak, and following that Eddi and Raddatz got a recounting of Blake's exploits on DMI—though Raddatz could hardly recall Blake at DMI when their service overlapped. Blake was an older guy. No legs. Like Vin with an exponent. Good for little but sitting and talking.

And talking.

That's how they differed, Blake and Vin. Vin hardly said a word. Blake wouldn't shut up.

"'You go in,' Wagner says," Blake said, "'and you step on the thing.' And that's what Wagner tried to do."

"Detective Blake . . ." Eddi tried to put a stop to things.

Didn't work. "So we're inside the building, Wagner steps on the freak . . . only, the freak shrinks even smaller, gets inside Warner's leg—"

"Detective . . ."

"Then expands again. Expands inside Wagner's leg. Can you imagine having a man pop out of your leg?"

Nardi—Frank Nardi, the ex–DMI cop they'd talked to before Blake—had been an easier interview. No nonsense. To the point. Helpful. Jack MacKay had been the easiest. MacKay was dead. Suicide. And there was Ed Blake and there were interviews yet to come with Houris Tynes and Marty Carlin. Raddatz and Eddi had profiled their suspect: ex–DMI cop. Ex allowed him a free hand to do his dirty chores and ex because the vics could all be cross-referenced with a DMI watch list that was four years stale. The suspect had no access to new intel—with a background in or knowledge of special weapons. That meant cops who'd worked A or D platoons or HIT.

Five guys fit the profile. Nardi, MacKay, Blake, Tynes and Carlin.

Wasn't MacKay.

Nardi had been easy, but maybe he was too easy. Too prepped. A guy with all the answers and ready to give 'em. To Eddi that made him hinky.

Blake wasn't hinky. Blake wasn't their guy. Unless he was out boring freaks to death.

Tynes was a strong possible, but if she had to take bets, Eddi was ready to bet on Carlin. Carlin's package . . . it was . . . well, it was interesting.

"I'll tell you what it was like having a guy pop out of his leg."

"Hold on one second." Raddatz did a hand-to-pocket, pulled out his cell. "Hello?" He listened, listened . . . "Jesus . . ." To Eddi: "It's Donatell."

Donatell? Donatell was dead.

Raddatz was up and moving as he repocketed his phone. "Gotta go." A couple of pats to Blake's shoulder.

Blake: "Bad one?"

"Metal morpher in Carson."

"Plastic," Blake said. "Come at it loaded up with plastic and the thing'll run from you like a politician runs from responsibility."

Raddatz, Eddi headed out. Thanked Blake for the tip. Left Blake with a smile. The knowledge there were still cops out there kicking superass.

Outside the house, walking to their car, Eddi to Raddatz: "Donatell?"

"First name I thought of."

"Could've just told Blake we had to go."

"Guy's got nobody. He wants to tell stories."

"So you take a fake phone call. You're a softy."

"Not about being soft. When I get to be like Blake, stuck on a shelf and forgotten, I hope somebody leaves me with the illusion that what I did mattered."

Now you fucking come? Now you're here? Where were you when I needed you? Where were you when he was pounding on me?"

Ramona Carlin sneered, bit at the thumb of the hand that held her cigarette that drifted smoke into her eyes. Red. Bleary. The redness, the bleariness were the cume effect of all the cigarettes she'd used methodically since turning fifteen. Twenty-seven hard years ago. She waited for Raddatz and Eddi to say something, defend themselves. She waited for them to open their mouths so she could take their words and shove them right back down their throats.

And they were hip to that. Same as any other wronged citizen who couldn't understand why they got such crappy police work for their tax dollars, Raddatz and Eddi got that Ramona was just warming up her rant. They didn't bother saying anything. And their passive-aggressiveness just got Ramona all the hotter.

"How many times did I call the cops, how many times did I try to get you involved? What'd you do?"

Nothing from Raddatz and Eddi.

Eddi figured Ramona to be in her early forties. Her looks offered up the proposition that she was years older. The smoking didn't help the texture of her skin. But the wrinkles her face displayed were more like stress fractures. Hard to tell in the two and a half minutes Eddi had been acquainted with Ramona if she had been born a touch high-strung. What was clear was that her years with her husband had done nothing to help her become any less anxious.

His package: Carlin had been with a Harbor MTac element that served a warrant on a firestarter. Had attempted to serve a warrant on a firestarter. Two of the element ended up a slick of ash. One of the operator's legs was charred up like an overroasted chicken leg. And Carlin, most of the right side of his body between neck and torso looked like some kind of sick joke of nature. A patch of something that wasn't flesh, wasn't human. It was a scarred, twisted, nasty, barren wasteland. His arm was the limb of a tree burned and burned and burned but was, in the end, too stubborn to fall away.

After that, Marty Carlin was useless for MTac.

He was good for DMI. For a while. Then there was an incident. Eddi and Raddatz didn't know what the incident was. The facts were left out of Carlin's package. As a rule when shit goes down, suspendable shit, and the cops who are doing the suspending think it's best even sealed records shouldn't reflect the shit, the shit was serious. Seriously bad. Potentially damaging to the department image-wise. Legal-wise.

However it was, whatever he'd done, the PD didn't think Carlin was fit for duty.

To Eddi's way of thinking, unfit equaled unbalanced.

An assumption affirmed by poor Ramona. Hard enough being married to a cop. Hard enough being married to a cop who decides to go MTac. But being married to one who barely survives serving a warrant on a freak. Then he apparently goes nuts. Then he, again apparently, decides he wants to use you to work off some misplaced aggression . . . can't beat the freaks, might as well beat the missus.

Eddi could forgive Ramona for her nature. Forgive, yeah, but that still didn't make the woman any easier to deal with.

Ramona: "You didn't do anything, that's what you did. You didn't do anything because he was a cop. I can't even . . ." Hands shaking as she tried to take a drag on her smoke. She'd worked herself into a state. "He detached the retina in my left eye. Can't even see out of it. Can barely see out of it," she modified. "That's how hard he used to hit me. One goddamn arm, and he could still . . . And I call the police, and they're all 'You two just work it out. You don't want any trouble.' You're the ones who didn't want trouble. You were supposed to arrest him! That's what you're supposed to do, a man beats his wife. But he was a cop, so you all didn't do shit!"

Nothing from Raddatz and Eddi.

Ramona stared, stared at them. Kept her anger to do some aikido; redirect Raddatz's and Eddi's compassion against them. But they gave her nothing.

Ramona gave to them: "Hell with you."

She moved from them, across the room, sat down. Her non-cigarette-smoking hand ran over her face.

"We're sorry for what happened to you." Raddatz, his

tone was calm. Assuring. "We're sorry other people didn't take action."

"Other people." Hand still manipulating her face, buffing her agitation, Ramona's words were slurred. "Always has to be other people. Nobody wants to take responsibility."

Addressing Ramona, but talking of things more sizable than her: "That's not always the case," Raddatz said.

"Yeah? Are you here to do something about what Marty did to me? Is that why you came around?"

It wasn't. Ramona knew it wasn't. Raddatz knew there was no point in lying that things were otherwise.

"I, you know, I stood by him." Ramona was cooling. Winding down. Her emotional fission had left her spent. "It was always about, our whole marriage was about what *he* wanted. Being a cop; that's what he wanted. Never mind what I . . . It wasn't about money. He could've been a FedEx guy for all I cared. What I cared about: that he came home every night. I cared he didn't have gang thugs taking shots at him because they were high, and that's what they do when they're high. But Marty wanted to be a cop. He wanted to be a cop, so I was there for him. Had an accident after a high-speed chase, fractured his pelvis—"

Eddi: "Mrs. Carlin—"

If she heard Eddi trying to cut her off, Ramona didn't care. "When I went to the hospital, I would not cry in front of him. Wouldn't. Would not. I wasn't going to let him know how I worried. I wasn't going to, I wasn't going to let me being scared for him keep him from what he wanted. And then he wanted . . . the day he came home and told me he wanted to be one of those antifreak cops . . . I just, I sat there and I stared at him . . . When do you ever get it in your head you want to do something like that? You read the papers, you see what's going on, how people are dying going after those . . . ," repugnant as she could make it, "*things,* and the person you love tells you that's how he wants to make a living?"

A long drag killed her cigarette. Ramona stubbed out the butt. Took another from the pack. Did not light it.

Ramona said: "You just . . . I mean, I shut down. I did. Might as well have told me he was going to kill himself. Somebody tells you that, how do you not turn off a part of you to them?"

Raddatz wondered. If somebody asked Helena, would she say the same about him?

Ramona: "But for a while I went on, like, okay, maybe he's going to be all right. Maybe nothing's going to happen to him. It wasn't even . . . maybe it was two months before . . ."

Ramona put the cigarette in her mouth. Took it out. It remained unlit.

"That thing," Ramona said, "whatever it was, it gave Marty third-degree burns over fifty-seven percent of him. I remember that. I remember the doctors telling me what percent of him was burned, and I remember thinking: How do you even measure that? That they knew how much of him was . . . how do you calculate that when so much of him was beyond just burned. Anyway, he lived. Obviously. But Marty, he should've died 'cause that was the end of him. As a human being he was done. He didn't even look human, and that's me, that's his wife saying that. He got moody and he got angry and he started . . ."

Ramona touched her left occipital lobe. Then, finally, she lit up her smoke. "Called the cops, but you all didn't do anything."

Raddatz, Eddi; they remained settled. Made sure Ramona had gotten it all out, had let all her emotion spill.

She sat. She smoked. Seemed as though she was done.

Raddatz looked to Eddi.

Eddi said: "I'm sorry for what happened to you. I'm sorry the right people didn't get involved."

Ramona nodded. Sarcastic. "Yes. You said."

Eddi said: "But your husband, your ex-husband—"

"Still is. Never put the papers through."

Ramona took a drag on her cigarette.

"Do you know where he is?" Raddatz asked.

Ramona looked at her cigarette. Rolled it in her fingers.

That bit of active inaction, Ramona's irresolution. It was something Raddatz on domestic violence calls . . . as a cop he'd seen it before. But every time, in every circumstance, he could not process the divide between logic and emotion. Her husband had treated her like a punching bag. Her body, and mentally too. She'd screamed for help, screamed for it. Claimed she had. Now when someone comes around looking to wrap the bastard up, someone offers her the payback she'd been wanting . . . she rolls her cigarette in her fingers, has to think about things?

Eddi got it.

Eddi was blunt with it: "You still love him."

Ramona asked: "Are you in love?"

In exchange of the question Eddi gave hesitation.

Ramona gave a bit of a laugh, a bit of a sneer. "You

can come in here and ask me what you want. I ask you something simple . . ."

"We're asking what we're asking as part of a police investigation." Raddatz put authority behind a statement that was mostly false.

"Do I look like I give a damn?" To Eddi: "Yes or no; are you in love?"

"There was a guy. A cop. He was killed."

"But you still love him."

"I think the circumstance is extremely different."

"The hell it is. If it was death, or a well-placed blow, emotions don't care. They stay with you. Your man died. How you feel about him is unkillable. A guy like Marty . . . he hit me, and I felt it. I don't mean it hurt. I felt his touch. So what'd he do wrong? This time."

"At this point," Raddatz said, "he's only a person of interest. We just want to talk with him."

Ramona wasn't going for that. "Yeah, right. You just want to talk, so I should just give him up."

"You should give him up because it's the right thing to do."

Ramona nodded, but it wasn't like she was acknowledging agreement.

"When he hit you," Eddi said, "maybe you felt something, and it was . . . I don't know. You took it. For whatever reason, you took it. Your choice. There are people being hurt and they don't have a choice about it. They're dying. They're being murdered. If your husband's got any information, we need it."

"You know what I said to him when it was over." Ramona talked on like whatever Eddi had to say wasn't worth listening to. "I told him he was a waste. I told him everything he thought he was, was nothing. He wanted to be a freak cop, and all he ended up was a freak not even good enough for going after his own kind. And he told me, you know what he said? He told me I was right. Said that, and just walked out that door. As many times as he hit me, when it came to it, I knew just how to hit him. That's the thing about being so in love with somebody. It gives you the secret knowledge you need to destroy them. You know the queer thing? Whatever you want Marty for, I think he's just trying to prove he's not nothing."

Eddi and Raddatz couldn't argue the point.

"We don't talk much. Every once in a while he sends me a letter, a little note. Tells me how sorry he is about what happened. That's what he calls beating me, abusing me. 'What happened.' I don't write him back. I'm not afraid of him, you know. I'm not." Ramona let that hang for a moment, then: "I think if I did, I think if I talked to him . . . love; it's just unkillable."

Eddi rolled the paper around in her fingers. A talisman. Carlin's address.

"How you want to play it?" she asked. "Go after Carlin or take a run at Tynes first?"

"Finish up with Carlin."

"Can we get any kind of backup?"

Raddatz shook his head to the negative. "We get it by telling MTac we know what we know how?"

"Same way DMI always gets backup."

"By presenting a chain of investigation. Look, if we were going after a freak, maybe we could count on the review being lax. But to go after a normal, an ex-cop who's killing freaks, you don't think questions are going to get asked? And that's if we could even put Carlin on this for sure. All we've got now is a guy who's hinky."

"You don't like him for this?"

"I love him for it. But that doesn't prove nothing, and it doesn't get us backup."

"Then some of your superfriends?"

"You've met my super*friend*."

Eddi wasn't ready for Raddatz's lack of engagement with the meta community. "That's it?"

"They're careful."

"They don't trust you."

"They won't let me get into a position where I could be forced to compromise them."

"Like I said: They don't trust you."

Raddatz gave a shrug, let it go. "We'd still have the same problem we've always had: How good would that be for the other side that metanormals are acting as vigilantes?"

"How good is it going to be if we get killed and Carlin gets away?"

"He's human. No matter what he can do, he's a normal. What was wrong with the Age of Heroes: It wasn't that the metanormals were trying to act like gods. It was that we forgot how to stand up for ourselves. This one's ours. We've gotta take the lead."

There was logic there. Logic wasn't what swayed Eddi. What swayed her, when Raddatz added: "What Carlin may have done, the people he might've killed: I've got no problem paying him back for that on my own."

Eddi thought of Soledad. She didn't have a problem handing out payback either.

The capper from Raddatz: "You were going to kill me. I'd at least like to know you don't hate me so much you wouldn't give the same courtesy to somebody else."

She gave a laugh.

"What?" Raddatz asked.

"Me protecting freaks, that's funny as hell."

"Life's queer like that sometimes."

"Yeah." And then Eddi said: "Normal or not, if we're going to do this, there's something I want to have."

She got herself killed. I'm not going to let other cops go down the same way." This was a hard, hard lie from Eddi. Hard to give.

Just as hard for Bo to take. Bo wasn't accepting it. "Soledad didn't get herself killed." His voice was even, nearly quiet. His tone was unmistakable: Shut up. Go away.

Eddi would not. "Her gun didn't work. It failed to fire. She died."

"That happens with sidearms."

"It wasn't supposed to happen with Soledad's. That it happened with an experimental weapon—"

"How many freaks has that thing brought down?"

"That it happened with an experimental weapon suggests the gun shouldn't be standard issue."

Bo, head ticking side to side: "How long have you been with DMI?"

"What does that have to—"

"A couple of weeks? A month? You talk like one of them."

"Wherever I'm assigned, I do my job. If you have

prejudice for one division over another, then that's your issue." She was plain, simple. Direct and unflinching.

Her facade was. Behind that: Real clear to Eddi was her first call. Going after a speed freak, too anxious with her trigger, too anxious about going BAMF. Ending up sailing a couple of slugs into Vin. When her world was falling apart, when she thought on the good end of things she was facing Admin discipline, on the bad end she was looking at discharge from the force, who was there to back her up? Bo. Soledad and Bo. Now Eddi was selling Soledad out and shining Bo on, and as far as Eddi could tell, the deceptions were only starting.

But then . . .

Someone had killed freaks, had killed some of the best freak-hunting cops on the PD. Had done it with harsh science. Harsh science was needed to fight back. Soledad's gun was needed, and Eddi could not be honest about her reasons. She'd already bitten a guy's ear to the cartilage and come *this* close to putting bullets into the back of another guy's head. So a couple of lies, what were a couple of lies even to and about people she really cared for?

Coming forward in his chair, leaning on his desk, locking eyes with Eddi: "Then how about this: How long have you been with DMI that you get to come around giving orders?"

"How long have you been 10-David you can't follow procedure? I'm not giving orders. I'm conducting an investigation."

"On Soledad's piece? That'd be for A Platoon."

"If Soledad's weapon had been issued by the department of the armorer. It wasn't, and it wasn't being tested under the auspices of HIT either. If it's an investigation pertaining to metanormal activity, then it belongs to DMI. The question is, did the freak"—Eddi made sure she threw in the word; she'd noticed she was using "metanormal" a lot. A lot more than most cops. She figured it'd be smart to make sure she talked the talk—"Soledad was surveying have some kind of an effect on her sidearm? The incident happened while she was detached to DMI, so it's a question for DMI to answer." Eddi was coming off like a five-hundred-dollar-an-hour lawyer. So slick she slipped and slid.

Problem was that cops hated lawyers, and Bo was cop to the bone.

"Then let me ask things this way . . ." That drawl of his made his subtext read: Maybe you think you can shine me, but I don't shine. "How long have you been at DMI *you* should be handling the situation?"

"I'm going to be fair."

A snide laugh from Bo.

"If the gun works, I want to know. If it doesn't, I want to know that too."

"Soledad always figured you were envious of her."

Beyond her playacting, Eddi bristled. She was hearing that too much; hearing people thought she was in competition with Soledad. Enough that it annoyed her. Enough that it might be true.

"Let's face things. You, well, you idolized her. Wanted to be her."

"If you're trying to make me feel something in particular . . ."

What Eddi felt: her breast. The sting of her tattoo. As fresh as the day she had it etched on the flesh of her chest.

"If you can't be as good as Soledad, might as well discredit her."

"You're better than that, Bo. I know you are. No reason to attack me. I miss her too."

Bo chewed the air in his mouth, chewed at it . . .

Bo asked: "Is there something I should know? As in why you're forcing the issue?"

To keep Bo at arm's length. To keep him from getting involved. Eddi was being the way she was because when things went south, and most likely they would, Eddi didn't want Bo heading down with her.

"These are . . . they're unique times. 'Unique' is hardly a strong enough word. All of us have to work from the gut now and figure out right and wrong later." It was veiled, but Eddi was speaking a truth beyond the subject. "But that's the point: later. Maybe we'll look back and see we made a mess of some things. A lot of things. But I'd rather be around five, ten years down the road to apologize *then*, knowing we bought ourselves the time *now* to be sorry about anything at all."

Veiled, yeah, but truth. And Bo was the sort, truth he always had to yield to.

"Okay, Eddi," Bo said. "Okay."

G Platoon had its own evidence lockup. Superfluous. For most crimes, if they went to trial, there might be questions. Reasonable doubt. Did that guy really rape that chick? Did that woman really pour gasoline on her husband while he slept, then toss a match on after? Ladies and gentlemen of the jury, evidence.

With freaks?

With freaks, if you were a freak, if you got caught being a freak—flying or shooting energy from your fingers or morphing metal—that and a little DNA sample positive with a meta gene was all the more evidence anyone really needed. "Anyone" being agents of the law.

So the evidence lockers for MTac were really more like souvenir storage. Leftover junk from calls gone bad. Slagged helmets. Uniforms shredded by animated steel. Punctured by hand-slung projectiles.

And there was Soledad's gun. And from her workroom in Parker Center all the prototypes, sketches and theory work she'd done in adapting her O'Dwyer. Eddi wasn't ready for that. It was nearly obsessive-compulsive the details Soledad put into the designing and the modifying and reworking and adapting the weapon. Yes, Eddi was aware Soledad had the background for it. Studied tech at Northwestern. But it was impressive taking into consideration that Soledad was still "just" a cop. Not a hardcore techie. Not a scientist. Merely a chick with a gun who wanted to make a difference. Made Eddi angry when she considered neither the department of the armorer nor the money drain that was HIT had come close to putting together what Soledad had. It just made Eddi feel all the shittier for what she was perpetrating.

Put that aside, she told herself. Eddi told herself she'd deal with her ill feelings, her guilt . . .

Later.

Right now she wanted to do something for Soledad: find the thing that killed her. Make sure it never killed again.

Action.

People like action. To hell with sitting and thinking and planning and considering. People want guns coughing, muzzles flashing, random objects taking bullet hits and fragmenting spectacularly. Balls-to-the-walls action. Which is why, you go to a movie, you hardly ever see police doing police work—filling out duty logs, filing reports, working phones. You just see cops kicking in doors and letting their guns do the verbalizing. And miraculously, no matter movie cops never seem to do surveillance or shadow a suspect or engage in an ongoing stakeout, they always seem to know exactly which door to kick in. They never seem to let their guns get verbal with the wrong person.

It was getting cool at night. Cool for LA. Eddi's blood had thinned since she'd moved West from Philly. She kept the car windows rolled against the chill. Except sitting in a car for hours with another person's got a way of making the air rank. Stale. So every once in a while Eddi had to crack the window, let fresh air inside. But that just made the car cold. She'd have to close the window. The air'd get stale. She had to do her little ballet all over again.

Sixteen hours of that. Sixteen hours and twenty-three minutes of rolling the window up and down while she eyed Carlin's little house on Folsom Street.

Not really sixteen-plus hours continually. Her and Raddatz had been swapping little naps in shifts when they hadn't been eating shitty drive-thru food, when they hadn't been just staring at Carlin's house looking for signs of life that hadn't presented themselves in the previous three-quarters of a day.

Heading for the seventeenth hour, things were going to get hard. Eddi was going to get . . . she *was* antsy. If you're a cop, there's only so much sitting and staring and bad-food eating you can do before you want to kick in doors and have conversations spoken in hot ounces. Before you become like any other paying customer who wants to see some action.

Eddi poked Raddatz in the shoulder. He was fully awake instantly. Eddi gave a quick update on how little the situation had changed.

She said: "Nothing."

Raddatz nodded, looked to the house. A little place at the end of a cul-de-sac. Wood that looked weakened. Paint that was worn. A yard full of junk. That's what filled the yard. Junk. Unrecognizable beyond anything more than metal that had rusted reddish orange. The place was a dive. A deep dive where a guy who was sinking same as a weighted rock would end up.

"What do we do?" Eddi hated asking that. Made her sound like a newbie. A good cop would just sit tight. But

Eddi was hoping Raddatz was getting antsy too. "Haven't seen a thing. What do you want to do?"

"Guy's got no job, no life. No reason for him to go in and out of the place. Not if he's stocked. He could hole up for days. Longer."

"Or he could be out killing freaks." Even when she used the word, she was using it with less conviction. Putting on a show.

"Could be doing that."

"Only one way to know for sure."

Raddatz checked his watch.

"More than sixteen hours," Eddi informed.

Raddatz shook his head, told Eddi that wasn't what he was thinking.

"Ought to call my wife."

"If you want."

"More trouble than it's worth."

"The inquisitive kind."

"Never learned to be a good cop's wife."

Eddi, lightly sarcastic: "That's tough; you having to settle for a good regular wife."

Just for a second Raddatz took his eyes off the house, looked to Eddi. Gave a smile. "You'd like her."

"You think?" Eddi asked, but didn't really care. Wouldn't let herself care. Getting wrapped up in Raddatz's personal life was counterproductive. What she cared about, what she had to focus on: Carlin and how they were going to handle him.

"She'd like you." Raddatz looked back for the house. "You're both no-nonsense, you know? That's the thing with her, she never—"

"Helena, yeah?"

"Yeah. Helena. She never went in for the bullshit. Like I said, I could do without her playing twenty questions all the time, but you gotta like a woman who just eliminates the bullshit."

"I'd take that in most people."

"I had no interest in marrying most people. I found it in her, I said that's the one. You should get to know her. After this is done, it'd be good of you to get to know her."

Oh, shit. Eddi knew what was going on. Oh, shit. Get to know her. Get to know Helena. "After this is done," get to know Helena. What Raddatz was saying without saying: After we do the job, if I don't make it, go have a conversation with my wife. Give her all the post-death clack: He was a good guy, an honest cop, he loved the hell out of you . . .

Eddi hated that kind of thinking, prepping for things going way south. It invited bad luck. Bad luck had a way of spilling around. She didn't want to have to have a conversation with Raddatz's wife. Raddatz's widow. The only thing she wanted less was for someone to have a similar conversation with . . .

It came to Eddi if the job did go south, if she didn't make it, who the hell would miss her? Her mo—

No.

Vin she had a relationship with. To some degree. Maybe a couple of other cops'd miss her for a while before she was reduced to a photo on a memorial wall. Something schoolkids on field trips would look at with mild curiosity.

More and more Eddi realized how similar she was to Soledad. How much of that was nature, how much was nurture?

Moving off the thought, moving back to what's what: "How do you want to play things?"

"Knock, see who's home."

"A guy who can kill freaks, and we're just going to—"

"We're two regular normal humans coming around to ask questions. He lets us in, we look around, see what we're dealing with."

"Because as psychos go he's one of the nice ones. He's got manners and all that."

"You're the one getting antsy."

"You're not?"

Raddatz, a smirk. Appreciative. He asked: "No one answers, are you ready to go in?"

"Whatever's next, I'm good for it."

"You'd really like my wife."

The third knock on the door got the same response as Raddatz's first two. None. Except for the bark of the dog on the inside of the house. The shades were drawn. Raddatz and Eddi couldn't see inside, couldn't see what kind of dog it was. The barking, its low octave, said it was sizable. Ill tempered. Pit or English bull terrier. Rottweiler.

The situation—the two of them standing around in plain sight for a returning Carlin should he be out—was less than good.

Raddatz pointed that out to Eddi.

Eddi agreed. Asked: "So?"

"I'd say bust in. Except for the dog."

"Not a problem." Eddi unholstered her gun.

"You are not going to shoot a dog."

"It's just a dog."

"You are not going to shoot a damn—"

"For Christ's sake, I get you've gone soft for freaks. It's a dog!"

Holding up a finger, slowing Eddi down: "That dog didn't do anything to anybody. It's got nothing to do with the job."

"You want in the house?"

Raddatz took a moment. Pressed his face to the front window, juked to see what little he could see past a slit in the shade. What he could see: straight through the house to a back door. "Break open the back door. The thing comes out around back, we head in the front."

"Nuts."

The two stood around awhile. Long enough Eddi got that Raddatz wasn't altering his position on things.

Eddi: "Freaking nuts."

"We knocked. A couple of times. If Carlin's here, he already knows we're looking for him. What happens next happens on the other side of this door, and I'm not letting a dog keep me from getting to it."

Shaking her head: "Easier just to shoot it."

"Never had a dog, have you?"

"Never."

"Talk to me after you've had one."

"I'll go around back, make the run."

"I'm missing my hand, not my legs. I can make the run."

"You can make the run like an old guy. I'll do it."

As she was heading around to the back of the house, as she was trudging around junk, Raddatz said to Eddi's back, his nature only kinda good: "Screw you, Aoki."

"Got the feeling I'm doing it to myself."

*   *   *

I'll make the run. That's what she'd told Raddatz. But Eddi hadn't factored in, hadn't even considered . . . how fast do dogs really run? They were tight on turns. They had, after all, four-wheel steering, so to speak. And Carlin had a yard full of shit. Crossing through the yard, Eddi saw the junk was pipes and rusted chairs, discarded appliances. A lawn mower that had given up the fight against grass that was wild with weeds and uncontrolled growth and ultimately very little grass. Eddi had to pick her way through all that to get to the rear door. There would be no time to step careful on the way back around.

Just pop the glass, open the door . . .

Yeah. Sure.

Her right hand brushed the butt of Soledad's holstered piece. Its action echoing her true belief: It'd be so much easier to . . .

Eddi's hand quit its fantasizing, picked up a ruler-length pipe from Carlin's junglized yard.

She schooled herself: Pop the glass, clean the frame real quick so you don't slash yourself to the bone reaching in, flip the lock. Hopefully *lock* and not *locks*. Open the door. Run. Well, dodge all the crap in the yard and run.

The simple plan was getting amended by the second.

She couldn't see into the house from the back door any better than she could from the front. But what she could hear was Raddatz pounding on the front door, distracting the dog. The dog barking.

The fact that their operation thus far came down to them playing head games on a dog . . .

With the pipe Eddi popped the glass . . .

Raddatz, she thought, better have that front door open.

"Raddatz," she yelled.

Eddi swirled the pipe over the wood frame, cleaned it of glass. Hand in, she reached around and threw the dead bolt.

Already there was the scratch of claws on linoleum. The dog wasn't barking, it was snarling.

"Raaaddatz!"

Door open. Run.

Down the porch to the weeds.

Behind her the dog crashed the door.

An obstacle course lay ahead of Eddi. The pipes, the equipment, the mower, lawn chairs, a legless table . . . more shit than she could remember. More junk than she could easily navigate.

Not the dog.

The dog wasn't having any trouble, not from the sound of its growl. The thunder—yeah, the rhythm—of thudding paws on dry earth that was like a coke-high drum solo done up midconcert Keith Moon–style. It was gaining by the millisecond. Eddi's estimation of distance would have to rely on audible approximation. No way she was turning around. No way—no matter that she thought, honest-to-God thought, she could feel the dog's breath on her ankles—was she turning for a look. Pillar of salt? Piece of meat. Assume it's right there, she told herself. She told herself to run her ass off like the animal's right there. That, and keep from getting snagged on the mower or the lawn chairs or the pipes or the—

A hot hurt to her lower leg. She'd cut too close to something and it'd cut back. She was thinking when she should be running and moving and dodging. She wanted to think about something, forget the pain in her leg: the dog. Think about how bad that would hurt. How bad would a mauling hurt? Think about that, and book.

There was Soledad's gun . . .

No time to pull, to turn, to take aim.

More fire to her leg.

The dog?

The dog was still chasing, closing.

Phantom pain she was feeling. Or maybe another jagged laceration. Worry about it later. Once in the house or tomorrow or anytime, Eddi told herself, when she wasn't getting chased.

The porch.

Eddi grabbed right hand to railing, let centripetal force swing her. Went up the stairs, dived for the threshold like a wideout stretching to make the goal line. She crossed it.

"Close the fucking—"

Raddatz was already on it. Eddi heard the door slam shut, the lock get thrown. Raddatz wasn't taking chances.

Eddi lay, sucked air.

"Should've let me shoot it."

Eddi lay, looked at her leg. Fabric of her pant torn. Flesh of her ankle rent.

"Should've—"

"Heard you."

Hand out, Raddatz helped heft Eddi up.

Eddi went to the door, peeled back the blind, looked to the dog jumping up, at the window. Throwing foamy spit at the window. A beast. It was much more beast than domesticated animal. Guessing as much as she knew for certain: It looked like a mastiff. It looked like how she'd imagined one of the hounds of the Baskervilles when she'd discovered reading could actually be fun, not just a chore, back in her senior year of high school. Snout bleeding from where it tried to get through the pane Raddatz had shattered to do the B and E. That was its freshest wound. Flesh a jigsaw of scars except where its fur was bare to the skin from lashings, from burnings, from beatings. The sadistic fuck. Carlin didn't have Ramona to slug around anymore. He'd gotten himself a new whipping horse.

Jumping. Snarling, no matter its slashed snout.

"The dog," Eddi said as it did all it could to get through the door to kill her, "that thing was bred for hating." She felt sorry she hadn't killed it. She felt like she oughta put it out of its misery.

"Come on," Raddatz said to her. "Come on."

From her holster Eddi took Soledad's appropriated gun, flicked the safety off. Unlike just about every other gun in the world, the piece audibly confirmed it was hot.

"What kind of load you using?" Raddatz asked.

"Soledad's red clip. Slugs tipped with Semtex. Explodes on contact, so do yourself a favor and don't get caught in the cross fire."

"Do me a favor and don't get me caught in one."

The outside of the house—the junk, the weedy yard—was barely a primer for the level of charm the interior had been allowed to degenerate to. Newspapers everywhere. Magazines everywhere. Everywhere there were dirty dishes. Rotting food. Unseen but smelled was excrement. Maybe from the dog. Maybe from Carlin. Whichever. The stench was a sock in the face square to the nose. It was a funk so rank it actually hurt. The only smell Eddi had ever taken in more putrid was the stink of a decaying, rancid, bloated, gaseous floater she once had to stand watch over off the Santa Monica pier. She was a newbie. The vets made her do it, made her mind the body. The vets wanted to have some fun. Make Eddi puke. Eddi was not about to toss in front of "the boys." Eddi stood there. Took the smell. Told "the boys" if LACFSC wasn't around soon to pick up the body, they should order her some lunch. She'd eat it right where she was. The boys fucked with her much less after that. And if it weren't for *that,* if it weren't for *that* smell giving her a primer on how bad something could reek, at that moment Eddi might real well have lost it. Thank God, too, for the shaded windows of Carlin's house. The California sun roasting the rot in the joint would've made the air toxic as alien atmosphere.

"Nice," Eddi said, looking around. "Early American psycho."

"Guy's nuts," Raddatz assessed. "But that doesn't make him a freak killer."

"You're not thinking he's clean?"

Raddatz shook his head to the negative. "I just want to know it for a fact. Especially before he comes home and we have to figure how to explain breaking and entering on a guy just for being supersloppy."

"He beats his wife, beats his dog, lives like he thrives on shit—"

"You almost dropped me for the wrong reason. Let's just be sure."

Raddatz, Jesus . . . toeing the line between unilateral action and moral justification, to Eddi he was coming off like a badassed Quaker.

Again: "Let's just be sure."

Raddatz pointed Eddi to a room off the entry that was, really, just a main trash area. He indicated he'd have a look into the kitchen.

All the while just outside, the dog—that poor kill-beast—barking. Snarling. Growling. Bleeding.

The room off the entry: papers, magazines and stench. Standard decor. And, in a corner, a tribe of roaches. The whole of it potential evidence to be sifted through.

And here was Eddi without any rubber gloves.

She started looking through some papers on a table. Might as well start high and work her way down. The paper at the very top of the mound was dated almost two years previously. So which was it: Carlin hadn't touched a paper in two years, or he read—actually sat and *read*— old papers? Eddi figured whichever was the crazier.

Digging through the mound: A paper sixteen months old. One that was outdated by another nineteen months. Five months. Sixteen, again. Four. Ten. Seven months. Not one fresher than three months. And not one that offered particular insight, that indicated a particular frame of mind. Nothing, that Eddi could see, regarding freak killings or MTac operations or cops getting hobbled by muties or obsessive consideration of any of that. Nothing more significant than yesterday's news.

Was there something else to be found? Elaborate plans for world domination merely left lying around? That was comic book stuff. That was the kind of thing La Femme would have done to taunt Nightshift back in the day. It was the kind of thing disorganized serial killers did because they were too crazy, too sloppy in mind to do otherwise. But even the kookiest of criminals, shy of their desire for direct notoriety, generally liked being free of incarceration too much to just leave a pointing finger for the cops.

Still . . .

Eddi kept looking. A *Chicago Trib* from eight months prior. An old *Time* magazine. An older *Better Homes and Gardens. Southern Living. Harper's.* A Chinese take-out menu.

A paper fetish. Maybe Carlin just had a paper fetish. And a metal fetish to go with his junk fetish. All around, as there'd been in the yard, were pipes and rods and siding. Welded. Twisted.

Art?

Didn't look like art. At least, if it had artistic value, it wasn't apparent to Eddi's eye.

Eddi, yelling across the space to Raddatz: "Anything?"

Raddatz yelling back: "Nothing."

The thing about metal sculpting, to Eddi it always seemed like a loopy kind of art—word used loosely—in the first place. You've got paint, you've got pencils. Clay. Even marble if you're desperate to chisel something. And marble work looked good when you were done with it. Looked classic. Metalwork? Looked like something the stoner kids did in some high school detention class. And this, what Carlin had . . . ? This crap—this crap on top of all the other crap he had lying around—was just . . . welded. Twisted. Bent and rent.

And Carlin called this . . .

Not art.

It wasn't art.

Twisted metal. Melted metal. It was practice.

Picking up a pipe, turning to Raddatz, moving for him: "Hey, this might be—"

The floor became ten thousand killer bees. In its instantaneous fragmentation it formed a swarm. Tiny piece of flying oak. Inanimate, but seeming to possess an instinct for delivering pain. The swarm rode a concussive wave for Eddi, stung her with their splinters. Slashed her with their jagged edges. Bare flesh was lacerated flesh. Bleeding flesh. Eddi's hands went on the defensive, jumped up, sacrificed themselves to protect her face from what hit with the force of a good-sized gas explosion. A small bomb. What it really was: Carlin irrupting up into the room from a crawl space. Up into the room *through* the floor.

His maximum arrival kicked Eddi back. She went limp, took the force. Didn't fight it, let it ride her down. Hit the floor. More unforgiving wood waiting for her.

The moment she landed Eddi was already making a move. Trying to get up. She did a simultaneous self-diagnosis. Nothing broken. Nothing broken so bad as to gimp her. Probably, she was cut pretty nastily on her exposed flesh; the splintered wood having worked like razors over her skin. Felt warm blood flowing from cuts. She didn't feel any hurt. Adrenaline was blocking her lower pain receptors. It was revving her heart, getting her ready for a fight.

She tried to look, tried to get her bearings. Eddi's right eye was functionless. Wouldn't open.

She hoped that was the deal: Her eye'd caught some wood and refused to uncover itself. The alternative was the eye was punctured. Or gone altogether. Either way at the minute it was useless. Staying alive meant working with the one good eye she had left.

Eddi was twisting, bringing Soledad's piece around. Taking aim . . .

Across the room: gray sweat-suited, hood up. Carlin. Carlin was bear-hugging Raddatz. Raddatz, without a weapon, was trying to fight, trying to fight back. Fighting back amounted to good-for-nothing flailing. Weak slapping with his hook and hand. Carlin's grip would not yield. Beneath the drape of his sweats, Carlin's Power-Assist suit. The hiss of air pumps. His grip constricted. The pain inflicted feebled further Raddatz's slaps. Then from Carlin, for good measure, an electric shock settled Raddatz the fuck down.

And Raddatz was right where Eddi didn't want him to be: in the line of fire.

"Raddatz!"

Raddatz turned. His face, beaten—power-punched—busted, was like a bloody rag.

Carlin turned. His face, darkened by the hood, wore a smile Eddi's blinded eye could not see but could real well sense.

Carlin torqued and Raddatz twisted. A scream. Raddatz's snapping spine. Impossible to tell if one preceded the other.

Raddatz oozed from Carlin. Puddled on the floor. His body was like that now. Hardly better than liquid. Hardly more sturdy than gelatin.

Eddi: "Fucker!"

Gone.

Before Eddi could pull the trigger of Soledad's gun Carlin jumped himself up through the roof of the house.

Up through the roof.

A rain of wood and shingles. The crumble of brick.

He was as much freak as he was normal. More.

Quiet.

Quiet.

Especially from Raddatz's body. Twisted up. No sound, motion. No breathing Eddi could hear.

Eddi looked up, looked at the hole in the roof. Light filling the darkness constricted her pupils. Her pupil. She held a hand against the sun. Saw nothing. Listened.

Just the quiet.

Nothing above her. No footsteps, not the creak and moan of motion.

Eddi eased for Raddatz. Newly acquired 2-D vision made her put effort into calculating proximity.

"Raddatz," she whispered, hand stretched for him. "Raddatz!"

No response.

Pointless. She'd seen what Carlin had done to him. Carlin could kill freaks. Carlin had taken out an invulnerable. Snapping Raddatz, burning Raddatz amounted to clipping a nail.

"Raddatz!"

Eddi kept up a constant sweep of the place with her inherited gun. The muzzle hole a surrogate eye that was doing duty where Eddi needed the slack picked up. Part of her wanted to do some tough-talking. Wanted to go MTac macho. Faux testosterone wanted to taunt the unseen: C'mon, motherfucker! I'm right here!

But the hard-guy part of Eddi usually had a trio of MTacs backing her up. Something like a game plan to go with them. Now she was fifty percent blind. All alone.

Up the block she could hear someone praying in Spanish. She could whiff mother's milk being suckled by a newborn. And every beat of a hummingbird's wings was clear to her.

A hypersense of the world. She'd read about that in Soledad's journal. She called it a sense of death. Simpler just to call it fear.

Queer.

It was weird to Eddi. First time in a long time she could recall feeling fear and it was hunting a normal instead of a full-blown freak.

Hissing. Eddi heard hissing. Carlin's freak-faking suit? Ruptured pipes? A gas leak? Figure it out later, get out of the house befo—"

Not gas. A breath. Raddatz was breathing. Poorly, slowly. Shallow, but he was . . .

"Radda—"

The chaos this time delivered a hail of glass, brick and wood. Carlin busting back into the house through a wall, the frame of the structure screaming as it took the wound.

Eddi brought her gun around. Tried to. Carlin was already on her, had her. Threw her. Just a flick of his wrist. Didn't feel like hardly more than that. Geared up, it was all that was needed to manipulate Eddi's 128 pounds. Eddi took air, punched through the glass of a window. The transit pass a three-inch gash slashed into Eddi's thigh. The ground outside no more benign to her fall than the floor had been. It caught her without kindness, with hard dirt, rocks slugging at her back and shoulders. Eddi rolled, still half blind. Now weaponless.

The earth shook. Carlin taking a leap from the house for Eddi.

Eddi clawed frantic.

The gun!

Her hand ripped at the ground, got ripped by the junk that booby-trapped the yard.

The gun!

Eddi's leg got grabbed. Shin snapped. Busted tibia tore through her flesh.

She screamed. Her own body getting turned against her.

Carlin was reeling her in. She could feel the pleasure in the measure of his motions. He was going to get her. He was going to hug her. He was going to break her. He was going to kill her.

The gun . . .

Reality. She wouldn't find it before death was delivered.

Carlin's grip was tightening.

Jasmine. Laughter. Tears.

Death was coming.

A stay of execution came leaping at Carlin. His dog. Whippings, beatings, burnings. Electrocutions for the sake of shocking something. The beast was looking for payback. The beast was serving it up with snapping jaws and tearing canines. Carlin wasn't its master anymore. There was a slave revolt. It was Juneteenth. The tortured was giving it to its tormentor.

The snarling was nearly hideous. The animal sounds . . . which was the dog, which was Carlin?

Eddi pulled herself, pulled her busted ankle along the ground.

The gun . . .

The crack of electricity. The stink of burned meat. A pathetic yelp.

Carlin tossed the animal away. A toy grown tiresome to a belligerent child.

Carlin had another toy to fill his interest. Eddi. His curiosity: how to break her.

His hands on her. *Back* on her, digging into her. Hardly a beat skipped after killing the dog and Carlin returned to pulling Eddi for him.

Eddi wildly padding down the ground.

The gun . . .

Her hands—her left, fractured, but still doing work—whipping around frantic for the gun.

Technology to fight technology. If she had any chance at all of living, Eddi had to resurrect Soledad and put a bullet . . .

The gun?

Not the gun. Anything but the gun. She was suiciding herself by even trying for it.

Eddi's hand felt metal. A pipe. It held warmth from the sun of the day. Hot to Eddi's touch. Heavy in her hand. It was just enough to do damage. Eddi swung it with purpose. She twisted in Carlin's grip. Her ankle gave her another injection of pain. She batted, batted at his midsection. Slugged at his ribs. Pointless. Carlin had sanctuary under his exoskeleton and Kevlar.

Eddi kept pounding. Two, three times. A fourth. The force of the hit running hand to shoulder. A major leaguer on GHB, Eddi was swinging for the fences.

Carlin's head took the strikes, recoiled. He slowed none. Under his hood, a helmet? He wasn't wearing the hood for nothing. He wouldn't be stupid enough to go after freaks naked upstairs.

He couldn't all be armored. Achilles had his heel. Carlin had some weak spot.

A blow to the shoulder, the chest, the gut, the neck, the—

A grunt from Carlin. He staggered.

The hum of batteries. He was charging up to juice Eddi.

Now. Eddi told herself: Now's the time to get macho.

"Let's go, motherfucker! C'mon, bitch! Do me like you did Soledad! Try and fucking ki-*aaaah!*"

Eddi's right wrist caught, then snapped twig-style. The pipe tumbled to the ground. Her brain had the natural re-action to the hurt, wanted to shut down.

Carlin pulling her close. An augmented hand on her neck. The squeeze was slow and steady. The flow of blood to Eddi's brain was dammed. For a moment she floated. Started to. Then her head throbbed like her brain was beating against the sides of the skull that was, second by second, becoming its casket.

. . . this is what I wanted . . .

Her thoughts going gray. Gray to black.

I wanted . . . I wanted him to kill me? I wanted . . .

Gray to black. Black. Just black.

I wa . . . wanted him to pull me close. I wanted . . .

A flop, a flop of her hand. A grab with her left hand. Wrist fractured, the grab would be weak. Decrepit. It had better be good 'cause it was the only one Eddi would get.

Hand to her belt. Hilt in her hand.

Deep in the black, one word slipped past her lips: "Daddy."

She brought the knife, the Hibben Bowie, out of its sheath. Drew it, thrust it in an upward arch taking aim as best her one eye, her fading vision would allow for

Carlin's vulnerable throat. She felt the blade catch, jam against bone. Eddi let her body fall forward, drive her arm upward. It was all about the follow-through. Like a golf swing. Like a tennis backhand. Like a deathblow. She pushed. Eddi pushed. The blade doing battle with Carlin's cervical vertebra. The knife lost the fight. Snapped off. Remained lodged. Then again, looking at it that way, having a piece of metal in his throat: Really, it was Carlin who was the loser.

He lost the battle.

He was losing his life.

He was losing it in a mist of blood that hissed from his carotid artery in a seemingly ceaseless spray.

Tangled together, Eddi and Carlin did a little tango to the ground.

Eddi lay among the junk, the oxidizing metal. She lay with a dead dog. The dying Carlin. Blood still geysering. Less, less. The spray subsided.

Was gone.

The end of fear.

No sirens.

All the ruckus done and no one in LA, at least in this part of LA, cared enough to call a first responder.

Eddi wouldn't be making the call.

She was broken up and she was bleeding out, and her abilities were at the moment limited to lying right where she was.

She could hear a child just pulled from its mother's womb take its first breath.

Eddi could hear the lips of two lovers meeting.

Eddi could feel the air generated by the flap of a butterfly's wing in China. Guiyang, to be precise.

Eddi had a sense of the world.

Loss of blood made her very relaxed. But she was also very sad. She did not wish to die. Obvious. Does anybody really want to die? Like cloudy skies on the day of a parade, it's just one of those things that happen. One of those things you can do nothing about.

One thing she could do.

She put on that grin of hers.

So how did you know?

What's that?

How did you know, Eddi?

I just . . . in the moment, I knew.

In the moment, while a guy is trying to snap your head clean from your body, you just—

When Raddatz took the cadre after Carlin their radios just happened to go down? Anytime Carlin was anywhere near a surveillance camera they just happened not to work? Cars just stalled? Technology vs. technology. Carlin . . . I figured he must have had a low-level electromagnetic pulse coming off his suit. Just enough to mess with electronics, digital cameras . . . Enough to mess with Soledad's gun. That's why it misfired. Even if I'd found it, if I'd tried to use it, it would have done the same. I quit trying. I went for my knife.

Ah, bullshit.

Look, I'm not a techie. I don't know how all that electronic stuff works. But I took a chance, and it—

That's not what I'm talking about. You figured all that out in one split second while somebody was working on separating your head from your body? Nah. What I think: When it came down to it, you wanted out of you know who's shadow. Wasn't going to happen dropping Carlin with that gun.

Wait . . .

So you went for your knife. Carlin could've killed you, but you went for it.

Wait, am I . . . I'm not having this conversation. I'm not . . . I'm talking, but I'm not . . . I'm dead. In Carlin's yard with the junk and the dog. I'm—

You had a better place of dying. Although, guess there's no perfect place.

I don't want to—

Glad you could make it, Eddi . . .

I don't want to die.

Even for just a minute. I'm proud of you.

The average human can survive about eight minutes without heartbeat before the brain, starved of oxygen-rich blood, begins to suffer permanent damage.

Eddi's heart stopped beating for nine and three-quarters minutes on the operating table of Valley Presbyterian Hospital. It would have remained still eternally except she'd lucked out, gotten an ER doc who was only in his second year. Jaded by the sight of people dropping off the face of the earth, he worked that extra minute and three-quarters to bring her back to *this* side.

No brain damage.

None that the docs could find with their MRIs and CAT scans. None that the psychologists could find testing her mind.

Except . . .

There was a conversation had that was absolutely indisputable in Eddi's mind. The words and tenor were vivid to her. The only thing she wasn't sure of: who she'd spoken with.

She told this to no one. Told no one about her conversation. She didn't need anyone thinking her head was messed up, her gray matter was fractured. Despite her snapped wrist, her snapped ankle, a left eye that's usability would be diminished by at least thirty-five percent, a face that would forever carry a lightning scar from left brow to right jaw . . . and possible but clandestine brain damage, Eddi still had designs on being a cop. Back in MTac if doable. DMI if she had to. She wasn't ready to quit the fight. The fight was just starting. And it was nothing like what Eddi thought it would be when she'd first suited up.

The question, the *questions* now as she rested, rehabbed, got ready to get back into things:

What is she going to do?

Who's she really fighting?

Who does she trust?

Who could Eddi even talk to about the new knowledge of the struggle? Not to Vin. Not that she couldn't trust his council, not that she couldn't trust him with the truth. Or the version of it she was carrying this week. Vin was beyond caring about anything that didn't pour from a bottle. Much like the city of Las Vegas, what happened with Vin would stay with Vin. But Eddi had no idea how to begin a deep meaningful politically dicey conversation with him. In her heart she didn't want one. Her feelings about him, for him were confused. Confusion was a thread not to be trifled with for fear of unraveling. So all the days Vin sat with Eddi, endured her recuperation with her, she said nothing to Vin of the incident.

That's the way it was talked about within the department. What other euphemism is there for cops going after an ex-cop who'd souped himself up so he could kill freaks? Wasn't one. Wasn't a good one. So it got called "the incident," and a lot of brass spent sweaty nights hoping no one at the *LA Times* got wind of the truth.

They didn't

It was Oscar season in Hollywood and the *Times* flooded the zone on that.

There were conversations to be had.

With Raddatz. That conversation was difficult. Carlin had done a job on him, had come up shy of killing him. Busted Raddatz's back, his spine at T9. His body was dead from the abdomen down. He was bed-bound. For a while. He had to wear diapers because he had absolutely no control over his bladder and bowels.

Other than all that . . .

Actually, other than that, Raddatz was still a prideful fighter. In private moments he would tell Eddi that what they had done together was perhaps the single most significant act in the *real* struggle between normals and metanormals since San Francisco.

Eddi worked really hard at cheering him up, cheering him on. The world at large didn't know the truth. The world at large still hated freaks as much as they did the day before Raddatz's body got busted.

There was a conversation to be had with Helena, Raddatz's wife. It wasn't quite the "he was a good man" chat Eddi was afraid she was going to have to have. It was an ugly cousin to it. He *is* a good man. You should be proud of him for what he did, even though we can't tell you what it was.

And Helena was all right with that. Not with . . . there was no part of her that wanted her husband to be a paraplegic. No part of her. But what she had wanted for so long, two things: That her husband should live to see their boys grow. That he would no longer be a cop.

Not like she'd hoped, but finally, she'd have both.

There was the talk Eddi had to have with Bo, the one where she came around and told him that all was good with Soledad's weapon. Bo, being MTac and not DMI, didn't know all the specifics of "the incident" beyond the rumors that bounced around inside the blue wall. Eddi gave no clarifications other than to say that with modifications Soledad's piece should be able to eliminate its only fault. Excel was a weapon. As dismissive as she'd previously been, Eddi was now effusive in praise for the gun. For Soledad.

For all that Bo didn't know of the reality of things, Eddi's contriteness was not lost on him.

As she began her hobble from his office, Bo said to her: "Why don't you do it?"

"I'm sorry?"

"Work on Soledad's piece. Modify it."

"I don't have the background for it."

"You got all her work as a starting point. You could do it in conjunction with A Platoon or HIT. And I can't believe you couldn't finish something Soledad started."

Bo tossed that line like bait. Not to antagonize. To encourage. Albeit encourage with a taunt. Bo believed the department—normals, period—needed cops like Eddi. The Eddi he thought he knew. And if he had to play her ego to keep her around, keep her in the fight, he was ready to play.

And there was one other conversation to be had.

Eddi took another sip of her Pom. A merchandised version of pomegranate juice. It was supposed to be good for her, but she wasn't sure how. The nutritional benefits were vaguely stated on the bottle. But Eddi was working on eating more healthfully as her physical activity was going to be greatly curtailed for the near future. Her ankle and wrist were quite jacked, and in her physical therapy she was still working on mobility. That is, a so-called therapist who was little more than the devil in disguise traveling among the unsuspecting under the obsequious name of Bonnie would spend about twenty minutes heating Eddi's mangled joints while talking Eddi through the slight increase in degree she was going to manipulate Eddi's injuries over the previous day. And then Bonnie would do the manipulating.

Eddi would do some screaming.

She'd taken a lot of hurt as an MTac, and more than she'd expected in her short time at DMI. She could remember grunting and groaning at various times. Couldn't recall any out-and-out screaming. Not that she was a tough guy. She chalked up lack of shrieks to adrenaline, focus—getting hurt but not letting the hurt take her off her game. Or maybe she'd screamed like a girl time and time again, but had excised the memory to make herself feel tough.

She'd remember, always, tribulations under the touch of Bonnie.

Then came Tashjian. Walking up the street for his house, not breaking stride as he saw Eddi parked on the steps of his porch. No matter what'd happened last time she greeted him, what she'd done to him, no matter his ear was a fright—looked like the pull toy of a junkyard dog—he did not visibly react to Eddi's presence other than to say, regarding her drink: "Is that stuff any good? I see it all the time, but I can never quite get myself to try it."

"You're a cool customer, know that?"

"How exactly should I react, Officer Aoki? Are you going to maul my other ear? Out in public, top of the evening, are you going to pistol-whip me again, threaten my life? It's not that I wouldn't put it beyond you. Killing me. But I think you'd pick a better opportunity than here and now."

Eddi quietly conceded Tashjian was right.

He took up a spot next to her.

Eddi asked: "Were you trying to give Soledad payback for squirreling away from you before? You put her in a situation with bad intel hoping she'd get killed. I mean this was . . . this just worked out perfect for you."

"I did not want Officer O'Roark dead."

"Whatever you really knew about what was happening at DMI you held it back from Soledad. Held it back from me."

"That's assuming you regard Tucker Raddatz with complete trust."

No doubt from Eddi. "I do. No matter how he was going about the job, right or wrong, I know for a fact his version of things is the true version."

"He led a cadre inside the Los Angeles Police Department that was friendly to metanormals."

"You've always known. I don't have to tell you. All I'm trying to figure: Did you want Soledad dead, Raddatz dead, or best of both worlds, they cancel each other out?"

"There is one other possibility."

A little laugh. Eddi settled back as much as the concrete would allow. This, Tashjian's reality, she wanted to hear.

"There is the possibility I knew that Raddatz was, is, sympathetic to metanormals. There is the possibility I knew that whatever Raddatz and his cadre were proceeding against was . . . well, it was beyond them. Did I know, did I suspect the perp was a self-enhanced normal human? Absolutely not. Regardless, that Raddatz was working above his station was obvious. But how to help Raddatz without exposing the fact that he was aiding those he was supposed to be enforcing the law against? Send in another player. Perhaps the most formidable one in the Los Angeles Police Department. Give her enough information to make the situation seem plausible and hope against hope that once inside, if not converted by Raddatz, she would be in position to aid him. What I could not count on, but I guess I should have realized: There was some*thing* even superior to Soledad O'Roark. What I also could not count on, but I guess I should have hoped: There was some*one* superior to both. I did not plan on you, Officer Aoki. But I do thank God for you."

Eddi heard that last part but didn't take it in any particular way. Really, before Tashjian was halfway through with his spin Eddi already knew what she was going to come back at him with.

"The problem with that," she said like she was stating the obvious (to her she was), "is that you'd have to be soft for metanormals."

"Didn't you used to refer to them as freaks?"

"I think if it was to your advantage, you'd have sympathy for them. You've sold your soul so many times the devil wouldn't want it. But there's no advantage to backing them. There's nothing for you to gain, no reason for you to be on their side. So I think you're full of shit."

"Eddi . . ."

His being familiar with her sounded very weird to Eddi's sensibilities.

Tashjian said: "There's so much to be gained, and there is so very much to be lost. Revelation is coming . . ." He turned his head slightly, peeled back the bandage that covered his ear. The ear Eddi had mangled with her dentition. Gave Eddi a real good look. Tashjian put forth the slightest amount of effort—a kid making faces on the school yard—and the torn, misshapen lobe filled itself out, formed new cartilage and flesh and blossomed fresh. It held an intact shape for a moment—for just a moment—then reverted to looking as Eddi had re-created it.

"The truth," Tashjian said, "will set us free."

Tashjian took Eddi's Pom bottle, took a drink of the

stuff. The twist of his lips said he didn't particularly care for it.

Eddi kept up a stare at his ear.

To Eddi: "I will see you later, Officer Aoki."

Tashjian got up from the steps, got himself inside his house.

I'm not going to say . . . I'm not going to say I'm stunned. I quit being stunned years ago. I quit having my sense knocked from me that day about three months after San Francisco when the government announced that they were going to stop trying to do any DNA testing to identify remains because there basically were no remains to get tested in the devastated part of the city. I'd lost my father, but I'd never really have any . . . closure is a word I've come to hate. The psychologists always sling that around as if at some point you can shut the book on tragedy, on loss. Do this and you can break with your hurt. Do that and you can move on from the past. Anyone who talks about closure is either some unfeeling bastard or someone who's never once in their life truly suffered loss. My intimate relationship with the incredible will forevermore be unaltering.

So something getting the best of Soledad, Raddatz working with the metanormals, a human making himself over into a metanormal, Tashjian being a metanormal. Me using metanormal over the F-word . . .

None of that is incredible to me.

It's only daunting.

Like Raddatz'd said: Power always is. And information is power. And I had a lot more, a shitload more info than most people walking around.

What to do with it? That's the question.

You don't go into the fight asking questions. You can't. You can't hesitate, you can't think too hard. There's a call to duty, you do your duty. You trust the people who are sending you to do the fighting, the killing, have already spent a lot of nights not sleeping but up thinking. Worrying. Considering.

Then the fight goes on a little too long. Then you start asking questions. You start thinking the people who sent you to do battle don't have one idea in hell what the battle's about. Or maybe they know too well what they're doing. Maybe their fight isn't really what you're fighting for. It's not about Archduke Ferdinand or the Tonkin Gulf or WMDs.

Excuses. Not reasons.

But by the time people like me start asking questions it's way too late for going back. All there is, is slogging forward in the normal as we know it.

So the struggle continues. Of course it does. Probably will beyond my lifetime. But in my lifetime how do I engage—how do I reengage—the struggle? Who am I fighting for? What am I fighting against? Even if I knew what the end objective was, I've got no idea what I've got to sacrifice to achieve it: the law or morality?

As I write this, I feel, I feel like a pugilist between rounds. Beaten about badly, trying to get bearings. Knowing no matter my hurt, when the bell sounds I've got to take center ring.

Okay.

That's okay.

Every other round I took to the fight with my fists, my balls and my father's knife. They've gotten me this far. But next time I go do battle I'll have one thing more.

I've got Soledad's gun.

About the Author

John Ridley is a triple-threat writer of novels, film, and television, plus he is a regular contributor to NPR on their "Morning Edition." Ridley gained considerable attention for his first novel, *Stray Dogs*, which was made into the motion picture *U Turn* directed by Oliver Stone. Ridley followed with the critically acclaimed, *Love is a Racket, Everybody Smokes in Hell, A Conversation with the Mann,* and *The Drift*. His science fiction titles include *Those Who Walk in Darkness* and its sequel *What Fire Cannot Burn*.

Nightshift was the first. He showed up and overnight the world changed. I was young then. Younger. And all I cared about were rock bands and movie stars, and didn't give much thought to the significance of things like his arrival. Except that it was cool, he was cool. In time, that, like everything else, would change too.

In the first weeks after he hit the scene the papers and news shows were fat with rumors and half-truths and speculations by experts.

Experts?

How were there going to be any experts when there'd never been anything like him, it, before?

It was his physiology, they said. It suggested that he may not be of this . . . They said he was the by-product of government experiments which caused his body to become . . . Mental superiority allowed him to project an aura which resulted in . . .

On and on. All that anybody really knew was somewhere in San Francisco, night after night, he . . . it. It was out there. Stopping a bank robbery, a gang drive-by, *keeping a kid from getting flattened by a runaway truck . . . whatever.*

And then, just as quick as he appeared, Nightshift got mundane. Oh, he kept a jewelry store from getting ripped off again? Another car jacking busted up? Well, sure, I mean it's good, but . . . .

I got used to it. I got used to them. We all did. And we all went back to being concerned with other things . . . rock bands and movie stars.

Like I said: That would change.

San Francisco. The dead. The EO that made them all outlaws.

We blame them. They deserve blame. But maybe it's our fault too. We never should've let them do our job for us. We never should've relied on them. We never should've slept while they stood guard; spectators at the foot of Mt. Olympus.

No.

Hell no. What happened was their fault and theirs alone. And for what they did they're all going to pay the price.

EVERY SINGLE ONE OF THEM.

J esus Christ.

It was the thought pumping through Soledad's head. A phrase. A prayer. Something to chant over and over to keep her mind off what was coming.

What was coming was what she'd spent her whole life working toward. Her whole life: only twenty-six years, nine months. But most of that was spent at Northwestern studying, at the police academy and on the force training, working her way from beat cop through SPU up to MTac—prepping for this moment: her first call.

Jesus. F'n. Christ.

The others in the APC, the others riding with Soledad, they looked calm. Serene, kind of. Mostly they didn't look like cops racing through LA traffic, lights and sirens at full tilt. Except for their weapons and body armor—none of it worn to regulation. Bo and Soledad the only two who bothered with Fritz helmets, and Soledad was pretty sure Bo sported his just so she wouldn't come off like the only weak sister in the bunch—they looked like people out for a Sunday drive. Not one of them seemed to carry the thought odds were, end of the night, all of them would be dead. Maybe that was the key, Soledad considered, to getting through this: don't think, just do.

Soledad adjusted the strap of her breastplate where it cut into the flesh of her underarm. Probably designed by a man, it didn't particularly fit a woman.

"Don't bother." It was Yarborough—Yar—playing cocky, giving Soledad shit for concerning herself with things like body armor, things that might keep her alive. His bravado was his tender. He spent it easy: a lazy grin, a wink tossed for no reason. He spent it heavy in the body armor he *didn't* wear, same as if he were among the rare breed too cool to die. "Might as well take that shit off. Doesn't do any good."

Soledad looked to Reese. Didn't mean to. Had told herself no matter what, especially this first call, never in a moment of doubt look to Reese. Soledad thought it was a sign of weakness, like looking to your mom when the corner bully went calling you names. But the action was reflexive. Reese was the only other woman on the element, one of the few female MTacs. So Soledad looked to her, as if femininity equated fidelity.

Reese, deep in her own thoughts, just stared straight ahead paying no attention to Soledad or anyone else.

Bo, jumping into things: "Leave her." His voice had a drawl. Slight. Cowpoke slow. Soledad had seen Bo with a gun on the target range. His drawl was the only thing slow about him. "We're supposed to be wearing it."

"You're not wearing your armor," Yar tossed back.

The APC juked hard to one side to avoid a Toyota that cut across an intersection never-minding the lights and sirens of the MTac vehicle. Typical LA. Didn't matter what the emergency was, everybody thinks they've got someplace to be.

"I did first call. First call I would've driven a tank if I could've."

Yar laughed. Not like what Bo had said was funny, like what Bo had said was plain ridiculous; as if a tank would make any difference in the world when you were facing down a freak. Bo was senior lead officer of the element, the oldest. Soledad thought: hell of a career choice she'd made where forty was considered a long-timer. The same thought jerked her hand to the case resting next to her thigh.

"Whatcha got?" Yarborough asked, using his chin to point at the case. It was small, hardcover-book-sized, zippered, made from synthetics.

Soledad wondered to herself why Yar was paying her so much attention. She hadn't been on Central long, but they'd all trained together, put in hours together. All that time Yar hardly looked in her direction. Here they were rolling on an M-norm, and all he could do was razz her every couple of—

"Whatcha got in the case? Bring a couple of books so you won't get bored?"

The APC stopped. Not even. It slowed some, but that was signal enough: time to move. Bo was first out, the door barely open. Yarborough, Reese just a step behind. Soledad, affixing the case to her back, was right with them hesitating not a second, not any amount of time anyone could say she froze, she was scared, she wasn't ready. Even if she was all that, no way she'd let anyone think it.

As she moved, Soledad's eyes worked the scene, took

in information and processed it on the fly. Downtown
LA. Rail yards. A warehouse, boarded windows showing
fire. Police cordoning off the area, keeping a good distance back.

A safe distance.

Inside the perimeter: a couple of burned-out fire trucks
and squads, the reek of their molten metal, plastic and
fabric strong enough to choke on deep breaths.

Outside the perimeter: Lookie-lous gathered. The
good citizens of Los Angeles. They stared. They pointed.
A couple had camcorders ready to do some taping, hoping a cop got offed in some spectacular manner so they
could sell the footage to CNN.

Bo wove his way to the officer in charge. Soledad got
the name on the sergeant's badge: Yost.

Bo, direct: "Whatcha got?"

"Pyrokinetic." Yost was sweaty from more than the
heat of the fires. He was wet with fear.

Soledad felt herself starting to share the dampness.

"Firestarter?" Bo's eyes swept the warehouse.

Yarborough swept it with IR goggles.

"If it was a firestarter, you think any of us would still
be here?" Yost answered. "Flamethrower, but it can toss
'em about thirty or forty feet. That's what happened to the
vehicles."

Reese worked the action of her piece. It was like she
wasn't even listening to the back-and-forth between Bo
and Yost. It was like all she cared about was putting a bullet in something.

Yost: "The freak won't let the bucket boys put out the
fire."

Yarborough kept moving his goggles across the warehouse.

"Probably started it just to get them down here, work up a body count. Fucking freak."

"That's good," Bo said. "Keep calling it names. That'll get us home early."

Yost mumbled something audible about MTacs being arrogant motherfu—

Yarborough: "Got him. Third floor, southeast corner."

"One?" Reese asked.

"That's all I'm reading. Hard to be sure with the fire."

"Thank God it ain't one of those mind readers." Yost was getting sweatier by the second.

Soledad: "Maybe it is." She hoped she sounded like she was just voicing a consideration and not bitch scared.

"Couldn't pay me to go in there, I'll tell you that." Yost said it, then said it again. "You couldn't pay me nothing to go in there."

Bo said: "Throw some light up top, make a little noise for cover. You'd take pay for that, right?" To his element: "Mike check. One."

"Two."

"Three."

Soledad: "Four."

Bo started to move, started for the warehouse. Soledad was ready to move with him. Something on her arm. Fear made every sensation feel like fire, like maybe she'd caught a little of what slagged those vehicles. A quick look: Reese giving a squeeze; reassuring. Saying stay close without saying a word.

Soledad eyed Reese's shoulder, her tattoo; the words

etched there. Tough words. Downright BAMF words that told it like it was, like it should be. Soledad kept close to Reese as the four went for the warehouse.

As they did, behind them, Yost managed to get his act together enough to put spotlights on the building. Third floor.

Bo had point. He carried a Colt .45 government model: more stopping power than the 9mms beat cops carried. A precision kill weapon. Reese and Yarborough toted HK MP5s, excellent for chopping freaks. Light, fast, and at full auto it could spray, baby, spray. Soledad had the Benelli, a semiauto shotgun loaded with one-ounce slugs. She was the fail-safe. If nothing else could stop what they were going after, the Benelli could put a hole in anything. Usually. All the weapons were Synthtech series, manufactured—like everything else they carried and wore—from synthetics and composite materials.

Inside.

The first thing they got hit with was the smell, the odor of perpetually burning flesh. And something else. The hint of another aroma that Soledad could just barely distinguish. The stink of smoked crack.

Oh, that's good, she thought. Not just a flamethrower. A hopped-up flamethrower. And this was her first call.

Stairway. Narrow. Not a good place to get caught. All four MTacs could go up like kindling. But it was the only approach.

Up the stairs.

First landing . . . nothing.

Second landing . . . more nothing, except the smells were strong and there was a voice. Strange, distorted like it was trying to make itself heard through the roar of a blast furnace.

All four MTacs had their weapons gripped hard and ready to do work. All four did a crab walk, step by step, inching upward for the third floor.

Bo's voice whispered into their earpieces: "Hold."

The air was hotter, thinner, some of its O_2 gone. The thing was burning it off. Her uniform was suffocating her. All that, anxiety; they didn't help Soledad's breathing any. Her chest rose and fell in a rapid pace. Her hand pushed sweat off her forehead. It was rolling from her now. Rolling in sheets. Chestplate crushing her. Felt like it was. Should've listened to Yar; ditched the body armor. Should've . . .

Jesus Christ.

In her mind her own voice repeating: This is it this is it this is it. Stay cool. This is it this is it . . .

More of the blast furnace rant. Clearer now.

"Muthafuckas! Ya want sum? Huh? C'mon, bitches! Come taste summa dis!"

All Soledad could think was that he . . . *it* sounded like a crazy waving a Saturday night special around a liquor store. Everything they can do, all their abilities, but get down to it, end of the day, they're just street punks. Nothing more. Nothing better.

Bo peeked up to the third floor. A lot of space broken up by vertical supports.

In Soledad's earpiece, Bo clipped and to the point: "Sixty feet. Back to us. Me, Yarborough left. Reese, Soledad right."

That was all the more instruction they got. All they needed. Bo moved out low and quick with Yarborough right behind him. Reese and Soledad moved opposite, Soledad's heart slamming away inside her chest. They eased across the floor using the vertical supports, thankfully many of them, for cover.

The smells were thicker: the never-ending stench of roasting carcass swallowed with every breath to form a nauseating mixture in the stomach.

From hiding, Soledad peeked around a vertical. She could see the freak engulfed in its own flames. She had never seen one this close—a pyrokinetic or any other kind of M-norm. Its body shimmered with heat and fire but refused to burn itself. The flames just crackled and danced continually, feeding on the flesh of its host: an endless human wick.

This is it this is it this . . .

Soledad couldn't take deep breaths, couldn't get her breathing to slow down.

"Muthafuckas!" it screamed at the cops down on the street. "Think you got sumthin'? Bitches, come up here an' show me sumthin'!" It thrust its arm out a window. It shot a tendril of flame, the fire howling as it scorched the air it rode on.

Outside, three stories down, Soledad heard the wail of men. Maybe burning. Maybe dying.

"Muthafuckas! Better recognize!"

Bo, in the earpieces: "Ready?"

Down the line:

"Ready."

"Ready."

This is . . . "Ready."

Bo twisted from behind the vertical.

Soledad's heart clutched, then double-pumped.

Bo spoke, yelled with pure authority. "This is the police! You are in violation of an Executive Ord—"

That was all Bo got out, all the thing would let him get out before it turned from the window and sent a finger of flame burning in Bo's direction.

Bo sprang back, tumbled. Moved on instinct. Thought would've taken too long. Thought would've left him standing where fire now cooked the floor. He would have been dead.

"Bitches come ta play?" the pyro shrieked over the crackle of the burning wood. The thing shot fire again. From its skin, from its flesh, from itself it generated fire.

Instinct wasn't fast enough. Not this time. This time Bo got sent sailing, ridden into the dark of the warehouse along a river of flame. "Show me sumthin', bitch! Whatcha got ta show me?"

Yarborough, Reese and Soledad up and out and shooting. A continual chant of 9mm fire interrupted by the low boom of Soledad's shells.

Why didn't, she wondered as her finger jerked the trigger, they just do this first off? You got a thing that can spit fire from its body, fuck warnings and police procedure. Kill 'em! They all deserved to die anywa—

Bullets no good. Lead turned to slag from the aura of heat around the freak before the shells could even touch it.

"What da fuck?" the thing snapped. "Was you 'bout ta shoot my ass?" A hand arched before it. Just like . . . that, . . . empty space burned hot. A wave of flame ran for Yarborough, Reese and Soledad in a violent ripple.

Soledad moved, tried to dodge the flames. Too slow. They picked her up, kicked her back. They slammed her down hard on the wood floor. She had sense enough to roll with the landing. Kept her from getting hurt. Badly hurt. The bits of pain that came with lightly singed flesh let her know she'd survived the assault.

She came up looking around: Yarborough down. Leg engulfed. He rolled, snuffed it out. He didn't scream. Bad as the burn was, bad as it looked even at a distance, he didn't scream.

Reese was clear. At least, Soledad didn't see her. So she was clear. Maybe. Maybe Reese'd just been turned to ash and there was nothing of her left to see.

The thing, the monster, stepped up, stretched a hand for Yarborough.

Soledad: "Yar!" She took aim. Fired. The shells, useless as ever, turning to molten lead as they sped for the burning man.

The thing's arm twisted away from Yar, gave its full attention to Soledad. Through the heat-distorted air, on the creature's face, Soledad could make out a jacked smile. It was there for just a second before being washed away by the flames the thing sent for her.

"How's dis, bitch? I'ma 'bout ta break me off my burnin' foot in yo ass!"

Soledad turned and curled and took the flames like a fist to the back. They batted her against a vertical, forcing the air from her body. Good thing. A breath in, and she would have sucked fire; she would have fried herself from the inside out. Bad as the hit hurt, it saved her life.

Vision blurred, head throbbing. Soledad sank to the floor, couldn't help herself from going down. She tried to lift herself, then sank again. Pain was the motivator to stay where she was. Brilliant pain. Arm burning. The

Nomex uniforms were fire-retardant, not fireproof, and not fire-anything against muties. She slapped the flames dead, then stared at charred fabric. Except it wasn't charred fabric. It was burned flesh beginning to boil and blister.

Soledad felt like she was swimming: light, buoyant, moving through a viscid fluid. She felt all that, and her burnt arm felt cool.

Shock. Coming on fast.

Soledad's empty hand groped for the Benelli but stayed empty.

Yarborough, still down. Still immobile.

Where was Bo? Where was Reese?

Soledad managed to get her head up. Coming toward her through dutch-angled vision was the thing. The floor sizzled where it stepped.

Soledad's long-standing fear, her cop nightmare: to be incapacitated by a perp, unable to run, unable to hide . . . a weapon touching-close but too far away to be of any use, she'd be unable to do anything but lie and watch Death take a stroll for her. It was a weak and helpless and frightening scenario, and she was staring right at it.

"What's da matter, ya bitchass skeez?" Slow burn to its voice. All of it burned slow. "Ain't got nothin' more ta show me?"

A hard struggle got Soledad nowhere near up to her feet.

"I'll show ya, sumthin'. Ya wanna see sum shit?"

The thing stopped moving. It stood over Yarborough. Its hand glowed, gathering heat and flame, ready to send it pouring over the cop. Ready to kill him.

"Too easy!" Soledad screaming, swooning with disorientation. "Kill a guy who can't fight?" Felt like she wanted to fall. Still on the floor, and she felt like . . . "You're the goddamn bitch, you two-dollar whore!" Burned, weaponless, weak; big talk, that's all she had.

Nothing. For a second, nothing.

Then the glow from the thing's hand spread over his body. He went hot with excitement as much as fire.

"Skeez got sumthin' after all. I'm gonna light you up. I'm gonna light up yo pussy!"

The man of fire stalked for Soledad, but took its time about it, each step prolonged for its max pleasure: the anticipation of the kill. Foreplay, then death.

Soledad felt the thing approaching, felt the heat of it pressing toward her more than she could see it. One eye was swelling shut, the other collecting the blood that ran from her head. A weak arm feebled for her back, for the pack she had attached there. Didn't have the strength to pull it free.

"How you want it, girl? Which hole you want it in?"

The heat, oppressive, burning oxygen and passing Soledad out. At least, she thought, she wouldn't be conscious for her own end. Through a curtain of blood she saw the thing's fiery hand reaching for her. It was an unnatural wonder. It was the last thing she'd ever see.

Blue, moving fast. Reese, throwing herself at the mutie, knocking it from Soledad's path.

Soledad rolled, scrambled for the cover of one of the verticals. The stay of execution injecting her with enough fight to keep alive.

Reese, on the floor; wounded animal sounds. The side of her body she'd slammed against the thing was black with burns.

Reese down. Yar down. Bo gone.

Time. It was only a matter of how much—a minute, a few seconds—before that thing killed them all.

Hand alive with desperation, Soledad pulled the pack from her back, worked the zipper. Inside: a gun.

The freak, only dazed by the open-field tackle, got its bearings, moved for Reese. "Bitch, I wasn't tryin' ta fuck wit you. Ain't nobody told you ta come in here an' git wit my shit. You better axe sumbody!"

No hesitation this time. The thing's hand to the chest-plate of Reese's body armor. A second later: a horrible sizzle, the smell of burnt meat.

From Reese, screams. Spastic jerking and twitching against the pain, and screams.

Shaky hands, Soledad fumbled for the clips in the pack. Which color, her mind unable to lock thoughts. Which color? Which— Red, the red clip. Grabbed it, she slid it into the back of the gun.

One deep breath.

Soledad stood, came into the open.

The thing rose to meet her.

Reese's body kept flopping around over the wood.

"Oh, now bitch wants sumthin'. You gonna play me like dat wit yo little bitchass gat. Let's get it on, girl. Bring it da fuck on!"

Yeah. Let's bring it on.

Soledad took aim with her piece. The DTT raced up, then locked.

The thing burned bright, ready to spatter fire. Ready to kill.

How do you shoot something like that? How do you use a bullet against a thing that can melt lead?

Soledad squeezed the trigger. No hammer fell. Just the same, her weapon spat. The slugs—four fired in instantaneous succession—touched air, then went white hot. They stayed white-hot as they cut through the freak's flames, hit it in the chest, tore it open. They were white-hot as they ripped and shredded flesh and muscle, broke bone and turned it into shrapnel, wounding from the inside outward. The slugs were just as hot when they opened four jagged defects in the freak's back and kept on going.

Phosphorous bullets. Soledad had answered a question with a question: How do you melt what's already on fire?

The thing stood unbelieving. Blood, like streams of lava, leaking from the tunnels Soledad had laced through its chest. It stood for a moment . . . stood . . . its light and fire dimmed. Then the thing went down felled-timber hard.

Quiet.

Soledad limped for the body, not having known until that moment she'd done damage to her leg. The pain of a twisted knee subordinate to that of smoldering flesh.

Step, drag. Step, drag.

Soledad stood over the pyro. She venom-dripped words down at its empty eyes. "Who's the bitch now? You bleed. Fucked-up-looking and hot, but you bleed."

Eulogy over.

Soledad turned for Reese. Reese's body. In the center of her chest, where her armor was melted away, was a burned-out crater. Cooked meat hanging off the bone.

"God . . ." Soledad lowered herself, repulsed by Reese's wound but unable to look away from it. Her hand out toward it to . . . to what? To touch it? Tend to it? What was the point? Nothing she could do. Not one—

A gurgle. A spasm from the body.

Soledad sprang back.

Reese in a death prattle . . . and then something else. A breath. Short, shallow, but a breath.

"Ten-thirty-three!" Soledad yelled, not knowing she was yelling. Not even sure if there was anyone to hear her. "Officer down! I need a rush on a bus at this loca—"

Real quick her words got choked out. Her throat was on fire. A painful jerk of her head to the side, through the corner of her eye: It was alive; the thing, the human flame. Alive just enough to ignite its hand, take Soledad by the neck and sear her skin.

". . . Youse sumthin', girl." Slurred words of the dying, but dying slow enough to drag Soledad with it. "Truth: youse the only bitch man enough ta be wit all da shit. Truth. It's da truth dat sets ya free, an' revelation is comin'. Come here, bitch, an' kiss me good-bye."

The thing worked up half a smile and got ready to end Soledad's life—choke it from her, squeeze it, burn it from her. One way or the other, kill her.

Three loud pops. Three large holes bust open in the thing's body just before it tipped and thudded against the floor.

Hand to her throat. Soledad could feel the dead flesh peel beneath her touch.

Across the warehouse: Bo, blood leaking from his skull, held his smoking .45.

Soledad saw that, then promptly passed out.

WORKING FOR THE DEVIL
Lilith Saintcrow
(0-446-61670-2)

Dante Valentine just got really busy. A licensed Necromancer with the emerald to prove it, she can raise the dead and wield a sword better than a samurai master. But one rainy Monday morning, she's offered a deal from Hell.

The score: the Devil hires her to hunt down Vardimal Santiago, a rogue demon. Her reward? Her life. With an offer like that, Dante can't refuse.

Rave Reviews for
WORKING FOR THE DEVIL

"This book just blew me away. I ate it up! I loved, loved, LOVED the book. Couldn't put it down. Darkly compelling, fascinatingly unique . . . I devoured this book."

—**Gena Showalter**, author of *Awaken Me Darkly*

"Lilith Saintcrow's *Working for the Devil* is pure fantasy and fun. A take into a different world, a fantastic escape. I enjoyed it tremendously."
—**Heather Graham**, *New York Times* bestselling author

"*Working for the Devil* combines dark urban fantasy with a splash of cyberpunk, a pinch of paranormal romance and a dash of gritty crime thriller to create a unique and engaging mélange."

—**Jacqueline Carey**, author of *Kushiel's Avatar*

Kitty and the Midnight Hour
CARRIE VAUGHN
(0-446-61641-9)

Kitty Norville is a midnight-shift DJ for a Denver radio station—and a werewolf in the closet. Her new late-night advice show for the supernaturally disadvantaged is a raging success, but it's Kitty who can use some help. With one sexy werewolf-hunter and a few homicidal undead on her tail, Kitty may have bitten off more than she can chew . . .

❧

Everyone Loves *Kitty*

"I relished this one. Carrie Vaughn's KITTY AND THE MIDNIGHT HOUR has enough excitement, astonishment, pathos, and victory to satisfy any reader."
>—*New York Times* bestselling author
>Charlaine Harris, author of *Dead as a Doornail*

"Fresh, hip, fantastic—Don't miss this one, you're in for a real treat!"
>—L.A. Banks, author of
>The Vampire Huntress Legends series

"You'll love this! This is vintage Anita Blake meets *The Howling*. Worth reading twice!"
>—Barb and J.C. Hendee, coauthors of *Dhampir*

❧